Purple Sunshine

sex & drugs, rock & roll, war, peace & Love

To Bruce,
The prose may be purple
But the sunshine's
heartfelt!
Bob Calverley

Bob Calverley

Disclaimer

This is a work of fiction, a product of the author's imagination. Any resemblance or similarity to any actual events or persons, living or dead, is purely coincidental. Although the author and publisher have made every effort to ensure there are no errors, inaccuracies, omissions, or inconsistencies herein, any slights or people, places, or organizations are unintentional.

*****

Credits

Cover photo courtesy Bigstock Photo
Editing and cover design by Harvey Stanbrough
Formatting by Debora Lewis arenapublishing.org

*****

ISBN-13: 978-1512344516
ISBN-10: 1512344516

To my comrades in the 187th Assault Helicopter Company, and those we loved, especially those who stood by us when the going got tough.

Prologue

May 3, 1945, 9:14 p.m., Berlin, Germany

Matthias Dorrinian shot the shuddering little girl in the back of her head with the Walther and watched her tumble into the big bomb crater with the others. She was about 13 years old, pretty, blonde and with a blossoming maturity that was still more potential than reality. That was the core of her appeal. He had trained her a few years earlier. She and her older sister had been two of the first and her sister one of the very best: compliant, delicately responsive, and well received by his clients. She had been a real moneymaker because she was Nordic, not Jewish. Not that the clients ever asked. He had forgotten about this girl and he wondered what had happened to the older sister. As soon as the girl stopped moving, Bucholz shot the last boy in the head. By Dorrinian's count, they had shot 37 children, mostly girls, ranging in age from seven to eighteen. Only a couple of the children had tried to run and Bucholz had quickly cut them down with a burst from his Schmeisser.

"A bad business," Bucholz said as he holstered his pistol and draped the Schmeisser by the sling over the remains of an iron fence. Dorrinian didn't say anything but placed his reloaded Walther carefully in a pocket. The two of them spent the next hour shoveling dirt and rubble into the crater to cover the bodies. Hard work, but the evening was cool. The bodies might be found, but there were thousands of bodies all over

Berlin now. Dorrinian thought most of the fighting was over. It had been difficult to gather the children while the fighting was going on, but he had spread word that he had shelter and food and many had found him. As long as they worked and obeyed him, he had always treated them well.

Dorrinian had heard that Russians were raping women, some of them very young, and killing civilians by the hundreds and maybe thousands. He wasn't sure that they had to cover the bodies, and killing the children had been a risk, but Bucholz had insisted. The children could identify not only him and Bucholz, but also dozens of their clients, who included many high-ranking government officials and wealthy businessmen. There were undoubtedly still some children out there who could do the same, but now there were 37 fewer of them.

A client had probably decided that eliminating the children was necessary. There were a few clients among the Gestapo, and Dorrinian suspected that Bucholz had been ordered to do it. Bucholz needed Dorrinian's help because only he knew where to find the children. On the other hand, only Bucholz knew about Dorrinian. Dorrinian had been careful never to deal with the clients directly, and he had tried not to let any of the children learn his name. His relationship with Bucholz had made both of them a lot of money and Bucholz trusted him. It had apparently not yet sunk in with Bucholz that his superiors were no longer in power.

Dorrinian worried that the gunshots might attract the Russians, but no one had noticed. They were still hearing sporadic gunfire and were in an area so flattened by bombing that people had left long ago.

As they shoveled dirt, Bucholz again related his plan to escape by slipping through the American lines. He expected to be detained, but was confident in his ability to convince the

Americans that he was a businessman. He did, technically, have a small security business in addition to his job in Department C of the Gestapo. Buchholz was a liaison to Albert Speer's operations, where Dorrinian was a little-known consultant. Bucholz had been spying on Speer for the Gestapo and everyone knew it. That was where Bucholz and Dorrinian had discovered their mutual interest in children and profit.

For the third or fourth time, Bucholz was telling Dorrinian that he had a list of German businessmen and party officials who were hiding financial assets. He had been working on the list for more than a year. "Millions, maybe billions," he said, smiling and patting his breast pocket. In his mind, he was already spending the money. He had offered to share with Dorrinian, but Dorrinian had declined.

Dorrinian didn't think Bucholz' escape plan had any chance of success. He had never been impressed with the man's intelligence, though keeping the list was a clever idea. Bucholz had probably stolen it. The Russians would just shoot him, and he was more likely to run into them than the Americans. The Americans might shoot him too, but they certainly wouldn't let him go when they found his list. But Dorrinian had decided that neither of those outcomes would occur.

With the bodies finally covered up, the gasping Bucholz, who was a large man, dropped his shovel and wiped the sleeve of his jacket across his brow. He had been a mediocre heavyweight boxer before the war, but now he was at least 20 kilos over his fighting weight. Dorrinian took the pistol out of his pocket and shot Bucholz in the head just as he completed the head wipe. He bent over and removed the packet of papers in Bucholz' breast pocket and stuffed them into his own pocket without looking at them.

He dropped the pistol beside the body. Looking carefully around one more time, he left the Schmeisser where it was. He thought carrying a weapon of any kind would increase his chances of being shot. He'd heard that the Germans had surrendered, but the sporadic gunfire indicated the fighting was not quite over. It was dangerous to be outside. However, among his many languages, Dorrinian spoke both English and Russian fluently and had documents to show he was from Azerbaijan. He wanted to get back to the bunker he had built in his basement and hide the papers he had taken from Bucholz.

He was already in contact with both an American and a Russian. Now he had a simple bargain to negotiate: his life for the papers. Now that he had the list, he was beginning to think it might work. He didn't want the money because that just increased his chances of being killed. He preferred to deal with the Americans. He was convinced the Russians would kill him no matter what they agreed to. He had already decided to hold back some of the papers, for years if necessary, in order to guarantee his continuing safety.

A full moon was rising, fat and a sickening pallid grayish-green, bathing the rubble in pale light and casting weak, ghostly shadows. Dorrinian barely noticed. Walking back to his underground hideout, he wasn't thinking of the moon or the looming negotiations for his survival. He was thinking about the blonde girl, remembering the pleasures of training her, and wondering whether he should have kept her alive for a few more days. But that would have been too great a risk, and besides, she was almost too old.

"Shit," he said. He had been thinking in Armenian but it was the same word in English.

CHAPTER 1

July 22, 1967, 3:35 p.m., Grosse Pointe, Michigan

She was five foot four, just like the song said, and her name was Gloria.

Maybe she wasn't quite five foot four. She'd been wearing shoes with small heels when she'd measured herself, right after the first time she'd listened to Them pounding out "Gloria" on a 45-rpm record. She'd never measured herself again. She'd learned to play the song on her guitar, the first real rock and roll song she ever played. She'd learned "Baby Please Don't Go" too, which was on the other side of the record and was actually the A-side. She'd wanted to change her name, Gloria being too ordinary, but decided that maybe it was cool after all. She couldn't think of anything better.

In the summertime, she'd be outside all day in her bathing suit singing and playing guitar, tanning to a rich dark brown that never really went away in the winter while her wavy golden hair got lighter and brighter. Her hair framed a glistening, smooth-skinned face ruled by wariness that sometimes gave way to a tentative smile. Slender but full-figured, she looked older than her 15 years, and she knew it. She'd been turning men's heads since she was 12.

Her guitar was a gorgeous Epiphone FT120 Excellente made of Brazilian rosewood with an ebony fingerboard decorated with little clouds and an abalone peg head inlay. The big black pointed pick guard was engraved with a golden eagle.

She should have sold it like the others, but she was too attached to it. Gina had bought it for her 15th birthday. But Gina was dead now.

Gloria was sitting in her stepfather's red 1967 Corvette Stingray, rain drumming on the garage roof as thunder rippled above. She hated the car but her stepfather loved it. He loved it more than he loved any human being. It reeked of cigarette ash, a sour bouquet of sweat, Jade East aftershave and very faint Juicy Fruit gum. Made her queasy. A weak brown aura surrounded the car; it would get stronger if she sat there doing nothing much longer.

"Gotta get away," she chirped. She preferred singing to speaking so much that she often spoke by pretending she was singing, her words coming out in a strange singsong lilt. In a song, there was a structure on which she could hang the words. She knew where she was going, what she was singing, and she could play her guitar to make it better, just like the blues. You sing a line and answer on guitar with notes that feel like the words, the emotion flowing through her long, articulate fingers and out through her guitar, sometimes generating colorful auras, happy colors, pinks, oranges and turquoises. Playing guitar gave her hands something to do. Her whole body worked in marvelous, coordinated ways that never happened any other time. But when speaking, she got mixed up or locked up or just couldn't keep going.

The rain stopped abruptly and she turned her attention back to the car. She'd been practicing driving up and down the long driveway for three months, ever since Gina had died. She no longer ground the gears. The car was so powerful that she squeaked the tires even though she tried not to. She'd made several middle-of-the-night runs around Grosse Pointe and onto the freeway when her stepfather was out of town. She'd learned to power shift, got it up to almost 100 miles an hour one night. She'd slowed down because she didn't want to get stopped. Yeah, she could drive the car—she could do anything if she tried—and she could do it better than the boys.

She opened her big purse and looked one more time. Four hundred twenty-three dollars and change. Her single suitcase was on the floor in front of the passenger seat. Her guitar, in its case, lay across the seat alongside the big handbag. She turned the key and the Corvette started. Her stepfather would be home from the airport soon from his long Asia trip and he'd have the whip. And she'd overheard him talking about taking her on his next trip and leaving her there.

Where would she go? Could she look for her real mother who might be in Las Vegas? She had no idea who her real father was. Could she drive to California? She wanted to see hippies and San Francisco. The magazines had called this the "Summer of Love," and she wanted to find somebody to love. The song "Somebody to Love" was special. She longed for somebody to love, and for somebody to love her. But before she got to San Francisco her stepfather would have reported his precious missing car to the police. What if she got stopped? Maybe she could go to Ann Arbor or East Lansing. There were universities there where she'd probably find some hippies.

"I have to leave," she said, then started singing "Gotta Get Away," tapping the dashboard in time to the Rolling Stones pulsing through her head.

She revved the engine and popped the clutch and the car screamed out of the garage, leaving two black smoking streaks of rubber on the dry concrete and then skidding and skittering on the wet pavement of the driveway. As she power shifted into second gear, one back wheel lurched into the grass, spraying a cloud of muddy dirt before she got the car back on the concrete. She kept the gas pedal all way to the floor through another power shift into third gear and then slammed on the brakes to skid to a stop at the end of the driveway. She couldn't see oncoming cars very well because of the hedges. She looked back at the steam rising from the wet pavement and grinned.

* * *

She drove to Belle Isle. It was cloudy and still raining a little, and there were few people. She finally parked on some grass by a fountain at one end of the island. She walked out to a point and looked at the Detroit River running by, deep and cold, then went back to the car and drove across the grass, stopping short of the point. No one was in sight. She took out her things and placed them on the wet grass, being careful to put her guitar in its case on top of the suitcase. Then she opened the little trunk where she found an old black leather briefcase she'd never seen before.

She picked up a flat, heavy rock and laid it on the front seat. Carefully, she depressed the clutch with her right foot and shoved the shifter into first gear with her right hand. Then she placed the rock on the gas pedal, making the engine roar. As she slid her foot off the clutch the car lunged forward, bumping her hip. It bounced up when it hit the rocks lining the shoreline. She was surprised at how high it went. It looked like an airplane taking off and sailed into the water tail first with a huge splash. It floated for a few seconds before sinking. The last thing visible was the menacing black stinger on the hood sliding into the water.

She brushed herself off, picked up her things and trudged back to the road thinking she was stupid, but not caring either because her hatred for her stepfather was so strong. She walked along the road until she came to a spot where the grass was not wet beneath a large elm tree and sat down. She took out her guitar and started strumming randomly until she found a sequence of chords that she liked. Just then the sun broke through the clouds and began to warm her.

And inspire her.

"My name is Sunshine," she chirped, "and I will love you."

And as a pink glow grew, words came to her:

"I got the blues when Gina left me out Eight Mile way.
A great big truck came and took that poor soul away.
She never meant to treat me bad; she was the only mom I ever had.
We never said good-bye, and it made me cry.
Got down so low that I thought I might die.

"Well I got four hundred dollars, and a few extra nickels and dimes.
Ain't never goin' home, or I just might lose my mind.
Be on the road for days, startin' brand new ways,
Walkin' across Belle Isle on a bright sunshiny day.

"Well, I'm sittin' under this damn tree, wonderin' what's in store for me,
Feelin' crazy, happy and lazy, but oh so ever so free
Might take a train, or maybe a bus, but I won't be feelin' down.
Gonna ride to the end of the line, no one's ever gonna see me frown.

"Well I barely got a nickel, or even a lousy dime.
My ol' man finds me, think I'm gonna lose my mind.
I ain't never going back to stay; I'm startin' a brand new day,
Walkin' across Belle Isle on a bright sunshiny day.
Walkin' across Belle Isle on a bright sunshiny day.

Walkin' across Belle Isle on a bright sunshiny day."

After awhile, she opened the old black leather briefcase and examined the bankbooks and papers, and stuffed them into her suitcase. She thought she understood it. Most of the bank books were from other countries, many of them places in Asia, and the few American ones were from big cities on the east and west coasts. Finally, there was a folder with strange documents that were difficult to read because they weren't written in English. The paper was very thin, almost fragile, and very dark with barely discernible tiny white print in a foreign language. She riffled through them in a few seconds and was going to throw them away, but they didn't take much room so she tossed them into her suitcase with everything else.

11:45 p.m., Detroit

Jimmy Hayes liked to live on the dangerous edge of blaring feedback and electronic distortion. By overdriving the amp, he produced an edgy, distorted tone with a hollow, wet sound that oozed into the big room without overwhelming the rest of the band. Give some credit to Roscoe because he had made Hayes crank the volume down. Well, it was Roscoe's blues band. Hayes loved to experiment with his Stratocaster and amps to find new noises. Loud ones. *It's supposed to be an electric guitar for God's sake!* he thought. *Playing the right chords and notes is just the beginning.* So he had spent a lot of time fiddling with the equipment to get something unique. Then halfway through their blues set, purely by accident, he'd found that if he crouched a few feet in front of the amp, he could generate a delicious distorted drone of fuzzy feedback that skittered into sharp, high harmonics and extended the notes when he moved his guitar into positions that exposed the strings to the sound blasting out of the speakers. He could control it, but just barely. And at the end of Hayes' solo there was a burst of applause and whistles.

Hayes could play the hell out of the blues and that solo had won over the audience. Unlike the college scene, this audience did not despise the military, so when Roscoe introduced him as "Jimmy Purple Hayes," and said "Jimmy's on leave and shipping out to Vietnam in two weeks," the rattle of applause had surprised him. Playing blues was not a lot different from the psychedelic rock he played with his own band, Universal Joint. Universal Joint was louder and his band mates weren't as good as Roscoe's. He hadn't played music with a band for months, and he was having one of the best nights of his life. After an hour and a half of blues, they took a break.

About the only other white person in the room was a girl sitting across the table where Hayes sat thirstily drinking a bottle of Stroh's beer. She had him under her spell. Has to be a hooker, thought Hayes. She was just too beautiful to be anything else and the place was crawling with hookers. There were some women present who weren't, but they were mostly older, there to dance, listen to the music and keep a close watch on husbands and boyfriends. *Why else would a young unattached white girl be here?*

She was wearing a bright, sleeveless dress that was green, pink and yellow. The neckline was high and the skirt was short, but it all clung tightly to every curve. She really had the curves too, along with wavy, golden hair that swirled with hints of other lighter colors whenever she moved. Her dusky, tan skin looked like she must lie in the sun all day. Green eyes sparkled under a hint of pink eye shadow and matched the green in her dress. Her green shoes matched too. And the lipstick on those full lips matched the pink in her dress and her eye shadow. Her earrings had all of those colors, and of course, the colors matched. She was so beautiful, so sexy looking, so matched up. And at the same time, she looked so young and innocent. In fact, she didn't look any older than him. *Probably younger,* he thought. *Then again, how old do you have to be, to be hooker?*

She was smiling just a little at Hayes but didn't say anything. He figured she might be a deeply tanned Scandinavian. Hayes was at least half Finnish and there were a lot of Finns living in the Upper Peninsula of Michigan where he'd grown up. She wasn't big, but her legs were long and her waist narrow, making the curve of her hips all the more dramatic.

She kept looking at him too, with a questioning expression on her face and those sexy lips. He wanted to feel them against his lips. Hayes smiled and she upped the wattage of her smile a little. He wanted to introduce himself and let her know that she was wasting her time with him. He was a 19 year old private first class in the U.S. Army making less than $80 a month, drinking beer in an illegal after-hours joint and sitting across from a really pretty and probably very expensive hooker. If only his Army buddies could see him now. He had been paid before going on leave. Could he possibly afford her? He had never been to a hooker. Maybe he should offer to buy her a drink, but she was already drinking a Pepsi. Instead he just sat there, paralyzed and unable to think of a way to break the ice.

It was almost midnight and still warm. Hayes' purple T-shirt stuck to his body and his jeans itched. *Too loose... must have lost weight in basic training.* He was exactly six feet tall, slender, perfectly proportioned, graceful and broadcasting his emotions with every movement. The soft features of his face drew people in. His blonde hair, barely an inch long, branded him military as much as a full-dress uniform. Though his vision was perfect, he wore rimless, pale, purple-tinted glasses. He reveled in his old PF Flyer tennis shoes after months of wearing Army combat boots. Felt like he could jump up and turn back flips. In fact he had done some jumping and spinning as he'd bathed the room in the scream from his Stratocaster.

Before World War II the place had been a neighborhood market. This night, the windows were tightly shut and no air was moving inside. His ears were ringing from 90 minutes in front of the amps, so the buzz of conversation and clink of glasses was a little otherworldly. He smelled sweaty bodies, spilled beer, cigarette smoke and some marijuana. He was a little high, but only a little. He, Roscoe, the drummer and the bass player had shared a joint before their blues set. Universal Joint was stoned more often than not when they played, so he was used to it.

Roscoe Lincoln was a stocky, slightly overweight Negro not yet 30 who was a studio musician and had taken Hayes to some recording sessions at Motown. He had introduced him to music producers and had gotten him hired for a three-week tour playing guitar in a band where Roscoe played sax. Hayes had played and been paid for it. Then as soon as he'd completed the tour, his own band had gotten a break. After more than a year of scraping by playing frat parties and dormitory mixers around Michigan State University, Universal Joint had landed a regular gig at one of the busiest campus bars. Universal Joint was good, but Hayes sensed they were not good enough to go much further. His band mates were more interested in drugs and girls than music, and the band was a means to both. Hayes liked drugs and girls too, but he didn't like looking for substitute bass players or drummers all the time because someone in the band was shacked up or too wasted to play. It had gotten hard to get his band to rehearse or work out new songs. He was making enough money to get himself a room instead of living in his car or in the university's underground steam tunnels or crashing with acquaintances.

Except he kept spending all his money on more music equipment. He was the hottest local guitar player, and Universal Joint was packing the bar every night they played and getting hired for other gigs. He was doing all of the singing and writing the songs, though he didn't think he was much of a songwriter or singer. Mostly, the band played amped-up, spacey, psychedelic covers of other people's songs. Hayes didn't have the courage to play more than a handful of his own songs on any given night. It all ended when he got drafted.

Ever fussy about his collection of musical gear, Roscoe was still fiddling with a guitar, a microphone and one of the amplifiers at the back of the stage while Hayes drank the Stroh's. The room was a blind pig catering mostly to Negro high rollers in search of music, liquor, drugs and women. If it had a name, Hayes didn't know it. The room sold a lot of liquor, though it had no license to do so, and you could get weed if you wanted it and probably harder stuff too. But the real business was the women. It was essentially a brothel, a place where you met women whom you paid for sex. There were no rooms on the premises, but there were several nearby motels.

Hayes found being a guitar player in an almost-whorehouse a lot more exciting than playing the college scene, though he mused that some of the college girls reminded him of the whores in the blind pig. Now that he was in the Army, he'd heard a lot about whores. He was no virgin. There was no doubt that playing in a rock and roll band attracted girls, but most of the time Hayes had no place to take them. When something happened, it only happened once. He'd never had a steady girlfriend, had never gone on a real date and had few close friends except for Roscoe. Even his band mates—who all had girlfriends, except for the drummer who was married—kept their distance. They were intimidated by his musical prowess. He had several good fake IDs to show he was 22 years old, and he'd told people he had graduated from high school and attended college, neither of which was true, though he wished it were.

Roscoe finished with the equipment and came to the table carrying a beautiful acoustic Epiphone guitar to which he had carefully taped an electronic pick-up on the inside with packaging tape. It was a gorgeous instrument, noted Hayes, who appreciated fine guitars. It was one of the best acoustics he'd ever seen. He ran his fingers over the colorful fret board, trying to feel the action of the strings, as the girl reached for the guitar. Her fingers touched Hayes' fingers and lingered. Their eyes met again.

"You ready?" Roscoe asked the girl.

She nodded.

Surprised, Hayes released the guitar.

"Careful," Roscoe said. "It's gonna be louder than you're used to, but you gotta play it just as strong. Don't back off 'cause you think it's too loud or it'll throw off your playing. You've got a great rhythmic style. It'll be better with this pickup. You won't have to keep it in front of the mike. You can move. Where'd you say you got those songs?"

The girl didn't say anything at first. Finally she mumbled, "Old blues songs... lately, been listening to Tom Rush." Hayes could barely hear her. Then she was repeating, "Just old blues songs. I can play lots of songs...." She looked at Hayes again. "I liked your playing. How do you...." She spoke softly and couldn't seem to complete a sentence. Then more loudly, and a little weird, like a bird singing, she said, "I thought that noise was a mistake, but you made it beautiful."

"Thanks," he said and nodded, smiling encouragement. She looked scared and it drew Hayes more to her. *Holy shit! She's here to play,* he thought. He felt like a fool. He had been so hung up on thinking she was a hooker that he hadn't noticed her nervousness. *A girl guitar player... wonder where Roscoe found her....*

"You're gonna like this, Hayes," Roscoe said, answering Hayes' unspoken question. "I ran into her on Belle Isle today. Man, wait'll you hear her sing. She's as good as anyone I've ever heard. And this girl plays a guitar like she's ringing a bell."

"You mean like Chuck Berry?" Hayes said sarcastically, making Roscoe glower. Roscoe had backed up Chuck Berry on a two-week tour and didn't like him. Hayes loved Chuck Berry's music and they argued about it all the time. The girl strapped the guitar around her neck and walked up to the stage, which was just a riser a foot above the floor level. Roscoe had set up a barstool in front of a microphone. She sat on it, looking uncomfortable.

"Help the lady with the mike," Roscoe said. "I'm going back to the amp to control the volume. I swear it's gonna sound better with that pickup than if we tried to put a mike in front of it."

Hayes adjusted the mike so it was a few inches from her mouth. He stepped back and then got down off the stage riser, catching her attention again, and suddenly looking right into her eyes. His heart jumped and his face flushed and he was suddenly as nervous as she was. *God, those green eyes....* And her dress hiked up past mid-thigh when she sat on the stool. She smiled shyly and then looked around the room. It was noisy, with people talking, laughing, drinking and smoking. Only a few were looking at the stage. He was thinking that Roscoe should have introduced her, but Hayes couldn't do it because he didn't know her name.

"Just start playing," Hayes finally said. He was flustered, barely able to think straight. "It'll quiet down and they'll listen. You're so pretty they'll like you even if you can't play."

Hayes instantly regretted the words, but from the very first moment, as she took a deep breath and prepared to play, he was a prisoner. With a flourish, she launched into a catchy progression of chords on her guitar. That was part of what captured Hayes. He expected girls with guitars to play soft folk music, but she was an aggressive player. She underwent a rapid transformation from quiet and nervous to powerful, confident, and fully engaged. Roscoe had been right. She had a strong sense of rhythm that seemed to pulsate from her core. Her guitar came on very loud, but Roscoe cut back the volume just as she began singing about a fat man.

She was singing about his "great big leg" and "he got a whoppin' thigh" and "get your fat leg off'a me" to the delight of the crowd.

She was working her guitar so hard that Hayes thought she might break something. She was putting her whole body into every chord, strumming it hard, picking out little runs with her fingers. She got up off the chair and leaned into the mike, except now it was too low for her. Hayes quickly climbed up and adjusted it. Everyone in the room was captivated by her music, but none more than Hayes. An electric flush swept over him and he knew his life would never be the same.

Her voice was deeper than he had expected, and just as Roscoe had said, she was a glorious singer. The purity of Joan Baez, the power of Gracie Slick and a tinge of bluesy, whisky-soaked Janis Joplin had her putting a song across the way Roscoe had been trying to teach Hayes. He couldn't believe she was doing it so naturally. She had the rich, resonant, polished control of a professional, a lot of vulnerable young-girl heart and more emotion than anyone he had seen. She made it seem like there was a fat man dancing in front of her. Which, not long after she started singing, there was. A fat woman and an even fatter man had begun dancing, much to the delight of the audience. Hayes looked around the room and everyone was watching her, swaying to the rhythm of her guitar. Instant love.

She played half a dozen songs. Hayes recognized "Drop Down Mama" and "Stagger Lee." She did a couple of Beatles songs: "I've Just Seen a Face" and "In My Life." She dazzled everyone with a two-handed sizzling guitar version of the keyboard solo from "In My Life." Hayes had tried to do a good solo for that song on guitar, but he'd never come up with anything that worked. Then she stopped for a minute to tune her guitar. It hadn't sounded out of tune so he was puzzled at first, but he soon figured it out. She was changing the tuning, and then she started playing strange, eerie chords interspersed with some slide guitar flourishes she did with a finger bar. It was a slow, hypnotic and melancholy number with a gentle, rolling rhythm like a boat rocking on long ocean swells. And it was complicated, endlessly changing chords and going in unexpected directions. She didn't sing, but she started humming into the mike. It was a beautiful, haunting melody, but one he'd never heard before. Had she forgotten the words? However, it didn't fit the rollicking ambience of the blind pig. Although everyone was still watching her, a restlessness was creeping in. She sensed it too, ended the song, quickly retuned her guitar and started in on a slow, bluesy version of "Baby Please Don't Go."

Hayes and Roscoe looked at each other. This was a song they had played together, though in a different key and faster. Hayes grabbed his Stratocaster and plugged into his amplifier. Roscoe got his saxophone and was motioning to the bass player and drummer. Before she was done with the first verse, they were a band. The five of them played together for another hour. It didn't matter what they played, the girl not only picked it up but put her own rhythmic stamp on it.

They finally took a break with Hayes drinking another Stroh's and trying to talk to the girl, who was drinking another Pepsi. He managed to find out that her name was Gloria, though she said she was calling herself Sunshine. She didn't say much, just nodded and smiled at him. She kept looking around wide-eyed at everything. She pulled her chair closer and leaned against him. He liked that, a lot. Roscoe and the rest of the band were all crowded at the same table with them. An additional two rounds of drinks had already been delivered from people in the audience. They were all discussing what to do next.

Roscoe looked at the girl. "We been playing here most nights, ten until maybe four in the morning. Can you make it tomorrow?"

She nodded.

"How 'bout you, Hayes? How long you in town?"

"You were correct... two weeks," Hayes said. "I have to report to Fort Dix New Jersey on August 6th. I was gonna go home, but my Uncle Sepp is out working on the boats so there's nobody up there. I tried to get my band together by phone, but I think it might be over. All I got is my guitar, my amp and my car and I could use the practice."

"Need a place to stay?" Roscoe asked. "You can sleep in the spare bedroom if you want."

Just then a large and very dark Negro with a big Afro and a menacing glare came over to their table. He was the main bouncer, and he'd given Hayes a hard time when he'd arrived. But he was in full friendly mode now, touching Hayes on the shoulder and nodding. "You play pretty damn good blues for a white boy," he said, then looked at Gloria. "And you even better. Better lookin' too." He turned to Roscoe. "We closin' down. The pigs busted a joint over on 12th Street. They arrestin' ever'body and it's startin' to get nasty outside. I don't know if they comin' here next or not, but we all ought'a get outta here while we can."

"Shit," Roscoe said. "Okay, but we gonna get paid?"

The big bouncer shrugged. "You speak to the man about that, but he ain't got time to deal with it tonight. Why don't you come by tomorrow mornin'?" Then he turned to Gloria, studying her for a few seconds as if he wasn't sure about something. He made up his mind. "Gentleman standing over there wants to offer you two hundred dollars to go home with him." He gestured toward a Negro richly dressed in a bright blue pinstripe suit with a purple tie and a white Stetson hat adorned with a plume of multi-colored feathers. He had a shiny black walking stick in one hand. The man was short and rotund, but he looked light on his feet. His eyes twinkled; he smiled and tipped his hat as they all looked.

"Jesus, that's Clyde Bonaventure," murmured Roscoe. "He runs the black rackets in Detroit and he owns this place. Shit, some people think he put a lot of the original money into Motown."

Gloria blushed and looked down at the table, then shook her head. "No."

Bonaventure, still looking at them, caught her headshake, smiled again, tipped his hat again, turned and left.

She slid even closer to Hayes, took his hand and whispered in his ear, "Can we leave?"

July 23, 2:25 a.m.

Opening the back of his 1959 Rambler station wagon, Hayes shoved his duffel bag to one side to make room for the cases containing his Stratocaster and Gloria's Epiphone. "Well, it isn't exactly cool, but it runs good." He opened the passenger-side door for her.

"Thank you," she said.

Hayes punched up WKNR on the radio as he started the car. "Some Kind of Wonderful" by the Soul Brothers Six was playing, a song that he had heard for the first time while driving into town, and he turned it up. She slid over close to him and rested her head on his shoulder. There were cars in front and back. Everyone was leaving. In the half-minute that it took them to get to the street, which was Clairmount, three police cars and an ambulance screamed past. When he got to the street he turned and headed in the other direction. He asked her where she lived, but she didn't answer. "Well, do you want to get some coffee?" he asked, and she nodded. He headed north and west until he found a restaurant called Biff's open on Grand River Avenue. They ordered breakfast.

Sitting across from him in the booth, pushing her scrambled eggs around with her fork, she looked directly at him and took a deep breath just like she had before she sang about the fat man. "I don't have a home," she said in that birdlike voice. She looked nervous again. "Can I stay with you? I'll pay you back when I make some money. I hope I can make some money playing guitar."

"What do you mean you don't have a home? Everybody has a home. Even I have a home, though I haven't been there recently. You must have come from some place." The girl was just too beautiful to be willing to go home with him, even if he'd had someplace to go besides Roscoe's. And he couldn't bring her to Roscoe's because Roscoe lived with his mother, a straight-laced, church-going woman who was suspicious of white people in general and who seem to dislike Hayes in particular. He had wondered why Roscoe had invited him to stay in the spare room.

Gloria was looking down at her food. She sniffed and blew her nose in a napkin.

He reached over and put his hand on hers. "It's okay. We'll find someplace."

They stared at each other for a long moment and Hayes held her hand with both of his. The fear seemed to melt away and she relaxed again. He said, "You know, I lived on campus at Michigan State for a couple of years without ever having my own place." He was just trying to make conversation and it wasn't easy. He finally looked away from her and carefully said, "Let's find a cheap motel and we can figure out what to do next."

"Okay," she said right away. Now she wasn't looking at him either, but when Hayes squeezed her hand, she squeezed back.

It was Sunday morning, about 5:30, when they pulled into a motel called the Cresthaven. Before he went to the office, Hayes studied Gloria. She had darker hair than him, but it wasn't that much different. He thought they resembled each other enough for what he had in mind. They were both young and slender.

"Okay Gloria, let's have you be my little sister. We can say that I've got orders for Vietnam, which is true, and you're here to see me off. Home is Sault Ste. Marie in the Upper Peninsula. I think we can sell that easier than saying you're my wife. You're too young to drive, so that way it makes sense that you don't have any ID if they ask."

"Well, I *don't* have any ID. I don't even have a driver's license but I can drive. I can even drive a stick."

"Good for you. And you play some pretty mean guitar. And oh, call me Jimmy. And pick on me like you would a brother."

"I don't have brothers or sisters."

"Neither do I, but we're gonna have to fake it."

It worked. The room cost $9.50, which was a little more than he'd expected, but it was also nice. It had a telephone with free local calls, a 21-inch color TV, a radio, one double bed, and one small desk with a chair, a tiny open closet and a clean bathroom with a shower over a bathtub. When Hayes explained he had orders for Vietnam, even offered up a copy of them, and said that he and his sister, who was his only family, had been driving all night from the Upper Peninsula, the motherly Negro woman running the desk told them she would enter the check-in time as past noon. That way, their $9.50 got them the room until checkout time the following day. And she as good as said she could stretch that checkout time by a few hours unless there was a sudden and unexpected flood of guests. He wasn't sure the lady was buying their story, but she didn't seem to care. By the time they hauled the duffel and her suitcase up to the room, the sun was coming up.

"I'm beat, but I want to take a shower," Hayes said. What he really wanted to do was kiss her. He wanted to lie down on the bed next to her, put his arms around her and kiss those intriguing lips. But he was afraid to make a move and they were both looking everywhere except at each other.

"You first," she finally said.

He didn't argue. He took a quick, militarily efficient shower, and came out a few minutes later with a towel wrapped around his waist.

She was looking at him, studying his body, and she blushed. So did he. When Gloria went to take a shower, he dropped the towel and rooted around in his duffel until he found clean boxer shorts. He put them on and saw that despite his fatigue he was very excited. So he got into the bed to cover his obvious desire. *Not surprising,* he thought. It had been almost five months since he'd even thought about the opposite sex. He had gone through basic training and then directly to a 15-week school to learn how to fix airplane propellers and helicopter rotor blades. There had been a few weekend passes, but Hayes hadn't tried to chase girls. He'd spent any spare time the Army gave him playing his old beat-up Gibson. Now he was lying in bed with a raging hard-on, his mind filled with visions of a naked Gloria just the other side of a thin wall as the thrum of the shower filled his ears. He began thinking about his time at Michigan State playing music gigs, constantly putting bands together and watching them fall apart, going to lectures on everything from electrical engineering to Chinese history, and sneaking into the dormitory cafeterias to eat. And in less than a minute, he fell asleep.

Just as quickly, he woke up with a naked body sliding against his.

"Sorry... you're kind of in the middle," she said.

There was a naked breast on his chest, naked legs against his own naked legs and one of her hips pressed against his thigh. He tried to shift away and when he did his excited cock escaped the weak confines of the boxers and sprang against her soft skin.

She looked at him. "Oh my goodness."

"Oh God," he said. "I'm sorry, but I can't help it."

She lightly gripped him, moving her hand up and down the shaft. As he tried to take her hand away, she pulled down the light coverlet with her other hand. "Oh," she said, staring at it, a smile on her face.

Hayes was staring at her breasts, ripe with dark brownish-red nipples. There were light tan lines from a two-piece bathing suit, but it still looked like she might have also been sunbathing in the nude. He was quickly overwhelmed by desire.

He reached up with both hands and caressed her breasts, making the nipples harden and pop up with his thumbs. He kissed each breast in turn and then buried his face in her soft belly. He licked her belly button and she gasped. Then he rose up on one elbow and kissed her lips, slowly moving his hand on a long, slow, exploratory expedition from her breasts to her hips, to her belly and ending in the tangle of soft, moist curls between her legs. Her legs parted and he felt her excited wetness.

She moaned and broke the kiss. "Do something quick! And hurry! Oh please hurry!" she groaned. She was still gripping him.

He rolled on top of her and tried to comply but her hand was in the way. Hayes reached down and took her hand away. "Let me," he said, and with his own hand he slowly started pushing inside her. He detected some tearing just as she squealed. *Is she a virgin?* He tried to keep from thrusting, but hot-blooded desire had seized control and he pushed all the way in. She squealed again, louder, then groaned and gasped, and then Hayes exploded inside her, issuing loud grunts and groans. He lay on top of her, supporting himself on his elbows, still deep inside her. "I'm sorry. Did I hurt you?"

"No, it was like getting a needle at the doctor's... but is that all?"

Hayes couldn't think of anything to say, so he kissed her instead. It was a long kiss and as she wrapped both her arms and legs around him, he rolled them over on their sides, still kissing her.

"Can we do it again?" she asked when he finally broke the kiss.

"Oh yes... and it'll be better next time." His desire was already starting to build. And it was better.

They made love repeatedly during the day, which was a long blur of half-sleep and sex. Much to his amazement, he discovered that she had absolutely no inhibitions about sucking his cock and skillfully bringing him to an exquisite orgasm. Sex got better each time, and each time they fell asleep in each other's arms, only to wake and start again.

One time Hayes was awake caressing Gloria's back as she lay on her stomach. He wasn't sure whether she was awake. He was hoping to softly arouse her so they could do it again. He was studying her buttocks as ran his fingers over her and he saw the marks in the light coming around the edges of the curtains in the window. About a dozen long, thin streaks were visible as lighter areas on her skin, and he could feel them as his fingers traced over them.

"What are these?" he said.

"Mmm?" she murmured.

"These lines?"

She shifted and turned her head back and up to look, groaned and then fell back.

"A whip," she whispered, more asleep than awake. "My stepfather whipped me. Cobra skin whip... it hurt...."

She stopped and then seemed to fully wake up. She lay still for a few moments, then rolled over and took his hand.

"Fuck me," she said. So he did, and he forgot all about the marks.

Finally, Hayes woke up after several hours of sleep and it was dark. During the day, they had been hearing sirens, but paid no attention. Now he was hearing them again, louder this time, and not only sirens but also the rumble of trucks, bells clanging and explosions. The room had a small window and he went to it and pulled the curtain. He couldn't see the street because the room faced sideways from it, but he could see the rhythmic flash of red lights reflecting off the side of a dirty brick building beside the motel. Deciding to investigate, he started pulling on his jeans and a T-shirt. He was sitting on the chair at the desk tying the laces of his tennis shoes when Gloria woke up.

"What is it?" she asked.

"Don't know," he answered. "There are a lot of sirens out there. Thought I'd go out and find out what's going on."

"I'll come with you." She got out of bed and when she started to squeeze past him her naked belly was only a few inches from his face.

He cupped her buttocks and pressed his face into her stomach.

"Uh oh," she said, and their hot blood boiled over again.

July 24, 2:45 a.m.

More than an hour later, they were freshly showered, dressed and ready to go out. Two police cars with their blue lights flashing sat in front of the motel and an ambulance with a flashing red light idled across the street in front of a building with hazy white smoke slowly drifting out of the back. Uniformed soldiers milled around a green Army truck and a Jeep with a big machinegun mounted on the back. Two attendants were loading a stretcher into the ambulance.

Immediately below them, two uniformed policemen and a big burly man in a rumpled grey suit were talking with the Negro lady who had rented them the room. The two policemen were white, as was the man in the rumpled suit. He slapped the Negro lady hard across the face. She said something and the two uniformed cops ran along the other wing of the motel, drawing their pistols. They stopped at a room and it sounded like one of the policemen had kicked open a door. Hayes and Gloria couldn't quite see, but there were screams and then the police reappeared, dragging two Negro boys. They looked like young teenagers. A Negro woman came out of the room and ran after the cops. One of the cops turned around and pointed his pistol at her.

"Leave my boys alone! They didn't do nothing!" she screamed without slowing her advance. Just as she reached the nearest policeman he fired twice and she dropped. A dark pool of blood began spreading around her head.

The boy that policeman had been dragging broke free and ran toward the fallen woman. "Momma! Momma!" he shouted.

The same policeman shouted at him to stop and then he fired again hitting the boy high in the back. The boy sprawled forward, his head hitting the pavement with a loud smack. He raised his head slightly and reached one arm forward like he was trying to crawl, and then he lay still.

Gloria gasped and emitted a soft, high-pitched keening.

Across the street, some of the soldiers were running and others were dropping to the ground. Tires screeched on pavement as the ambulance skidded out onto the street. The burly man in the suit ran toward the two uniformed policeman, cursing as he pulled a small pistol from his belt and pointed it at the woman and the boy on the pavement. Then he lurched back toward the office and grabbed the Negro woman from the motel, yanking her hard by her hair and slamming her into the side of the office. He pointed his pistol at her head and cocked it.

Hayes thought he was going to shoot her when there was a loud boom from the balcony on their left. A spray of red enveloped the burly man's face. He fell to his knees, dropped the pistol, then flopped onto his face. Two more big booms followed and both uniformed policemen fell to the ground. The second Negro boy looked up at the balcony, seeming to look right at Hayes and Gloria, then turned and ran hard along the street away from the motel. One policeman and the man in the rumpled suit were both lying still on the pavement, and the other policeman was rolling around in agony clutching his stomach. There was a fourth boom, but he kept moving. Then footsteps came toward them from the balcony on their left. A short tubby Negro man carrying a shotgun came around the corner, heading for the stairs. He stopped when he saw them. It was Clyde Bonaventure and he looked surprisingly calm. He was wearing dark blue work clothes and a blue Detroit Tigers baseball cap.

"We didn't see anything," Hayes said. He stepped in front of Gloria, his arms spread, his palms up.

Hayes flinched as Bonaventure racked the shotgun's pump, ejecting an unfired shell. He stooped to pick it up and put it in his pocket. "Okay, you didn't see anything," Bonaventure said, starting to back away.

Just then, there was a series of deep, booming, fast gunshots and the corridor 25 feet behind Bonaventure exploded in a shower of bits of concrete, wood splinters and glass.

"Jesus Christ!" Hayes shouted. All three of them dropped to the floor and started scrambling on their hands and knees down the corridor in the other direction. Hayes was holding Gloria by one hand. They got to the corridor leading to the back wing of the hotel, got to their feet and ran. The shooting had stopped and didn't start again. Bonaventure had disappeared.

Hayes and Gloria stopped at their room, trying to decide what to do. He pointed out that they had seen one of the police kill at least two people who hadn't done anything wrong. "I bet that big guy in the suit was another cop, the boss maybe. I thought he was gonna shoot the motel lady," he said. "I think we'd better get out of here before someone shoots us. That Bonaventure guy might come back, and we don't know what he's gonna do."

She nodded. "I-I... I ran away from home, and the police might send me back and my stepfather beats me up and...." She shook her head.

They grabbed their things and went down the stairs at the back of the motel. They jumped in the Rambler and drove out the back of the parking lot. Hayes got on the freeway, then remembered that Roscoe's house was in this part of town. He got off at the next interchange and made his way along Grand River Avenue and into the residential area where Roscoe lived. In Roscoe's driveway, they decided not to say anything about what had happened at the motel. They listened to the news on the radio and learned that there had been a big disturbance in the city. The news announcer was calling it a riot. Sometime after sunrise, Roscoe found them asleep in the car.

The Next 10 Days, Detroit

For the next 10 days they played music in Roscoe's big garage where he kept all of his instruments and other music gear, and where he had just finished building his own recording studio. Sometime during that period, people started saying "Black" instead of "Negro" and both Hayes and Roscoe learned that treating Gloria as anything less than equal to them was guaranteed to upset her. The first blowup came when Roscoe asked her to make some coffee.

At first, they were just having fun and Roscoe was recording some of the music so he could practice using the new equipment. Hayes got very interested in what his guitar sounded like in a recording as opposed to live. They were playing around with songs they all liked, working out arrangements. Once they'd worked out a song, they would record a take. When they listened to it, they always found things they wanted to improve, but they never got bogged down. Then Hayes started offering his own songs, not the ones he'd done with Universal Joint, but brand new ones. They were collaborations with Gloria. He liked to keep things simple, like Chuck Berry.

"I never heard a Chuck Berry song I didn't like," he claimed.

Roscoe gave him a pained look.

He started playing "Promised Land," which he thought was one of the very best Chuck Berry songs.

Gloria was even less impressed than Roscoe. "Sounds like 'Wabash Cannonball,'" she said. And she was right.

"Shit, you're right," Hayes said after thinking about it. But he could usually find some chords that sounded good together. They were rooted in the countless surf instrumentals that he had learned in California. Then Gloria would improve the music markedly. She had a knack for creating melodies from the chords but seemed to have a block when it came to lyrics. Then again, it was often her ideas that spurred Hayes to write lyrics. Hayes could play killer guitar solos and Gloria was the best singer. She also was an amazing rhythm guitar player, though sensitive about being confined to that role.

"You're better than the Everly Brothers," observed Roscoe, who had played shows with them, "and they're the best."

Gloria liked Jimmy's lyrics, which he dismissed as "stupid love poems." Roscoe didn't write any music, but he was the most polished and versatile musician. He knew how to capture the sound on tape, though Hayes was soon making adjustments to create unique sounds. Roscoe played all the drums, saxophone, and keyboards, and most of the bass. Sometimes he played guitar. He seemed to know just what kind of touch—piano chords or a drum flourish or a bigger bass line—could make a song better, and he helped both Gloria and Jimmy play better. They would record some music and then make careful overdubs. Usually all three of them would lay down a rhythm track and then dub the singing and guitar or sax solos over it. Roscoe heard their mistakes and he came up with a lot of different arrangements. He had a Gibson Les Paul guitar, and Hayes found he could coax some new sounds from it that he couldn't achieve with his Stratocaster. When he played the Gibson, Gloria was thrilled to play Hayes' Stratocaster. Then Roscoe picked up her electrified Epiphone and they did a completely spontaneous three-guitar instrumental that was almost 15 minutes long.

Roscoe's mother was away visiting her own elderly sick mother in Tennessee, so Gloria and Jimmy slept in the spare bedroom on a bed with one sheet, a cotton quilt and two pillows. But they hardly slept. If they weren't making music, they were making love. Neither of them spoke about what they'd seen at the motel. Music and lovemaking pushed those thoughts away, at least for the time being. For 10 days, they only left the house when they ran out of food or drink. But they also barely stopped to eat.

Near the end of the 10 days they finally got stuck. They were doing the song Gloria had played with the special tuning at the blind pig. She told them that it was Hawaiian slack key. This time she and Jimmy had worked on some words, though he claimed she had written most of it just by talking about what she was thinking. She had told him that she was thinking about her mother and her stepmother, whose name was Gina and who had recently been killed in an accident. Hayes recalled the moment in the motel when she'd confessed to running away from home because her stepfather beat her.

"Gina never once said she loved me," Gloria said, "and the one time I met my real mother, she laughed at me. I think she was crazy. I saw Las Vegas on her airline luggage tag, so maybe she lives there."

It was the most she'd ever opened up about herself. Hayes looked at her, and he was glad he had told her earlier that he loved her. But secretly, he wondered whether it was love or raw lust.

He had a hard time understanding her mother thing though. "I can't write a song about a mother," Hayes grumbled. "My Uncle Sepp never told me about my mother, which was his own sister. I figure she abandoned me and I think there's bad stuff that he didn't tell me."

"What about your father?" Gloria asked.

"What about him?" he said. "I'm a bastard... a *real* bastard. I have no idea who my father is, and I don't care. Hell, my mother might not know who he is."

She thought he sounded too bitter and it made her sad. "Don't you ever wonder about your mother? Where she is? What she's doing?"

"Nope. She decided not to have anything to do with me, so why should I care about her?"

He maintained that the song was about lost love or love that never was or how not to lose love. But if Gloria thought about mothers when she sang the song, that was okay with him. It made the song real to her and he knew that was important. They had been working on that song longer than any other and all three of them were unhappy with the results. The chords were complicated and they'd tried several different tempos. Hayes couldn't find a guitar sound that pleased him and Roscoe was sick of playing drums because it just wasn't working. They played it one more time:

> If I somehow lost your love
> Did you love me?
> If I didn't know your love
> Did you love me?

If love is lost, is it gone
Or does it keep going on and on?

I may love and never say
That I love you.
Then my love isn't lost;
I still love you
But if you never knew my love
Did I really love you?

I didn't lose your love;
I never knew it.
Your secret love's no good;
I never knew it.
If you love and never show it,
Love's been lost 'cause I don't know it.

When you love you have to say
That I love you.
One-way love is always lost;
Say I love you.
The love you give comes back in turn,
So say I love you

Love's great risk is if you lose it
And I love you.
My love goes on and on;
I'll always love you.
Love me back; you'll never lose it.
Say I love you.

"It's a good song," Hayes said, smiling at Gloria, and making her smile. "We're just not playing it right."

"I like it too," Roscoe said, punctuating his remark with a drum roll. "It's such a rich blend. I just can't seem to find a beat that works. There's no bottom."

Gloria was looking at her guitar over in the corner of the garage and then she looked up. Let's call it 'Say I Love You.'"

They all thought about it until first Hayes and then Roscoe nodded. Then they all thought about it for a long time. Gloria got up and went outside. Hayes and Roscoe had both grown accustomed to her lack of communication.

"I think you're right about the bottom, but I don't like the guitar sound either," Hayes said finally. "When she first played it that night, it was slower than we've been playing it. I remember thinking it was like waves on the ocean."

Roscoe nodded slowly.

So they slowed the song down, and Gloria came back. Right away, she felt more comfortable singing. They could hear the difference in her phrasing. Roscoe came up with a new bass line that was similar to the way Gloria had originally played it. She had been singing and not playing her guitar, but as she picked up her Epiphone and added a catchy backbeat, her singing seemed to gain emotion. Suddenly, the song's rhythm was as complex as the chord structure.

Hayes borrowed Gloria's finger bar and began playing slide on the Les Paul. He didn't play slide very often, irrationally feeling that it was cheating. The fuzzy, surfy sound he'd been unhappy with took on a whole new character. He backed off on the volume, letting Gloria's rhythm guitar take on more prominence. They worked for a couple of hours, recording several takes that they loved. In the last take, Roscoe sang some harmony with Gloria and Hayes thought it was a masterpiece, maybe the best piece of music he had ever participated in.

They were sitting around the kitchen table drinking coffee late in the evening when a knock sounded on the front door. When Roscoe opened the door, it was Clyde Bonaventure. He glanced past Roscoe, taking in Hayes and Gloria before looking at Roscoe again. He reached into his back pocket and took out his wallet. "I never paid you and the band for that night we had to close early," he said. He took out some bills and pressed them into Roscoe's hand.

"Thanks," Roscoe said, examining the money. He was clearly surprised. He motioned for Bonaventure to come in "Want some coffee?" Roscoe gestured toward a chair at the table.

Bonaventure shook his head. He was wearing a dark-plaid three-piece suit, mostly purple with brown leather buttons. His shirt was somewhere between pink and orange and his tie looked like it had come from a Middle Eastern rug maker. He removed a black felt fedora with a small red feather and placed it on the table. The ensemble was more subdued than what he had been wearing at the blind pig, but not by much. This time he had no walking stick.

He was not more than five foot four or five and rotund, but once again Hayes was struck by the lightness with which he moved. His expression was light too, almost merry, like a leprechaun. He beamed at Gloria and then Hayes, and bowed to take Gloria's hand. For a moment, Hayes thought he was going kiss it, but after nodding at Hayes he sat. His skin was light for a black man and was glistening, either from sweat or some sort of cream. His slick hair was cut across his forehead in a line as straight as a ruler. Hayes wondered whether he used a razor on it. Bonaventure looked at Roscoe. "Didn't Edgar tell you to come by? We haven't been open, but I left the money for you."

Roscoe shrugged. "We've been holed up here, making music. Having a blast if you want to know the truth. I guess there's been trouble out there, but we haven't been out of the house except twice to get some groceries."

Bonaventure kept glancing at the other two. Hayes thought he wanted to talk about what had happened at the motel, but not in front of Roscoe. He must have ascertained that Roscoe didn't know about it, or at least Hayes hoped he had. Hayes would have liked to talk to Bonaventure, but the man stayed for only a few awkward minutes. He was friendly enough, but after he gave Roscoe the money, the conversation died. Bonaventure said his goodbyes and left.

"Man, I wonder what that was all about?" Roscoe said, puzzled. "He's never paid me like that before. Hardly ever said anything to me before."

He looked at the money. It was a hundred and sixty dollars, all in twenty-dollar bills. He peeled off a hundred dollars and passed it to them.

"Huh, the band never got paid more than a hundred bucks, and that was only on good weekend nights. You guys keep this and I'll pay Lionel and Arthur. Shit, you guys made the night, especially Gloria."

Hayes pushed the hundred dollars over to Gloria. She still hadn't said much to him about her plans, but he knew she was striking out on her own and would need the money. He shrugged. "Can't spend it where I'm going."

And Hayes' time was up. They had one short night filled with desperate lovemaking. Then, early in the morning, he put on his khaki summer dress uniform. Gloria said he looked handsome. Roscoe said he would work on the music some more. They had recorded 17 songs, seven of them covers of songs they all liked.

"Man," Roscoe said. "There's more than enough for an album. Could be too much because some of these pieces are long."

"It's a hundred and nine minutes and twenty-three seconds total," Gloria said.

Hayes and Roscoe both looked at her.

She shrugged. "You always told us how long the final takes were."

"Yeah, but...." Roscoe started adding up the minutes and seconds. Math was not his strong point. He got mixed up a couple of times and after a few minutes he said, "She's right. A hundred and nine minutes and twenty-three seconds. How'd you do that?"

"I'm good at math, and I remember everything," she said. "If it's something I'm interested in."

"Wow," Hayes said.

On the way to the airport, they stopped at a Kresge's and Gloria and Jimmy crammed into a photo booth to take a strip of photos. Jimmy carefully cut it in half so they each had two pictures of the two of them together. Then each of them took a strip of individual pictures. Then all three of them squeezed into the booth at once and they tried to take pictures. That was tough without cutting off parts of their faces. They kept feeding money into the booth trying different combinations, laughing and causing a stir in the store. They left most of the pictures with Roscoe.

Roscoe laughed. "Album art. It'll be like 'A Hard Day's Night.'"

Reaching the airport, Gloria clung to Jimmy at the gate and couldn't stop kissing him until one of the airline employees pried them apart. He was the last one to get on the plane, and as he disappeared down the entry ramp he promised to write every day. Roscoe drove Gloria back to his house where, after hugging him, she got into Jimmy's Rambler and drove away in the rain, crying both happy and sad tears.

She loved somebody, and somebody loved her. She was sure of it. Or was she? Almost immediately, she had doubts. Why had she jumped into bed with him so quickly? Maybe that was why he'd told her he loved her. Isn't that what boys did? He had told her she could drive his car while he was away. She thought that must mean something. She had wanted so badly to be held and loved. Then, with horror, she couldn't remember saying "I love you" to Jimmy.

But the worst thing of all was that he was gone, gone, gone.

September 14, 2:36 a.m., Grosse Pointe

When the telephone rang in Matthew Doran's home in the middle of the night, he picked it up on the third ring. His daughter started singing before he could say a word. He heard a blaring electric guitar so loud that it almost drowned out the singing.

> "Do you remember me?"
> "I used to blow you for free
>
> "I took your precious car
> Didn't drive very far
>
> "Took it over to Belle Isle
> Where I thought a little while
>
> "Hope you're not too drunk
> 'Cause I opened up the trunk
>
> "Got that briefcase you were keeping
> Guess you should start weeping

"Giving half to my boyfriend
Yeah, I've really got a boyfriend

"Now your car is underwater
And I'm not your loving daughter.

"You can fuck yourself, Fat Matt, you piece of Armenian shit!"

The last line, which mimicked some of the conversations she had overheard as a child, wasn't sung but screamed and ended when she slammed the phone down.

Three days later Doran watched as a police wrecker fished his Stingray out of the Detroit River, and when he looked in the trunk, it was empty.

"You stupid little cunt," he said, loudly smacking his fist on the slippery wet fiberglass car body and startling a nearby policeman, who turned his head to look.

When Doran got home, he started making telephone calls.

September 15, 10:30 a.m., Detroit

Slick Percy Dupree was a tall, lean, and hard-muscled black man. At six foot two and 205 pounds, he was often mistaken for a professional athlete. He sometimes told people, especially women, that he was a boxer. And he did spend hours every week in a gym on Detroit's east side where a number of professional boxers trained. He lifted weights and hit the big bag. Sometimes, when he thought no one was watching, he'd try to get a rhythm going on the small punching bag. He'd resisted boxing lessons because Slick Percy wouldn't admit to anyone that he needed tips on how to fight. And he didn't. He also avoided requests from the professionals who trained there to spar. For one thing, it wouldn't do to lose, but more important, he didn't want to damage his face. Slick Percy was handsome. He knew it and worked on it.

Today he was wearing a dark blue Brooks Brothers suit and a mostly yellow paisley-patterned shirt open at the neck. An early fall chill was in the air, so he had donned a long dark-brown leather coat and a newsboy cap made from the same leather as the coat. His hair, done up in a burgeoning Afro, threatened to overwhelm the cap. His hand-made boots weren't the same leather, but they were close. Both the coat and the suit jacket were tailored to make room for a Colt .357 magnum. In his pockets were a pair of brass knuckles and a folding Gerber knife with a locking blade. The blade was razor sharp. Percy could flick it open in a flash with his thumbnail and a flick of his wrist. He could also throw it and stick it within an inch of his aiming point up to 25 feet.

When visiting someone, he would politely remove the cap and the leather coat but keep the suit coat on and buttoned. That way the gun wasn't so obvious. If he felt the need, he'd casually tweak open a button to display the gun. However, most of the time he could get people to do what he wanted with a hard stare from his luminous brown unblinking eyes. He had dressed far more spectacularly when he had been a pimp, but those days were over. Percy had not been a very good pimp. Beating women so badly that they could no longer work wasn't good for business. Before that, he had been dishonorably discharged from the U.S. Army for beating up young German prostitutes.

Percy was, however, ambitious. There was elegance in the way he spoke and presented himself. He dressed for success. With the white people who paid him, he exuded a smooth confidence but an undeniable toughness. That's where the "Slick" had come from. On the job, his "fighting clothes" consisted of a shorter, carefully scuffed, bomber-style black leather jacket, blue jeans, and black, steel-toed motorcycle boots. Around other blacks, he became blacker in both speech and dress.

He went into Matthew Doran's office, carefully taking off his cap and leather coat, laying them on the couch and sitting in the chair in front of the desk. They talked. Doran told Dupree what he wanted him to do and the request startled him.

"You want me to find your daughter and maybe kill her?"

Doran nodded. "Can you do that?"

"Yeah... but why?" He was a little worried about asking the question because Doran could be unpredictable, but killing a 15 year old girl was unusual to say the least.

"She's not really my daughter," Doran said matter of factly. His voice was flat and his black eyes bored into Dupree with cold indifference. Doran was colder than anyone Dupree had ever met. Doran slid a picture across the desk. "She's adopted and she's been threatening me. You don't have to kill her. Find her and bring her to me. I'll take it from there. Maybe I can still send her to Asia. They like white girls over there. That would get her out of the way. But I can't have her running loose and shooting her mouth off to the wrong people. If you can't bring her here, get rid of her. I don't care how, but you did a good job with Gina."

"Okay." Dupree looked at the picture. She was an attractive girl. That got him thinking about some other options. He liked his sex violent, but he always held back with the local prostitutes. He wouldn't have to hold back with the girl.

Doran slid open a drawer and handed him a wad of currency. Dupree picked up the money and smiled. He didn't have to count it to know it was more than he usually got.

"More when you do it," Doran said.

Dupree smiled again.

"I'm paying you so much because the job isn't quite that simple," Doran said.

In the process of putting the money in his pocket, Dupree paused.

"The girl has a boyfriend," Doran said. "Him, I want dead, and I don't know who he is either."

"So two of them—"

"I'll pay for two, and I want it done yesterday."

* * *

That evening, Dupree knocked on Clyde Bonaventure's door. Bonaventure's home was a fine, three-story Craftsman not far from the Manoogian Mansion, the official residence of Detroit's mayor. Dupree removed his leather coat and hat, this time laying them on the red leather couch where he was sitting. He talked to Bonaventure for a quarter-hour, drinking two glasses of Irish whiskey. He could tell Bonaventure had a woman upstairs and wanted to get back to her.

Bonaventure also had a request, one that was less audacious than Doran's had been. He too handed Dupree some money, an amount that was less than he had received from Doran but adequate for what Bonaventure asked him to do.

Dupree smiled as he took the money. The information he'd received from Bonaventure was more important than the money. He too wanted to find Doran's daughter, and the boyfriend too. More important, he had a pretty good idea where Dupree might find them, and he knew the boyfriend's name. Dupree displayed no reaction as he folded the money into his pocket, and he didn't tell Bonaventure anything about Doran.

"I just need to talk to them," Bonaventure said as he glanced at the stairs. "No rough stuff. Just bring them to me."

Later that night, Dupree met with an Italian gentleman in a darkened booth in a quiet little Italian restaurant owned by the Italian gentleman's large family. The Italian gentleman was more often called a greaseball than a gentleman. He did not offer Dupree any money and he made no effort to hide the pistol under his coat. This time, after he carefully laid his cap and leather coat in the corner of the booth, Dupree popped the button open on his suit coat. The two of them talked for almost an hour, though the Italian gentleman did almost all of the talking. Dupree learned nothing useful and said nothing about either Doran or Bonaventure. Dupree just wanted to keep on the greaseball's good side.

Finally, Dupree went home to his apartment, which was not too far from the gym. He thought about going to the gym. It had a very nice steam room, and a good steam before he went to sleep was tempting. Instead he counted the money he had received. Twice.

CHAPTER 2

Fall 1967, Republic of Vietnam

It was like a bad dream heading for nightmare status. The first thing Hayes noticed about Vietnam was the heat and humidity, which slapped him as soon as he stumbled off the Boeing 707 and into the blazing midday sun. Then the smell hit.

The soldier behind Hayes said, "Motherfucker! Is something dead?" Staggering under their bulky duffel bags, the soldiers crammed onto dusty buses and soon, the heat and the rotting smell got worse as they traveled through a horrific landscape of stinking squalor. Shacks were jammed together, made of scrap lumber, old signs, pieces of plastic, tarps, or drop cloths and topped with corrugated roofs.

"Jesus!" Hayes said. "Makes home look like a fuckin' palace."

Toothless old people, not clearly male or female, leered; small children wearing no pants and playing in mud puddles stared wide-eyed at them; and astonishingly, pretty girls in long white tops open to reveal black silk trousers seemed to be watching them out of the corners of their eyes, and sometimes they smiled. Bicycles, scooters, three-wheeled vehicles resembling rickety golf carts, water buffalo laden with heavy sacks, dripping cans and huge bundles, and throngs of pedestrians all parted magically just as the buses were about to hit them. Eventually, the buses slowed at a gate adjacent to a big sandbagged bunker surrounded by barbed wire and then wound past military buildings until they stopped in a place identified by the driver as the "Repo Depot."

A sergeant pointed them toward a two-story barracks and presently, Hayes found an empty bunk, dropped his duffel bag beside it and collapsed on the bed. Even drenched in sweat, he still fell asleep almost instantly, only to be awakened by a Spec Four who told him he had to stand in a formation and listen for his name. He stood, but they didn't call his name.

In two days, he got outfitted with a new set of clothing: jungle fatigues. He went to half a dozen formations every day, got stuck with KP once and became casually acquainted with a dozen other soldiers in his barracks. Finally, in the first formation on the third morning, his name was called for the 99th Assault Helicopter Company.

The 99th Assault Helicopter Company was almost within sight of the Cambodian border in Nui Binh Base Camp, situated near one of the branches of the Ho Chi Minh Trail that snaked into Vietnam. The company's radio call sign was Blackjacks and there were blackjacks painted on the noses of all of the helicopters and on the patches that the members of the company wore. The company had two platoons of Huey helicopters, called "slicks," that carried troops and cargo, and one platoon of Huey gunships. The slicks were mostly UH-1Ds, save for a few new UH-1Hs, and the gunships were all UH-1Cs, Charley models, equipped with miniguns or rockets or both. The gun platoon's radio call was Headhunters. The noses of those helicopters were painted with a cannibal spouting flames from his nose, and Headhunter personnel wore cannibal patches. Hayes thought the cannibal patch was pretty cool.

All of the helicopters flew with two door gunners, one of whom served as the crew chief. They also had two pilots, who were usually warrant officers, but sometimes commissioned officers. One was the aircraft commander and the other was the co-pilot, or peter pilot. There was a large attached maintenance platoon that kept the machines flying, a small headquarters platoon, a motor pool, and a medical detachment with a flight surgeon. There was a supply room and a mess hall with sections for officers and enlisted men. There was an armorer, an avionics unit, an operations bunker, small officers' and enlisted men's clubs and an orderly room. A lieutenant colonel commanded the company.

The buildings were wood framed huts with corrugated roofs that had the top halves of the sides open and screened. They had concrete floors and were called hootches. The men slept on beds with mattresses. Some of them had found time to drape parachutes around their beds for some privacy and others were building plywood walls within the hootches to create rooms. Low, sandbagged bunkers were dug into the ground between the hootches. Water from scavenged aircraft drop tanks flowed to crude showers and a few faucets at outdoor bathrooms with separate facilities for enlisted men and officers. Urinals consisted of smelly screened pipes dug into stony drain fields, and there were also outhouses. The waste in the outhouses dropped into the bottom halves of 55-gallon steel drums and was burned daily using jet fuel.

A big diesel generator provided sporadic electricity. Some of the men had acquired fans and stereos. The food was not bad, though it would get worse. The weather was humid and hot but there was usually cold milk and Kool-Aid at the mess hall. The enlisted men's club usually had beer or sodas, sometimes both, and some of the men kept bottles of liquor there. Young Vietnamese women came into the base camp every day to do laundry and work in the kitchen, so there was no KP. The company was supposed to have about 300 men, but Hayes learned right away that it was very short of personnel and would remain so for the duration of his time in Vietnam. It was not what he had expected. He thought it was a lot better than being in the bush carrying a rifle and a heavy load as a grunt, which when he was drafted was what he thought would be his fate. And it was better than sleeping in his car or in the steam tunnels or guesting on someone's couch back in Michigan. In fact, Hayes thought he had hit it pretty damn lucky for a draftee.

"Prop and rotor repair specialist," the first sergeant said, looking at the file Hayes had been carrying. Hayes was standing in the 99th Assault Helicopter Company's orderly room. The first sergeant was sullen, overweight and sweaty, and he appeared older than even a first sergeant should be. He radiated an energy driven by frustration, and his default mode appeared to be pissed off. His name was Sypher, and after noting Hayes' specialty, he picked up the phone and asked someone about prop and rotor repair. He listened for a few minutes before finally smacking the phone down.

"Shit, so we got a slot for one of those, but we don't fix any fuckin' rotors," Sypher said.

Hayes wasn't sure whether the first sergeant was talking to him or to himself.

"Nobody wants to fly on a patched rotor. We just put on new ones and use the old ones for walkways across the fuckin' mud. So you're pretty fucking useless." He glared at Hayes, then looked at a big white board on the wall behind his desk. It listed every authorized position in the company and had names filled in with grease pencil for most of them. But there were a lot of blank spaces. "We need gunners, but I guess I could put you in Maintenance. They're short too and you must be a little mechanical," he said. "Been to college I see. Another fucking waste of time. Probably didn't learn anything useful there either. What did you do in civilian life? Ever had an actual job?"

"Uh, well... I played guitar in a band," Hayes said. This wasn't going well.

The first sergeant looked at him incredulously. "Were you one those long-haired fucking hippies?"

Hayes nodded slowly, but kept his mouth shut.

"Jesus H. Christ," Sypher muttered. He leafed through the personnel file. "Well, you shot sharpshooter, so at least you can shoot." He turned a page. "Upper Michigan—you do any hunting?"

"Sure, every fall. My uncle and I hunt deer." Hayes had gone home to hunt deer even after he'd moved out. "I usually hunt deer with a bow, and I like duck hunting too."

"You some kind of fuckin' Robin Hood? You ever get a deer with a bow and arrow?" Sypher, who had done a little deer hunting, was curious. He had never bagged a deer.

"Sure," Hayes said, not mentioning that he preferred to use a bow because it was silent and he often hunted out of season. "You got to get close with a bow. I once put an arrow clean through a doe's neck, but I couldn't have been more than about fifteen feet away."

Sypher looked up from the file.

"Hard to believe. Duck hunting too.... You want to be a gunner?"

Hayes shrugged. Mostly, he wanted to get out of there. "I guess I could do that," he said. Later, he would wonder why he'd said it.

Scratching the stubble on his head, the first sergeant made a decision and slapped the personnel file down. "Okay, you'll be a gunner in second platoon." Then he picked up the file again and leafed through it one more time. "Lately, most replacements are already spec fours, but you're still a PFC. Did you fuck up Stateside? You must have."

"No, First Sergeant," Hayes answered. "I was top of my class too."

"Top of a *useless* class," said Sypher. He eyed Hayes suspiciously, then turned to one side and called to the clerk: "Gillette, take PFC Hayes down to second platoon, introduce him, and tell Sergeant Johnson I want to see him. He's gonna have to give up a gunner for the Headhunters."

Being a gunner wasn't bad the first month. Hayes learned what he had to do quickly and he was a good gunner as far as he could tell. He never skipped cleaning the machineguns, even if they hadn't been fired, which was often the case that first month. The very first time he fired an M60 machinegun in the Armament Hut, he fired a long burst and loved it.

A hard-looking guy in dirty jungle fatigues with a cannibal patch whacked him on the shoulder and snarled, "You fire too many long bursts like that and you'll burn out the fuckin' barrel." He didn't say anything else but looked at Hayes like he was a particularly slow child and then walked away. Hayes later found out his name was Frank Rivera and he was practically a legend in the gun platoon. He felt like a moron, because he should have known better. If he emptied his 12-gauge pump shotgun too fast at home, the barrel was almost too hot to touch, so he took the advice to heart.

He made friends quickly but didn't get too close to anyone. He got used to eating C-rations most days for lunch. Getting used to the temperature extremes was harder. Several thousand feet in the air, it could be cold, especially if it was also wet. And then on the ground, it was uncomfortably hot and humid. By the end of the first week, he had fallen in with the pot smokers, most of whom were not in the flight platoons.

But there were more than a few pot smokers in the flight platoons too, and the marijuana was very potent. He flew every day and got high every night, but he tried not to get high before flying. Twice he got picked for night missions and went out stoned. Even though it was strong, he didn't think the marijuana affected him much. He was sure he could handle it.

After two weeks, he learned that he could get bennies. Flight crews were getting up before the sun, flying all day or waiting to fly somewhere, coming back late in the day, usually cleaning guns and pulling maintenance after dark, and doing it all seven days a week. The bennies were prescribed by the flight surgeon, or so he'd heard. Hayes was always tired, but he didn't like the Benzedrine jag. When he'd gone on tour with Roscoe, he'd met musicians who popped bennies and he'd tried it. Take a bennie and you were awake and sharp, but you were still jacked up when it was time to sleep. And when it wore off, you crashed big-time. He thought it made things worse. He did better with coffee.

He wrote letters to Gloria, care of Roscoe. He'd sent the first two from the Repo Depot. For the first couple of weeks, he wrote almost every day. He described everything that was happening. He told her he loved her in every letter, though he again wondered whether what he felt was lust rather than love. Still, he wrote her love poems and said she should put them to music. She was good at that, better than him. Besides, he had no guitar to do it himself. In the evenings, he would pass a pipe with some of the potheads and if it wasn't raining, he would lie on top of one of the bunkers staring up at the stars and think about her. He thought of how her long golden hair hung over her shoulders and down her back, how her shiny Epiphone guitar pressed against her breast, what her fingers looked like as they danced around the fret board and the timbre of her voice as she sang. He tried to remember everything she had said and concluded for the umpteenth time that she sang far more than she spoke. He thought a lot about her being naked, and once he'd seized on that image, he couldn't get it out of his mind. He would sometimes fall asleep and dream of making love to her, then awaken with ejaculate soiling his pants.

Thirty days after he arrived, he saw his first real war. Three times during that first month the 99th had made combat assaults and they had been ordered to shoot at the tree lines: full suppression. Hayes fired and like everyone else was pleased with the opportunity to do so. And he fired short bursts. They had not received any return fire from the trees though. The other gunners and crew chiefs had been talking about how quiet it was, and how it couldn't last. One night, White, a tall skinny black guy who was a crew chief and one of the potheads, said the Headhunters were seeing more and more VC.

"Motherfuckin' naptime is over," he predicted. "There's a shitstorm coming."

The next day, they went into the landing zone (LZ) and got the order to deploy suppressive fire. Hayes had thought that no enemy could survive, let alone fight back, with 16 machineguns simultaneously blasting 7.62-millimeter rounds from the eight slicks. He was wrong. He was firing into the trees when they approached the ground, and as the helicopter touched down, there were green twinkles in the trees and tracers were flying past him on either side.

Jesus! he thought. *Somebody's shooting at me!* His heart pounded and he felt like he'd just stepped off a cliff. He was terrified, but he shifted his M60 slightly to the right so that his orange tracers were going toward the green twinkles. He thought they were the ones that were the closest and they were clearly the biggest ones, as big as basketballs and coming almost exactly toward him. He couldn't remember ever being so afraid, but he wasn't frozen by the fear. He kept shooting. Grunts tumbled off the helicopter, flopping down in the grass and firing toward the trees. If they could do it, so could he. His headphones exploded with excited voices as the helicopter lurched up again:

The first voice was surprisingly calm. "Fifty-one at four o'clock."

"Chalk three taking fire!"

"We're hit!"

"Shoot 'em!"

"Blackjack 23, we're losing hydraulics!"

"Christ almighty!"

At some point, Hayes realized that the reason the tracers on the right had seemed bigger and closer was that they must have been coming from a .51 caliber anti-aircraft gun. It was serious trouble and his fear drove him. He kept firing into the area where he'd seen the basketball-sized tracers. They had barely climbed 30 feet off the ground and Hayes was still firing furiously when out of the excited chatter he heard, "Chalk three, you're on fire. Get down, get down!"

Hayes' machine was Chalk Two. He looked around. Black smoke was pouring out of one side of the helicopter behind him. The helicopter sank quickly, flared out and settled on the ground. The main rotor stopped turning right away, which wasn't normal, but at least the pilot had had enough control to get down in one piece. Someone was asking for permission to pick up the downed crew.

"We're coming in to get you, Chalk Three," and only when the helicopter lurched around in a tight circle did Hayes figure out that the last voice he had heard was his own pilot, Moss. They landed behind and slightly to the side of Chalk Three. Smoke was swirling around the helicopter but there were no flames, and they weren't under fire as far as he could tell.

Without thinking, he unstrapped his belt, unplugged the helmet's radio jack and jumped out. It was difficult for a pilot to open the front door of the helicopter from the inside. He ran to the front of the smoking machine and popped open the pilot's door, but the pilot wasn't in the seat. *Must have gone out the back,* Hayes thought. The peter pilot was still there so he ran to the other side and opened that door. He helped the peter pilot pull himself out. The man immediately fell to his knees and started coughing violently. Hayes picked him up and half-dragged the stumbling pilot back to his own machine. Then he ran back to the burning helicopter. *Where the fuck is McLean?* McLean was his own crew chief. When he got to the burning helicopter, the pilot was trying to pull someone out of the smoky machine by one arm. The smoke seemed to be getting thicker. Hayes grabbed the victim's other arm, producing a loud scream.

"He's hit!" the pilot shouted.

Now his hands were slippery with blood, so Hayes reached under the man's knees and lifted. Between the two of them, they were able to get the wounded man back to the undamaged helicopter. Hayes caught a glimpse through the side of the windshield of his own peter pilot—*What the fuck was his name?*—making a winding motion with his hand. He wanted Hayes to hurry. *No shit,* Hayes thought. Then he thought, *No one's shooting at us.* They were only a few hundred meters from the original LZ where a firefight was still going on, but there were no bullets coming his way. That was good.

"Where's my fuckin' crew chief?" Hayes muttered. Then he said loudly to the rescued pilot, who was sitting on the floor of the helicopter and coughing, "Where's your other crew?"

The pilot stopped coughing said something, but Hayes couldn't hear. He bent over and put his ear next to the pilot's face.

"Dead. He's dead."

The last word came out in an explosive cough. Hayes plugged in the radio jack and keyed the mike. He shouted into the mike, "There's one more. Pilot says he's dead. I'm going back to look."

"Roger," came the reply.

He ran back to the other side of the burning machine. The smoke was very thick but he still couldn't see any flames. The crew chief was strapped in, his machinegun hanging vertically in front of him. Hayes bent close and squinted in the smoke. There was a very large hole in his face, right where his nose should have been. He felt himself start to retch, then controlled it and unsnapped the dead man's seatbelt. He remembered to unplug the radio cord and hoisted him over his shoulder. The body was heavy and by now Hayes was coughing and couldn't stop. He got to his ship, dumped the body into the middle of the floor, climbed into this seat and keyed the mike. "Clear!" he coughed into the mike. The machine immediately lifted off.

"Gimme a sitrep, Hayes," Moss ordered.

"The crew chief's dead for sure." He coughed several times before he could go on. "I think it's White. Shot in the head. The gunner is fucked up. Looks like his arm, or maybe the shoulder. The two pilots can't stop coughing but I think they're gonna be okay."

When they landed at the evac hospital in Cu Chi, medics pulled the wounded man and the dead soldier out and dragged them into the hospital. The two coughing pilots were able to walk on their own. Hayes got up and slowly walked around to the other side of the helicopter where the crew chief was. He was pissed that McLean hadn't helped him.

Moss was already there. He was bent over, looking at McLean, who was slumped in his seat. "Jesus fuckin' Christ, Hayes, you should have checked on him."

Hayes shouted toward the hospital, "We need some help here!" But it was too late. McLean was bathed in blood from his neck to his thighs and Hayes was sure he was dead.

Moss looked at him. There were tears in his eyes. "Damn it all, I'm sorry. You did okay, Hayes."

After awhile, the peter pilot, whose name he still couldn't remember, suggested they get a bucket of water to wash the blood out of the helicopter.

That night, Hayes, his hands still shaking with fear, wrote to Gloria, but with only a vague outline of what had happened. It was hard to write with his hands shaking. Every few minutes, he'd have another bout of coughing. He told her he needed her love or he couldn't get through the war. He tried to elaborate but couldn't. He smoked some marijuana and drank two cans of warm beer, trying to make himself sleepy. His hands mostly stopped trembling. Then he wrote to his Uncle Sepp and told him everything that had happened that day. And he told him about Gloria and enclosed a picture. He wrote, *Uncle Sepp, I love her. I need to hear from her.*

Still unable to sleep, he walked out to the flight line and to the helicopter he had flown in that day. He just wanted to see it because he still couldn't believe McLean had been killed while the helicopter hadn't been hit. And all of the fire had been coming from Hayes' side. As he approached it, the pinpoint of a cigarette brightened, revealing a figure sitting against the revetment. It was Moss.

"Mr. Moss," he said as a greeting. He felt awkward because he barely knew Moss. It had been the first time he'd flown with him. Moss didn't say anything but passed him a bottle. It was a fifth of Jim Beam, a little more than half-full. He didn't care for whiskey, but he took a healthy swig, managing not to choke, and handed the bottle back. Moss took a pack of cigarettes out of his fatigue shirt pocket and offered him one. He didn't smoke, but he took it. Moss lit it for him. He coughed but sucked more smoke into his lungs. It was harsher than marijuana and he wondered why he was smoking it, why anyone smoked it.

Moss was talking and drinking whiskey. "McLean and I came over together from Rucker with the 99th. He was my fuckin' gunner the very first time I flew here. I was the worst goddamn peter pilot in the history of this fucked-up war. Fuckin' near died just taking off. And the A/C wasn't a hell of a lot better."

He took a long drink.

"Crimmins, that's who it was. Got infused into the 115th. I heard he flew into a mountain in the fog. Whole fuckin' crew got killed. But that McLean, he had his shit together from day one."

Another drink.

"Motherfucker saved my ass more than once. Smart guy. They made him a crew chief 'cause he was so smart. Never went to school for it. He was the best fuckin' crew I ever flew with and it took me almost five months before I made A/C. I was a shitty pilot when I got here, but I eventually figured out that I'd better get unshitty."

Another long drink.

"Fuckin' warrant officers and enlisted men aren't s'posed to socialize. Me and McLean, we were buddies. Fuckin' A, he was as good a friend as I ever had. Goddamnit, I loved that guy. We were both goin' home in a few months. We were goin' down to the Keys to fish and chase pussy. That's all we were gonna do, all we cared about: pussy and fish or fish and pussy, dependin' on the time of day."

Another pull on the bottle.

"What's this fuckin' war about? I hate those commie motherfuckers, but why the fuck are they my fuckin' problem? They aren't about to hit the beaches in Hawaii or L.A., and they sure as fuck aren't worth McLean getting blown away. Nobody fuckin' cares except his friends and his family. Fuckin' LBJ can kiss my fuckin' ass."

A long pull on the bottle.

Moss handed the bottle to Hayes. There were tears in Moss's eyes and his cheeks were wet.

"I hardly knew McLean," Hayes said. "I knew White a little better, but I've only been here a month."

"McLean said you were okay for a pothead," Moss said. He was very drunk. They kept drinking until the bottle was empty, and Moss kept talking until he dropped the empty bottle in mid-sentence. "Shit," he said. "I am one fucked-up motherfucker. I don't usually fuckin' drink like this."

Hayes helped Moss up. He got one of Moss's arms over his shoulder and they began staggering toward the officers' quarters. Hayes was drunk, but he had been drunker and was in better shape than Moss. Luckily, they ran into another officer dressed only in a towel and flip flops, picking his way carefully along the boards and old helicopter blades that ran from the officers' shower to the officers' quarters. Hayes didn't recognize the officer.

"It's Mr. Moss," Hayes said. "He's a little under the weather."

"I'd say he's drunk, and not just a little drunk," said the officer.

"Yup, he's shitfaced," Hayes said.

The officer eyed Hayes with some malice, then grabbed Moss around the waist.

The two of them got Moss inside his hootch, where he collapsed face-first on his bunk. The other officer disappeared, muttering something about Jesus and Hayes thought he was swearing. Someone grunted and rolled over in the adjacent bunk. He untied Moss's shoelaces, pulled his boots off, and turned his head to the side so he could breathe better and wouldn't choke to death if he vomited. Then he walked back to his hootch.

He was drunk enough to sleep, and as he drifted off, he wondered whether he would ever hear from Gloria again.

CHAPTER 3

Fall 1967, Michigan

Gloria wrote to Jimmy every day, though she didn't always complete a letter every day. She could usually finish a letter once a week. Writing was difficult for her, so they were short letters, especially the first ones. Nevertheless, she enjoyed writing them and could feel the writing getting easier. She had no address so she addressed them to *Jimmy Hayes, Republic of Vietnam* and wrote on the envelope *(Please forward)*. At first she was afraid the letters might not get to him, but by the second or third one, she had convinced herself they would. She never put a return address on the letters. Jimmy had promised to write to her as soon as he had an address. Roscoe had told them he was scheduled to go to a recording session and then he'd be on the road for a tour that might last two or three weeks, maybe even a month.

Jimmy had said he would send letters in care of Roscoe, so after three weeks, Gloria drove to Detroit to see if she could find Roscoe. She managed to find his house, but his car wasn't there. The house looked deserted and when she knocked on the door, no one answered. No one answered Roscoe's phone when she called either. She assumed that he was still touring, and that his mother wasn't back from taking care of her sick mother in Tennessee.

She went to East Lansing, Ann Arbor, Ypsilanti, Battle Creek and Grand Rapids. She thought about getting a post office box but she couldn't make up her mind where to get it. She assumed her stepfather was looking for her, so she kept moving. She regretted calling him in the middle of the night from the bar in Ann Arbor where she had played two nights using Jimmy's Stratocaster, but it was done.

She stayed in boarding houses near the universities, which were full of students. She tried to pick houses that had at least some girls in them because she felt a little safer. Before she left home she had enjoyed attracting the attention of men and boys. Now she wanted to avoid it. She had often fantasized about having lots of boyfriends. After Jimmy left, she didn't want another boyfriend. She felt a fierce loyalty to Jimmy, and that was completely new to her. Boys, especially those in the boarding houses, tried to persuade her to sleep with them. She was asked repeatedly to go on dates, but she turned all of them down.

At first she bought clothing at the best department stores, reveling in the freedom to buy whatever clothes she wanted and spending more than she should have. Gina had always closely monitored her shopping. As she spent more money she started going to discount stores and finally second-hand stores. She had just one good pair of jeans that she'd brought from home. So she splurged on a brand new pair, but regretted the decision almost immediately because new unfaded jeans were not the fashion. So she bleached them. She cut down secondhand jeans that were too short into shorts and tied up secondhand men's shirts in a Daisy Mae look. She tie-dyed T-shirts and embroidered flowers on them or sewed on a border and made some colorful headbands. She bought peace symbol earrings and necklaces and bracelets and sandals, though it was soon too cold for sandals. She found a couple of old colorful long dresses and a pair of inexpensive leather boots that looked nice but turned out to be uncomfortable.

Then the sole tore loose on one of them so she threw them out. When the weather grew cooler she had to invest in sweatshirts, sweaters and then a jacket. She was looking for a sleeping bag and bought an old ugly green scratchy wool blanket instead at an army surplus store. They had sleeping bags but they cost more than she thought she could afford.

The hundred dollars she'd made playing in Clyde Bonaventure's club had convinced her that making money singing and playing her guitar would be easy. It wasn't. She was out on the streets playing her guitar almost every day unless it was raining. Rainy days usually meant no money, so she would lie in bed in whatever room she was renting, try to sleep and avoid spending money on food. Then she would get so hungry that she felt sick. Or she would go into a dorm and try to sneak into the cafeteria line or hang around a TV room, or she'd go to a library. If she was lucky, she could earn a meal or some money playing in a restaurant.

On a typical day, she would go out in the morning and start playing her guitar and singing on a downtown street. People occasionally dropped dimes and quarters, or even a dollar, into her guitar case. One day she was near the University of Michigan music school, playing mostly classical music, like "Ave Maria," "Beethoven's 5th Symphony" and other pieces she had heard on the classical music radio station but for which she didn't know the titles. She used her voice to fill in some instrumental parts while picking out lines on her guitar. Sometimes there were parts that just didn't work on a guitar, or parts she couldn't play because too many musical things were going on at once. She would improvise her way through the unplayable parts with something new. She improvised transitions from one piece to another too, and that wasn't easy, especially if she had to change the key. She would add rhythm too, a spicy rock and roll flavor. That was easier because she almost couldn't play without rhythm. She wasn't as fast as the violins, but she could come close. It was challenging and good practice and fun, and she became totally immersed in the music, closing her eyes as she hummed, strummed, trilled, picked, danced, jumped, spun around and slapped her guitar. The pink glow she felt and saw was so strong that she could barely see the dozen or so people she'd attracted and they were dropping many coins into her guitar case. Two older men, one with a beard, had stopped to listen.

"That sounds like Bach," said the bearded man when she stopped for a second to retune a string. She was panting but she shrugged.

"Are you a music student here?" said the other man. "I haven't seen you before."

Gloria shook her head. "Just trying to make a few dimes," she said with an explosion of chords on her guitar. Music always lifted her spirits, and she was trying to hold onto the pink glow. "My name is Sunshine, and I'm singing for my supper."

"Well that was just remarkable. I've never heard anything quite like it. You are a simply beautiful and gifted young lady," said the bearded man. He took out his wallet and dropped a ten-dollar bill into her guitar case. "I'm Professor Herman Rosen and I think you should consider enrolling in the music school. I'd be very pleased to write you a letter of recommendation."

The other man, who was younger, reached into his wallet and found a five-dollar bill. He dropped it into her guitar case. "I too was very impressed."

It was the most she had ever made in a single day, but it wasn't enough. Her money was dwindling. She had to buy gas for Jimmy's car and be careful where she parked. She kept getting parking tickets, which she threw on the floor in front of the back seat.

* * *

One cold night when she was between boarding houses, she tried sleeping in Jimmy's car. The two front seats could be folded back to form a bed. She was wearing sweat pants over her jeans, a T-shirt, a sweater and a sweatshirt and extra socks, and she huddled under the scratchy Army blanket, but she was still cold. She idled the car with the heater on to get warm, then turned it off, fell asleep and woke up from the cold a short time later. She thought again about investing in a sleeping bag, but she had never seen one in a secondhand store, and the Army surplus ones weren't cheap. She was sure her stepfather was looking for her and maybe Clyde Bonaventure was looking too. Though she used false names when she rented rooms, she was afraid to stay at any of them for more than a couple of weeks, and usually less than that.

October 12, Detroit

One day, some hippies who were passing out flyers saw Gloria playing on the street in Ann Arbor and asked her if she could play "Blowin' in the Wind." She played it for them. She knew the words and thought it was a pretty song. They invited her to a Vietnam War teach-in that was going to be held at Wayne State University in Detroit. So on a sunny Indian summer Thursday, Columbus Day, she drove to Detroit. Driving past burned-out buildings, she found Wayne State, then the rally and finally, a parking spot on the street.

She wasn't sure whether she was for or against the war. After all, Jimmy was part of it. Then again, thinking about it, who would ever favor war? She had been reading newspapers and watching the TV news whenever she could, and every time she saw something about the war, fear gripped her. It seemed to seize her entire body. Soldiers had started fighting in a place called Khe Sanh. She wondered whether Jimmy was there, but the stories said that those in Khe Sanh were Marines. Jimmy was in the Army. That was a little bit of a relief. But there were other stories about Army soldiers in Vietnam, and there were always helicopters. Jimmy had said he had been trained to fix helicopters, the rotors, so she hoped he was back somewhere safe fixing helicopters.

At the teach-in, a couple of hundred people were chanting, "One, two, three, four, we don't want your fucking war." Students were holding hand-lettered signs: *Stop the War, Down with U.S. Imperialism, All You Need is Love, Black Power, Resist the Pigs,* and *Equal Rights*. A man with a thin moustache and slightly shaggy hair and dressed in a faded blue work shirt and khaki pants was speaking into a microphone. He was older than most of the students she'd met. For about 20 minutes she listened to him drone on about the history of Vietnam, American and French imperialism, the Geneva Convention, and the CIA. He said he was a member of Students for a Democratic Society, and then he read something called the Port Huron Statement. Whatever it was, she didn't understand it and she thought he was boring.

Then another, younger man, a black man with a bright red headband cutting his Afro, took his place at the microphone. He was wearing green trousers and shirt that looked military with a red peace symbol on the front pocket. He was very handsome, tall and perfectly proportioned, his skin a smooth and glistening bronze. His shirt was open in the front and the sleeves were rolled up, revealing well-defined muscles. At first she thought it was more of the same but he started calling on the crowd to join him in a revolution. He called U.S. soldiers in Vietnam "pigs who are worse than the local pigs" and he pointed at a cluster of policemen around two police cars out on the street. "Our local pigs only got to kill 43 innocent people! Our soldier pigs are killing thousands!" he yelled, and the crowd roared with angry cheers. He shook his fist and led several chants. He got people worked up. He was rambling abruptly from one subject to another, but always coming back to calling soldiers pigs, and the crowd screamed every time he did.

Thinking of Jimmy, Gloria started to get angry but most of the people seemed to like the speaker. She was thinking of leaving, but she had drifted closer to the front. As was her habit when at loose ends, she was strumming her guitar. There was a lull and several people on the platform were huddled around the speaker, apparently trying to decide what to do next. By now Gloria was right at the front.

One of the hippies who had been passing out flyers was with the group standing around the speaker. She remembered him because of his English accent. He pointed at her. "Hey, there she is. That's the bird I was telling you about. She's great. Just what we need."

They motioned her up to the microphone. The young man who was at the microphone looked miffed, and he quickly started talking again. Then he got a better look at her. She was wearing bleached jeans and a too-small but warm red V-neck sweater that she'd found at the Salvation Army. She wasn't wearing a bra because she'd found none that fit and were clean. She seemed to be in a growth spurt, or at least her breasts were, as they felt like they were getting bigger.

She climbed up on the stage and saw that there was a second mike. She lowered the second mike down to the level of her guitar. She was already strumming the chords to "Blowin' in the Wind."

Peering at her chest, the speaker lost track of what he had been saying. He whispered, "What's your name, Baby?"

"Sunshine," she said.

He smirked, and looked down the front of her sweater, making no effort to disguise his interest. Then he said into the mike, "Here's Sunshine. She's gonna sing for us."

She sang "Blowin' in the Wind" and as she ended there was applause and someone shouted, "I ain't marchin' anymore." She remembered hearing the song though she had never played it. But she could usually play a song she'd heard on the radio and get it right the first time, provided she liked the song. This one had a catchy, jumpy guitar part that she liked. She started playing it. It was a long song with a lot of verses but she remembered most of the words. Everyone grew quiet as she sang the final refrain slowly. It was about old people starting the wars in which young people died. She was thinking of Jimmy and her passion was genuine.

She received a big ovation and crowd seemed to be growing. She had never played in front of so many people and found she wasn't afraid at all when she was singing. In fact, she was jazzed and a pinkish orange glow was building around her. Remembering the sign, she played "All You Need Is Love." She loved that song and she'd been hearing it on the radio. And she had seen the international television broadcast when the Beatles recorded it. People sang along and when that one was over she received her biggest ovation of all. But now, she could feel that some of the rally people around her on the stage were getting impatient and she couldn't think of any other antiwar songs. She didn't want to stop because she could tell the crowd liked her. She quickly re-tuned her guitar and mumbled into the mike, "Here's one that I wrote." She started playing "Say I Love You." She used her back beat rhythm, and in the middle she came as close as she could to re-creating some of the slide guitar solo that Jimmy had played. She hadn't played the song since Roscoe's garage and she was unable to focus on her original thoughts about her mother and stepmother. She was battered by a storm of conflicting emotions. She was thinking of Jimmy, thinking of the war and it spawned a wrenching fear that Jimmy would die. It became so strong that it pushed out the longing for her mother and the sadness about Gina. By the end of the song, tears had started down her cheeks. She got another good ovation though and said "Thank you" as the young man who had been speaking before her moved quickly to take back the mike. Her glow had faded anyway.

"We're here because we're against the war, not to sell your motherfucking records," he snapped as he grabbed for the microphone. The microphone picked it up and the comment echoed across the plaza.

Her hackles up, she leaned back in toward the mike. "Who's in favor of war? I bet the boys fighting are more against it than any of us. And I don't have any records to sell. My boyfriend's in Vietnam and he's not a pig. He got drafted and I just want him to come home safe."

There were some whistles and a few people clapped. Behind her, the hippie with the English accent said, "Righto! You bloody tell him, Baby!"

"He's a *pig,* you stupid little bitch!" shouted the young man, his face a few inches from her. "Every soldier is a cog in the imperialist war machine. He could have gone to Canada. He could have gone underground. But he wants to kill women and children instead." He pushed her away roughly, his hand on her breast, and that was the last straw.

She spun around, striking him on the cheek near his eye with one of the pegs on her guitar. It was mostly accidental, but she didn't regret it. He jumped back in surprise and she ended up in front of the mike again. She started smashing out the chords to the Beatles' song "Revolution" on her guitar.

He lunged at her again, smacking into her guitar and knocking her back. She whirled again, aiming the end of the guitar at his face. He jumped back, stumbled and then fell over backwards, landing with a thump on his ass.

She went back to the mike and started singing "Revolution," the part about wanting to see the plan to change the world. She slowed and segued into the chorus from "All You Need Is Love." People started singing along again and she slowly backed away from the mike.

"Bloody fool!" the English hippie said from behind her. He put his arm over her shoulder when he noticed the tears on her face. "Hey, what's the matter? You were a big hit. Don't pay any attention to *him*." He gestured with his head toward the speaker, who was breathing hard. He was being held back by two other men.

Gloria glared at him. "Asshole!" she growled. "Keep your fucking hands off my boobs!"

Then the previous speaker in the blue work shirt approached her. He looked concerned. "Are you okay?" He maneuvered between her and the younger man.

"Yeah." She nodded. She was getting control, taking deep breaths.

"Listen, that guy's a hot head. SDS supports our soldiers. Heck, my cousin got drafted. We just want to bring them all home," he said. "I'm sure your boyfriend wants to come home."

Gloria nodded again and wiped a hand across her wet eyes. She wasn't sure she believed him. She was feeling stupid, regretting getting so upset. Looking over the crowd she saw there were now four police cars out on the street. One policeman was leaning on the roof of a car and appeared to be looking at them with binoculars. She hurried off the stage with the English hippie following. She lost him in the crowd, which still seemed to be growing. She had parked the car around the corner from where she'd seen the police and presently she came to it. The crowd was chanting again. Clouds had replaced the sun and a chilly breeze had sprung up. There were no police in sight, but there was another parking ticket. She took it off the windshield and threw it behind the front seat with the others just as a very small man suddenly stepped between her and the front door of the car.

Where did he come from so quickly? He reminded her of a banty rooster. He was small but he stood with his legs apart, his hands balled into fists and his chin aggressively jutting forward. "Al Checchi, Detroit Police Homicide," he said, reaching into a pocket and flipping open a leather case with a shiny gold badge in it.

She looked, but didn't see as she stood frozen.

"I'd like to ask you some questions."

"Questions?" She slowly walked to the back of the Rambler. She opened the back and carefully placed her guitar in its case.

"Is your name really Sunshine? What's your last name?"

She didn't answer right away. She fumbled to close the guitar case and adjusted its position in the back of the car.

"I'm Sunshine when I sing and Gloria the rest of the time." *Why did I tell him my name?*

"Do you know Roscoe Lincoln?"

She shut the back of the car and walked back until she was standing in front of him. "Ah, maybe... I know a guy named Roscoe... I'm not sure of his last name." Gloria was a little smaller than the average girl, but she looked down at Checchi, and for the first time he seemed a little uncomfortable. She had never seen a policeman who was so small.

He was staring hard at her, but even though her breasts were almost at eye level, he was looking up at her face. She was wary of the scrutiny and he started to regain his composure.

She thought he was far too small to really be a policeman. Still, he looked like he might want to start a fight. "We played together, along with my... ah, boyfriend."

"James Hayes?"

She nodded.

"What did you say your last name was?"

This time she consciously ignored the question.

Checchi asked, "Okay, when did you last see Lincoln?"

"He took Jimmy and me to the airport... early in August... a Sunday. Jimmy had to be at Fort Dix... didn't want to be AWOL." Finally she managed to ask, "What's this all about?"

Checchi shrugged and fished his wallet out of his back pocket. He took his eyes off of her as he started pulling at the wallet's contents and she took the opportunity slide past him. She quietly opened the front door of the car.

He finally pulled out a card as she eased into the front seat. He looked at her, exasperated and then squinted at the card before showing it to her. It was a little calendar from a bank. "Was it August sixth?" he asked.

Now that she was sitting, his face was at the same level as hers and she smelled garlic and cigarettes on his breath. She looked at the calendar for a few seconds and nodded.

"What airline did he take?" asked Checchi.

"Uhh, Northwest."

"Where is Jimmy Hayes now?"

"Vietnam," Gloria said.

She looked up from the card and found herself looking into his eyes. They were bright and very dark brown, almost black. He seemed concerned and curious rather than threatening.

The look was at odds with his aggressive posture. She forced herself to smile and he started to smile back. But the smile disappeared as she pulled the car door shut. "Look... why... all these questions?"

He shrugged and started putting the little calendar back in the wallet. She was thinking that she wanted to get out of there before he asked any more questions. He made her nervous, and when she was nervous she couldn't think.

"You know, you should be more careful parking." He glanced into the back of the car. "You've gotten quite a few tickets."

She started the car.

"Hey wait a minute," he said. "I have some more questions."

She shifted into first gear and started driving away. When she looked in the rear-view mirror, he was gesturing unhappily at her. She stuck a hand out the window and waved.

5:15 p.m.

After getting lost a few times and driving past the remains of more burned-out buildings, she found Roscoe's home in northwest Detroit. There were no burned buildings in this area. This time there was an Oldsmobile parked in the long driveway that she hadn't seen before and lights were on inside the house in the late-afternoon gloom. She pulled off the concrete driveway and parked in the same gravel area where Jimmy had parked three months earlier. She was strangely sick to her stomach but hungry at the same time. She'd thought about stopping to eat, especially when she'd seen the Biff's where she and Jimmy had their first breakfast together, but she didn't want to spend the money. Tentatively, she rapped softly with the brass knocker on the door.

The door opened almost immediately and a tall, stern black woman with grey hair and suspicious eyes made bigger by thick, dark-rimmed spectacles looked out at her. Her dark blue dress was simple but made of fine wool. A pearl necklace with real pearls peeked from behind a cream-colored blouse, visible under a brown suede coat. A big brown purse hung from her shoulder. "Who are you?" Her tone wasn't friendly and she seemed startled.

"Ah, I'm a... I'm a friend of Roscoe's... Gloria. You must be his mother." She had to concentrate to talk, and was feeling more queasy by the second. "I just wanted to see if there were any letters for me from Jimmy."

The woman stared at her for a long moment. "You'd better come in. I was on my way to the church, but that can wait."

She opened the door wider and led Gloria to the living room where she gestured toward a couch covered with a flowery slipcover. It was the first time she'd actually been in the room though she had passed it when she and Jimmy had been there earlier with Roscoe. They had only used the kitchen and the spare bedroom. She took a seat on a chair with a matching flowery cover. There was a large picture of Roscoe on the mantle over the fireplace. She didn't think it had been there before.

"What's your last name, Gloria? I'm Frances Lincoln, Roscoe's mother," said the woman, her manner thawing a little. "Can I get you something? Some tea? Or coffee? Or a soft drink? You look a little... piqued."

"That's okay," Gloria said. She was weak, on the verge of dizziness, and gulping air. "Thank you. I'm feeling a little unsettled, probably because I've hardly eaten today." She shook her head. "Sorry, I'm okay. My last name is... ah, Dorchester...."

Her voice trailed off. She didn't like lying.

"Dorchester?" Frances said. "Not Sunshine?"

"Sunshine?" Gloria said. "Well, ah... sometimes I go by Sunshine... when I sing."

"By Jimmy, you mean Jimmy Hayes, a white boy with long blonde hair? Plays a guitar and sometimes played with my son? I think he uses drugs too. I didn't approve of him, all that long hair and the beads and the purple glasses and the drugs."

"Yes, that sounds like Jimmy," she said, remembering that Jimmy had told her he'd had long hair before he got drafted.

"Wait here," Frances said. She walked out of the room and Gloria heard her climbing the stairs. She came back a few minutes later with a sheaf of letters in her hand. She gave them to Gloria. "I think these must be for you."

There appeared to be a couple of dozen letters. They were from PFC or SP4 Jimmy Hayes and addressed to *Gloria Sunshine* or *Sunshine Gloria* and on one of them she saw *P.S. I love you.* With a sickening feeling, Gloria realized that Jimmy didn't know her last name. *I never told him!* "Oh my God! Oh thank you! Thank you!" For the second time that afternoon, she was crying, but this time they were happy tears. She wanted to rip open the letters and start reading.

"Come into the kitchen," Mrs. Lincoln said. "We need to talk and I'll heat up some spaghetti for you. Do you know the police want to talk to you? And so do I."

Mrs. Lincoln took a covered bowl of spaghetti and meatballs out of the refrigerator and dumped it into a pot. Then she lit the gas stove.

Soon, Gloria was hungrily devouring it and drinking a glass of milk. "Thank you. I'm very hungry."

"I want to talk to you about my son's passing," Frances Lincoln said when Gloria was almost finished.

Gloria gasped. "What?" She choked on some spaghetti and coughed it back into the bowl. She tried to speak a couple of times, but her mouth seemed to be paralyzed.

Mrs. Lincoln took a newspaper clipping from a cardboard box on the table and handed it to her.

It was from the *Detroit Free Press* and dated several days earlier. Gloria emitted a groan as she read it, and a chill spread through her. The headline read, *Area Musicians Stage Benefit Concert for Slain Colleague.* There was a picture of Roscoe above it. His full name under the picture was Roscoe J. Lincoln. He was described as an up-and-coming studio musician who had played on several Motown recordings. Apparently he hadn't made as much money as she and Jimmy had thought because his musician friends had staged the concert in a VFW Hall to help his mother pay for his funeral. The last paragraph really caught Gloria's attention:

> Lincoln was found dead Sept. 18 in an alley near Eight Mile Road and Southfield Freeway. Detectives said he might have he died of a drug overdose but also may have been beaten. No arrests have been made.

Frances Lincoln had learned of her son's murder the same day she had placed her own mother in a nursing home. It had taken police a long time to track her down.

Mrs. Lincoln had been talking as Gloria read the newspaper clipping. Her voice faded into Gloria's consciousness: "Mother has lost her mind, poor dear. Sometimes she doesn't even remember who I am. Hope I don't ever get that way. But I don't think she's gonna last long, because she's got the cancer too." Mrs. Lincoln was speaking slowly, looking around the room as if she was trying to push back the overpowering sadness. When she talked about Roscoe's death, she got choked up and dabbed at her eyes with a handkerchief she quickly produced from the big purse. She clearly didn't think much of the two homicide detectives from the police department who were investigating the murder. "The big one is dumber than dog poop," she said. "But that little one is sneaky."

The police seemed to believe that Roscoe had died from drugs. They told her he had been severely beaten and they believed he had been in a fight over drugs and money. She thought the detectives were not telling her everything. They didn't believe her when she said her son didn't use drugs and didn't usually go to the part of town where he had been found.

Gloria knew Roscoe and Jimmy had both smoked marijuana but that didn't seem out of the ordinary. It was illegal, but since leaving home, she had seen a lot of people smoking it, especially around the universities. She had tried marijuana only once, the first time Jimmy and Roscoe lit a joint. At first it didn't seem to do anything. Then she got sleepy and scared, and it screwed up her memory. She didn't like marijuana.

However, the police had learned from talking to neighbors that Roscoe had been seen with two young white people, a man and a woman, both with blonde hair. And the neighbors had heard music coming out of the garage at all hours for more than a week, and then it had stopped. It was loud enough for them to hear, but not loud enough to complain about. Roscoe had brought tapes to Motown where he had been asking people to listen and he had been working on them, mixing them. Some of the music people were interested, Mrs. Lincoln said, and there was talk of putting out a record. It wasn't Motown, but a small company started by former Motown people. The police didn't think there was any connection to Roscoe's murder from his work at Motown, except that they seemed to believe most musicians, especially if they were black, were drug addicts.

"I think there's gonna be a record album, but they want to know who the girl singer was," she said. "Was that you?"

She nodded. "And Jimmy was singing and playing guitar too. In fact all three of us were. But Roscoe mostly played sax, piano, bass and drums. He's a really good musician and it's awful what happened to him."

"Oh dear! Are you sure? I thought he played all the instruments. He told me he could do that with all that equipment he was buying. But I knew there had to be a girl doing that singing. I thought he might have finally found a girlfriend." She sighed. "But you're Jimmy's girlfriend?"

Gloria nodded and told Roscoe's mother how they'd spent the time making music in the garage. She didn't mention Clyde Bonaventure or the motel shootings. They hadn't said anything to Roscoe about that.

"Where's Jimmy Hayes now? San Francisco?" Mrs. Lincoln asked. "That's what the return address on the letters say. I told those two detectives about those letters the last time they called. Said they ought to talk to Jimmy Hayes who was in San Francisco. They didn't seem very interested. They were supposed to drop by to pick up the letters, but that was more than a week ago."

Gloria said, "Jimmy's in Vietnam and I'm really scared about what could happen to him. I'm so glad to get these letters. Now I have an address where I can write to him." She sniffed, then got back to the original question. "Roscoe drove us to the airport and we put Jimmy on a plane to Fort Dix in New Jersey. That's where he was supposed to ship out to Vietnam."

"Oh."

Gloria opened her purse and took out the two Kresge photos cut from the filmstrip. She showed them to Mrs. Lincoln.

"That's me and Jimmy. He doesn't look the same as the last time you saw him."

Mrs. Lincoln just glanced at the pictures and Gloria realized that she didn't care much about Jimmy, just her son.

Gloria had found her voice and they talked more. She had decided that there was no harm in confiding in Frances Lincoln, who was so grief-stricken about Roscoe's death. She told her a little more about the recording session in the garage and that she agreed with her, that her son didn't use drugs. Marijuana, she decided, didn't count. Finally, Gloria hugged the stern black woman and told her again how sorry she was about Roscoe. They both cried. She thanked her for the letters and the meal, and said she had to leave. She had to get away from the woman's sadness, and a different kind of fear was taking hold. Now the police were probably looking for her too. That's why the little detective had been asking her questions.

"You know, I'll have to tell the police you were here," Mrs. Lincoln said. "I'm sure they'll still come by for those letters sooner or later."

It was clear that Mrs. Lincoln didn't like the police very much, but Gloria clutched the letters more tightly. "Okay," she said.

"They might want to talk to you."

"I don't know anything, just what I told you."

"Can I tell them where they can find you?"

"I don't think so," Gloria said a little slyly. "I mean, you don't know where to find me, and I won't tell you where I'll be. I'm not even sure myself and I'm too afraid to talk to the police right now. Thanks again for your help, and I'm so sorry for your loss."

Before Mrs. Lincoln could say anything else, she left.

CHAPTER 4

10 November, 1705 Hours, Nui Binh Base Camp

Hayes had been promoted to Specialist Fourth Class and transferred to the gun platoon. The firefight that had claimed White and McLean also had drawn attention to Hayes. When second platoon's Staff Sergeant Homer Johnson was asked to give up another gunner for the gun platoon, he offered Hayes to Staff Sergeant Ernie Metcalf, the Headhunters' platoon sergeant. Metcalf hesitated only momentarily, being somewhat apprehensive about Hayes' burgeoning reputation as a pothead. But he wouldn't be the only pot smoker in the gun platoon. More important to Metcalf was the fact that Hayes had not panicked during his first exposure to combat. The wounded gunner whom he'd helped rescue swore that Hayes had gotten the .51. So did Warrant Officer Moss, and so did a pilot on another ship. Hayes' actions made it clear that he had his shit together under fire, and that was Metcalf's main concern.

A couple of days later, Hayes had done something even more remarkable. The 99th had been assigned to insert an ARVN unit—a unit of the Army of the Republic of Vietnam—into the same LZ, which was supposed to be secure. Unless they were ARVN Rangers or from other American-trained units, the ARVNs were often reluctant to get off the helicopters to go into battle, and that day the flight crews had been given orders to throw them off if necessary.

The ARVNs, having heard about the earlier fighting, were even more skittish than usual. Hayes and the crew chief he was flying with that day, a Cajun from Louisiana named Smokey St. Clair, had to throw all of the ARVNs off the chopper and threaten them with their weapons to keep them from clambering back on.

Hayes had just gotten back down behind his machinegun when one of the ARVNs turned and fired his M79 grenade launcher at the helicopter. The 40-millimeter explosive round hit the lower front of the helicopter, blowing out the chin bubble and peppering the peter pilot's lower legs with shrapnel. As the man screamed, Hayes killed the ARVN with a short burst from his M60. The helicopter took off and headed for 12th Evac hospital with the wounded co-pilot. The last Hayes saw of the ARVN were his comrades clustered around him. Hayes was sure he was dead because he'd been close enough to see bullets hitting his face and punching though his helmet.

At the hospital, Hayes was interviewed by Lieutenant Colonel Blair, their new commanding officer. Blair was a medium-sized slender man who'd recently turned thirty. When the colonel's gray eyes locked on him as he stood at attention in a daze beside the helicopter, Hayes remembered to salute.

Blair returned the salute crisply. "Tell me what happened, Specialist...." He squinted as looked at Hayes' nametag. "Specialist Hayes. And stand easy."

"Sir, he... ah, that ARVN took a shot at us with a grenade launcher. Hit the front of our ship. I heard somebody scream and I just hit him with a burst from my sixty," Hayes said. "Jesus, I think I must have killed him."

Blair looked at Hayes going from his face down to his feet and back up to his face. "Are you okay, Specialist?"

"Yeah... yes Sir, I think so," Hayes said. He still had his flight helmet on. He removed it so he could hear the CO better. He rubbed his head, which was itchy with sweat. "Yeah, I'm okay. He didn't hit me."

Blair walked over to the front of the helicopter and looked through the open front door where they'd pulled the peter pilot out. The pedals and the front of the seat were splattered with blood and there was big puddle of blood on the floor. He winced at the sight. "What were you thinking, Specialist?"

The question rattled Hayes for a moment. He figured he was in deep trouble. "I wasn't thinking, Sir," he finally admitted. "He shot at us so I shot back." He looked away from Blair and shook his head. "Man, he must be dead. I know I got him in the head," Hayes groaned. He wrapped his arms around himself as a chill spread through his body. "Why did he have to shoot at us?"

"It's okay, Son," said Blair. "I don't believe you did anything wrong."

Blair had the company clerk type up a statement for him to sign. Half a dozen others, including the peter pilot who had been wounded, also signed statements. Everyone told him he hadn't done anything wrong. Still, he felt bad about killing the ARVN and worried about it despite the reassurance he was receiving.

Hayes hadn't wanted to go to the gun platoon but he hadn't said anything, figuring he had no choice. When Johnson and Metcalf asked him if was willing to go to the gun platoon, he'd just shrugged, said "Okay" and began throwing his stuff into his footlocker. Metcalf helped him with the footlocker and brought him over to one of the two gun platoon hootches. It was messier than his old hootch, and the alcove where Metcalf gestured to the top bunk was the only orderly place. Hayes and Metcalf dropped the footlocker on the concrete floor.

"Rivera, this is Hayes, gunner from second platoon who's now with Headhunters. Help get him squared away," the sergeant said, then left.

Hayes looked warily at Rivera, who was a Spec Five crew chief and a Cuban from Florida. Hayes hadn't forgotten about his mistake with the long burst. Rivera had light skin, but his kinky hair and most of his facial features looked Negroid. Hayes wasn't sure whether he considered himself black or white, and he never asked him about it. He'd been with the 99th since shortly after it had come to Vietnam, and he'd been a grunt before that. He was quiet and experienced, the most competent crew chief in the platoon. Hayes had never seen him smoking pot or drunk, though he occasionally had a beer in the EM Club. He was quiet and one of the most respected men in the company.

"Hear you like to smoke pot," Rivera said evenly.

Hayes just nodded.

"I don't want to fly with anyone who smokes. Might get me killed."

After a long moment, Hayes said, "What about drinking? I've seen some guys so hung over they're might still be drunk."

"I don't like that either. We're in combat; it's stupid to do any of that stuff. I heard you're smart and a good gunner, so I don't understand why you'd do something so stupid."

Hayes sat down on his footlocker and thought about it, remembering all the nights he and Universal Joint had played while they were high. One night somebody had taped some of their show, and when he listened to it, he remembered being shocked at all of the mistakes he'd made. "Okay, I'll stop smoking pot. You were right about long bursts and you're right about this."

Rivera looked surprised, then stuck out his hand, a gesture of formality that surprised Hayes as they shook. "Welcome to the Headhunters," Rivera said. "Wasting that ARVN cocksucker was something else. I've been here almost two years and never got a chance to do that."

"Well, I've been here three months and the only person I've for sure killed was supposed to be on our side."

CHAPTER 5

November 13, 9:15 a.m., Ann Arbor, Michigan

Gloria knelt on the bathroom floor, bent over the toilet and very carefully threw up. She remained kneeling for several minutes until she was sure she wasn't going to be sick again. Then she pulled down her jeans, sat on the toilet, urinated and flushed. She washed her hands and thought about taking a shower. *Will that calm down my stomach?* But she had taken a shower before going to bed and there were a dozen or more people living in the house. This was the only shower and the hot water often ran out. She liked the house. Everyone living there was young like her. Most of them were students, though not all of them. She was one of the few not sharing a room, but having a room to herself was a luxury that she would not be able to afford much longer. Sometimes she would come down in the mornings to find several complete strangers sleeping on couches and the floor of the living room. Maybe she liked the place because for the first time in her life, she was starting to make friends.

She sighed and settled for washing her face, arms and torso with a washcloth. By the time she walked out of the bathroom, she was starting to feel queasy again. She headed for the kitchen. *Some oatmeal might help.*

"Hey Gloria baby, you were great last night at the Gables," said Lenny Papineau, a skinny, unshaven guy with long, untidy hair that he kept out of his eyes with a flowery bandana.

He had a strong body odor, and the pungent aroma from the spicy omelet he was making increased her queasiness.

Hippies, she had learned, were not as romantic and were considerably smellier than she had imagined. And Lenny was a true hippie. Still, Lenny was one of the nicest people in the house and she could talk to him. He hadn't made a single pass at her and he didn't get into drunken squabbles, though he sometimes went on bad acid trips. Lenny didn't do much of anything except smoke pot or drop acid, read J.R.R. Tolkien novels and go to an occasional class. He had said he was a pre-law student and Gloria liked him because he treated her with friendly respect.

"You want some of this omelet? It's got green chilies, onions, coriander, cashew nuts, paprika, oregano, cumin, and eggs. It's Indian, I guess," he said, his face tightening as he thought about it. He looked a little stoned. He glanced through the doorway to the living room as Gloria shook her head, trying to hold her breath as she brushed past him to get a pot to make oatmeal. For once the living room was empty. "Anyway, you're really fuckin' cool on guitar. Call yourself Sunshine, huh? Neat name. You ever think of starting your own band?"

"Well, I'm sort of in a band already," she grinned. Then she remembered that she and Jimmy and Roscoe would never play together again and she felt sicker. But she ought to be feeling better and made an effort to try. She had made a week's rent money playing at the bar. They hadn't asked for ID, paid her in cash and asked her to come back. And it had been fun because she'd used Jimmy's electric guitar and amplifier. She wasn't as good as Jimmy was at getting the right sounds, but she was learning and the audience seemed to like her.

Lenny looked around again, this time also checking to see whether anyone was in the dining room, which was off the other end of the kitchen. He spoke in a low voice. "You want some really fuckin' bad acid? It's Owsley. I got a friend in San Francisco and we bought a bunch of it. I mean, this stuff is killer. I'm the only one around here that's got Owsley."

"Why would I want bad acid?"

"I don't mean it's *bad,*" said Lenny. "It's baaaaaaaaad. This is powerful shit. Took me a couple of days to come all the way down the first time. Dropped too much. I was trippy for days, but I'm getting' used to it now. Man, I was so far out that first time. I was thinkin' you could give away a few hits when you play. Bands in San Francisco do that. Or you could sell it if you need the bread. You could get two or three bucks a hit easy, probably five, maybe more, though Owsley don't want nobody chargin' more than two bucks a hit. Strange fuckin' guy. Most of the acid around here costs twice that and it's for shit."

Lenny pulled a little envelope from one of the big pockets on his faded blue work shirt. Then he took a big bottle of pills from a suede pouch hanging from his belt. He carefully poured a dozen capsules into the envelope.

"Anyway, you wouldn't want to take more than about half of one of these, especially the first time. That's probably two hundred micrograms, enough to launch you into outer space." He carefully put the bottle back into his pouch, looking at it as if it were a religious icon, and then handed the little envelope to her.

"Sunshine, eh. Cool," He studied her for several seconds until something clicked in his eyes. "I'm gonna call this stuff Purple Sunshine. Gotta call it somethin' and the capsules look kinda purple. Purple Sunshine, yeah."

Gloria laughed. She was going to give it back, but decided she didn't want to hurt Lenny's feelings. Lenny thought she was cool and that made her feel good. She had thought about trying LSD, thinking it might be better than marijuana, but she was too afraid to try it. Maybe she would send some to Jimmy. He'd told her that he had dropped acid before.

"Thanks," she said.

"I heard you getting sick again," Lenny said, concern in his voice. "Don't take any acid if you feel sick."

"I'm okay," she said. "Just a little upset. Some oatmeal will fix me up."

"You could go over to the free clinic," he said. "Won't cost anything. They even give you free pills if you need them."

Two hours later, Gloria was sitting in a crowded storefront clinic waiting room reading the *Detroit Free Press*. She let out a loud gasp that turned few heads. The headline read *Police Say Detroit Musician Was Murdered*. The worst paragraphs of the story were about a third of the way down:

Lincoln was found dead last September in an alley off Eight Mile Road in Northwest Detroit. Detectives said they ruled out a possible suspect who was a soldier because he was stationed in Vietnam at the time of the murder.

"We cleared him, but we are now actively looking for the soldier's girlfriend," said Sergeant Al Checchi, a homicide investigator. "We spoke to her briefly, but we now believe she knows more about this murder. We know the young woman's first name is Gloria and that she sometimes calls herself Sunshine."

The woman is believed to be a singer and street musician. Checchi said she had been seen in both Ann Arbor and East Lansing and might be in another university community. Checchi said the woman was of medium height or a little smaller, young, possibly a teenager, with dark blonde hair.

"She sang at an anti-war rally at Wayne State University last Columbus Day," said Checchi, "so she might also be in Detroit."

Gloria was still staring at the newspaper when a young nurse in jeans and a white coat called her name. The nurse led her into a small office, told her to sit down, and took the chair across the desk from her. "You're pregnant," the nurse said. "I'd say three or four months along. You should stop getting sick soon." She paused for second and looked at Gloria. "How old are you, and please tell me the truth. I won't tell anyone else. Right now, this is just between the two of us. Oh, and I'm Vicky Osgood, by the way. I'm in the graduate nursing program at University of Michigan and I'm a volunteer here. I'm probably not much older than you are."

Gloria didn't answer right away, still thinking about the newspaper story. Both of her hands had involuntarily gone to her belly. A hot, frightening feeling from deep inside surged over her. It was like when she'd learned that Gina had been killed. She had heard "pregnant," and it shouldn't have been a surprise. It seemed that the part of her brain devoted to understanding had stopped working. "I'm fifteen," she finally said. It was the first time since leaving home that she had admitted her real age to anyone. She hadn't told Jimmy how old she was and he had never asked. Neither of them had told the other much about themselves, though Jimmy had divulged more than she had. She thought ruefully that they had spent almost every waking moment they were together either making love or making music. It would have been a miracle if she hadn't gotten pregnant. She had been so stupid. Her knowledge about the facts of life had been vague before she left home, but she had learned a lot about sex in the past few months. However, she had completely overlooked the fact that her periods had stopped.

"Fifteen," the nurse said, a note of surprise in her voice. She swallowed and nodded. "I thought you were older, maybe a college student."

"What am I gonna do?" she murmured.

"Do you need help telling your parents?"

Gloria shook her head.

"What are you going to tell them?"

She shook her head again. "My mother died and my stepfather... well, he beats me up... and he does other things. I left home in the summer."

"Who's the baby's father? You're not by chance married are you?"

"No. My boyfriend's in Vietnam, in the Army," Gloria said. "My letters might not have been getting through to him, but I just got his right address."

She had been struggling with a long letter to Jimmy after reading all of his letters. Now she would have to start over. She vowed to do it as soon as she left the clinic.

Osgood looked at her. "I know someone who might help... you know, get rid of it. I mean, no coat hangers or anything like that. It's really quite a simple procedure. This guy's an OB resident, and I heard he's helped some girls."

Gloria's hands tightened on her belly. It was like she could feel a baby in there. "No... I couldn't do that."

"Well, it might be best for your situation. You should at least think about it." They sat silently for another long moment. "Will he—your boyfriend—will he do the right thing?" the nurse finally asked.

"What do you mean?"

"Do you think your Army boyfriend might marry you?"

Gloria's eyes grew moist, and presently a tear rolled down one cheek. *Is Jimmy really my boyfriend?* They'd barely known each other for two weeks. He'd been in a rock and roll band and maybe he had other girlfriends. *What am I gonna do?* She sniffed once, then again, and started crying, softly at first. Soon she was producing big wet sobs. Vicky Osgood came around the desk and put one arm around her.

"Jimmy loves me. I know he does. And I love him. My stepfather hates me. He hits me when I boil his eggs wrong. He hits me a lot. He uses a whip. He makes me do... other things. He'll kill me if he finds out."

"No, no," Osgood said, but she sounded like she hadn't heard anything Gloria had said. "You're going to be okay. We won't let anyone hurt you. But you're a minor and we are supposed to tell the state. What they'll want to do is get word to your family, in this case, your stepfather. The State of Michigan doesn't want to pay for anything if there's family who can pay. Maybe I can persuade them to forget about your stepfather, and try to contact your boyfriend in the Army. It's worth a try. Meanwhile, you have to take care of yourself, especially if you want to have the baby." She handed Gloria a large amber bottle of big pills. "These are vitamins. Take one every day, and make sure you eat good meals, and eat regularly. Try to keep something in your stomach all the time. That helps with morning sickness. Do you drink alcohol?"

Gloria shook her head.

"Do any drugs?"

She shook her head again.

"Good," said the nurse. "You should do fine, even though you're... young. Let's go make an appointment with Dr. Schmeling. He's an OB/GYN who's here on Wednesday evenings. And think about what I said. Please don't say anything to Dr. Schmeling about that though."

She led Gloria out of the office to the big reception desk in the waiting room, but the chair behind the desk was empty.

"Wait here," Osgood said. "I'll go find Edna and we can make that appointment."

As soon as Osgood was out of sight, Gloria walked quickly out of the clinic.

November 25, 12:05 a.m., Detroit

Gloria woke from a bad dream to loud knocking on her door. She struggled out of bed, unfastened the chain lock and the deadbolt, and then opened the door. It was Mrs. Murphy, her new landlady.

"Telephone call," she said. "You'll have to take it downstairs. I told you no calls on my phone so make sure they don't call back again. My husband doesn't like getting woke up, especially on a holiday."

"I don't understand. I didn't give the number to anyone," Gloria said.

"And another thing—the caller said you were Gloria Doran. Did you give me a false name?"

Gloria ignored the question but a chill ran through her. She went out the door into the hall and headed for the stairs.

"Don't you have a robe or something? You shouldn't be parading around half-naked in front of my husband," said Mrs. Murphy. Gloria was wearing a T-shirt that just covered her butt and panties. She didn't have a robe. She started back to the room to put clothes on.

"Oh, never mind. Maybe the poor man deserves a treat after getting woke up," she said, a touch of mirth in her voice. "But mind you, don't take too long."

Gloria hurried down the stairs to the kitchen. Mr. Murphy, a fat man in his sixties, was dressed in old blue-flannel pajamas that didn't look too clean. He was holding the phone and looking unashamedly at her semi-nakedness. He smelled like stale beer and dirty laundry. She grabbed the phone and sat down at the kitchen table so it obscured her lower half. "Hello," she said.

"Gloria this is your father, and I am ordering you to come home right now." He was trying to speak calmly but Gloria could tell he was angry. His voice grew into a low growl and started to rise. "I know you're pregnant. I told you that could happen, you stupid bitch. But I'll take care of that problem and no one has to know. I want you home. Now."

Gloria glared at Mr. Murphy, but he showed no signs of leaving.

"I'm not coming home," she said. "Not now. Not ever."

"I know a doctor who can help. We'll get rid of it and a couple of months from now you'll barely remember. You can forget about that boyfriend too. Either you come home right now or I'll drag you home. And if I have to come get you, it'll be worse... a lot worse. You'll find out what a real whipping feels like. There's no reason to worry about scars now."

"You leave me alone or I'll give that stuff you had in your briefcase to the police," she said. Then she rattled off the names of a couple of banks and the amounts in the accounts.

He was silent for a few seconds.

"Jimmy knows about it... he knows about everything. And I sent some of that stuff to him too. I used to listen to you talking on the phone and talking to people in your office. I know all about the money and the companies and the Garganos. Everything. I can remember stuff like that from when I was little. Gina said I had a photographic memory. You beat up Gina, but I'll never let you beat me again."

Again he was silent but he was breathing heavily, so she started talking about two companies he had started for the Garganos. She told him the exact amount of money that had gone into them. It was from one of his early conversations and the companies no longer existed, but she wanted to prove that she wasn't lying about her memory.

"You don't know what you're doing, you little cunt," he said in a hoarse whisper. "You want to end up like that nigger musician?" He was enraged and Gloria knew he'd be hitting her if he were in the same room. "I know where your goddamn boyfriend Jimmy Hayes is too," he sputtered.

She hung up abruptly.

At the beginning of the call she thought she had heard the faint sound of breathing on the phone. Was Mrs. Murphy listening in? *I wouldn't be surprised. The old bat seems pretty nosey. Or it might have been another of the boarders.* She remained at the kitchen table for a minute, thinking.

Mr. Murphy had moved a little to one side and slumped down in his chair, trying to see more of her legs. She wasn't anxious to get up to give him another display and he showed no signs of leaving. Finally, Mrs. Murphy came into the room. She looked sternly at her husband, who slowly got up and waddled out of the kitchen.

"Sorry," Gloria said. She had wrapped her arms around herself and was rocking back and forth in the chair, frightened, suddenly cold and very angry.

Mrs. Murphy studied her carefully. "You're not Gloria Darnell, are you?"

Gloria shook her head.

"You're in trouble?"

Gloria stared at the tablecloth and slowly nodded.

"You're gonna have a baby?"

She nodded again.

"Father?"

"Vietnam," she said, almost in a whisper.

"You're not married to him?"

She shook her head.

"Does he know?"

She shrugged, then shook her head. Only her anger was keeping her from tears.

Mrs. Murphy looked at her.

Gloria decided anger was better than tears and started talking rapidly. "I wrote him a letter but now I think it might have been stolen. My stepfather must have it."

When she was coming back to the Ann Arbor house, she had seen a big, tough-looking black man open the mailbox and then walk quickly to a car parked just down the street. Less than a minute later, a police car with its siren on and lights flashing had rolled to a stop in front of the house. She had fled, leaving many of her clothes behind. Luckily, her suitcase had been in the car. She slept in the Rambler for a night. It had been too cold to sleep much. Then she'd stayed in a very bad motel in an industrial area near the Rouge Plant. They'd let her stay despite having no identification. But the people in the motel frightened her, and paying for it had used a good deal of her remaining money. The weather had turned cold, making it difficult to play her guitar outside. Besides, she was afraid to play on the streets because the police were looking for her. So she had holed up in the motel and had written several letters to Jimmy. It had taken her a long time to write them because she was scared. Unlike in the letter that had disappeared, she didn't tell him that she was pregnant. Now she was afraid to tell him. She was trying not to think about it.

"He's written to me though. I got thirty-two letters last month," Gloria said. "I got them through a friend who's dead now... murdered. But Jimmy doesn't have my address because I keep moving, and I didn't give him a place to write. All I know is that he's in Vietnam. I know he loves me... well, he says so in the letters. Maybe he doesn't care about me now because he probably hasn't gotten any letters from me. It sure sounded like he cared in the letters I got from him though." She stopped and closed her eyes tightly, thinking of the TV news and the stories about Vietnam that she read in the newspapers. Maybe Jimmy had enough to worry about and that was another reason she hadn't told him about her being pregnant. She fought the darkness she felt closing in around her. "I'm so scared that he might get killed over there. I know he's in the fighting and he's flying in helicopters. He told me he's a gunner now. I thought he was supposed to fix helicopters, not fly in them."

"And your stepfather wants you to get an abortion?"

"Yeah, and the nurse at the clinic does too," she said a little crossly. "Gee, did you listen to the whole call?"

Mrs. Murphy said, "Missed the very beginning, but he sounded like a mean bastard, if you don't mind me saying so. Let me make some tea for you and you can tell me more. You should tell someone. I don't believe in minding my own business all the time, and you can talk to me, especially about this kind of thing."

Thinking of Jimmy, Gloria lost her grip and began sobbing. She couldn't speak for another minute. She finally got hold of herself by thinking of her stepfather, which made her angry again. *Angry's better than crying.* "Okay," she said. "But I'd better get out of here pretty quick. I think he'll come here." Warily, Gloria decided she liked Mrs. Murphy, who reminded her of Roscoe's mother. Mrs. Murphy was Irish Catholic, and the very thought of abortion was abhorrent to her. Gloria thought the older woman wouldn't believe her when she said her stepfather was a Detroit gangster. They brought their tea up to her room and her thoughts tumbled out in a disorganized torrent, like the water below a waterfall.

"He keeps books for the Mafia, the Italians. He's a CPA—you know, an accountant—and he's a lawyer too. He moves their money around, and he's always talking about tax laws and the IRS. I don't understand that part so well, but I know the money part, what happens to it, where it goes. I've been listening to him through the heating vent in my bedroom since I was little, and I can remember all the money stuff. Anything with numbers. Well, I can remember music too, but that's not anything he ever talked about. He puts their money into companies that he starts, or sometimes they buy companies. It's millions and millions of dollars. He does it for other crooks too.

"I think my stepfather might have already had one of my friends killed. You heard what he said about that musician? He must have been talking about Roscoe, because I just found out Roscoe was murdered. It's been in the paper too." She stopped and was looking at the floor, thinking about it. She had heard his words on the telephone, but they were just now sinking in. *Would he really kill someone?* "I'm not sure what I believe," she said, looking up at Mrs. Murphy again. "I never heard him talk about killing people before. He's not very nice. He really does beat me, and he started using a whip. He got it in Asia. He beat Gina—she was my stepmother—so bad she had to go to the hospital half a dozen times. And he did other things to me... called it training...."

It had just dawned on her that sometimes she could speak just fine. She had been forced to speak more, and it was getting easier to talk than it had been a few months ago. Here she was, babbling on like never before.

Mrs. Murphy reached over and took one of her hands in both of her own hands. "Honey, I believe you. Let's talk about what else he did, those other things you've mentioned. Are you talking about sex?"

Gloria locked up again and at first she wouldn't answer. Finally, she said, "You won't believe it." She was looking at the floor again.

Mrs. Murphy put her fingers under Gloria's chin to raise it, furrowed her eyebrows and looked her in the eye. It was a strangely comfortable feeling, maybe because the older woman appeared to care.

"Well," Gloria said, "he... when I was little, he used to spank my bare ass, and he... he would touch me... and then he made me touch him and... put it in my mouth."

"Oh Lord Jesus!" said Mrs. Murphy. She sighed, then groaned, and then slapped the table with her hand. She looked at Gloria. "What else? There's more, isn't there? What else did he do to you?"

"He brought me to some other men too. Not very many... maybe a dozen times, especially this fat Oriental man who would take pictures. And earlier this year he was trying to fuck me in my ass. It was important to him that I remain a virgin."

"Oh Jesus, Mary and Joseph! Oh you poor girl!"

"He called it training," Gloria said angrily. "He said it was how I could be a good girl and please men. He says pleasing men is what girls are for. And it isn't just sex, but cooking and cleaning... everything. When Gina died, I had to do all that and when he didn't like something, he'd beat me." She shook her head. "Gina just took it, but not me. I fought back, and I got loose from him sometimes. I think he might have been planning to take me to Asia and leave me there. I figured I had to run away."

Talking about it was making her angrier, and anger was something she could organize her thoughts around. "Gina was my stepmother. I'm pretty sure she knew what was happening and she never did anything. I hated her for that, but I guess she tried to be good to me. Then she died this spring. He used to beat her a lot more than he did me. That was another thing about training. I could sometimes keep him from beating Gina, but then after she died, he started beating me more and more. He brought a Cobra-skin whip home from Asia," she said sharply, and then stopped again. Her mind was racing faster than she could speak. *He might show up any minute now.*

"Something similar happened to me when I was young," said Mrs. Murphy, taking advantage of the silence.

Gloria started pulling her clothes on as she listened to Mrs. Murphy. She hurriedly stuffed the few things she had unpacked back into her suitcase.

"My brother was raping me and my father used to slap both me and my mother around. Both my parents eventually learned about my brother and didn't do anything about it. They blamed me, not him. They said I was a slut. They were both drunks. Threw me out of the house when I was seventeen and pregnant. My... my oldest daughter is also my niece. My husband doesn't know this and neither does my daughter Agnes. My parents are dead now and my brother—" She smacked her fist hard on a little bedside table, rattling the empty teacups. "I wish I'd killed him when I was younger. I had the fire then," she said bitterly. "He's a real loser. He's a drunk too. Been to prison twice, and he's been through four wives. And he's hurt them all. I haven't spoken to him for almost forty years, not one word. But I have a big family so I have to hear about him from the others. They think he's had a hard life. Well, not hard enough."

"You really thought about killing him?" Gloria asked.

Mrs. Murphy shrugged. "I wouldn't do it now, but I probably could have thirty-five years ago if I'd known what I know now. Back then, I thought everything was my fault. Now I know that what he was doing to me wasn't my fault. It was rape, pure and simple. And what happened to you is rape. My fault was never doing anything about it, letting it go on. I hated my mother and father because they never helped me, but you know, I never helped myself either. My brother just got away with it. And he's still a right bastard. You did the right thing in running away. Good for you." She stopped and seemed to consider what she had been saying. "But you shouldn't think about killing your stepfather. You'll just end up in prison. But at least you've run away, which is more than I did. Getting thrown out ended up being the best thing that ever happened to me."

"I have to get out of here," Gloria said, grabbing her suitcase. "He's probably gonna be here soon. I just know it, and I don't want him to find me. He's very dangerous, so be careful. I don't know how he found me here, but he's smart. I wouldn't tell him about anything you heard or what we talked about. If he comes here, you should call the police."

She slung her big purse over her shoulder and hurried down the stairs with her suitcase. She opened the front door to leave.

A tall black man with an Afro and dressed in a black leather jacket and jeans had his hand up. He was about to knock. He was almost as startled as Gloria was. In an instant, she recognized him as the man she'd seen taking letters from the mailbox.

"That's her! Grab her!" someone shouted. The voice was distant, coming from down the street somewhere. Two more men were on the sidewalk directly in front the house. They were both black. All the men were big, but one them was huge. The huge man on the sidewalk was pulling something out of his coat pocket.

Gloria saw that it was gun, and it was coming up to point at her.

CHAPTER 6

30 November, 0630 Hours, Nui Binh Base Camp

Thanksgiving started well enough. Everyone was supposed to eat a turkey dinner with all the trimmings, and Hayes was looking forward to it. He had settled into the gun platoon and was feeling better about it. The Headhunters were a wilder group. The two Headhunter hootches for the enlisted men were notoriously messy. Pictures of naked women torn out of magazines were tacked to walls with crude comments scrawled on them. Somebody had acquired an ashtray that looked like a human skull. You had to look closely to see that it wasn't real. The lower jaw was moveable and there was usually a pipe clamped in the mouth. People tapped cigarette ash in through the eyeholes. Also tacked to the walls were Polaroids of dead bodies with captions: *Another day at the office, Honey, I'll be late* and *Your taxes at work,* which had been crossed out and replaced with *Your Headhunters at work*. The pictures would be torn down whenever a senior NCO happened on them, but soon they were replaced with new ones. One of the gunners had a brother who owned a small novelty shop in Madison, Wisconsin and he had printed up colorful fluorescent stickers that decorated several lockers: *The Great Society: Bombs, Bullets and Bullshit, Vietnam, Love It or Leave It, Fuck The Army* and *Peace Through Superior Firepower*.

The gun platoon also had a dog named Fuck You. Fuck You was a mostly white medium-sized shepherd mix with short fur and he was about a year and a half old. He had been rescued from a dinner date with a Vietnamese cooking pot. Fuck You was a survivor, perhaps the brightest of his litter, and he was likeable. Dogs were not allowed in Nui Binh Base Camp, but Fuck You had ingratiated himself not only into the hardened hearts of the Headhunters but most of rest of the company as well. He seemed to have a sixth sense for the few officers and NCOs who might be inclined to do him harm. The CO pretended not to see him. Fuck You had gone on several short helicopter rides and enjoyed it. Some of the pilots wanted to train him to crap by the door of the XO's hootch, but the enlisted men were against it because it would surely seal the dog's fate. When the god-fearing XO learned the dog's name was Fuck You, he demanded that it be changed. So on Rivera's suggestion Fuck You's name was changed to Jesus.

"I have a cousin named Jesus," Rivera said, which wasn't actually true, or at least his cousin's name wasn't pronounced the same. It didn't matter anyway, because the dog had learned his name was Fuck You; he heard it constantly, and he never did get the hang of Jesus.

"That unChristian son of a bitch," observed Arnie Walters, who had just been promoted to CW2.

The pilots seemed closer to the crewmen in the gun platoon and there was less formality about rank. Hayes had been accepted immediately. He was a naturally good shot. He instinctively compensated for the helicopter's motion and speed when he was shooting and usually hit what he was aiming at, but he was also careful about where he fired. He was meticulous about cleaning the machineguns and had enough mechanical smarts to learn to troubleshoot the armament systems. And he was strong enough to manhandle the heavy rockets when they were re-arming. He didn't avoid any of the work. He was good enough at fixing the armament systems that there was some talk of putting him to work in the armament hut. More than half the time he flew with Rivera and they mostly got along, almost like family. He hadn't wanted to get close to anyone, but Rivera was becoming a good friend. As he'd promised, Hayes had stopped smoking pot. He realized that he cared about what people thought of him, perhaps more than he had been prepared to admit. He didn't like being known primarily as a pothead.

Hayes found gunships more interesting than slicks. He felt like he was riding around in a giant, heavily armed bird of prey. Every day they went out and killed people, or tried to. Killing was their mission and Hayes got used to it. Most of the killing was done with the rockets and the miniguns. Most of their ships had rocket pods that held seven rockets on each side as well as miniguns. A couple of ships that had larger rocket pods held a total of 38. They were called Hogs.

He hadn't wanted to be part of the killing, but he got over it quickly. He remembered that he hadn't liked it the first time he'd killed a deer either. Killing was part of war, the main part. He decided it was better to kill than to be killed. On the slicks, he had been riding around as a target. Might as well have a bulls eye painted on his forehead. He had changed since coming to the 99th. Now the Vietnamese were "dinks" or "gooks" or "slopes." Seeing White and McLean get killed had triggered the change. At first he had doubts that all the people they killed were enemy soldiers. There were free-fire zones where all civilians were supposed to be gone. Sometimes they saw people who looked like civilians and they didn't usually fire on them, but sometimes they did. Even before he'd killed the ARVN, he hadn't liked ARVNs very much. Every day Americans were dying in Vietnam but Hayes thought the average ARVN was a cowardly bastard doing everything he could to avoid combat. And it was their country. The Vietnamese Rangers were better, and they were the only Vietnamese soldiers that he had any respect for. Well, them and the enemy. They were tough little bastards, and they were trying to kill him.

He was sure that most, and maybe even all, of the Vietnamese workers in Nui Binh were Vietcong spies. Some of the young women who worked as hootch maids washing clothes and shining boots were very pretty. Some of them would blow you for a few bucks and every once in awhile, he heard that somebody had gotten laid in a bunker. He didn't actually hate the hootch maids even if he thought they were all spying for the VC. They probably didn't have a choice. He was always friendly to the one who washed his clothing. She was darker and skinnier than most of the others. Cambodian, she said. Actually, she had said "Khmer," and Hayes learned that she had two kids and her husband had been killed in the war. He didn't know her name, which was very long. He called her Jane and gave her C rations when he could.

He tried, but he couldn't stop thinking about the ARVN he had killed. Instead of Gloria, now he dreamed about the ARVN almost every night.

Hayes didn't see the hootch maids much because he was usually flying before they came into Nui Binh in the morning and they were gone by the time he got back at night. That was good, because they reminded him of Gloria, and Gloria was an ache that wouldn't go away. It had been almost four months and he had heard nothing from her. The last letter he had written to her was two weeks ago and he wasn't sure he would write again. It hurt too much, though it was also because of the changes he was experiencing. There wasn't a lot of room anymore to think about love, or even lust. His days were long and exhausting and sometimes included killing and near-death experiences. When he had a little time in the evening, he'd think about getting high, especially when he smelled someone else smoking. Sometimes he and Rivera would go and get a beer at the Enlisted Men's Club.

Other evenings, he'd work himself up to thinking about Gloria again, and would write a letter saying how much he loved her. Then after he mailed it, he felt like a sucker. Every time there was no mail for him, he'd crash into the depths of despair. He tried to avoid mail call. He was sure she had dumped him for someone else. She's probably banging someone else now... *or several someone elses,* he thought ruefully. *God, she's so beautiful, and no girl that beautiful would ever go for me.* He hadn't heard from Roscoe either, which made him just a little suspicious that maybe she had taken up with him.

He had written to Roscoe, and there had been nothing back. Roscoe had known Gloria longer than Hayes, though only by a few hours. *Or so he said.* He knew so little about Gloria. *Christ, I don't even know her last name, just that she's calling herself Sunshine sometimes. She's a hippie chick, so what did I expect? She's probably into free love.* He told himself he should be thankful for the time they'd spent together, that it was the best two weeks of his entire life. She was the most beautiful girl he had ever known and she had loved him for a little while. *Didn't she?*

There was a minor argument underway by the Operations Bunker when Hayes arrived. Mike Daltrey and Metcalf, the platoon sergeant, had been assigned to fly the smoke ship for a big combat assault. Metcalf had assigned himself. Brigade Operations was worried about a nearby firebase that had been attacked the previous night and no one was sure the fight was over. Two Headhunter ships had been out providing support most of the night. Hayes was glad he hadn't been on them because those guys were in for a long day.

Daltrey was a crew chief who didn't like flying the smoke ship and avoided doing so. Maybe it was fear, or maybe it was the fact that they had to do a lot of messy cleanup afterwards. Metcalf, the platoon sergeant, flew only once in awhile and had never flown the smoke ship before. He wasn't likely to help much in the cleanup either, but he wanted to get some experience with it. He said it would help him make decisions. Rivera, on the other hand, loved flying Smokey and had been bugging everyone to let him fly it again so he could show Hayes what was involved. There had been a debate in the Headhunters about who should fly Smokey. Was it better to have the same crew every time, or should it be spread around pilots and other crew so that everyone learned how to do it? There was even talk of having one of the slick platoons operate the smoke ship. One factor fueling the debate was that the smoke ship was undeniably dangerous. In the past four months, two of them had been shot down, killing the pilot and a crew chief in one of the crashes. That had happened just before Hayes arrived. The second crash had destroyed the smoke ship, but everyone got out. The two pilots assigned to it this Thanksgiving morning were Barnhart and Ziegler. Hayes didn't know whether Barnhart had an opinion on flying the smoke ship, but he was a good pilot. Ziegler had only been in-country for three weeks and Hayes hadn't flown with him.

The smoke ship was the first to enter the landing zone, flying very low and steady and spewing a stream of smoke along the edge of the LZ while the gunners raked the tree line. The flying demanded good piloting skills, but low-level flying was also a lot of fun. If there was going to be an ambush, the smoke ship often triggered it.

Rivera was telling Metcalf, "For Chrissakes, let Hayes and me do it. Daltrey fuckin' hates flying Smokey."

"Aw shit, Rivera, you'll have another chance soon enough," Metcalf said. He was smiling, but Hayes could tell he was getting pissed off. The argument must have started well before Hayes got there. And Metcalf was probably hung over. Metcalf was a good guy, but he was a lifer who had just re-enlisted for a big bonus and was now in line for a promotion, so he'd been celebrating the night before.

"Christ, don't get the ass, Sarge, I'm just tryin' to do you a favor," said Rivera.

Then CW2 Walters opened his mouth. He had become acting platoon commander of the Headhunters after Captain Kenny Detwiller had rotated home and there was no captain or lieutenant in the company to take his place. Walters looked at Barnhart. "Might not be a bad idea if I fly Smokey with Ziegler, and Rivera and Hayes crew. This is very likely to get hairy." Walters was a fabulous pilot but he had been in a command position for less than a week. The suggestion was a poor one, Hayes thought. Walters was supposed to command the Headhunters and that would be a lot more difficult if he was flying Smokey. Besides, it sounded like he had made a suggestion, not given an order.

Major Lehman, the 99th executive officer, who was by far the worst pilot in the company and unpopular with everyone, had been listening to the discussion and decided to exert his authority. He snapped, "Barnhart will fly the smoke ship with Ziegler, and with Sergeant Metcalf and Specialist Daltrey."

Walters said, "Major, I think—"

"No. That's an order Mr. Walters. You're not just a pilot today; you have a platoon to command."

"Yes Sir," Walters said, finally realizing he had fucked up.

So the argument ended and everyone was okay with the outcome.

Rivera shrugged, and then walked out to the helicopters with Metcalf, talking about some of the things he should do, like helping with the cleanup. "It's a real pain in the ass. I really was trying to help you."

"Yeah, I know," said Metcalf. "I just want to see for myself what Smokey's all about."

No sooner did they get out to the helicopters than the operations clerk trotted up and said the whole insert had been delayed. Then it started to rain hard. Most of the gun platoon pilots and crewmen, lugging their machineguns, hurried through the rain to the Officers' Club, which was close to the revetments where the helicopters were parked. They told the clerk he could find them there. Walters got Cokes out of an ice chest and passed them around. Ziegler reached behind the plywood bar and came out with a guitar, a worn but serviceable Harmony.

Hayes' gaze locked on the guitar. He hadn't seen one since he'd gotten to the 99th.

Ziegler said, "I told myself that while I was over here, I'd learn to play the fuckin' guitar or die trying." He started softly strumming, pausing each time he changed to another chord to carefully place his fingers on fret board. It was clear he knew very few chords. Hayes couldn't stop looking at the guitar. It was like he had a hard-on for it. It was all he could do to keep from snatching it away from Ziegler.

Finally, Ziegler stopped to take a drink of Coke and Hayes held out his hand for the guitar. "Could I try? Maybe, I could show you a few things."

"Sure," said Ziegler handing the guitar to Hayes. "You play?"

"A little," Hayes said. He adjusted the tuning on a couple of the strings and then started playing Beatles songs. For two hours they stayed in the Officers' Club while Hayes and Ziegler played guitar. Ziegler, although he could barely play, had a great voice and wasn't shy about singing. Everyone, in fact, ended up singing some of the songs. Hayes showed Ziegler some new chords and helped him practice. Ziegler seemed to be learning and Hayes thought he could learn to play well with practice. Hayes agreed to keep teaching him.

It was almost 1100 hours before the operations clerk showed up to tell them to get their asses out to the helicopters and saddle up. There was still some light rain and they had been soaked through earlier. At 3000 feet with the slipstream blasting him, Hayes was wet and shivering from the cold.

The insert went badly from the very beginning. There was no rain at the LZ, but it was cloudy and the air was leaden with humidity. They watched as Barnhart roared into the LZ, low and maybe not quite slow enough, but acceptable. The smoke trailed out of the machine and seemed to be drifting into the trees just right. There was hardly any wind but they had gotten the direction correct. Smokey was two thirds of the way down one side of the LZ, with Daltrey and Metcalf firing at the respective tree lines when the entire LZ exploded. Tracers seemed to come at the smoke ship from every direction, and at least two rockets narrowly missed it.

The ship was tilted almost to a 45-degree angle in the middle of a sharp turn that would bring it around to smoke the other side of the LZ when the ambush caught up with it. Hayes thought he might have seen some pieces flying off of the rotor, though he would never be sure because it all happened so fast. The ship wobbled and dipped down no more than a few feet. But it was enough for a rotor blade to catch the ground, instantly spraying a cloud of dirt and shredded rotor bits into the air and slamming the helicopter nose first into the turf. It cart-wheeled end over tail once before a huge orange fireball engulfed it. Still shivering from the cold, Hayes swore he could feel the heat from the explosion. Burning wreckage sprayed over a couple of hundred yards.

Four gunships immediately rolled in on the LZ, firing volleys of rockets and hosing the tree lines with their miniguns. Then Walters told the others to provide cover as he went down to check for survivors. It was a stupid action. It was necessary, and everyone agreed with it, but Walters shouldn't have been the one doing it and he hadn't asked permission. The CO clicked onto the air, paused, and then said, "Roger that."

No one thought anyone could have survived the crash, but none of the Headhunters or anyone else in the 99th was prepared to say so until they looked. No one was surprised that Walters was leading from the front. They received no fire as they descended. They cruised slowly past the burning wreckage, but Hayes couldn't see it because it was on the other side of the helicopter. He peered at the tree line, but couldn't see anything. Ironically it was obscured by smoke. Nevertheless, he directed a steady stream of fire from his machinegun through the smoke toward the trees.

The helicopter settled on the ground and Walters ordered Rivera to get out and see what he could find. "We'll cover you." That was dicey, Hayes thought. Rivera wouldn't have a chance if the enemy was still there. Then the ship lifted slightly and swiveled and Walters cut loose with the miniguns. Walters pivoted the ship around slowly, firing bursts into different areas of the tree line. Hayes kept firing too. The other three gunships continued to pour fire in as well, with Walters directing them and keeping track of Rivera. At one point Hayes glimpsed Rivera, his arm across his face to shield it from the heat, trying to edge closer to the wreckage.

Finally the helicopter landed again and Rivera came on the intercom. "I might have seen one body burning, but I didn't see anyone alive. We could go to the other side and check that. I couldn't see everything over there."

They did, and this time Hayes went out. He didn't find anyone either, though he got a little closer to the wreckage than Rivera had because the fire was dying. It had started raining again and once more Hayes was soaked. He got back on board and heard the CO ordering Walters to leave. Then some of the slicks landed with troops to secure the area around the wreck. Hayes felt sorry for the grunts because they'd be out there in the rain all night, though it was nothing new for them. Not for the first time, he thought how lucky he'd been. At least he got to sleep on a mattress and eat in a mess hall.

The assault had been called off. It was clear they weren't going to surprise the enemy, who had apparently made a speedy withdrawal. Walters sent two gunships to re-arm and refuel while the remaining two provided cover. They worked shifts for the rest of the day, and before nightfall the grunts had recovered the four charred remains. Walters' ship was the last in the company to shut down back at Nui Binh.

Hayes and Rivera stumbled into the mess hall and sat at a table with six other Headhunter crewmen. They and the officers sitting at another table were the last ones in the mess hall. They were all tired and dirty, and they were numb. No one was talking. One of the pilots slammed his fist loudly on the table and shouted "Motherfucker!" but Hayes didn't even look up to see who it was. The meal was a breaded cutlet of some kind of meat that might or might not have been turkey. It was cold and so were the mashed potatoes, the congealed gravy, the green beans, and the apple cobbler. The cobbler was good though. In fact, even though it was cold, all of it was good. Under better circumstances Hayes might have enjoyed it cold because it was light years ahead of the C-rations they would have had to eat if the mess hall had closed down, which increasingly had been the case in recent weeks. Sometimes even when the mess hall was still open, some of the food ran out. He had finished his food and was halfway through a second glass of milk when Cartwright, the new company clerk, wandered in with a handful of letters.

"You got a letter, Hayes," he said, dropping an envelope on the table in front of him. He started tossing letters to some of the others. Hayes looked in astonishment at the name in the return address: Gloria Doran. "Holy shit!" Hayes said, and he started tearing it open.

Cartwright had started walking away, but turned back and reached into a leather pouch he was carrying. He dropped two more letters on the table.

"These came last week," said Cartwright. "I couldn't find you. In fact I didn't know who you were. I think this is the first time we've met."

"Goddamn!" Hayes said, looking at Cartwright.

"Sorry," said Cartwright.

"What's the matter?" asked Rivera, but Hayes held up his hand as he tore open the first letter and started reading.

Dear Jimmy,

I know it's been a long time and as I told you before, lots has happened. I didn't get any letters from you until October. I wrote a lot of letters but didn't have your address. Wrote to you when I first got those letters, but I think the letter was stolen. I have no address where you can write to me now 'cause I'm on the run. Like I told you in my last letter, Roscoe is dead and now the police are saying he was murdered. His mother's having a hard time. I visited her and she was good to me, but it has been difficult for her because Roscoe was supporting her. The murder happened a few weeks after you left. There was a story in the Detroit Free Press about how the po-

lice are looking for me and I'm scared. You are mentioned too, but they know you were in Vietnam when it happened. I thought that Roscoe might have been killed by you know who looking for you and me because of what we saw, but I don't think so now. It has something to do with my stepfather.

I have been playing guitar on the street and a few places and making some money, but am starting to run a little low on money. It's too cold to play outside most of the time now. Besides, the police are looking for me, and they know I play on the streets. If the police find me, they'll send me back to my stepfather.

"Oh shit, oh shit, oh shit," Hayes said, bending over with his head on the table.

"What's the matter?" Rivera asked. Others were looking at him too. Hayes waved them off and kept reading.

There's a lot more. As I told you before, my name's Gloria Doran. I ran away from home because my stepfather (he's not my real father) beats me up and did other bad things. Couldn't stay there. He's a big gangster with a lot of money and he's looking for me.

In those early letters, when I had no address for you, I sent you some papers in another language that belonged to my stepfather. I hope you got them, but maybe not. They might have been in German and I don't know German, but you told me once that your uncle was in the army in Germany. I was hoping that you might understand it or could send it to him.

It's hard for me to write, but I will keep trying. Sorry if this is all a big surprise. I'm so scared.

I love you Jimmy, with all my heart. You are the most important person in the world for me. I'll try to write again soon. Please don't take chances.

All my love,
Gloria

"Holy shit," Hayes said again and there were tears running down his face. "Oh God, oh God."

He put his head down on the table. He wasn't sure if the tears were happiness at getting a letter and her saying she loved him, or sadness at her predicament, or a delayed reaction to what had happened that day.

Rivera put his hand on his shoulder. "What's the matter?"

Hayes just tried to shake his head, which was still down on the table. "Tell you later," he mumbled.

He sat with his head down on the table for a long time. It was too much all at once. He raised his head and glanced around, pulled himself together. He didn't want anyone to see the tears. Rivera had left and there were only two others in the mess hall, both of them reading letters. They hadn't seemed to notice his sobbing, or they were leaving him alone.

He picked up the envelope. There was no return address but the postmark was from Ann Arbor. He looked at the other two letters. They were postmarked from Wyandotte. He decided to save them for later.

"Get your goddamn shit together, Hayes," he muttered, angrily wiping tears from his cheeks . The two remaining people in the mess hall looked at him.

"I'm okay," he said as he got up. "I'm okay."

CHAPTER 7

November 25, 1:15 a.m., Detroit

The gun in the hand of the giant man on Mrs. Murphy's front walk didn't quite register in Gloria's brain. Her attention was focused on the black man at the door. Almost in slow motion, he had turned to look at the street when someone cried out, "That's her!" but he was turning back again, his legs slightly apart, when Gloria rammed the big suitcase she was holding right into his crotch.

"Oomph!" He doubled over.

She swung the suitcase back behind her and then, with both hands, slammed it as hard as she could into the side of his head. He fell to his hands and knees. She was going to hit him again when there was a loud, cracking boom and the door jamb exploded beside her head. Eyes wide, she looked toward the street. On the sidewalk, the huge man's arm was extended in front of him, the man slightly in front of him starting to duck and lean away. A flash and a second cracking boom echoed down the street.

He's shooting at me! She jumped back and shut the door just as a third shot sounded and a bullet smashed through the wall beside the door. She found the lock and turned it.

The man at the door yelled, "Stop shooting, you crazy motherfucker! You almost hit me!"

Gloria turned and raced through the house. Mrs. Murphy was standing at the top of the stairs, both hands holding her face. Gloria shouted, "Call the police!" Something banged hard into the front door and Mrs. Murphy screamed. Gloria kept going, threw open the back door and stepped out. She stopped, turned back and shut the door, carefully and as quietly as she could just as the front door splintered with a crash. Behind the house she ran past the garage and into the alley. It bisected the block and was lined with trash barrels. She turned right and raced toward the street where she had parked the Rambler.

Just short of the corner she slowed, then stopped. She crept forward just far enough so she could look down to the front of Mrs. Murphy's house. The big man had his back to her and was still in front of the house, his pistol in one hand at his side. Lights were coming on in houses up and down the street. A porch light about three houses down the street popped on and illuminated a cream-colored station wagon with someone sitting in it. Her stepfather had an Oldsmobile station wagon that color. She squinted but couldn't make out the occupant. Another scream came from inside Mrs. Murphy's house. It was a big house with at least half a dozen boarders.

Confident she was out of their view, she backed up and opened the door to the Rambler. The dome light popped on and she quickly closed the door and tossed her suitcase into the back seat. She had just put the keys in the ignition when she thought, *They might hear the car start.* Instinctively she slouched low in the seat and pondered. There was a chance that no one knew about Jimmy's car. It was dark, and fortunately she had parked far from the nearest streetlight.

She cranked down her car window so she could hear and then peeked out. The man who had been at the front door was in the alley. Light glinted faintly on one of the zippers of his black leather jacket. He looked down the alley, one way and then the other, then walked back toward the house. A minute later, car doors slammed and a car started. She waited a half-minute or so, then started the Rambler and drove slowly to the corner without turning on her lights. The car that had been parked over the sidewalk in front the house was gone, and so was the station wagon that had been parked farther down the street. Mrs. Murphy was standing at the front of the house talking to someone, gesturing her excitement with her hands. It wasn't her husband so it must have been a neighbor or one of the other boarders. Gloria drove through the intersection and turned on her lights when she was two blocks away.

Without thinking, she found herself heading toward her Grosse Pointe home. She was enraged and growing angrier. She felt sparkly, like she might catch fire. Her stepfather had beaten her and raped her. He'd wanted to end her pregnancy and he had just tried to kill her. How much did he have to do with what had happened to Roscoe? And he'd threatened Jimmy. Could he really harm Jimmy in Vietnam? Vietnam itself is bad enough.

She thought about church. Gina, who would have gone to church every day if she could, had taken Gloria to church starting when she was baby. Gloria had continued singing in the youth choir even after Gina had died. Church hadn't meant more than a place where she could sing, or so she thought. She didn't like the nuns, and most of the priests were boring, and some were hypocritical, but she remembered about the sanctity of life. Her stepfather had made it clear that he was going to get rid of the baby, and that struck her as the single worst thing. The baby was going to be a real person. It was her baby. It was part of her, and part of Jimmy too. She would do everything she could to protect it. Killing the baby would be as terrible as losing Jimmy in the war. Her emotions were all mixed up, but she was growing from an angry teenager into an angry young woman.

The Grosse Pointe house was dark and appeared empty. She stopped at the end of the long driveway, then drove around a curve down the wooded street and parked deep in the shadows behind some bushes. She walked back along the street and up the long driveway, looking over her shoulder every few seconds to make sure no cars were coming. At the house, she took out her house key and very quietly opened the front door. She stepped inside then waited without moving, listening intently. She moved through the ground floor, looking in the living room, kitchen, breakfast nook, family room and office. From the kitchen, she opened the door to the garage. The garage normally held three cars. Two of them were inside. Gina's Mercury looked like it hadn't moved for months and the Oldsmobile wasn't there. Her stepfather had a new Corvette, a black one this time with a red stinger on the hood. She went back into the house and crept up the carpeted stairs, avoiding the one stair near the top that she remembered had a creak.

She glided along the hallway carpet to the master bedroom. The door was open. Normally her stepfather slept with the door closed. She waited at the doorway, scarcely breathing. Finally she eased into the bedroom, leaning forward just enough to see the bed past the closet wall. It was empty, and hadn't been slept in. *He isn't home.* Her own former bedroom was completely empty. Even the bed and dresser were gone and the closet was empty. That upset her a little, but she couldn't think of anything she wanted and she didn't linger. *Maybe I'll see if my winter coat is still in the downstairs closet.* She went back to the master bedroom and got the flashlight that her stepfather kept beside the bed, then went back down the stairs.

She went through the desk in his office. She found $260 in twenty dollar bills in an envelope in the top drawer. Smiling, she folded the money in half and stuffed it into her right front jeans pocket. In the right hand drawer, she found a revolver. She tucked it into the back pocket of her jeans.

In the kitchen she got a shopping bag. She opened the refrigerator and drank some milk from the bottle, then grabbed a package of extra sharp cheese and dropped it into the shopping bag along with an unopened package of sliced ham. She found a loaf of bread and a few other things in the pantry. In the entry hall, her winter coat was still in the back of the closet near the front door. She folded it into the bag and set the bag by the front door.

She returned to the garage, walked through it and out the far side door to the tank on the outside wall where her stepfather kept a supply of special high-octane gasoline for his Corvette. She filled a big red can, carried it into the garage, and splashed gas over both cars. She retrieved several rags from a big box, wadded them under the vehicles' gas tanks and soaked them with gas as well. Then she splashed gas on the wall to the house and carried the gas can inside, splashing gas all the way and leaving the door to the garage propped open. She took a box of matches from the kitchen cabinet, then splashed gas on the kitchen floor, on the bottom few stairs and around the living room, then ended with a trail of gas that led to the front door. She threw the gas can toward the stairs, then picked up her shopping bag. After she'd carried it outside and put it down, she lit a match and tossed it through the open door.

Whump! As flames began spreading inside, she picked up the shopping bag and raced down the driveway. Soon another explosion sounded and she ran faster. She had almost made it to the end of the driveway when a car came around the corner of the winding street, its headlights sweeping above her as she dropped to the ground. She rolled to the side and into a hedge, pulling her shopping bag with her. The Oldsmobile station wagon pulled into the driveway and sped past her just as there was another, even louder explosion.

Gloria craned her neck around. The garage door had blown off and the cars were burning fiercely inside. As if in slow motion the Oldsmobile rolled to a stop by the garage. Her stepfather flung open the driver's door and got out. She thought *He's too close to the fire* just as the gas tank beside the garage exploded.

The force of the blast knocked her stepfather back and he started running away. She stood, pulled the gun out of her back pocket and pointed it toward him. He was almost a hundred yards away. She cocked the hammer like she had seen Wyatt Earp do on TV and pulled the trigger. *Blam!* The sound hurt her ears as the gun bucked in her hand. She kept pulling the trigger until it finally clicked.

She wanted to run, but she forced herself to walk down the street to the Rambler. Lights were coming on in the few houses that she could see. She drove out of the neighborhood by a longer back route that the fire trucks wouldn't use and went to Belle Isle. She parked and just sat for about a half-hour, calming herself down. Finally, she made a sandwich of cheese and bread, then took out a notebook to write a letter to Jimmy. *But so much has happened... what should I say?*

She thought about it. She had burned down her stepfather's house and destroyed all of his precious cars. *Will he buy another Corvette?* And she had shot at him. *Did I hit him?* She didn't think so, but told herself she wouldn't regret it even if she had killed him. *But this whole thing will make him angrier. He'll try harder than ever to find me, and the police might try harder too.* She had pushed back hard, but she didn't feel good about it. As her anger drained away, she realized she loved Jimmy and she loved the baby. Love made her feel good. Anger made her feel bad. For a long time she tried to write the letter, but she couldn't. When the sun rose, she gave up and drove away.

December 1, 4:25 p.m., Detroit

Pietro Gargano, head of the Gargano crime family in Detroit, his son Pietro Jr. and Vincent Ayala, who was married to the old man's only daughter, sat around a polished walnut table in the elder Pietro's office on the 38th floor of the Guardian Building in downtown Detroit. Ever since the riot, his son and son-in-law had been trying to persuade him to move to the suburbs, but the old man loved the exuberant art deco architecture and was proud to be in The Cathedral of Commerce.

That morning, Pietro Jr. had learned that the Detroit office of the FBI had assembled a task force to look into an incident involving the Detroit Police Department at the Cresthaven Motel that had occurred during the riot the previous summer. Two police officers had been killed and another seriously wounded. This was of little interest to the Garganos, except that there had been at least one other witness, and probably two, who hadn't been found. The FBI had learned that the Detroit police were conducting an additional, secretive investigation into the incident in hopes of finding the witness or witnesses and preventing the story from getting out about what their officers had done before they were killed.

Unlike the Detroit police, the FBI had learned that one witness was a young white man. It had taken the FBI less than a day to identify him as James Hayes, and they quickly determined that he was in the Army and stationed in Vietnam. It had taken the FBI almost two weeks to run down Hayes' uncle, who had been working as a bosun on a Great Lakes ore boat, and interview him in Gary, Indiana as the boat was unloaded at a steel mill.

The uncle, Sepp Hayha, hadn't been much help but they did learn that his nephew had a girlfriend by the name of Gloria. Hayha didn't know the girl's last name. That explained the girl who had been registered at the motel with Hayes as his sister, Gloria Hayes. Sepp Hayha also had a photograph of the girl that his nephew had sent to him.

The FBI had been unable to identify the girl or to find her, but a secretary who worked in their office recognized Matthew Doran's daughter at once. The secretary was from an Italian immigrant family, so she had said nothing to the FBI. Instead she had gone to see Pietro, Jr., whom she knew from high school, and told him.

The Garganos had been discussing their problem for almost an hour but no strategy had yet emerged. Pietro Jr. had suggested killing her.

"The girl wouldn't know enough about us to hurt us," Vinnie argued.

"Besides, we don't kill women or children," the old man said. "But if they talk to the girl, they'll probably talk to her stepfather, especially if it's the feds. And no one knows more about us than he does." He shook his head. "I never liked that Armenian prick."

His son said, "Goddamn lawyers. Ought to drown 'em all at birth."

"Maybe we should kill him," Vinnie said. "He's the danger. And it would send a message to the girl. She'd be more likely to keep her mouth shut."

The younger Pietro gave his brother-in-law a curious look. "He was your good friend from Germany. You brought him to us and you've always supported him."

"Well, maybe I made a mistake," Vinnie said, "but I'm willing to put it right. I can take care of this personally."

The old man stood, walked over to a window and stared out at the Detroit River. Then he plodded back to his desk, shaking his head. "If we do that, we might call a lot of attention to ourselves. We can be sure the authorities already have an idea about what Fat Matt does for us. His death might start another federal investigation. And if you were that fat cocksucker, wouldn't you put something away in case a day came when the nice people you worked for ceased being friendly? He's not stupid. That's why we have him doing what he's doing. But he's not part of our family either. I've always watched him very closely because I've never thought he had any honor. We might have to replace him, but that's a problem for tomorrow. Today's problem is the girl. I am afraid we have to kill the girl, and if we need to, Fat Matt too." He looked at his son and son-in-law. "And we have to do this ourselves. No one else can know,"

"I'll handle it," Vinnie said hoarsely, looking first at his father-in-law and then his brother-in-law.

"I'll help," said Pietro, Jr., mostly because he didn't trust Vinnie.

8:30 p.m., Detroit

Matthew Doran carefully wiped his mouth with one of the soft cloth napkins at the Book Cadillac Hotel. He was finally getting the staff trained. They sent three napkins whenever he ordered a meal in the restaurant or from room service. Since his stepdaughter had burned down his Grosse Pointe home, he had been living in a suite atop the hotel, which was one of Detroit's finest. To his surprise, he liked many of the changes that the fire had forced on him. He was getting laid every day, often by a brand new beautiful young woman. Of course, they weren't young enough, but he had long since accepted that he had to go to Asia to fulfill those desires. He was taking taxis whenever the weather was bad and he was eating either at the hotel or at Detroit's finest restaurants. The restaurants and hotels provided many pay phones where he could have telephone conversations that were less likely to be monitored by the FBI than his home or office. He wondered why he hadn't thought of this sooner.

Thinking of the fire and his stepdaughter ignited a little explosion of anger. *She has to be exterminated, and the sooner the better.* She no longer had any value and indeed posed a major threat. Her obstinacy made him so angry that it had affected his judgment. *I wasn't forceful enough in training her... she never learned her proper place.* He threw his napkin to the table. *She's worse than her mother.* Saija, her mother, had been, and still was potentially a problem too. He should have had the mother eliminated a long time ago, despite her being Vinnie's secret ex-wife. *Damn kid... damn spoiled brat....* He had to find her, and soon. Doran wiped his mouth one more time with the third fresh napkin. He patted his expanding belly and belched loudly enough for a woman at the next table to glance at him.

CHAPTER 8

25 December, Nui Binh Base Camp

Christmas Day was unlike any other for the 99th Assault Helicopter Company. It was a rare day that they didn't fly. In fact, it was the first time they hadn't flown since Hayes had been there. There was supposed to be a truce, a ceasefire negotiated with the enemy that had started on Christmas Eve at 1800 hours. There had been truces in the past, and they had often been broken, so the Headhunters were supposed to be on standby, ready fly on a moment's notice. A few men had attended a Christmas Eve non-denominational church service with a chaplain, but most of the officers were watching eight-millimeter stag films in the Officers' Club. Most of the enlisted men had been in the EM Club drinking 10-cent cans of Schlitz or Carling Black Label beer.

Hayes spent most of Christmas Eve sitting next to a bunker on the wall of sandbags surrounding the club, playing the guitar and singing songs with dozens of others, all of them drinking beer and passing joints around. Hayes got high, and when he saw Rivera looking at him, he just shrugged. *He can fly with someone else if he wants to. I'm tired of being a saint.*

Cartwright, the company clerk, had painted *The Ellsworth Bunker* on a big piece of shrapnel from an incoming rocket and hung it by the bunker entrance. Someone from the Headhunters had placed a sign on the side of the Enlisted Men's Club: *Peace on Earth, Firepower to All* with the platoon's cannibal patch. Cartwright was painting another shrapnel chunk with *The Henry Cabot Lodge*. He was going to hang it at the entrance to his own hootch. Someone from Maintenance had a reel-to-reel tape recorder and was recording the dirty versions of Christmas carols and songs about the XO as they made them up. Several soldiers were pounding out rhythms on coffee cans and an ammo box. There were both blacks and whites in the group, which was a little unusual. A few of the warrant officers and lifers were there too. Hayes played some soul and some country and western. The last song he played was the Animals "We Gotta Get Out of This Place," and everyone sang along loudly. They all stayed up later than usual and slept-in on Christmas Day.

Christmas morning Hayes and Rivera had gone out to their gunship and given it a thorough 100-hour inspection. Hayes had disassembled both of the miniguns and replaced several parts that looked worn. By afternoon they were talking about knocking off and going back to the hootch to take a nap when the first sergeant and the executive officer approached. First Sergeant Jubal Sypher had quickly become unpopular for a myriad of reasons, not the least of which was handing out Article 15s.

"I wonder what the hell they want," Hayes said.

"Hide your pot," Rivera said.

"I don't have any."

The first sergeant said, "Rivera, you can bugger off."

"No, stay," Lehman said, and turned to Sypher. "Won't hurt to have a witness here."

Sypher nodded, his upper lip curling, and handed several sheets of paper to Hayes. "It's an Article 15. We have three witnesses who saw you smoking marijuana outside the Enlisted Men's Club last night. You will be fined seventy-five dollars. That'll be taken out of your pay, twenty-five bucks for each of the next three months, and you are demoted to PFC. You're getting off lightly."

"Who are the witnesses?" asked Hayes.

Sypher sneered. "It'll take a fuckin' court martial for you to find that out."

Lehman looked harshly at Sypher.

"Specialist Hayes," said Lehman. His tone was neutral and he spoke carefully. "An Article 15 is non-judicial punishment imposed by the commanding officer. You don't have to accept it. You can ask for a court martial instead. If you do that, we'll appoint an officer to act as your defense counsel and you'll be tried before a board. You'll have an opportunity to argue against the charge and confront the witnesses against you. If you lose, the punishment will probably be considerably more severe. It will be up to the board. With three eyewitnesses, I'd advise against that course of action. Frankly, I agree that you're getting off lightly here. However, this is a first offense. From what I've heard, you're the worst drug user in this company. I'm determined to put a stop to the use of marijuana around here."

Hayes looked at the papers but he was too flustered to read. He thought briefly about going the court martial route if for no other reason than to find out whom the witnesses were. "Okay Sir," he said finally. "I'll take the Article 15."

"Sign where your name is on the last page," said Lehman.

Hayes signed his name and handed the papers back.

"Stop by the Orderly Room and I'll give you a copy for your fuckin' scrap book," Sypher said sarcastically.

Lehman glared at him. "Sergeant!" The two started to turn around to leave.

Hayes said, "Sir, I've been trying since Thanksgiving to get my life insurance signed over to my girl and to get her an allotment. She doesn't have any money. How come the Army can type up an Article 15 in one day, but after six weeks still can't help me with my life insurance or an allotment?"

Lehman looked at Sypher. "Is this true?"

"Well, he's not married to her," said Sypher. "I don't think you can do that when you're not married. Besides, he doesn't even have an address for her."

"If I get killed, she'll get nothing," Hayes said.

Lehman scratched his chin, thinking, then turned to Sypher. "First sergeant, you will submit the paperwork for the insurance and the allotment. Maybe it will go through. Go to the Red Cross if you must and get their help on the address."

"Yes Sir," Sypher said, glaring at Hayes.

The two turned and walked away.

Rivera took out a pack of Pall Malls and offered one to Hayes. He took it and Rivera lit both cigarettes with his Zippo. It had a Headhunters cannibal on it and Hayes wanted to get one. They smoked in silence for a couple of minutes.

"Shit," Hayes said finally. "That goddamn Sypher has been after my ass ever since I got here."

"You gonna stop smoking pot?" asked Rivera.

Hayes shrugged. "I did stop. Last night was the first time since I came to the Headhunters. But I'm sure as shit gonna be more careful about it if I do it again. You know, I've been here four months. I don't know if I can take this place if I don't get out of my head sometimes. I do my job. I got my shit together. What's the fuckin' problem? There are a lot of guys, including pilots, who are flying with hangovers. Some of them are probably still drunk. Metcalf was hung over when he bought it. Marijuana's not that big a deal. Back in the World, half the people I knew were smokin' it."

This time Rivera shrugged. "The first sergeant isn't gonna stop trying to get you. I've been stoned a few times when I was home on leave. Mostly I didn't like it. It was like I couldn't control my thoughts. I got real scared once. That was the last time I smoked it. I don't see how anyone can function when they're stoned. You amaze me, Hayes, 'cause you're as good a gunner as I've flown with." He clapped Hayes on the shoulder.

Hayes nodded. "Thanks. When I get high, I feel like I'm living each moment more intensely. It's like time slows down, but my brain is still going normal speed. When I was playing with my band, I could be playing these really fast breakouts on my guitar and it felt like I was concentrating on every single note. Maybe that's what it is, concentration." He paused, remembering the recording back in the States. *It felt good but there were a lot of mistakes on that tape.*

"When I'm stoned, I can shut out all of the unimportant stuff and focus entirely on doing something. It's like putting on those glasses at a 3D movie or listening to music through a pair of headphones. Everything's brighter, sharper, clearer, louder... it's all better. And I need some of the all-better because everything's all bad over here. Sometimes I want to get stoned and listen to music or think about my girl and get all that bad shit out of my head."

Back at their hootch, they found out that Hayes was one of six people who had been given Article 15s for smoking marijuana. All six had accepted them. In each case, there had been three witnesses. There was much speculation about who the three witnesses were. A lot of names came up and a few soldiers made threats. There was some talk of having one of the six who had been punished change his mind and take the court martial so they could all find out who the witnesses were, but no one was willing to do that.

Hayes stopped smoking again and stopped hanging around the company area because he was afraid he'd be tempted. He would go out to the flight line with the guitar and sit on one of the revetments and play music.

Hayes strongly suspected the first sergeant was up to something. He didn't care, but he also didn't want to get a court martial. He just wanted to serve his year and go home.

"Why worry about it? You stopped smoking that shit so there's nothing he can do," Rivera said one night as they finished their maintenance.

"Yeah," Hayes said as he carried the machineguns to the Armament Hut. "Be nice if I could get away for a bit so I can put up with all this shit."

Back at the Headhunter hootch, he picked up the guitar and began playing one of his surfy love songs, one that Universal Joint had played. He imagined that he was hearing his amplified Fender. Rivera watched him, his eyes drinking in Hayes' persona and all the talent. He could almost hear it the same way Hayes said he did.

CHAPTER 9

December 23, 9:30 a.m., Michigan

Ever since she had burned down the house and emptied the revolver at her stepfather, Gloria had been depressed and troubled. She couldn't stop thinking about losing her temper and trying to shoot her stepfather. The only newspaper story she saw said the house had been unoccupied, and there was no mention of the shooting. She continued to dwell on the anger.

After burning the house, she thought it best to go someplace she'd never been before. She had driven to Kalamazoo and found a room in a house several miles south of town. But the room was expensive, and after a few weeks she had stayed longer than she thought was safe, so she headed for Detroit.

It was Saturday, and Monday would be Christmas. She stopped at the Northland Shopping Center on Eight Mile Road to walk around and look at the Christmas decorations. She hoped doing so would cheer her up. She brought her guitar on the chance that she might be able make a little money. She wondered briefly why she was risking being spotted by police. *Do I want to get caught?*

A group of four singers, three women and a man, all dressed in Victorian style clothes, were singing Christmas carols. After listening to a few carols, she wandered away from them, took out her guitar and started singing "Joy to the World." A crowd quickly gathered and a few of them dropped change into her guitar case. She sang "Silent Night," which she had been working on after reading about it in the library. She had worked out a long, elaborate guitar arrangement. People dropped more change into her guitar case, but near the end of the song, two security guards approached. They let her finish to a smattering of applause.

"That sure was pretty," said one of the security guards, an older black man with kinky gray hair and a large belly. "But you have to stop. You have to get permission from the management, and the only ones allowed are the singers from the Salvation Army. Sorry."

She nodded and packed up her guitar, noting that the two songs had generated several dollars. She felt guilty, like she was stealing from the Salvation Army. The security guard was still looking at her, though not in a threatening way and she was suddenly aware of how shabby she looked. Her winter coat, once an attractive imitation fur made out of lighter synthetic material had been soaked through several times by the rain. It was dirty and the fake fur was ratty with threads and other debris tangled in it. She had cleaned it as best she could, but it wasn't washable. She could no longer fit into any of her jeans or other pants. She was wearing old sweat pants with stains that wouldn't wash out. She walked away, but she felt a little better. Music always helped.

There was a long line of children at a big department store waiting to sit on Santa's lap. There were lots of families, mothers and fathers and little girls and boys. There were babies too. She wondered whether she and Jimmy and their baby would ever be able to do this. She watched a little girl climb onto Santa's lap and tug at his beard. The beard was real and Santa laughed. Then he erupted with a loud "Ho, ho, ho!" Children smiled and laughed, and Gloria smiled too. It was a long line and the littlest children were squirming and restless in their mothers' arms. She looked around and didn't see any security guards. She took out her guitar again and this time closed the case. She sang "Rudolph the Red Nosed Reindeer" to everyone's delight, then segued into "Here Comes Santa Claus" and then "Frosty the Snowman." She must have played for half an hour and was in the middle of "Run, Run Rudolph" when the security guard approached again. When she finished, she said, "I'm not collecting any money. I'm just singing a few songs."

He nodded and took a deep breath. "Well, you have to stop or I could lose my job. And I really need it," he said. A second security guard was standing back by a display beside two stern men in suits who were watching her closely. The three of them, all white, looked like they had severe indigestion. She put her guitar back in its case.

"I'm real sorry about this, but I have to escort you out." He led her through the center toward the lot where she had parked the Rambler.

She noticed the other guard and the two men in suits were following at a distance. "Why are they so upset?"

"You think Christmas is about peace on earth?" he asked bitterly. "Not around here. Here it's about 'I got to get my piece on this earth while I can.' Stores make most of their money at the holidays, and the owners get real worried anytime they think something might interfere with their trade. They didn't even want the Salvation Army here."

She had stopped at the Rambler and was putting the guitar in the back.

"I'm real sorry," he said again, "but I ain't worked since the riot. They wanted to call the cops on you but I told them it would be better if we didn't make a scene. If you don't leave they will call the cops and I'll get fired."

She nodded and climbed into the car.

"I really liked your playing," he said. "Especially that last one. That Chuck sure knows how to do a song."

"You'd like my boyfriend," she said.

"Now you try to have a merry Christmas," he said, and watched as she drove off.

3:56 p.m., Ann Arbor

She decided to drive to Ann Arbor, her favorite place to hide out. It was also the most dangerous, but depressed and lethargic, she was tired of running.

She parked outside the restaurant and bar where she had played the night before she'd learned she was pregnant, wondering whether she might persuade the owner to let her play for a meal. Just one meal and a chance at some tips. A short distance down the street, a man sat in a wheelchair bundled up against the wind and cold in a heavy coat with the hood up. He had made it across the street but he couldn't get the wheel chair over the curb. She got out of the Rambler and walked over to help him. She turned him around and then pulled the big back wheels up over the curb.

"Thanks," the man said, spinning the chair around to look at her. It was Lenny Papineau, the hippie from the Ann Arbor boarding house. He broke into a big smile. "Well, if it isn't Sunshine, girl guitar whiz! Good to see you, Baby!"

"Lenny, what happened to you?"

"I got the shit beat out me," he said. He looked at the restaurant. "Let's go in there. I'm cold."

They went into the restaurant. He ordered coffee and she got hot chocolate, first warning him that she couldn't afford to pay for it.

He waved that off. "My legs were broken, but they've pretty much healed. I had a broken wrist too, broke it pretty bad, compound fracture and all, and my right hand is still weak.

That's why I couldn't pull myself up. It's my back that's the real problem though. Son of a bitch threw me down the stairs and I broke two vertebrae. I was lucky because my cord's okay, but it'll take time before I can walk again. It gets a little better every week. Six more months I'll be doing the twist."

"Who did it?"

"Big Negro guy."

"Why would anyone beat you up, Lenny?" She had a sinking feeling that it had to do with her.

He didn't answer right away. He shrugged. "He was looking for you. He was sure I knew where you were 'cause the others in the house said you and I were... ah, close. Would you believe that some of them thought we were together?" He laughed nervously. "As if I could ever have a girlfriend as pretty as you," he said softly. He sipped his coffee, glancing off to either side, trying to avoid looking at her, but his gaze kept coming back to her.

"My stepfather's after me," Gloria said. "He tried to kill me."

"Man, that's harsh. Why? What's this about?"

"It's complicated, and it's a long story. I'm not sure about a lot of things. It's probably safer if you don't know, but I'm really sorry, Lenny. I don't know how to make it up to you. Let me tell you something else though."

He looked at her expectantly.

"I'm pregnant," she said. "Remember when you told me to go to the clinic? Well, that's why I was feeling sick. I'm gonna have a baby."

"Wow," he said. Then he gave her a sad look, maybe with a touch of jealousy. "I didn't know you were with anyone. Are you married?"

"Well, I have a boyfriend. He's in Vietnam. His name's Jimmy Hayes. He's a guitar player, just like me. He was in a band called Universal Joint in East Lansing before he got drafted." She immediately regretted telling Lenny that much because she could see he was a little hurt. And she didn't know for sure that Jimmy was still her boyfriend.

Lenny looked up at the ceiling for a moment, thinking. "I think I might have heard of them. A couple of my friends went to MSU last winter for a basketball game and they were talking about a great band they heard at some bar. Universal Joint. I remember when they told me 'cause I thought it was a cool name for a band. They said the guitar player was really good." He stopped and looked at her. "So why haven't you gone to the police?"

She shook her head. "Can't. The police are looking for me too. I didn't do anything except leave home, but one of my friends, Jimmy's friend too, was murdered. Really, the less you know about all of this the better. You've already gotten hurt because of it."

He sipped his coffee and looked at it. "You know, this happening to me wasn't all bad. My parents had to take care of me." He shrugged. "I saw how much of a disappointment I've been, so I started getting my act together. I really do want to be a lawyer some day and help people. My dad, he's a big lawyer in Detroit and he's done a lot of good things." He paused for a long moment. "So you've gone underground?"

She thought about it and smiled. "Yeah, underground."

When they'd been in the restaurant for about an hour, Lenny bought them supper. When he learned she had no place to stay, he invited her to spend the night at his apartment. "You'll be safe," he laughed. "I'm not much of a threat like this. And as much as I hate that war, I wouldn't go after a soldier's girl, especially you. You are one fine lady."

She was touched. She couldn't remember anyone ever calling her a lady, except for the music professor.

At the apartment, she played her guitar and sang for him until they both got tired. Then, over his protests, she insisted that he sleep in his own bed and she sleep on his couch. Before she fell asleep, she thought about going into the bedroom and giving Lenny a blowjob. It would be easy, and she knew she was good at it. No one but Lenny ever had to know. She hadn't heard from Jimmy for a long time. *Would Jimmy care? Would I care if Jimmy was with someone else?* She decided that she would care. Then she had a disturbing thought. *There must be women in Vietnam. Lots of soldiers go to prostitutes.* She tried to push all thoughts of sex away. She curled up, holding the growing bump in her belly, and eventually fell into a restless sleep. She woke up in the middle of the night and lay awake thinking. She made some decisions and was able to sleep more soundly.

December 24, East Lansing

She got up early on a cold, bleak Christmas Eve morning, left a note for Lenny, and drove from Ann Arbor to East Lansing. She bundled up and wandered around the deserted campus at Michigan State University, continuing to think about everything. Jimmy had lived on this campus for almost two years. She wanted to see some of the places he had talked about. But with her troubles heavy on her mind, she found a phone book, looked up the address and in the middle of the afternoon drove to a Roman Catholic cathedral in Lansing.

She got in line for confession. Although Gina had taken her to church every Sunday, she had never been confirmed. She had gone to the classes and learned about confession, but her stepfather wouldn't let her formally become a Roman Catholic. She knew the confession procedure, or at least thought she did. After waiting 15 minutes, she entered the confessional.

The priest sounded old and gentle to her, and he had an Irish accent.

When he asked her how long it had been since her last confession, she said, "I'm not sure. But it's several years, and I have committed many sins."

"And what troubles you the most?" asked the priest.

"I burned down my stepfather's house, and I tried to shoot him," she said flatly.

There was a long pause.

"I'm pretty sure I didn't hit him. And before that, I drove his precious Corvette into the Detroit River. I wanted to hurt him because he has committed so many sins against me. I was very angry."

"Sins are committed against God," said the priest.

"Well he beat me up and he did things to me sexually," snapped Gloria. "I hate him, and hatred is one of my biggest sins, the one that bothers me the most... that and anger. The anger might be the same sin as the hatred. I'm not sure, but it troubles me a lot."

Again, the priest didn't speak. She could hear him breathing a little faster than he had been, and she thought she detected a slight odor of wine.

"I have also committed the sin of fornication," she said.

"With your stepfather?" the priest asked in a shocked voice.

"No, with my boyfriend," she said. "But my stepfather made me suck his... thing. I'm not sure what you call that sin. In fact, why would it be a sin if he made me do it?" She thought momentarily about not confessing everything, but decided that God already knew anyway. "I did that same sin with other men. And one of them was a priest. That troubles me a lot because I didn't have to do it."

"A priest! Dear God!"

"And I did the sucking thing with my boyfriend too," she added. "And he did it to me. Well, I don't feel bad about that."

"How many times did you fornicate with your boyfriend?" the priest asked quickly.

She sensed his discomfort, but there was no turning back now. "I don't know. I didn't count. It must have been dozens of times at least over two weeks, but that doesn't bother me very much even though I'm pregnant now."

The priest gasped but she kept going.

"I have stolen food several times because I was hungry and didn't have very much money." She thought about it. "Maybe I could have paid sometimes. I have lied about who I am on many occasions but that really doesn't trouble me because I can't let my stepfather find me. He'll hurt me if he finds me and he wants to get rid of my baby."

"How old are you?" asked the priest.

This time she paused. "Do I have to tell you?"

"No, but I'm having trouble sorting out your sins. Sins are not the same for children as they are for adults, and you sound very young."

"I'm fifteen."

There was a very long pause, maybe half a minute. "Say a dozen Hail Marys and half a dozen Our Fathers before you leave the church. Then go and sin no more."

She didn't get up. "Father?" she asked carefully. "I have a request."

"Is it another confession? I thought you were through."

"No. I wish to ask for sanctuary. I remember learning in school that the church used to offer sanctuary to those who were fleeing. Do you still do that?"

"From whom are you fleeing? Your stepfather?"

"Yes," she said. "As I said, he beats me up and he beat my stepmother many, many times. When he found out I was pregnant, he said he would get rid of the baby. And I think he may have murdered someone when he was trying to find me. I'm very afraid of what he will do to me and the baby."

The priest groaned and thought for a long moment. "I think you should tell the authorities about all of this."

"I can't do that." She sniffled and fought back tears. "It's complicated, but if I go to the police, they will send me back to my stepfather because I'm only fifteen and he's a respectable lawyer as far as they know. I'm just a teenager. Who do you think they'll believe, me or him?"

"I can go with you to the police," said the priest. "I can make sure you receive fair treatment."

She didn't want to tell him the rest of it, about the police looking for her or the shooting at the motel. She could sense that the priest was close to the limit of what he would accept from her. On the other hand, he was a priest. "Father, it's Christmas Eve. It's cold outside. I'm hungry, pregnant and scared, and I have nowhere to stay tonight."

This wasn't strictly true because she had another place in mind where she might stay, though it was getting late. And she could probably drive back to Lenny's. She clenched her teeth, realizing that she had committed another sin of lying.

The priest answered almost immediately. "You shame me. Of course you can stay here tonight, with our sisters. Meet me at five o'clock just inside the main entrance. I should be finished with confessions by then."

"Thank you," Gloria said. "I have one more request, a suggestion really, and that is that you let me sing at Mass tonight. I can sing Silent Night and accompany myself on guitar. I truly want to earn my keep, and I promise you won't be disappointed. Father, did you know that Silent Night was written by a priest who originally performed it on a guitar on a

Christmas Eve about a hundred and fifty years ago? I learned that in a library last week."

"Go and do your penance," the priest said firmly. "You've been in here a long time and people are waiting."

Gloria went to the second row in the front of the church and knelt in a pew. She stayed there for a long time, reciting her penance and thinking about herself and Jimmy and their baby and God. She wasn't sure she was praying. She had always just closed her eyes and recited something because she could always remember the prayers she read in the books. She remembered some of them now and tried to think about the words. Mostly though, she thought about Jimmy and that she didn't want him to die in Vietnam. She tried to think of Jesus and God and the Holy Ghost and Mary, but she couldn't form a clear vision of them. "Please God, let Jimmy live," she begged. "Don't let him die. He's a good boy."

She thought about how badly she had behaved, about her hatred and her anger, and about the terrible things she had done. She didn't want to be like her stepfather, or even her stepmother. Ashamed, she sat in the pew choking back for several minutes. Some people looked at her. Then, she raised her arms up and looked up at the icon of Jesus on the Cross. "Forgive me. I will try to do better."

She slumped down and after a few minutes had almost fallen asleep. A soft yellow aura grew around her and she felt immensely better, more peaceful than she had felt for many months. She looked around the church, taking in the decorations: spruce boughs flocked with snow and tied with red ribbon, joyful white angels, glittering gold and silver bells, and an elaborate manger scene. Then she got up and walked to the church entrance. A stooped, elderly white-haired priest was standing by the door talking to two young nuns. They looked different and nicer than the nuns she remembered from school. He turned and looked at her, a question in his eyes, and she nodded, smiling. The old priest motioned to someone behind her and presently another priest appeared.

She froze. The new priest was smiling, but it looked forced. His black eyes were not smiling. The hood of his robe was up, giving him a sinister look. His name was Father Andres and he was the last choir director when she sang in the youth choir. One night she had lingered after choir practice and asked him if she could play her guitar instead of him playing the piano. She had persuaded him with a blowjob. She had been 14 then and just learning to use the power that sex gave her over some men. She reasoned that if she had done it with her stepfather, there was nothing wrong with her doing it for her own gain. However, Father Andres had never been content with just the single act. He had always wanted more.

"Father Andres, this girl wants to sing "Silent Night" tonight at Mass, and I see no reason not to allow her," said the old priest. "The first one, not the Midnight Mass."

Father Andres continued to smile at Gloria, and then turned to the older priest. "I've heard her before. She's very talented." He looked at her. "Very, very talented."

"Father Andres is our choir director," said the old priest. "Do you know him?"

"Yes." She almost added that she had mentioned him before. Father Andres kept smiling but said no more. She was sure he didn't like what was going on but he inclined his head slightly as she left with the two nuns.

They took her to an adjacent building where they showed her a cubicle where she could spend the night. She would be sharing it with one of the nuns. There were more nuns there and most of them were young. In fact, they were novices. Gloria had her guitar and she played "Silent Night" for them. Then she went back to the church to meet Father Andres.

Father Andres was solicitous. He helped her adjust the sound levels and the microphones though he seemed distracted. He was looking at his watch for the second time when another priest came striding up the aisle trailed by a bulky man. It was her stepfather. She turned to run, but Father Andres was between her and the nearest door, apparently ready to grab her. She couldn't get away.

Father Andres bowed his head slightly to the new priest, who was wearing fancier robes than the others. "Monsignor Napoli."

The monsignor turned to her stepfather. "Is this your daughter?"

"Yes." He turned to Gloria. "Time for you to come home, Gloria," he said pleasantly.

Her heart pounded and she looked around. She considered begging the monsignor for help, but she knew that wouldn't work. She thought about smashing them with her guitar and making a run for it, but there were two of them. Three, counting the monsignor. She looked up at the Jesus on the Cross over the sanctuary. *Why have You let me down?* But she knew the answer almost immediately: *It isn't over yet.*

"I just went to confession," she said to the monsignor. "I'd like to stay for Mass. And I was gonna sing."

The monsignor shook his head. "Our choir has been practicing for weeks. We can't have an unknown spoil the most important night of the year," he said, and then turned to her stepfather. "But surely you will allow her to stay for Mass?"

Doran was trapped and he knew it. He nodded begrudgingly. "Okay. I will be waiting by the main entrance when Mass has ended." He turned to the monsignor. "I'm Armenian you see, and I would prefer not to be in the church during your Mass." He turned back to Gloria. "And by the way," he said to Gloria. "I have men from Pinkerton's stationed at all of the church doors in case you're thinking of running again. You're not getting away this time, so enjoy the Mass." He moved to put his arms around her, but Gloria drew quickly away. "Ahh, teenagers," he said pleasantly to the monsignor. The two walked away together. Gloria guessed that her stepfather was agreeing to a large donation to the church.

"I'm sorry," said Father Andres, though he didn't sound sincere. It was more like he was sorry there wasn't time to renew their previous relationship.

Gloria shrugged, but she touched his arm. A plan was forming and she needed to get on his good side. It might work. They were alone in the nave, though that wasn't likely to last long. The earliest arrivals for the early Christmas Eve Mass would be coming soon. They walked to the back and outside to the convent building where the nuns lived. A man in a green nylon flight jacket was at the door, watching her closely. Gloria said she needed to get her bag so she could be ready to leave as soon as Mass ended. The man accompanied them to the building and Gloria took her time, pleased to see the early arrivals pulling into the parking lot in their cars.

When she returned to the church with her bag, she turned to Father Andres, smiled and stepped very close to him. "Would you mind hearing a quick confession? I need to be at peace for Mass tonight and I've just had some unclean thoughts... very, very unclean." She let her breast brush against his arm and smiled. "Could we have just a few minutes?"

"Okay." His voice quavered slightly. This time his smile was genuine. They stopped at one of the confessionals and she leaned her guitar case and suitcase against the wall. She held onto her big handbag.

"I seem to be very sinful today," she said, touching his arm again and stepping closer. He guided her into the confessional and went in with her instead of going into the priest's side. She didn't stop him when his hand slid down her hip. The, space was very tight. They pressed together and barely got the door closed.

She bent over slightly, letting her butt slide against him as she reached into her bag. She pulled out the pistol she'd taken from her stepfather's office. Pointing it at his face, she cocked it. The click sounded loud in the confined space. "Now, you can take off all of your clothes."

"What?" he gasped, but then he smiled lasciviously.

"Be quiet about it," she said quietly, still smiling. "If you attract attention, I'll have to shoot you. Now off with your clothes."

She had no bullets and the gun was empty. She kept it pointing at his nose, but he seemed to think it was part of a game. Slowly he began taking his clothes off until he had only boxer shorts left. He had an erection.

"Those too," she whispered throatily. "I want to see if it's as big as I remember."

He slid the shorts down and stepped out of them.

"Now turn around," she whispered, but with an edge this time. "The gun is real."

Quickly, she put on the priest's robes over her own clothes. She pulled out a white headband to cover her hair and put the hood up. She gathered up all of Father Andres clothes and stuffed them into her bag. It was a large bag and she had emptied most of it when she went back to get her suitcase. The pistol went into one of the deep side pockets in the robes.

"Enjoy the mass, Father," she said, cracking open the door. "Goodness, there are lots of people out there already... hardly any empty seats." She stepped out and grabbed her guitar and suitcase, then walked with her head down until she reached the side door that she calculated was nearest to where she'd parked the car on the street. Outside, there was a different man wearing the same kind of green nylon flight jacket. He looked at her and murmured, "Father" as she glided past. She found the Rambler, threw the bag and guitar onto the back seat and drove toward East Lansing.

She turned into the Michigan State University campus and entered a parking structure that she'd checked earlier. Most of the students were gone, but a few, mainly foreign students, were staying through the holidays. Those with cars were parking in this garage. She took off the robes and walked a route she had taken earlier to a circular, ground-level opening in a concrete alley between two buildings. A light veil of steam wafted up from a heavy grate. She slid the grate to the side, then climbed down the metal ladder until she was standing with just her head outside of the opening. She dragged the grate back into place and climbed the rest of the way down. It was hot and smelled of acrid, dirty steam. She heard distant machinery sounds, metallic creaking and clanking, but she felt safe.

Jimmy had told her about the university's steam tunnels and that he had spent many a cold winter night in them.

She spent the next several hours exploring outwards from the point where she entered. She found two doors that opened into laboratories or office buildings. Although the tunnels had lights in them, the lights in the basements of the buildings were turned off and she was afraid to turn them on even if she could find the switches. At 3:35 a.m., she found a third unlocked door. After her eyes adjusted to the dark, she crept through a basement until she discovered some stairs and found she was in a big kitchen. Dim light filtered in through the windows. After making sure the door wouldn't lock when she let it shut, she started exploring the kitchen. She was hungry. In a refrigerator, she found a big block of cheese slices and started eating them. There were also a few eggs, but she left them. She drank heartily from a gallon jug of orange juice that was more than half full. She found an assortment of cereal in individual serving-sized boxes, but couldn't find any milk. She ate out of a box of sugared cereal as she wandered around. A big walk-in freezer contained a treasure trove of frozen meats. She was satisfied that she wouldn't starve anytime soon.

After exploring the kitchen she began wandering through the dormitory, always making sure no doors locked behind her. She walked quietly down the long halls lined with doors to the student rooms, trying each door. Most of the students had locked their doors but few students had not remembered. On the second floor, she came upon an unlocked door for a room that appeared to be for three students. It had a set of bunk beds and a single bed and there were three dressers. The sun was just starting to come up and enough light was coming through the windows to reveal that the beds were only haphazardly made. Tired, she considered lying down on one of the beds. Instead, she took a towel from a dresser and went to the big bathroom across the hall. She had to turn on the bathroom lights because the room had no windows and was pitch black. The urinals made it clear that she was in a boys' dormitory. The showers were in one big, open, tiled room. She turned one on, waited until the water was hot and then stripped off all of her clothes. After her shower she picked up her clothing and walked naked back to the room, pausing in front of the big bathroom mirror to look at her swelling belly. She ran her fingers lightly over her expanding abdomen and smiled. "Jimmy and I are gonna have a baby," she said as she turned out the light.

Before she climbed into the single bed, Gloria sank to her knees, bowed her head and prayed again. How many sins had she committed? *Many,* she thought, but almost none of it bothered her. However, for a brief moment she had doubted God, so she asked for forgiveness and crossed herself. For the first time in many months, she felt absolutely safe. Her stepfather would not find her here and she was sure that no one would be coming to the dormitory on Christmas Day. She fell asleep thinking of Jimmy and the baby and slept for a long time.

December 31, 11:22 p.m., Detroit

Clyde Bonaventure, alone in his immaculate home, was sitting in his favorite red leather chair working his way through a quart bottle of Crown Royal Special Reserve Canadian whiskey. He hadn't felt this uneasy since the war. It was the same feeling he got when he wasn't sure what was going on around him while flying his P-51 Mustang over occupied Europe.

He was thinking about Matthew Doran. He had first met Doran in Germany in the late forties. Then, Europe was a more comfortable place for a black man than the U.S. He knew the military and he made a good living providing prostitutes, mostly for American soldiers. There was an endless supply of desperate women willing to work as prostitutes. In those days Doran was known as Dorrinian, and he brought Bonaventure some of the most beautiful, and most desperate women. Dorrinian was smuggling people from Europe to Canada and America, and the women he brought to Bonaventure needed to pay him for a one-way trip. They had done business and been casual friends for several years, until Doran had left for America to work for the Gargano Family. It was Doran who had suggested that Bonaventure come to Detroit and had helped him get established. If not exactly a friend, Doran had remained a steadfast business partner.

Then a few months ago, Doran had asked for help moving high-grade heroin from Southeast Asia to America. The Hmong tribes in the Golden Triangle of Southeast Asia were backing the CIA in Laos. The Hmong grew opium poppies and made heroin. It was the basis of their economy, and the CIA wasn't about to stop them. Indeed, the CIA wanted the Hmong to prosper. Doran was working with a shadowy intelligence operative who wasn't in the CIA but was connected to them. Bonaventure had never met the man, but he had agreed to help Doran. Specifically, he had arranged with the military contacts he still had for the heroin to travel on military aircraft. As a result, he and Doran were sending surplus pharmaceuticals back to Southeast Asia, another source of profit. Bonaventure's rationalization was that heroin was bad, but someone was going to make money selling it so it might as well be him, at least in Detroit.

Doran, however, had bigger plans.

When the Detroit heroin business was working, Bonaventure helped expand the operation to Chicago. They were talking to people in both Cleveland and Buffalo, and New York was on the horizon. It wasn't until the system started working that Bonaventure figured out Doran wasn't working for the Garganos. This was his own operation... and Bonaventure's. The Gargano Family, mainly Vinnie Ayala, knew they were getting good heroin from a new source, but that was all the Garganos knew. Doran and Bonaventure were making money on everything going to the other cities and paying off the military people. It was more money than Bonaventure had ever made, and his criminal life had changed dramatically. He had become a supplier of heroin to inner cities, and the customers were primarily poor urban blacks. And when the high-grade heroin first hit the streets of Detroit, people died. He shook his head and raised the whiskey bottle. The business was more unsavory than anything else he had ever done, but he told himself he could do good things with the money.

Despite his criminal life, Bonaventure saw himself as a moral man. He had been a war hero. He'd shot down four German planes in World War II only to find he was unwelcome in Stateside officers' clubs. When he and some of his fellow black officers protested, he was court martialed. That's when he decided he would not follow the white man's rules, although he had nothing against most white people.

Bonaventure also thought of himself as a community leader. Lots of Bonaventure's money went to Detroit's churches and their charitable works, and only a few pastors refused his gifts. He had helped countless blacks start small businesses; he had helped the black unions; and he was one of the biggest political contributors in the city though rarely acknowledged as such.

Thinking about Doran was unsettling. He had always been disturbed by Doran's perverse sexual relations with children, which he had first heard about in Germany. Back then he had decided it was none of his business. More recently, Doran hadn't seemed to care about his wife when she was killed in an accident. Bonaventure had heard whispers that her death might not have been an accident, but he had never met her so he put that out of his mind too.

Then there was Doran's daughter. Bonaventure would never forget the day Doran had brought him to his home to meet his daughter. The sight of the girl playing her guitar in a bikini bathing suit had unnerved Doran more than it had Bonaventure. He was sure Doran hadn't expected to find her in that state. Doran had planned on introducing her to him, but he was so upset that he turned around and the two of them left. The girl was so wrapped up in her music that she hadn't noticed them. Then, driving away from the aborted meeting at his home, Doran had offered her to Bonaventure as a wife, or just as a girlfriend. Doran had assured him that the girl was still a virgin, but that she was "well-trained," whatever that meant. Eventually, Bonaventure decided that Doran was really making a business proposition, akin to an arranged marriage. He had been flattered that Doran would consider him, a black man, important enough to marry his daughter. But what about the girl? Apparently, she had no say in the matter.

He was halfway through the bottle of Crown Royal and still flying solo in dangerous territory. He put aside the matter of the girl and thought about other aspects of Doran. The man was a financial genius. Doran had learned about the CIA's dilemma from a shadowy associate, someone he had known in Germany before Bonaventure met him. The old associate had apparently surfaced and solicited his advice on how to set up a deceptive front company for the CIA, something at which Doran was skilled.

Doran started legitimate companies that made enormous amounts of money and were incorporated in foreign countries, making examination difficult for outsiders. And on the surface, Doran was completely lacking in greed and generous with favors and advice. In that way, he learned a great deal about many different criminal operations. *Doran knows everything about where my money comes from and where it goes, so he must know the same things about a lot of others. He probably knows more details about the Gargano finances than the Garganos know themselves.* Then the Crown Royal loosened something in his brain. Suddenly a big piece of the puzzle about the girl slid into place. "Oh shit," he said. "Oh shit!"

He started doing the math using a pad of paper and a ballpoint pen. Impaired by whiskey, he had to do the simple addition three times and consult a calendar before he was sure that it was possible. He stared at the Crown Royal bottle. It was two-thirds gone. He picked it up, got up slowly and deliberately from the deep leather chair, and walked very carefully out of the family room.

He climbed carefully up the stairs to a room he used as an office. It was a room that he didn't visit very often. The walls were covered with family pictures. He examined the pictures as a warmth spread through him from more than the whiskey. Finally, he stopped at a picture of his grandmother, his father's mother, Grandma Persephone, an extraordinary woman who had raised 13 children. She'd been born a slave and was freed by Lincoln's Emancipation Proclamation when she was still a baby. The picture had been taken when she was just 26. She was dressed in a long, frilly dress that she was holding up in front to reveal shapely legs encased in silk stockings that went up to mid-thigh and were held by garters. There were three others in the picture, all of them dance hall girls in Dallas. She was the most beautiful of the four. Whenever the family got together, the picture was the subject of much discussion, because all four women appeared to be white.

He took the picture off its hook and slowly slid down the wall to sit on the floor and look at it some more. "Jesus H. Christ on the cross."

Bonaventure gulped the last big mouthful of whiskey and let go of the bottle. It slid off his leg and clattered onto the hardwood floor. He looked at the picture, thought about the girl, his family and his life, and he started to sob. The picture was clearer now, but Bonaventure didn't know what he wanted to do about it. He finally slid sideways onto the floor and passed out.

January 4, 1968, East Lansing

Not sure when the students would return and the dormitories would go back to normal operations, Gloria stopped going into the dorms the day after New Year's. She carted pillows, blankets and some cushions from a big dormitory sofa out to one of the garage-sized rooms in the tunnels. She found a spot that was hidden behind some machinery where there was some ventilation. She had a supply of canned food and several tins of Sterno that she'd found in a dorm room during a foraging expedition. Most of the time, she lay awake in her blankets wondering where else she could hide and trying not to think about being pregnant. *What if something goes wrong? How would I know? What will I do when I finally start to give birth?* Sometimes she felt a strange fluttering in her belly. It was like a small muscle was out of control. She worried about it.

She ached with fear about Jimmy. She wrote letters, but she couldn't mail them. She had only one stamp left. She thought about going to the post office. She thought about going to see Roscoe's mother or Mrs. Murphy again. Would Jimmy mail more letters to Roscoe's address? She wasn't sure whether Frances Lincoln was completely a friend, but Gloria didn't think she was an enemy. She was restless and anxious. She fought against being angry, but she needed to do something. On the Thursday after New Year's at 8:30, she climbed out of the tunnels in the same alley where she had originally entered, not even sure whether it was morning or evening.

It was morning. Lights were on in the library so she went in. For more than an hour, she read about pregnancy and finally concluded that she was doing okay so far. She wasn't exhibiting any of the problems she'd read about, and the fluttering she sometimes felt in her abdomen was probably the baby moving. She felt better. She walked to a small restaurant on Grand River Avenue and splurged on a late breakfast of French toast and sausage. All the time she kept thinking and the name she thought most about was Clyde Bonaventure.

Her stepfather was looking for her, and the police were looking for her, especially that sneaky little detective. How about Clyde Bonaventure? Was he looking for her too? When she'd first learned of Roscoe's murder, she'd thought Clyde Bonaventure might be responsible. Now, she didn't think he had done it, but he might know something. Was Roscoe's murder related to what had happened at the Cresthaven?

So late in the afternoon in the washed-out cold gray winter gloom, Gloria was parked in the Rambler directly across the street from Clyde Bonaventure's impressive brick house. She had looked up the address in a phone book in the library and gotten a Detroit street map at a gas station.

She was still in the car putting her handbag in order when the front door of the house opened and two women came out. They were both black, but one had bleached blonde hair in a wild Afro that spilled over a beige fur jacket. The other one was wearing sunglasses despite the darkening sky. Both were young and pretty and dressed in skin-tight ski pants. She couldn't tell for sure, but she thought she caught a glimpse of Bonaventure in the door. As the two women got into a dirty two-year old Pontiac, Gloria saw that they were both heavily made up. *A couple of Bonaventure's women*, she thought.

She waited until they had driven off, hoisted her big handbag onto her shoulder, and tramped up the sidewalk to the front door. She was about to ring the doorbell when she heard singing inside. It was a man, maybe two men, singing loudly and off key.

> "We are the heroes of the night
> To hell with the Axis might
> Fight! Fight! Fight!"

She rang the doorbell and was about to ring it a second time when the door opened and Clyde Bonaventure, a drink in his hand, opened the door.

He gaped at her. He was wearing a tan camel-hair sports jacket over a wine-red turtleneck stretching over his belly, black pressed slacks and shiny cordovan loafers. But his clothes looked like they'd been thrown on in a hurry. He smiled when he saw her, an expression of smug self-confidence on his face.

She pulled the revolver from the handbag and pointed at his nose. "I want to talk to you, and it's cold out here."

He raised his hands carefully so he wouldn't spill his drink and backed up as she moved inside. He looked concerned, but not frightened. He was still smiling. She pushed the door shut behind her with her foot and backed him up around the corner into a big room with red leather furniture. Another black man was sitting on the red leather couch. She took in a big color TV, an expensive-looking stereo, two whiskey bottles and an assortment of mixers on a coffee table, along with an ashtray loaded with cigarette butts. Cigarette smoke still hung in the air.

"Holy shit!" said the other man. "What the fuck's going on, Clyde? Who'd you piss off now?"

"Put the gun down before it goes off," Bonaventure said calmly. He had stopped backing up and looked as if he might move toward her.

She cocked the revolver, the click loud enough for all of them to hear.

His smile disappeared.

"Sit down," she said, letting the barrel wander to point at the other man. He tried to duck but she followed his moving head and then pointed it back at Bonaventure, who had already sat down. A matching smaller couch on the other side of the coffee table faced the couch with the two men. She sat on it, got comfortable and used both hands to hold the gun.

"Who's this?" she asked Bonaventure, using the gun to gesture at the stranger.

"That's my good friend Logan Carlton," Bonaventure said. "He's a state senator."

"Christ, you didn't have to tell her that! What is this Clyde?" Carlton asked. He was light-skinned, though not as light as Bonaventure, and his face was spotted with freckles. "Is this another one of your girls? She catch you banging some other cookie?" He glanced at Gloria. "Don't get your panties in a wad, Honey. You ought'a know you're not the only one. And put the gun away. Shit, I'll help you mess with this crazy motherfucker." He started laughing.

Bonaventure said, "Damnit Logan, shut up."

They sounded like they'd had quite a bit to drink. Gloria shrank down, and for a few seconds she couldn't breathe. *Getting angry,* she thought, and tried to control it. She started rocking back and forth, the gun wavering but always pointing in the general direction of the two men. She took several deep breaths as she silently recited the rosary. It helped, but only a little.

She looked at Carlton and snarled, "I'm not one of his girls, but I am pissed off."

"I won't hurt you," Bonaventure said, looking at her. There was worry in his voice. She had cracked his relaxed demeanor. "That's the last thing I want to do."

Gloria looked over the tops of the glasses on the coffee table.

"Okay," she said.

He glanced at Carlton. "I'd like to talk to her alone."

Carlton snickered, but Gloria kept her eyes on Bonaventure.

Bonaventure said, "I have something very important to tell you, and you might not want anyone else to know this. At the very least, you need to know first so you can decide who else should know. It's about your family."

"My family?" she asked. "What about my family?"

She kept looking at Bonaventure, who looked at Carlton, who was focused on the gun.

"Please Logan," Bonaventure said. "We need to talk privately."

"Sure, I'll leave you two lovebirds alone," Carlton said with blatantly false good humor. He started to get up.

Gloria moved the gun to point at his face. "No," she said. "Stay right where you are."

"Okay, okay," he said sinking back in the couch. He tried to keep it light but there was a sheen of sweat on his forehead. "I've known Clyde a long time. We were in the war together. He's a wild motherfucker, but you can count on him. Really, you can. He's one of the good guys even if the authorities see it a little different. It's true that I'm a state senator. Clyde's well-known to churches and unions... he's even a campaign contributor though you won't find his name on any of my lists." Carlton looked pleased with himself.

Bonaventure looked at her. "Your birthday's coming up soon, right?"

"January 18," she said. "How did you know that?"

"You'll be sixteen?"

She looked at him with a puzzled expression. "I haven't told anyone how old I am. How do you know?"

"I believe I'm your father," he said. He smiled tentatively, but with some of the same smugness he'd shown when he answered the door. It was like he was fishing for compliments after a good round of golf. "I didn't know I had fathered a child until just a few days ago, but I wasn't really surprised when I thought about it."

"No shit," Carlton muttered under his breath, but she heard it, and the start of a snicker, which stopped when the gun moved his way again.

Gloria glared at Bonaventure. "That's a *terrible* thing to say! How could that be true? For one thing, you're black and I'm white. Why are you making up an awful story like that?"

"Jesus H. Christ," Carlton said, laughing. "Are you shitting me, Clyde? You, a fucking daddy? I don't believe it!"

Bonaventure looked at Carlton, momentarily upset, but then he relaxed. "Had to happen sooner or later. Might even be a few more around."

Gloria bit her lip, seething with anger. She felt the anger taking over despite her efforts, and she lost control. She was almost shouting and she waved the gun around as she said, "I thought my stepfather was a terrible man because of what he did to me and Gina! But you are *awful*! *Both* of you! You have all the fucking money and power, but you're real assholes, making our boys fight your stupid war! No *wonder* kids hate grownups! Shit, there's something wrong with calling you two grownups. I'm more grown up than you are. I always wanted to know who my father was, but I am pretty sure he's not another crooked asshole who hangs around with one of the fucking politicians who sent Jimmy to Vietnam. You in your fucking conservative clothes, drinking your fucking booze and fucking your cheap whores... and thinking I'm one of them! I ought to shoot you both!" She stopped, swallowed with a gulp and momentarily felt better. She forced a thin, bitter smile. "But I believe in peace," she chirped. "All you need is love."

Carlton said, "Hey don't blame me for that fuckin' mess in Vietnam. I've been—"

Bonaventure drowned him out. "Please... I'm sorry, Honey. I—"

"Don't *fucking* call me honey!"

Bonaventure swallowed and then nodded, his smugness gone. "Let me have your hand, but please be careful with that gun." He reached across the table, took her hand and laid it on the table next to his. "I'm very light skinned for a black man, but I'm the darkest of all my brothers and sisters. Most of them can pass for white if they try. Look at your hand and mine. Mine is only slightly darker than yours, and your mother was a very fair-skinned woman. If you come upstairs I'll show you an old photograph of my grandmother that'll prove all of this."

Gloria peered at their hands. Then she studied his face. She turned his hand over and her own hand over so she could look at the palms. "Oh my God no! No, it can't be true!"

Carlton looked at her and then Bonaventure, his gaze slipping back and forth. "Christ Clyde, you're not shitting us, are you?"

She looked into Bonaventure's eyes and studied his face some more.

That brought just a hint of a smile. Some of his confidence was seeping back. "You might not want anyone to know your father is black. I can appreciate that. I won't tell anyone, and I haven't told anyone. The only other person who knows is Logan here and that's only because you didn't want him to leave. Most of the time you can trust him. And as for me, I only want to help you."

She glanced at Carlton and wished he wasn't there, but she was afraid to let him go.

He was dressed in a grey suit, though his red and yellow striped tie was just strung around his collar and not tied.

Sweating profusely, he picked up a glass on the table that was about half-full and drained it.

Gloria turned back to Bonaventure. She needed to get to the original reason she had come. "Look... I know my stepfather is trying to find me, and so are the Detroit police. Have you been looking for me because of what Jimmy and I saw at that motel? Did you have anything to do with Roscoe Lincoln being murdered?"

Bonaventure was shaking his head but avoided looking at her, as if he was hiding something. He stole a glance at Carlton, who was looking upset again. "Ah shit... sorry. I'm not a hundred percent sure who killed Roscoe, but—" He stopped and looked up at the ceiling. "It might have been a very dangerous man by the name of Slick Percy Dupree who used to work for me... well, sometimes he still does." He lowered his gaze and looked at Carlton and then back at Gloria. "Remember when I saw you and your boyfriend and Roscoe at Roscoe's place? When I saw you, I just wanted to talk to you, to see if you were going to do anything about what you'd seen. I couldn't talk to you in front of Roscoe because I figured he probably didn't know about it. So after that, I asked Percy to look for you and your friend Jimmy. But now I know Slick Percy was working for someone else too."

"My stepfather?" asked Gloria.

Bonaventure nodded. "Yeah. I don't understand why Fat Matt's so anxious to find you. Seems more than just because you ran away."

"You know what he does? You know who he works for?"

Bonaventure nodded.

She was feeling a little more secure. "Well, I know all about it too. I used to overhear him talking all the time from when I was little and I can remember the numbers. I can remember how much money is in what bank. I remember everything I hear about numbers. I don't know why I can do that, but I know you have one million, eight hundred and ninety two thousand dollars in a bank in Switzerland and two million, four hundred and thirty seven thousand, two hundred and ninety one dollars in the Bank of Montreal branch in Windsor... or at least you did last May. I have a bunch of his papers with some of the bank stuff too, and some strange ones in a foreign language. I don't know what it is or what it means. I think its German."

Bonaventure looked at her incredulously.

"Holy shit, Clyde," said Carlton. "You need to up your campaign contribution."

"And the Gargano family? What about them?" Bonaventure asked.

She started reciting amounts and banks and dates when the money moved and companies that it moved into.

He stopped her. "And he knows you can do this?"

She nodded. "I think so. I told him but I don't know how much he believes. But I remember everything like that. Gina said I had a photographic memory."

"Christ, that's it! The feds could put him and the Garganos away for a long time if they talked to you. And if the Garganos knew, they'd be after you too. And it might be all over for him. You could put me in prison too, first for what you saw at the motel and second, for the money. What you can tell them is how the Garganos—and me too—how we hide our money. Even if you couldn't remember every detail, you could give them enough so they would know where to look."

"I remember the details," she said.

"Jesus Christ, Clyde," Carlton said. "I really don't like hearing this shit."

Bonaventure glared at him but didn't say anything.

Gloria shrugged. "Too bad." She looked at Bonaventure again. "Tell me about my mother." He hadn't convinced her yet, but she wanted to know more. "Who is she and how did you meet her? Where is she now?" Suddenly, she was nervous.

"Well, it's maybe not a story you really want to hear," Bonaventure said.

"Please, I do want to know, even if it's bad. I need to know where I came from."

"Okay, let me go back to the beginning. I went to Germany after the war. I lived near Berlin, doing some of the same things I do now. Lately, I'm not so proud of that, but back then I liked making the money and being the big man."

"He ain't shittin' us," Carlton said. "Clyde's a bigger motherfucker now, but during the war he was so skinny we had to tie a board to his ass to make sure he didn't go down the shower drain."

Bonaventure ignored the dig and was looking at the window behind Gloria. But Gloria, no stranger to foul language, stared at Carlton. That shut him up.

"Maybe I still like being the man. I ran clubs where men, mostly American soldiers, could meet women. They were like the club you played in that night. The women were prostitutes, so I guess you'd call me a pimp."

He'd lowered his head but he was still looking at her. He shifted uncomfortably on the couch.

Carlton was looking at him, shaking his head. "Shit Clyde, do we have to do this?"

Bonaventure didn't pay any attention to him. "I was in the Air Force during the war. The 332nd Fighter Group. I was a fighter pilot, and damn good. Shot down four Germans and would have been an ace if they hadn't sent me back to the

States. I don't think they wanted any colored aces. Logan, he was a bomber pilot, but we knew each other."

Carlton opened his mouth to say something but then shut it.

"But back in the U.S., I couldn't even get a drink in the Officers' Club," he said bitterly. "No niggers allowed. That's when Logan and I got to be good friends. A bunch of us black officers just went into the Officers' Club one day. I got court martialed. They made an example of me... me and some others. We're known as the Tuskegee Airmen, though most white people never heard of us."

Gloria moved the gun from her right hand to her left.

"Sorry, I'm getting off target," he said. "Anyway, I got out of the Air Force and went back to Germany and started making money with night clubs and girls. I was good at that and I liked it over there. I knew your stepfather first as Matthias Dorrinian. We worked together some. He brought me some women. He was smuggling refugees from Europe to Canada and the States. He brought me women so they could earn money to pay him. Your mother was one of those women."

"What was her name?" Gloria asked, her voice hoarse.

"Well, I don't think she gave me her real name. She was introduced to me as Sasha, but I heard her call herself Saija Hayha. Pretty close to Sasha. She was Finnish, very blonde and very, very beautiful. Also strange. She hardly spoke. It was like she was daydreaming or distracted. Dorrinian told me she needed a lot of money because she had a brother who was going to be difficult to move. But two days later, Dorrinian came back and got her, and I never saw her again."

"So you and she...."

Bonaventure nodded. He looked right over the gun into her eyes.

Carlton said, "Trying 'em out, were you? Need to make sure everything's in the right place?"

"Aw c'mon, Logan... for Chrissakes shut up!" Bonaventure said loudly. He turned to Gloria and said just as loudly, "I know you're pregnant, so you know how that happens. As I said, I didn't figure out what must have happened until a few days ago."

"How? Who told you?"

"Nobody told me. I don't know if you were aware of this, but your stepfather brought me to your home in Grosse Pointe last May, not long after your mother died. You were out in the sun in a little two-piece bathing suit playing your guitar and it got him real upset."

Gloria blushed, but she nodded, remembering that her stepfather had given her a whipping over the bathing suit. It was the first time he had used the whip on her.

"Something about the way you looked and even the way you moved, was familiar," he said. "It was rolling around in my mind for weeks and weeks, not even consciously, and finally it just clicked. I remembered your mother and then looked at the picture of my grandmother. You really have to see it because when you do, you'll have no doubt."

So they went upstairs, Gloria holding the gun and making the two men walk in front of her. Carlton kept looking back at the gun, but Bonaventure seemed almost in a hurry. They entered his office and Bonaventure pointed to the picture.

"Holy shit, Clyde!" Carlton said. "You must—"

"Logan, shut *up*! Mind your dirty mouth!" Bonaventure snapped. "This is my daughter! Now damnit, clean it up!"

Gloria looked at the picture and it was almost like looking in a mirror. The resemblance was remarkable. Though it wasn't a color picture, even the hair color seemed to be hers. "Your grandmother?"

Bonaventure nodded.

"That would make her my great-grandmother...." Gloria spent the next several minutes staring at the picture, and then at the other family pictures. Suddenly, she had a lot of aunts and uncles. "Ah, okay," she said, her voice rasping with emotion. "Holy cow."

She believed him and it was going down like a small snake swallowing a big rodent. What was she supposed to think? She'd always assumed that she would like what she found out about herself. But a black father who was another criminal like her stepfather? A mother who was a prostitute? And she was half-black. *Well, so what?* she finally thought. *But what will Jimmy think? Will he still love me? Did he ever love me?* The thought simmered in her mind, a sour stew with new and strange ingredients. The tide of emotion was rising again, and it wasn't the happiness for which she longed. There was some anger, and some disgust and fear about what kind of a person she really was.

Other thoughts bubbled up. "So that night when Jimmy and I played, the night the riot started, you tried to pay me two hundred dollars to sleep with you? Your own fifteen year old daughter?" she said sharply. She moved the gun back to her right hand, braced it with her left and extended it toward him. "You're sick! You *disgust* me! I hate my stepfather for the things he did, but you're bad too!"

Carlton leaned away from Bonaventure.

"No, no," Bonaventure said, shaking his head. This time he sounded genuinely frightened. "I didn't know you were my daughter then. Didn't you know your stepfather had offered you to me? I didn't know what to make of it. I wasn't sure what he meant. I think he might have been trying to arrange a marriage, you know, like a business deal, because we'd been doing some new business together. I didn't know how old you were then. I don't sleep with teenage girls. And I wasn't interested in marrying one either. Did you know about that?"

She sputtered, "He *offered* me? Like I was car, or a horse? Or one of your girls?" She rocked back and forth, the gun moving around, causing both of the men to duck and lean out of the way. Some of what Bonaventure had said, maybe all of it, was a lie. He had wanted to sleep with her; he might not have known she was 15, but he had to have known she was young. *And how old was my mother when he slept with her?*

"Christ Clyde," Carlton said quietly, "can you stop talking about your business? I don't want to know about it."

But Bonaventure cut him off as he saw the storm gathering in Gloria.

"Logan, shut up," Bonaventure said. There was real anger in his voice and on his face. "We're old friends, and we're good friends, but there's a limit. This girl's fifteen years old and in a lot of trouble. I'm trying to help her, and as long as you're here if you can't help, please keep your goddamn mouth shut." He looked back at Gloria and opened his hands in a supplicating expansive shrug, but she wasn't buying anything he said.

She looked at him, both hands now holding the gun tightly, her mind in turmoil. Carlton had moved away from Bonaventure again. Gloria loosened her grip, pointed the gun up at the corner of the ceiling away from them and pulled the trigger. The hammer snapped on the empty chamber and both men flinched. "I don't have any bullets," she said with a wet snort and then sniffed loudly. She let the gun drop. It gouged the edge of the desk and landed on the floor with a thud. "I shot them all at my stepfather after he tried to kill me." She held her head in her hands and concentrated on not crying. She was determined to be strong. She thought about her breathing and recited the rosary again, this time in a dull monotone.

Then she spent half a minute breathing deeply and trying to settle herself. Finally, she looked up to see Carlton wiping the sweat off his face with his handkerchief.

Bonaventure knew enough to give her some space. He had picked up the gun, opened the cylinder and ejected the empty casings into his palm. He held one up to the light from the window. "Huh. Thirty-eight special. I thought so," he said. He dropped the gun into his jacket pocket.

Gloria was trying to take in what she had learned, trying to accept it, trying to find some good in it. "I believe you. I've always wondered about my dark skin. I thought I was just naturally tan," she said. She didn't care for him or his friend Carlton. Unsure of her feelings, she did know she was suddenly very tired. "What about my stepfather? Does he know?"

Bonaventure considered that but shook his head. "No, he doesn't know." He took the gun out of his pocket and placed it on the desk.

Carlton put his handkerchief away and picked up his empty glass. He looked at Bonaventure, who nodded. "Can he get you a Coke or something?"

Lost in thought, Gloria didn't respond and Carlton walked out of the room.

"I can't really fathom Doran at all, but I'm sure he doesn't know I'm your father. It is possible that he thinks he is actually your father. He probably... well, you know... he probably did it with her too. I'm sorry, but your mother was being used. She was also married to someone else, but I don't know to whom. Your stepfather knew who it was though. I think they were friends."

That was enough to give her an idea of whom that might be, but she didn't say anything.

"The more I've thought about Dorrinian, or Doran, the less I seem to understand him."

Carlton came back in, cradling three glasses in his hands.

"Is everything okay now?" he asked brightly. He put two drinks on the desk and handed Gloria a tumbler of Coke.

"Well, it's better," Bonaventure said. "Maybe a little better."

Gloria was shaking her head.

"I sincerely apologize for my foul language and thoughtlessness," said Carlton. "I've always had trouble with my mouth."

Gloria nodded, wondering about his sincerity, then drank most of the Coke and sat back with her hand on her stomach. There was a flutter.

Bonaventure was looking right through her, lost in thought. "Well," he said, finally leaning back in his chair, "maybe you should tell Logan here about what happened at the motel. I could go to prison, but secrets are not doing either of us any good. Truth time. I did what I did, and I would do it again. It's better that Logan here know the score, and besides, he's real interested in the Detroit Police Department. He doesn't like them. You need to know that about him. Might make you feel better."

That surprised her, but Gloria nodded, then recounted what had happened at the Cresthaven. It got Carlton's full attention. He took out a notebook to scribble notes with a ballpoint pen. When she got to the end she described how the black teenage boy had been running away and had stopped.

"He looked back and up at the motel. Jimmy was standing in front. I'm sure the boy saw him... maybe me too."

Carlton didn't say anything right away, staring at his notes. He looked at Gloria. "You can't go to the Detroit Police. Probably good they haven't been able to find you," he said glumly. "You can't trust any of those motherfuckers. What a sorry fucking state when you can't trust the damn cops." He smacked the desk, got up and walked in a little circle. "Motherfuckers!" he said bitterly. He walked back to his chair and sat down. "I could have you write out a sworn statement, and maybe that's worth doing. Let's draft something." He looked at his friend. "We'll leave your name out of it, Clyde. The girl saw what she saw, but all she knows is that it was a black man with a shotgun." He looked at Gloria again. "How about your boyfriend, this Jimmy? Will he say the same thing?"

"Well yeah... I think so, but he's in Vietnam, so maybe not. I don't know what he might say."

"You can put my name in if you want to," Bonaventure said. "I can live with that. I did what I did. And Logan, you shouldn't lie about a police murder."

Gloria looked at him, surprised, and drank the rest of her Coke.

"I'll bet the Garganos are looking for her as well," Carlton said. He thought for a minute. "I can get someone in my office to take her in."

"Oh, she can stay here," Bonaventure said. "No one will look for her here. I'll get some people to watch the place when I go out."

"Or we could get Wayne County to put her in foster care," Carlton said. "It's a confidential system. Yeah, that might be the best way to do it."

Gloria started to get angry again. "Stop talking about me as if I'm not even here! I don't want to go any of those places. I can take care of myself and I've got a place to go."

"You're fifteen, a minor," Bonaventure said. "I'm sorry, but you don't really have any choice here. Don't worry, we'll take care of you. I'm your father. We're family now."

He was stating a fact but she didn't feel any affection attached to it. He studied her. "You don't look like you're doing all that well."

Carlton was looking at his notebook.

"We have a chance to nail some of those cocksuckers in the Detroit Police Department," Carlton said as Bonaventure winced. Carlton drained his drink, and announced that he was leaving. "You're quite the young woman, and only fifteen," he said. "Clyde, you got yourself one hell of a kid. I think I like her."

He stuck out his hand. Gloria looked at it, and finally offered her own hand, which he shook. Then he was gone.

Gloria watched him go out the door, no longer sure what she thought of him. After a minute, she told Bonaventure about her running away, and she kept it factual. When she described how she had put her stepfather's Corvette into the Detroit River, he laughed. She told him about the papers she had found in the car and said she had hidden them. She didn't tell him where, and Bonaventure didn't ask her.

"There were more of these German papers," she added. "I sent about half of them to Jimmy in Vietnam. I didn't know what they said and his uncle used to be in the German army."

"Oh, shit," Bonaventure said. "Does Matthew know that?"

"Yes, I told him. Why's that important?"

He just shook his head. He seemed to be deep in thought. Finally, appearing distressed, he leaned back on the couch and put his hand on his belly. There was a gurgling rumble and then he farted loudly. He grinned. "Guess we're really family now. I have to go to the can." He shrugged out of his jacket and dropped it on the couch. He looked at her as if worried that she might still be a threat. "Stay right here," he ordered. "I'll be back in a few minutes and we'll talk some more."

She wasn't sure what to make of him, but he certainly didn't know her very well. As soon as he left the room, Gloria was out the front door and driving away in the Rambler.

She was emotionally drained and didn't want to talk to Bonaventure anymore. *Why is everyone so bad?* Her stepfather and now her real father, the police who were after her, the Garganos. Wherever she turned, there were bad people and they were after her. She didn't want to talk about it or even think about it anymore. And Logan Carlton? He might not be a crook but he reminded her of how crude she could be. She had more in common with him than she liked to admit. She did like how he wanted to do something about the police. Maybe she would sign a statement. Much as she didn't want to stay with Bonaventure, she didn't want him to go to jail. But she wasn't ready to trust either Bonaventure or Carlton yet. She would make her own way.

6:33 p.m., Detroit

Less than half an hour later, an emotionally exhausted Gloria drove up the driveway to Frances Lincoln's house. A few inches of snow had fallen several days before and then had partially melted. Tires had smashed the snow into dirty, slushy ruts and then the slush had frozen. It looked slippery and she carefully parked the car on a patch of mostly bare, frozen gravel. The Oldsmobile was there so Gloria was sure the woman was home. Before she could ring the doorbell the door opened and Frances Lincoln, dressed in a voluminous flowered housedress, said, "Thought you might come back," she said. "Come in. I don't want to heat the outside."

"You're not gonna call the police are you?" asked Gloria as she entered.

"I should, but I won't," she said. "I think you've been honest in what you said, though I wish you would tell me more. Let me take your coat."

Gloria took off her parka and Mrs. Lincoln inspected it before hanging it in a closet beside the front door.

"Are you hungry?" asked Mrs. Lincoln. "Of course you're hungry. If you can wait I'll cook some ham and make mashed potatoes and gravy. Collard greens too. Take an hour, a little more maybe. I don't like doing a big meal like that just for myself."

"Well I... I don't know." She'd been eating enough, but it was all canned food. The session with Bonaventure and Carlton had left her hungry and so tired that driving back to East Lansing wouldn't be easy. She needed to regain some strength first.

"Come. You can help me and we can talk in the kitchen. I'm doing better than I was, and you look like you could use some help," she said looking at Gloria's dirty sweat pants and sweater. It was warm but very dirty in the steam tunnels.

And they did talk. Although she was exhausted, Gloria started to grow more comfortable with the reserved black woman. She wasn't a criminal and Gloria liked her more all the time. "Tell me, Mrs. Lincoln, do you think I could ever pass for being black, or maybe part black?"

Startled, Frances Lincoln stopped in the middle of the kitchen floor, a big roasting pan in her hands. She looked at Gloria intently. "Funny... when you first came here, before we'd even said a word to each other, I thought you might be one of those black girls I sometimes see at the shows or recording sessions that Roscoe brought me to. There are always a few doing everything they can to pass as white. Bleached straightened hair, makeup, wearing those hippie outfits or bleached blue jeans. Sometimes when they have lighter skin, it works," she said. "And when I first saw you, I thought you were one of them. Probably where I got the idea you could be Roscoe's girlfriend. Soon as you opened your mouth though, I knew you were white. Why are you asking?"

Gloria shrugged. "Just curious."

"You might be able to pass for black if you tried, but why on earth you would want to is beyond me. Never heard of anyone trying to do that. Your skin's a little dark, and your hair is the kind of blonde that you can't get out of a bottle but you see on some black women. Wavy too, and those lips? Well, they're fuller than most white girls. You're very pretty and I'm not one who sees the white race as the standard for what's good looking. You're beautiful by any standard."

"Thank you," Gloria said. She told her more about the time she and Jimmy and Roscoe had spent at her house.

"I found out they want to release a record of the music Roscoe gave them. You know, you, your boyfriend Jimmy and Roscoe. Actually, they've already let some radio stations play a few of the songs. I just found out about that, and they did it weeks ago. You didn't hear any of them? Oh, and I told them we'd split the money. Half for you and your boyfriend and half for... ahh, Roscoe's estate."

Gloria thought a three way split was fairer. *Well, maybe not.* Roscoe must have worked more on the music after she and Jimmy left. But she and Jimmy had written all the songs except for the covers. She didn't say anything. She didn't care about the money very much and thought Jimmy felt the same way. Then she started thinking that she certainly could use some money now.

"They'll want you and your boyfriend to sign some papers. We can go over there and talk to them tomorrow. Tell the truth, I need the money. My son was supporting me and I have bills to pay. Do you think we could mail papers to your boyfriend in Vietnam?"

"I'm running out of money too," Gloria said, thinking about her situation.

"There you go," said the woman. "This will work out for both of us. I'm so glad you came to visit."

"I don't know. I have other problems, worse problems than money," Gloria said.

"What problems?"

She hesitated and took a breath.

"I'm pregnant," Gloria said. "I'm gonna have Jimmy's baby, and he's in Vietnam and could get killed. I'm so scared."

Frances Lincoln stopped stirring the sauce she was making and didn't speak for several seconds. Gloria continued peeling a potato and didn't look at her.

"Oh dear," Mrs. Lincoln said, " but that's probably another reason you'll need money. Babies are expensive."

Gloria was standing at the sink. Mrs. Lincoln came over and put her arm around her as Gloria nodded. "I'm so scared," Gloria said. "I haven't told Jimmy. I've written to him about a lot of things, about what happened to Roscoe and about my stepfather trying to kill me, but I haven't heard back. He wouldn't know where to write to me because I don't have an address. Maybe he doesn't care anymore. He could get killed. I keep seeing stories in the paper about the soldiers dying." Tears were coming and she fought them back.

Mrs. Lincoln squeezed her tight with both arms. "You need to tell him," said Mrs. Lincoln. "It's his baby too."

She nodded.

"There are some other things," Gloria said. Maybe it was because it was so fresh in her mind, but she told Mrs. Lincoln about what had happened at the motel. When she got to the part about Clyde Bonaventure, she stopped, not sure whether she should say his name. "This man in the motel shot all three policemen and when he was running away, he ran right into Jimmy and me. He didn't do anything to us, though."

"Do you know who it was?" asked Mrs. Lincoln.

Gloria finally nodded. "I don't want to say who it was."

Mrs. Lincoln looked at Gloria. "Did my Roscoe know about this?"

"No," she said. "Jimmy and I didn't tell anyone else. I don't care if he never gets caught. Those policemen killed innocent people. I sometimes dream about the boy they shot 'cause I saw his face real clearly. It was awful to see and sometimes at night I can't stop thinking about it."

Mrs. Lincoln tasted the gravy and added a little sugar.

"Then there's my stepfather. I ran away from home just before all this. My stepmother was killed last April. She was run down by a truck in a church parking lot. My stepfather used to beat her up all the time, and me too. Then he started hitting me more. He used a whip on me." She hesitated. "He did other things to me."

Mrs. Lincoln, her mouth hanging open, had stopped stirring the gravy and was staring at her. "Are you talking about sex?" she asked. She looked down at the gravy, trying to find words. "You'd be surprised how many men do that to their daughters. No one wants to talk about it."

Gloria stared at the floor. "Well, I can see why people don't talk about it. I don't like talking about it."

"Well, you were telling me you had problems, and I can see that it's true. You can stop anytime you want to, Dear. But I think I know where you're heading with this."

They both sat down at the kitchen table. Gloria took a close look at her. She appeared noticeably older than just a few weeks ago. Her hair was grayer and the lines on her face deeper. She looked very tired.

"Roscoe was my only child. My husband died years ago, so Roscoe was everything. He was such a good boy, so talented and he worked so hard. He was making it in the music business. He told me that someday he was gonna buy me a big mansion and a Cadillac. I told him I didn't want that. I like this house and my car is fine. I just wanted him to be happy. I was hoping he'd find a nice girl, but he was more interested in music than girls."

She sighed, and then sniffed, her eyes watery. "He's gone though. I'm gonna have to start selling all that music equipment. I'll have to get a job, which will probably be good. All I do now is sit around crying about Roscoe, or I go over to the church. But I can't afford to keep everything up more than a couple more months. There just isn't any money. That's why I'm hoping this record coming out will help."

Gloria shrugged. "I'll sign the papers. I'll send them to Jimmy too. I'm sure he'll sign," Gloria said. "But I'm afraid to go out where I might be seen. We'll have to be very careful. I don't want to go to the police because I saw what those policemen were doing. They shot that lady and her son for no reason. Maybe just because they were black. Even if they don't do anything to me, they would send me back to my stepfather. He's very rich and even though he's a crook, the police don't know that. They wouldn't believe me over him. I wasn't kidding when I said he tried to kill me. He shot at me," she said.

For the second time, Frances Lincoln was looking at her in horror.

"I'm not lying. He knows that I know about how he breaks the law. He's a lawyer and an accountant and he takes care of a lot of money for bad people. Millions and millions of dollars. Have you ever heard of Pietro Gargano? I found some of my stepfather's papers and I overheard him talking about what he does for the Garganos. I can remember everything about numbers and money, and he knows that. I think that's why he wants to kill me.

"Then there's the man who shot the policemen. When I first heard about Roscoe from you, I thought it might have been him. But now I'm sure it was my stepfather. Just before I came here, I found out that my stepfather hired someone to find me and that person probably went to Roscoe 'cause he thought Roscoe knew where to find me and Jimmy. He's a bad man named Slick Percy Dupree. You should tell that to the police.

"My stepfather almost caught me on Christmas Eve. He's hired people to help find me. Pinkerton's. He wants to find me awful bad. And if he tried to kill me once already, his own stepdaughter...." She shrugged.

Mrs. Lincoln stood up. Gloria had succeeded in penetrating her grief. "Let's eat and not talk anymore about this," she said

But Gloria pressed on. "You should also tell the police to talk to a Mrs. Murphy. I don't know her first name. She owns the boarding house where I was staying when my stepfather tried to kill me. And she overheard him talking to me on the telephone. She knows I'm not making this up, and she's a nice lady like you." She gave Frances Lincoln the address, and when she thought about it more, she remembered the telephone number. "Okay, now I can stop talking about it," she said.

It was the best meal Gloria had eaten since she had run away. They both tried hard to cheer each other up. Mrs. Lincoln told her funny things about the two lawyers she had been talking to, and about Sergeant Checchi. She called him "the midget detective," which Gloria didn't think was very nice. Gloria told her about playing her guitar on the streets and about getting kicked out of the Northland Mall. She went out to the car and got her guitar and played some of the songs that she and Jimmy and Roscoe had done. They both felt better. Mrs. Lincoln invited her to stay the night and Gloria found herself in the same bedroom and the same bed where she and Jimmy had made love so many times. She fell asleep thinking of him.

January 5, Detroit

Gloria awoke very early the next morning and lay in bed thinking about all that she had learned for almost an hour before she got up. She had a bowl of oatmeal and then she and Frances Lincoln cooked and ate an omelet together. She had no good clothes to wear so Mrs. Lincoln loaned her a dress with a bright orange and blue pattern. The dress would normally have been too big and certainly wasn't anything she'd have chosen for herself, but it accommodated, even hid, her pregnant shape and was better than the stained sweat suit she had been wearing. She had thrown her dirty clothes into the washing machine anyway. Gloria borrowed a matching patterned scarf and made it into a headband for herself. Mrs. Lincoln called the lawyers and made an appointment for them to go downtown to sign documents.

"Do you trust these lawyers?" Gloria asked.

"They've always been very nice to me, and they've already given me some money," she said with some embarrassment. Then she added, "I'm sure they'll give you some too. In fact, let's insist on that."

Gloria didn't trust anyone. She had an idea. She looked up Clyde Bonaventure in the phone book and called him. He answered on the second ring. She made no apology for leaving the night before and he said nothing about it. She told him what she was doing. "Why don't you join us if you'd like to be of some help, and bring your friend Mr. Carlton if you like," she said. "But don't bring anyone else."

"I'll try to get there," he said, "but I probably can't. I can call some people I know at Motown though."

"It's not Motown," Gloria said. "I don't know the name of the company yet, but I know it's not Motown."

She gave Bonaventure the names of the lawyers. He didn't sound very encouraging and she decided he was unhappy about her abrupt departure. She hung up with Frances Lincoln looking at her curiously.

"How does a girl like you know Clyde Bonaventure?"

"Roscoe, Jimmy and I played at his club," she said. "Having him on our side might be good, don't you think?"

They drove downtown in Mrs. Lincoln's Oldsmobile. After taking an elevator almost to the top of a big building, they were met by a tall black man wearing an expensive suit and an attractive white woman with blonde hair piled on top of her head and held in place with hairpins, clasps and probably half a can of hairspray. She was also wearing a suit and was as tall as the black man if you counted hair and high heels. They introduced themselves as Allen Fortune and Samantha Golightly. The two lawyers led them into a conference room with a stack of papers on the table. There was a big silver coffee percolator on a little table at one end of the conference room, but nobody offered them any coffee.

"These are standard contracts to arrange for the distribution of any profits from the sales of this record," said Fortune. I've marked the places for you to sign. And you say that you can get copies of this to the third party, James Hayes, and that he'll sign as well?"

"Yes, I have his address in Vietnam," Gloria said.

"How long will that take?" Fortune asked, concern in his voice.

Gloria shrugged. "Might be a couple of weeks," Gloria said. "I don't know how long mail to Vietnam takes and it depends on how fast Jimmy replies."

She was wondering whether Jimmy might be able to write to her at this office.

She had the first sheaf of papers in front of her and started reading it, hunching over the papers to concentrate. The two lawyers seemed surprised that she wanted to read it. A little over a minute later she looked up.

"This seems to be about the rights to the songs themselves. I think it's saying that we agree to give up all of those rights," she said. She looked at Frances Lincoln. "I don't know whether we should do that. Does that mean other people can use our music and we don't get paid?"

"Oh dear," said Mrs. Lincoln. "I don't want any problems."

"No problem," Gloria said, and looked at the attorneys. "Is giving up the rights to your songs standard?"

Fortune and Golightly looked at each other. Gloria grabbed the next set of papers that were paper-clipped together before they could react further. They were filled with numbers and she digested them rapidly.

"Very interesting," she said. "It says that the company will pay Frances Lincoln an advance of five thousand dollars. There's nothing in here about paying Jimmy or me anything, and our names are here just once. Then, there's all of these expenses that are listed, promotion and marketing, and the cost of production. It goes on and on. Even includes attorney fees. Then it says that any profit after expenses and the advance are paid back will be split, with the company getting ninety percent, Frances Lincoln getting five percent and any other artists getting five percent, but even that goes to you first."

Gloria looked at Mrs. Lincoln whose face was darkening in embarrassment.

"Then there's a formula where the more profit there is, an increasing percentage of the profit goes to the company. Until at $500,000, it all goes to the company. So, ten percent of half a million is $50,000, half to Mrs. Lincoln and half to Jimmy and me, except with that stupid formula it would be quite a bit less." She paused and looked up at the ceiling, squinting her eyes. "A little over $28,000. But the contract also says that we might have to pay additional expenses. I don't know how much that would leave us... if anything. There seem to be a lot of expenses." She pushed that sheaf of papers away and started to reach for the next one. "Maybe we do have a problem here."

Golightly stopped her from grabbing the next set of papers. "How old are you, young lady?"

"Not very polite of you to ask a lady her age," Gloria said. "How old are you?"

"Well, I don't think you've had much experience with this sort of thing," said Golightly. "You need to understand that the record company has invested a lot of its money in you already and will continue to invest money. Those recording studios cost thousands of dollars, for example, and you have to pay a lot of people like engineers and other musicians."

"Wait a minute," Gloria said. "We recorded this in Roscoe's garage with his equipment and we were the only musicians. And I know Roscoe worked on the music after we did the recording."

"And Roscoe bought that equipment with his own money," added Mrs. Lincoln.

Just then the door opened and her stepfather strode in, followed by two big men. One was bigger than just about anyone Gloria had ever seen and neither of them looked fat. Immediately, she recognized the biggest one as the big man who had been at Mrs. Murphy's house and had shot at her. The other one had probably been there too. They both locked their eyes on her. She tensed, terrified, but she tried not to let it show.

"How are you, my dear?" her stepfather said, smiling broadly. He surveyed the room, his gaze lingering on Mrs. Lincoln. "How is everyone here?"

Gloria looked straight ahead at the coffee percolator and didn't move. Her heart was pounding and she counted each beat. Then she remembered reading that it was best to confront your fears, so she turned and looked at her stepfather. He looked a little fatter than before, but his massive shoulders masked the fat. In addition to overhearing his conversations through the heating register in her room, the clanking of the weights he'd lifted in his office had awakened her almost every morning when she was growing up.

"I am Matthew Doran, Miss Gloria Doran's father. My dear daughter ran away from home last July. I am here to take her home, and these two gentlemen are going to ensure that she does come home this time. Unfortunately, she has been quite clever and more than a little lucky in eluding me."

Gloria looked from her stepfather to each of the two men and then to the lawyers, and finally back to her stepfather.

She was trapped.

January 5, 10:40 a.m.

Matthew Doran looked around the conference room beaming, exuding his persuasive false charm. "Good morning, Sam," he said to Samantha Golightly and took her hand. Releasing it, he extended his hand to the other lawyer. "I don't believe we've met. I'm Matt Doran."

"Allen Fortune," said the lawyer, looking a little puzzled.

Frances Lincoln rose from her chair and extended her hand.

"I'm Frances Lincoln," she said. "I've been taking care of Gloria, and she's staying with me."

"I don't think so," Doran said, no longer smiling. "I'm her father and she's coming with me."

He glanced at the two large black men. They were both wearing knee-length hooded coats, the kind that football players wore on the sidelines during cold games. They had their hands in their pockets. "As I said, these two gentleman are security agents to ensure that Gloria doesn't run away again," Doran said. Then his eyes fixed on the coffee percolator.

"What about the papers?" asked Golightly.

"Oh, she can sign them, Sam, but why don't we have some coffee first? I've not had any coffee this morning, and I've heard you talk about your coffee. Frankly, that's one thing the hotel doesn't do very well."

"I'll get the secretary to make it," said Golightly.

"No need for that, Sam," Doran said, frowning just a little. He didn't want anyone else in the room in case there was trouble. And the presence of the two thugs indicated that he was prepared for trouble. "We don't need a secretary. Gloria here can make it. She knows exactly how I like my coffee and she's good at it." He turned to her and smiled, but there was serious menace lurking in his eyes. "You still know how to whip up a pot of coffee, don't you, Dear?"

Gloria recognized the threat in those darting black eyes. His morning coffee was very important to him and she had been beaten for not making it correctly. It had been one of the first jobs she had been given by him. She got up quickly and walked over to the percolator, trying to think of something she could do.

"There's distilled water in the cupboard," Fortune said slowly. "We don't use tap water. Got chlorine in it."

Gloria opened the cupboard above the table and took down one of the large bottles of water and a silver container of ground coffee.

"We get our coffee directly from Hawaii... Kona coffee. It's very special, the best coffee in the world, and we just ground some beans fresh this morning," Fortune added. He and Golightly relaxed a little. "No rush on signing the papers."

"Absolutely," Doran said. "Sam here was telling me about this coffee at the bar meeting a couple of months ago. Distilled water, coffee imported from Hawaii! I'm looking forward to trying some."

Gloria spotted her large handbag, which she had put down on the floor near the table with the percolator. While she was opening the silver container with the coffee, she reached out with one foot and slid the bag over until it was in front of her and under the table. Mrs. Lincoln had started talking about the contracts and the problems Gloria had found. The two big men were both standing beside the door at the other end of the room to ensure that Gloria didn't try to make a break, but neither was watching her closely. She bent over and reached into the bag going all the way to the bottom. She frequently unpacked and repacked it and knew exactly where everything was. She went right to one corner and pulled up the envelope that Lenny Papineau had given her on the day that she'd found out she was pregnant. She had sent one of the capsules to Jimmy as a Christmas present, but the rest were still there. She opened the envelope and slipped the remaining capsules into her hand. She glanced around. No one was watching. With each spoonful of coffee, she crushed open a capsule and dribbled the powder into the top of the percolator with the coffee. She also poured some of it into the water. Then she turned on the percolator.

"It's gonna be a little while because it's a big percolator," she said. She went back to the table and sat down beside Mrs. Lincoln. "They're telling me these are standard contracts, but it sure seems to me that almost all the money is gonna end up with the record company," Gloria said.

"Don't worry about the money," her stepfather said, flashing his smile again. "We have lots of money and I'll make sure Mrs. Lincoln here is taken care of too." He smiled warmly at her and Golightly was nodding, but Gloria detected a subtle threatening emphasis when he said "taken care of."

"Of course," said Golightly. "We'll make this right. I appreciate you coming down, Matt. I knew as soon as I saw her name that you'd want to be involved."

The lawyers talked some more while Gloria and Mrs. Lincoln were silent. The two big men avoided looking directly at anyone but stood resolutely guarding the door. They kept their coats on and their hands in their pockets. The coffee pot had been percolating for some time and Gloria had been timing it by a clock on the wall.

"Coffee should be ready," Gloria said, getting up. She poured mugs for everyone except herself and Mrs. Lincoln. She added one sugar cube and stirred it into the mug for her stepfather and carried it over to him.

"There you are, Daddy," she said. "Just the way you like it."

He eyed her suspiciously because she never called him Daddy.

"It's getting rough out there on the streets. It's cold, not like it was in the summer, so maybe it is time to come home." She tried to sound like she was resigned to it. She was as capable of guile and charm as he was. "You never liked me playing my guitar, but it looks like I'm gonna make some money from it, so maybe I've proven something too."

Her father took a sip, and then a larger one and several more, drinking almost half the mug. "Excellent," he said. "You haven't lost your touch." He turned to Golightly. "It's even better than I expected, Sam."

Gloria served the mugs for the others and put sugar and cream in the middle of the table. She also brought a mug to each of the security men. She noticed that they both took the mugs with their left hands and kept their right hands in their pockets.

"Don't worry, I won't run," she said to them. They both accepted the coffee after looking at her stepfather, who nodded. Mrs. Lincoln gave her a questioning look. She seemed about to ask for coffee, thinking Gloria had forgotten her.

"We had coffee just before we came down, so I assumed you didn't want any," Gloria said. She tried to shake her head ever so slightly, but Mrs. Lincoln still looked like she was going to speak. "You know the doctor told you too much coffee's not good for your heart problem."

"You have a heart problem?" asked Fortune, though there was no concern in his voice.

Mrs. Lincoln looked at Gloria, still puzzled. Finally she said, "It's nothing serious."

Half an hour later Gloria thought her plan had failed. Her stepfather had consumed two cups and most of a third, as had the larger of the two big men. In fact, everyone was working on a third cup, or at least a warm-up. Golightly had almost finished a third cup. Nothing seemed to have changed and the conversation was petering out. Then the big man looked up at the ceiling.

"Ahh, spiders," he groaned, and he held up his hand as if warding off something. "Get away... get away!"

"What spiders?" the other thug asked, looking up.

"Awful hot in here," Golightly said. She stuck a finger in the front of her suit and started unbuttoning her jacket. Then she shook her head as if she was trying to clear it. "I feel like I'm dreaming."

Doran was holding onto the table like he was dizzy. He suddenly let go and started jabbering in Armenian. He pushed back from the table so hard that he crashed the chair into the wall. He looked at the wall in shock. "What's wrong? The wall is moving too!" He rubbed his eyes with his knuckles. "Jesus Christ, it's melting!"

Fortune giggled, but he stopped abruptly, looked around the table, hunched down in his chair, looked at the floor, and started to snicker again. He looked at Golightly. "I feel so strange. It's a very funny feeling."

Golightly said, "I'm hot, and I'm feeling... I don't know... dreamy. I think I could fly. This must be a dream so I'm gonna take off my clothes." She pulled at the buttons on her blouse, then stripped it off along with her suit jacket in one motion. Her bra quickly followed. She reached behind her for the zipper of her skirt. "I love naked dreams and flying dreams."

Gloria grabbed Mrs. Lincoln by the arm and gestured with her head toward the door. Fortune had gotten out of his chair and was cowering in a corner of the room. The smaller of Doran's two men was holding the larger one's arm

Fortune said, "Oh shit... oh shit...."

"Come on, let's get out of here," Gloria whispered. Mrs. Lincoln was looking around the room in amazement, but she picked up her handbag and followed Gloria. Gloria grabbed her big bag, which was still by the coffee percolator, and as she walked through her father's field of vision he fixed his eyes on her. He looked scared.

She remembered Lenny's bad acid trips and stared into Doran's black eyes. She hissed, "I know all your secrets!"

He shrank away from her and fell off his chair.

"Big fucking spiders!" shouted the big man. He had a gun in his hand. He fired at the ceiling, then fired again. The gunshots were deafening in the room. Someone was screaming as Gloria ran out the door, pushing Mrs. Lincoln in front of her. They ran down the hall where office doors were opening, heads popping out like prairie dogs. They stopped at the front of the suite, where the secretary who had escorted them down to the office earlier was crouched behind her desk, a telephone in her hand.

"Are you calling the police?" asked Gloria.

"Yes," said the woman. "What's happening?"

"They have drugs down there. They were trying to get me to sign some things and they're trying to gyp Mrs. Lincoln here out her son's money. But they must have taken too many drugs because they're all going crazy. We'd all better get out of here because somebody pulled out a gun."

They grabbed their coats from the coat rack and got on the elevator. They were pulling out of the parking lot when the first police car skidded around the corner and stopped in front of the building. They made the 15-minute drive to the Lincoln house in silence, for which Gloria was thankful. They went into the house and stopped at the kitchen table.

"I think I'd like some coffee, and I'll make it myself," Mrs. Lincoln said. "Why don't you tell me what you did?"

"Okay, just let me use the phone first," Gloria said.

Mrs. Lincoln shook her head in exasperation but gestured at the phone as she got coffee out of a cupboard.

Gloria got the phone book out and looked up the number for the *Detroit Free Press*. She called and told the woman who answered that she wanted to talk to someone about a story. "There was just a shooting downtown, and I was there."

After saying her name was Sunshine and refusing to give any other name, she was transferred to a reporter.

"City desk, Briggs," said a bored male voice.

"My name is Sunshine. I'm a singer and I was just at a lawyer's office downtown and there was some shooting. I was supposed to sign some papers and they were trying to get me to take drugs. They wanted to screw Mrs. Lincoln out of her son Roscoe's money, and me too, and my boyfriend Jimmy as well," she was talking fast, making it up as she went along, but she felt sharply focused. "See, we made this record back last summer and then Jimmy got sent to Vietnam and Roscoe was murdered, but they want to sell the record and someone told me that some of the songs are already on the radio. I haven't heard them, but I haven't listened to the radio very much recently and—"

"Hold on, hold on," interrupted Briggs. "Tell me who you are. Your full name, and slow down. I can't write as fast as you can talk."

"My name is Sunshine. I just go by Sunshine," she said slowly.

"You must have a last name," said Briggs. "What's on your driver's license?"

"I don't have a license," she said, "but I can drive a stick."

"Huh? Okay, tell me about the shooting. Where, when, who and what happened," he said.

"Well, it was in a big gray building, very pretty. I remember the street was Griswold," she said trying to remember whether the building had a name on it.

"Penobscot Building?" Briggs asked.

"Yes, that's probably the one," she said. "We were almost on the top floor, the fortieth floor. I don't know the name of the law firm, but the names of the two lawyers were Allen Fortune and Samantha Golightly. I was supposed to sign these papers about where the profits from the record would go, except when I read it, the record company was gonna get almost all of it. Even the rights to the songs Jimmy and I wrote. And they really wanted to screw Mrs. Lincoln out of Roscoe's share. He was a great musician and played on the record with us. Roscoe also owned all the recording equipment and he did a lot of work on the recordings after we made them. Anyway, they took drugs at the meeting, and I think they were high on something. The worst lawyer there was this Matthew Doran. He had two big guys with him and at least one of them had a gun. He started shooting and I got out of there," she said.

"Who made the record again?" asked Briggs. "You're still talking too fast. Take a breath and slow down."

"Me. My friends and I made the record. My name's Sunshine. And my boyfriend is Jimmy. Jimmy Hayes. He's in the Army in Vietnam now. Had a band named Universal Joint in East Lansing before he was drafted. And Roscoe Lincoln. He was a musician here in Detroit. We recorded it in Roscoe's garage. He built his own recording studio there. His mother was depending on him and now the record company is trying to take all the money. You've had stories in your paper about Roscoe's murder."

"We did?" asked Briggs. "The murdered man was Roscoe Lincoln you say? Like the president?"

"That's right, except it's Roscoe, not Abraham."

"Right." Briggs chuckled. "You said there were drugs there. What kind of drugs?"

"Well, I don't take drugs," she said carefully. Now she was speaking slower because she wasn't as sure as she had been about what she wanted to say. "They started acting strange, like they were seeing things. Then one of those big goons pulled out a gun and started shooting. It might it might have been acid, you know, LSD. They all seemed to go crazy. The woman lawyer started taking off her clothes and that goon who started shooting said he saw giant spiders."

"What? The woman lawyer took off her clothes? All of them?" asked Briggs.

"She sure did. She was completely naked when we got out of there."

"Wow!" said Briggs.

"Listen, I'm scared. I'm sure they're gonna tell lies about me, and that's why I called. That Matthew Doran's gonna claim he's my father, but he's not. I don't want them to find me. I don't care that much about the money, but it's important for Roscoe's mother, Mrs. Lincoln. I don't think Jimmy cares about the money either. I just want him to come home from that terrible war." Her voice caught. Thinking of Jimmy was hard. She snorted and it took her several seconds to regain her composure. "My friend Roscoe's gone. He was so nice to Jimmy and me and he was an incredible musician. He could play everything. And I'm scared about losing Jimmy next. Mrs. Lincoln, she needs the money, because she doesn't have Roscoe anymore. Those lawyers were trying to screw us. Look, I have to go."

She dropped the phone back in the cradle and wiped her eyes with the heels of her hands.

"Good lord, Girl, you can certainly spin some yarn when you get going," said Mrs. Lincoln.

Gloria smiled ruefully. "Well, I meant it. They're gonna tell lies about me. And maybe about you. No one believes me when I tell the truth, so why should I bother? I really only told one lie to that reporter. I said they were trying to get me to take drugs. That wasn't true. But they were taking drugs, and that was the truth, and those contracts were not what they claimed."

"What did you put in the coffee?" asked Mrs. Lincoln.

"I'm not gonna answer that, except to say that I think they took LSD. I don't take drugs, but I don't want to say where the LSD came from. The police might ask you about it. I've always tried to tell you the truth, Mrs. Lincoln. My stepfather tried to kill me once already. That's the truth. He's beaten up my stepmother and me. Hurt her bad enough to send her to the hospital many times. Made me... made me...."

She stopped and looked down. Then she took a deep breath, squared her shoulders, looked right into Frances Lincoln's eyes and spit it out: "He made me suck his cock!" She swallowed and hiccupped several times but this time she didn't start crying. "All of that is true. I swear. I'm sure my stepfather is behind Roscoe's murder. He sent that Percy Dupree to look for me and Jimmy, and he was probably trying to find out where I was from Roscoe. My stepfather's a really big criminal but everyone thinks he's an important lawyer and accountant. You were there, in that room. Nobody will believe me. I'm just a teenager and he's too important, but he's very bad."

With that she went upstairs and changed back into her sweats, which were still stained, but clean and dry. As she said goodbye, she told Mrs. Lincoln, "I probably can't come back. My stepfather knows you now and he'll be watching this place. Maybe Mr. Bonaventure will be able to help with the money and the record company. I don't like a lot of things about him, but he's not all bad. That's our only hope. I'm sorry, but those lawyers just weren't telling you the truth."

Ninety minutes later, she was safely back in the tunnels under the Michigan State University campus.

CHAPTER 10

January, 1968, Vietnam

January was a bad month for the 99th Assault Helicopter Company as the war began to heat up. January opened with a disturbing incident that almost led to open conflict between the Headhunters and the Filipinos. The Filipinos had an engineering battalion stationed in Nui Binh Base Camp. The Filipinos built most of the hootches and other structures in the base camp, and they were in charge of the truck convoys that brought in heavy supplies. Most units wanted to stay on their good side because the Filipinos never seemed to run short of beer, sodas or other luxury items that routinely ran out in American units. They were willing to share, for a price, and were notoriously hard bargainers. No hootches for them; they lived in elaborate and well-appointed bunkers. They had established a flourishing black market trade with the Vietnamese in Nui Binh village and they were making a fortune exchanging currency between the Military Payment Currency, or MPC, used by American soldiers, American dollars and Vietnamese piasters. On New Year's Day evening, a group of warrant officers, most of them from the Headhunters, had dinner at the Filipino compound with a group of the Filipino officers. The Americans were hoping to persuade the Filipinos to pour a big concrete pad between the officers' and enlisted men's' hootches that could serve as a basketball court. They had hopes there would eventually be enough replacements so they would have time for a basketball game.

The warrant officers arrived with gifts of several captured Communist weapons, three bottles of Courvoisier, a stag film and half a dozen large fruitcakes. The fruitcakes were an afterthought. The company had been flooded with them in Christmas parcels.

The Filipinos were excited about a special stew that they had been cooking all day. It was loaded with rice, Asian spices and chunks of vegetables that were difficult to identify. The meat, cut up in small pieces that the Filipinos wolfed down with chopsticks, had a unique flavor and the Filipinos were evasive about what it was. Walters declared that it tasted gamey and joked that it was probably "boiled rat." One of the other Southerners said it tasted like possum. They all ate it, though some ate more than others. They all drank lots of Filipino beer and Courvoisier and were happily singing dirty songs about the XO when they left. The Filipinos had agreed to pour the concrete pad sometime in the next two weeks.

The next day, Cartwright, the company clerk, ambled over to the Filipino compound to talk to a Filipino clerk whom he knew. It took a half-hour of prying before he learned that the meat in the stew had been dog. It wasn't until he returned to the 99th and was talking to the only Headhunter enlisted man not flying that day that he learned that no one had seen Fuck You for a couple of days. To a man, the Headhunters were enraged. Some of the pilots wanted to hit the Filipino compound with rockets and claim it had been an accident. Cooler heads finally prevailed and nothing was done. For one thing, they still wanted the basketball court.

Two days after New Year's one of the slicks on an ash and trash mission to a firebase suffered an engine failure. The engine quit as the helicopter was preparing to land on the firebase. A helicopter is capable of gliding as its unpowered rotor continues to spin. As the helicopter drops, the rotor acts like a windmill, slowing the descent as the air roars through the rotor blades. The pilot retains some control and the landing, while hard, is usually survivable. The aircraft commander, WO1 Randy Stoessal, did a textbook autorotation, but there was no level ground and the ship smashed hard onto the steep side of the rocky hill atop which the firebase was located. The gunner was killed, the peter pilot was paralyzed with a broken back, the crew chief broke his hip and his arm, and Stoessal escaped with cuts and bruises. The dead gunner was Private Abercrombie, one of those who'd received an Article 15 for smoking pot on Christmas Eve. He was trying to earn back some respect by volunteering.

Out on the flight line that night, Hayes said a quick prayer and smoked a joint, unleashing a surprisingly spiritual reaction. Hayes' thoughts careened over the finality of death and the infinite possibilities of a life cut short. It was like a religious epiphany that surprised him because he had never felt particularly religious or close to Abercrombie. He stayed awake most of the night and fell asleep the next morning as he stood beside the helicopter refueling it. The JP4 splashing on his hands startled him awake.

"Jesus Christ, Hayes!" Rivera said. "What the fuck is the matter with you?"

All month, the Headhunters had been leaving at dawn and getting back after dark. Some long days were filled with hours of excruciating boredom. On one of those days, the entire 99th was parked in a field along with several hundred grunts, everyone waiting for some high-ranking officer to make up his mind about a combat assault. It was one of those days when the 99th had been given no C rations to eat, and Hayes and

Rivera had wandered out among the grunts to see if they could scrounge some lunch.

Someone shouted, "Hey Hayes, you sack of Finnish fertilizer! You got a bow and arrow on that fuckin' helicopter?"

Hayes turned and saw Pierre Lemaire grinning at him. "Jesus, Lemaire! How in hell are you able to wipe your ass? There's no birch trees anywhere around here."

Lemaire was a Chippewa Indian from Sugar Island where Hayes and grown up. He, his two brothers and their cousin had gotten into a dispute with Hayes over a deer that Hayes had killed out of season with his bow and arrow. The Indians had been drinking, insults and then blows were exchanged, and the Indians took the deer away from Hayes. He took it back when he pulled his uncle's Walther PPK pistol and fired over their heads. But the game warden heard the shots, arrested Hayes and put him in the local jail for the weekend, and no one got the deer. Hayes ended up on probation and became known as Junior Nazi at school. His uncle was Senior Nazi. He got in a lot of fights and eventually dropped out of school. He left home to hitchhike to California. Oddly, by the time he left home, Pierre Lemaire, the youngest of the Lemaire brothers, had become his best and almost only friend.

The two of them embraced. Hayes hadn't seen Lemaire since he'd left home. He quickly learned that Lemaire was a brand new buck sergeant. He had completed the quickie "shake and bake" instant NCO course. Like Hayes, Lemaire had been drafted, but he had re-enlisted for an additional year to get the sergeant's stripes. Lemaire had married a girl from high school that Hayes couldn't remember and he said she was pregnant. He needed the sergeant's pay. Lemaire gave them some C rations and Rivera took them back to the pilots while Hayes continued talking to Lemaire. He found out that Lemaire's next oldest brother, Henri, and his cousin Orville had both enlisted in the Navy. His oldest brother Claude was at home taking care of everything. They showed each other pictures of their respective girls.

"I'm still real sorry about what happened to you over that fuckin' deer," Lemaire said seriously. "Me and my brothers, and cousin Orville too, we always felt bad about it."

"You know, it's kind of funny but in the end, it worked out for me," Hayes said. "I went to California and got pretty good on guitar. By the time I got drafted, I had my own band going down in East Lansing. I think I can make a living at music when I get home, so no hard feelings. Besides, it was as much my fault as anyone's. Maybe more."

They talked for more than an hour and then the waiting abruptly ended. The 99th flew the grunts in and the Headhunters spent parts of the next four days flying support for them. The fighting was persistent, but not heavy, and there were only light casualties. Only one grunt died in the entire operation. An American artillery round that landed short of its intended target killed Sergeant Pierre Lemaire. When Hayes heard the news, he cried. He wanted to smoke another joint, but he was able to fight off the temptation.

January 23rd was the worst day. In the middle of the month, the Vietcong started hitting Nui Binh almost every night with rockets, leavened with the odd mortar round. Late the first night, four 240-millimeter rockets hit the company area. One of them hit between the Headhunters' two enlisted hootches, peppering both with shrapnel that miraculously injured no one. Another one demolished the tiny hootch that served as the senior NCOs' club, which was not a great loss in Hayes' opinion. There were no injuries there either, the drinking lifers all having gone back to their hootches and passed out before the rocket landed.

The next night, two-dozen rockets, the more standard 122s this time, with more than a few mortar rounds in the mix, landed over the course of the night and no one got any sleep. A half-dozen men suffered shrapnel wounds, including two who had to be evacuated. Then the Headhunters started running shifts of gunships so at least one was up flying a counter mortar mission for the entire night, and nothing happened for the next two nights. The following night, they kept a ship ready and when someone saw tube flashes from the tower beside the airstrip, the gunship was airborne almost before the mortars landed. They hit the area where the flashes had been spotted with their rockets and the next morning a grunt patrol found blood trails, but no bodies.

"We took that round on points," Rivera said.

Hayes didn't say so, but he thought the VC were still ahead. After another two nights, he was sure of it. The VC aim improved. A rocket hit a hootch where some of the Maintenance enlisted men slept and killed Spec Four Eddie Quigley, whom Hayes didn't know well. Another half-dozen men were wounded, two of them badly enough to be evacuated. The following night a rocket hit an officers' hootch. Several suffered minor shrapnel wounds but no one was evacuated. By now, many men had moved their mattresses to the floor up against the sandbagged walls around the hootches. Others were taking their chances and sleeping with the scorpions in the bunkers. The entire company was nervous, grumpy and sleep-deprived.

"I feel like a kitten living on a desert island full of starving Rottweilers," CW2 Walters said as he pulled pitch with WO1 Rex Danvers, Rivera and Hayes at 0235 hours to chase after yet another report of tube flashes. They expended rockets but a patrol found no evidence anyone had been hit. They got back just in time to refuel and rearm for that day's adventures, but there wasn't enough time for Hayes and Rivera to eat breakfast, and there was nothing for lunch.

That night, which was the 23rd, the game changed again. First, Nui Binh Operations placed the entire base on red alert because a ground attack was supposed to be imminent. That meant no more hootch maids or KP personnel came into the camp, and everyone was supposed wear flak jackets and helmets all the time. It was stupid because a few Vietnamese workers who were considered essential, like the shitburners, were still allowed into the base camp. And most soldiers were already wearing the heavy protective clothing.

One of the fire support bases near Nui Binh had been attacked earlier in the day. The firefight lasted a long time and as the night wore on, the base ran out of flares. The 99th was asked to send out a ship to drop parachute flares. It wasn't something that the 99th did very often. A pickup volunteer flight crew loaded one of the slicks with the hundred pound magnesium flares. Each of the flares put out a million candlepower of light.

The aircraft commander was CW4 Abe Rollins, the test pilot from Maintenance who usually flew aircraft after repairs to make sure everything was working. He was an amiable guy, well-liked by everyone, and the oldest man in the company. He had flown P38 Lightnings in the Pacific at the end of World War II. WO1 Gordie Profumo, the peter pilot, who had just turned 19, had arrived in-country the previous week. Unlike many new arrivals, he was an excellent pilot. Spec Five Barney Curtis, the crew chief, had returned that same day from R&R in Bangkok and Spec Four Kevin Bailey, the gunner, was a supply clerk who wanted to honestly earn an extra $65 a month flight pay. The fifth crew, who would actually push the flares out of the helicopter, was the former company clerk, Randy Gillette, who had fled to Operations shortly after

Sypher had arrived. He was now a Spec Five and due to DEROS home in a couple of weeks. He claimed he had thrown flares before but Hayes thought he was lying. Still, he wanted to do his share and Hayes had always liked him.

The ship arrived at the threatened fire support base without incident. Two Headhunter gunships were along to provide cover. Then a flare ignited. The parachute lines might have gotten tangled in the huey's skids, or it might have ignited prematurely inside the helicopter after a lucky hit from ground fire. The two pilots were unable to see anything outside. It was like turning on the dome light in a car at night, only many times worse. The two gunships flew alongside the flare ship and tried to talk the doomed pilots down. The old A/C never panicked but several hundred feet from the ground, the rest of the flares ignited, along with the fuel, and the ship exploded in a blazing white-hot conflagration brighter than the noonday sun. All five men died. Their bodies were burned beyond the ability of Graves Registration personnel even to identify them. There were no faces, no fingers for fingerprints, no intact jaws or teeth for dental records. The only one immediately identified was Gillette, who apparently jumped out before he was completely consumed by the flames.

For almost a month, the families of the other four heard only that their loved ones were missing in action. Everyone in the 99th knew they were dead. Graves Registration knew they were dead. Graves Registration eventually solved the problem by taking a series of signed and witnessed statements about each individual documenting that they had boarded the aircraft, that the aircraft had exploded and that remains had been found. It made Hayes sick. He tried as hard as he could to put the names of all five out of his mind, and no matter how tired or hungry he was at the end of the day, he went out to the flight line alone and prayed. He prayed not only for those lost but to resist the strong urge to smoke a joint. He didn't understand his newfound spirituality, only that he had a need to engage with it.

He didn't get any letters from Gloria all month and at first he felt his love dying like a late night campfire. That self-pity soon gave way to a new kind of fear for her. She'd told him that her stepfather had tried to kill her, a statement that was so absurd and far-fetched that he couldn't, and didn't, believe it. Not only that, but everything else she'd said was also suspect. Had Roscoe really been murdered? And then slowly, he did believe. He hadn't heard anything from Roscoe, and he knew Roscoe would have written him back. Writing letters was clearly not easy for Gloria. Why would she make up such a story? Or anything else? Finally, Hayes trusted his instincts, and the first time he had read that astonishing claim, he had believed every word. It was only after thinking about it and talking to Rivera about it that he had become skeptical. He had come full circle. She was in trouble, and not hearing from her could only mean that the trouble was worse. All through the month, his last jumbled thoughts every night before he fell asleep were of Gloria. He couldn't stop thinking about her and he longed to get high. Was she still alive? His good friends Roscoe and Lemaire were dead and people were trying kill the girl he loved. She was supposed to be safe; he was supposed to be the one in danger. Oddly, the biggest danger he felt wasn't from enemy soldiers but from the first sergeant. As frustration and rage built up in him it was only a matter of time before he exploded.

CHAPTER 11

January 25, 1:15 p.m., Dearborn

Clyde Bonaventure wiped marinara sauce off of his lips and looked at the others sitting around the table. They were in a private room at an Italian restaurant in Dearborn. The room reeked of garlic and marinara. Al Checchi, the Detroit homicide sergeant, had wanted to meet at police headquarters but both Logan Carlton and Bonaventure had refused. Part of persuading Checchi had been offering lunch in a good restaurant chosen by Checchi. Then Checchi had unexpectedly shown up with Frances Lincoln.

Checchi got things rolling. "So Mr. Bonaventure, what is it you want to talk to me about?" Barely five feet tall, Checchi was the shortest cop in the Detroit Police Department. He was thin and had curly black hair that was shiny with cream and slicked back. He was wearing a bright blue suit that looked like it had come off the clearance rack from the boy's section of Sears. The bulge on his hip from his pistol was blatantly obvious. He topped off the ensemble with an ugly pea-soup green clip-on tie. He had a crinkled, boney face with the dark beginnings of a five o'clock shadow surrounding a world-weary half smile. His fingers were yellow with nicotine but his dark eyes glittered with an intelligence that made Bonaventure nervous. Shortly before the meeting, Carlton had informed Bonaventure that Checchi had the highest clearance rate of any detective in Homicide. Carlton laughed when he added that he'd heard stories about Checchi punching people in the balls if they gave him trouble. The "mister" was a clear indication that it was time to turn to business as they had been on a first-name basis all during lunch. "Anything you can do to help solve a homicide will be greatly appreciated."

"Well, I might be able to help you, or at least tell you something interesting," Bonaventure said. He tried to exude a self-confidence that was lacking. "Do you know Slick Percy Dupree? Sometimes he works for me but mostly he works for others now. I would think he's known to the police."

Checchi nodded. "I've heard the name."

"I believe he murdered Roscoe Lincoln," Bonaventure said.

The words visibly startled Checchi, but he recovered quickly. "I thought Dupree was your muscle," he said, with some hostility in his voice. Once he got down to business, the homicide sergeant was always anxious to get to the point. This time Bonaventure had beat him to the punch, but the ex-fighter pilot reacted to his tone by mopping his brow. This wasn't going to get any easier.

"He started with me, and that was some time ago, but he's a freelancer now. Last summer, I asked Slick Percy for help. I had a big problem. You know about what happened at the Cresthaven Motel?

"Yeah, we lost two officers there during the riot," Checchi said, looking at a large ring on one of fingers as he twisted it. "I haven't worked on it, but that's a big case. Two policemen were shot dead and we haven't found out who did it. Do you know who did it?"

"I do, " Bonaventure said, surprising Checchi even more than the first time. "And it was three policemen who were shot, though one didn't die. The person who did it was at the motel to do some business that I'm not going to tell you about. He was supposed meet someone there, and he had a shotgun because that someone was possibly dangerous. His visitor never showed up. He was probably scared away by the uprising."

"I should run you in if you say you know who killed two policemen. And we never released anything about a shotgun," Checchi said sharply. "Tell me more."

All four were looking at him intently. Bonaventure had been there to get the first shipment of high-grade heroin coming from Asia. For the past several months, a large amount of high quality heroin had hit the streets every month. The heroin had been extremely profitable for both him and Doran. Even after it had been stepped on by Bonaventure, it was still powerful enough to kill addicts who were careless. And there were a lot of new addicts.

"There was a lot of commotion outside. Remember, this was just about the peak of the disturbance. This man was on the second floor with his shotgun. He saw the police beating the woman who runs the front desk, a very nice lady whom I happen to know. The police officers had just shot and killed a woman and a boy and they were about to shoot the lady from the front desk when this guy on the second floor opened up on the police with his shotgun." Bonaventure leaned forward, looked directly at Checchi, and spoke with an intensity that belied his quiet voice. "I'm not going to tell you who the man is. He did the right thing as far as I'm concerned. Policemen shooting women and children... some cops truly are pigs."

Checchi bristled at the word "pigs," then calmed himself. "So why are you here? Why are you telling me this? Why shouldn't I take you downtown and sweat the name out of you? How do you know this guy's telling the truth?"

"Well, for one thing, you'll never get his name out of me. I don't care what you do. I don't mean to imply that all police are like the ones at the Cresthaven, but this story is a lot more involved than what I've just told you. There were several witnesses. There was another boy who I believe was the brother of the boy who was killed. The dead woman was their mother. Incidentally, the dead boy was only 12 and the surviving one was 14. When the shooter was leaving—remember, he was on the second floor—he ran into two young people, both of them white, who might have seen him. I don't know exactly what they saw, but I am quite sure they saw some of what happened... maybe all of it."

He paused and settled back in his chair. "The shooter came to me and told me everything because I'm known in the black community as someone who can be trusted and who can help with these kinds of problems. I expected the police to look for him, and I was prepared to hide him, but nothing happened. I heard nothing about police searching for my friend or any indication that they had spoken to the witnesses. At least not then. So I asked Percy Dupree to find those two witnesses. I wasn't sure what I was going to do when I found them. I wanted to know what they'd seen and what they were going to do about it. I just wanted to talk to them. That's God's honest truth.

"I was able to determine who they were from the description I was given and some other providential information. By sheer coincidence, I had seen both of them the night before at one of my clubs. They are musicians. The girl was quite striking, someone you would notice and not forget."

"Girl?" asked Checchi.

"Sorry, the witnesses were a boy and a girl, teenagers. I found out who the boy was almost immediately. He was home on leave from the Army and went to Vietnam less than two weeks after the shootings. I guess that makes him a man now.

"Slick Percy came to me and told me who both the witnesses were. I think he wanted to see if I'd pay him to have them killed. I told him no. That would make my friend and me no better than the police. And whatever you've heard about me, I don't kill people. Anyway, Slick Percy's not my muscle anymore. He's a freelancer, but I still talk to him from time to time."

Bonaventure paused and drained his water glass. He was tiptoeing around Roscoe Lincoln because he felt bad about it, and Lincoln's mother's gaze was boring into him.

Checchi finally grew impatient. "Who's the girl, and who's her boyfriend?"

"The girl's name is Gloria Doran. She's from Grosse Pointe. She ran away from home last summer. She's fifteen years old—no, she's sixteen now—and she's pregnant by the soldier who is the other witness. His name is Jimmy Hayes. He was a musician from the East Lansing area, and the Upper Peninsula before that. I just heard that Slick Percy has gone to Vietnam, and he might be going there to kill him."

He reached for his water glass. Suddenly he felt like he'd felt when a German fighter plane had suddenly appeared on his tail. He realized that he'd set in motion an action that might kill the father of his own unborn grandchild.

Checchi said, "This is all interesting, and I think I've spoken to that girl. If it's who I think, I've been looking for her. I didn't know what to make of her at first, but you're right. She's someone you can't help but notice. Mrs. Lincoln here also knows her."

Frances Lincoln nodded as Bonaventure stared at his empty water glass. "The girl is the stepdaughter of Matthew Doran. Do you know who Matthew Doran is?"

Checchi had taken out a notebook and was writing in it. He stopped and looked up. "Should I?"

"You know who the Gargano Family is, right?"

"Of course."

"Doran is a lawyer and an accountant who does legal and financial work for the Gargano Family. I won't lie; I know him too."

"So let me understand this," Checchi said. "This girl, Gloria Doran, runs away from home, and she and a boyfriend happen to be at the Cresthaven Motel making whoopee and they see who shot and killed two Detroit police officers and wounded a third. But you say you don't know if those two can identify the man who murdered the police."

"That's right," Bonaventure said. It didn't sound as convincing coming from Checchi.

"That girl knows who killed the policemen," Mrs. Lincoln said. "She told me she knew who it was, but she didn't want to tell me the name. She and that boy saw everything, and it was just the way Mr. Bonaventure described it. Those policemen murdered two innocent people and that's why she's so afraid of the police."

They all looked at her. Carlton looked nervous, like he wanted to leave. Bonaventure swallowed hard and eyed his empty water glass again.

Mrs. Lincoln was clutching her purse. There was an edgy, creaky quality to her voice, which got higher as she continued. "She's the same girl I told you about who's been to my place twice now, the one who got the mail from her boyfriend Jimmy. Jimmy was a friend of my Roscoe's. I didn't care for him, but he was Roscoe's friend. This girl Gloria, the boy Jimmy, who's a soldier now, and Roscoe spent almost two weeks at my house while I was out of town with my sick mother. They were in the garage recording music, and there's gonna be a record." She took a handkerchief out of her purse, blew her nose and dabbed at her eyes. "That girl has a gorgeous voice.

All three of them are very talented. I thought Roscoe had finally found himself a girlfriend, but she was that other boy's girlfriend, and now she's pregnant and her Jimmy's in that war, and people are trying to kill her... and my Roscoe is... is gone." There were tears in her eyes but she sat up straight and stoic in her chair.

Carlton and Bonaventure looked at each other like they wanted to talk, but Checchi was looking at Mrs. Lincoln with sympathetic eyes, encouraging her to continue.

Checchi said, "She's the same girl who calls herself Sunshine that a couple of our patrol officers saw singing at that anti-war rally. I learned about her from you and put the description out that I was looking for a girl called Sunshine. One of the patrol guys remembered. I thought we caught a good break there, but nothing came of it. I spoke to her very briefly and I should have brought her in. We haven't been able to find her since."

Mrs. Lincoln regained her composure. "Two weeks ago, she and I went downtown to see these lawyers and sign papers about the record. Those lawyers—well, they were trying to cheat us—but more important, they called her stepfather, that disgraceful Mr. Doran. He showed up with two great big ruffians. They had guns too. They were ready to drag her out of there. But somehow, they all got high on LSD and went crazy. One of those big ruffians started shooting. Said he saw giant spiders."

Bonaventure started laughing. "I read about that in the *Free Press*," he said. "Funny story, though maybe not if you were there. But no one was sure what happened. Apparently one of those lawyers, the woman, took all her clothes off."

The *Free Press* story had more about the naked lawyer, Samantha Golightly, than anything else.

"We couldn't get a coherent story out of anyone," Checchi said. "I talked to the patrolmen who filed the report. I think the girl might have had something to do with it." He looked at Mrs. Lincoln. "Interesting... I didn't know you were there." Checchi stopped, drummed his fingers on the table and looked up at the ceiling, thinking. "Tell me more about how the Lincoln murder fits in here."

Bonaventure said, "Yeah, there's more. I asked Slick Percy to find the two teenagers, but someone else wanted them even more than I did."

"And who was that?" asked Checchi.

"Matthew Doran," Bonaventure said.

"Okay, his daughter—"

"Stepdaughter."

"Right, stepdaughter. She runs away from home, gets herself knocked up and he wants to find her. That hardly seems like enough to kill someone over."

"I thought so too," Bonaventure said. "It took awhile, but I know why now. The girl has an extraordinary photographic memory, at least for numbers, and she's mathematical."

"That's true," Mrs. Lincoln said. "She figured out how those lawyers were going cheat us as soon as she read those papers. Didn't take her more than a minute or two."

Bonaventure nodded. "Growing up, she apparently overheard her stepfather talking to the Garganos about their money. She overheard a lot. She knows details about amounts, banks, and companies that were set up. She knows enough to put them all away for a long time. And Matthew Doran found out that she knows. And she really hates her stepfather. So Doran hired Percy to track her and her boyfriend down, and he had no scruples about how Percy did it."

"What's he got against her boyfriend?" asked Checchi. "I mean, besides the fact that he knocked up his stepdaughter."

"She told her boyfriend about him and the Garganos. This one doesn't make a lot of sense to me either, but I don't pretend to know everything here. Doran is a strange duck. He's hired Pinkerton's to help look for the girl now, and he's already tried to kill her at least one time that I heard about.

"I knew Detroit police were looking for the girl and trying to find out who shot the cops at the Cresthaven. Your police department has a very quiet investigation going on to find those witnesses. Trouble is, they didn't make much progress for a long time. At least that's what I hear. They might be getting closer now. Anyway, I'm telling you who they are. Even before the uprising ended, the police were investigating this incident. First, they questioned the desk clerk from the motel. They learned from her that the police had shot and killed that mother and her son and beat her up. They know this isn't just an unfortunate case of two policemen being killed in the uprising."

"Why do you keep calling it an uprising?" Checchi asked.

"It's what many of my people call it. That's all. Some of us see it as the beginning of a revolution."

Carlton nodded but said nothing.

"Do you?" Checchi asked.

Bonaventure shrugged and shook his head. "Uprising, revolution, riot—whatever you want to call it, a lot of black people were pissed off." He glanced at Frances Lincoln. "Excuse my coarse language, but it's true. We've been pissed off for a long time. My friend was pissed off when he saw those white policemen beating up that lady, and when they murdered the woman and the boy in cold blood he lost his temper. They'd never do that to white people. He lost it and he had a shotgun, so he killed them. That's a form of self-defense in my opinion. I think what happened—the uprising, the riot—surprised white folks, but it didn't surprise black people."

Mrs. Lincoln and Logan Carlton were both nodding.

"But you don't want to hear this. The police investigators figured out that they had a problem, so they've conducted a very quiet investigation almost from the beginning. They want to find out who killed their officers, but they don't want the circumstances to get out because it could cause another riot. That's what I've heard.

"They've been tracking down all of the registered guests from the motel to question them and asking the motel lady what she remembers about them. They were smart enough to apologize to her and gave her some compensation, and of course she's far too frightened to speak out."

"So you think we'll learn who killed the officers?" asked Checchi.

"And the murder of a black woman and her son at the motel still isn't very important, is it?" Carlton said sharply.

Checchi looked at him but didn't answer, then turned his attention back to Bonaventure.

Bonaventure shook his head. "I don't think they'll come across my friend. He wasn't registered. No one else knew he was there except the man he was supposed to meet. Besides, he's long gone, out of the country. Even the lady at the motel didn't know he was there.

"It took the police some time to get around to the two young people. They were white, and the police assumed that whoever killed their officers and anyone who saw it was black. Most of the people staying at the motel were black and, of course, from out of town. It wasn't easy for Detroit Police, almost all of whom are white, to question black people from out of town and keep it quiet. You have white cops trying to get information from black people who don't trust the police, especially the Detroit police. Everything has taken much longer than a regular investigation would."

Checchi nodded dejectedly and Bonaventure continued.

"The two white kids registered as brother and sister. The police don't know the girl's last name. The car the two were driving was registered to the soldier's uncle who lives in the Upper Peninsula. I heard that the police, or maybe it was the FBI, paid the uncle a visit a few weeks ago and learned that the boy has no sister. His uncle had no idea who the girl was and he told them his nephew was in Vietnam. He also didn't know where the car was.

"There's another complication too. The boy who escaped, the one whose brother and mother were murdered by the police, found his way to the NAACP and they went to the feds. So I believe there is, or soon will be, a federal investigation into what went on at the Cresthaven."

Checchi's breath caught at the mention of a federal investigation. "Aw no, not the feds." He looked at Bonaventure closely. "You're very well informed, Mr. Bonaventure. How do you know all of this?"

"I have good sources within the Detroit PD, and of course on the streets of Detroit I'm better informed than anyone, including the police. I have sources around Lansing and Ann Arbor too." Bonaventure indicated Logan Carlton. "One of them is right here."

"How much of this does this Doran know?" Checchi asked.

Bonaventure thought for a moment. "Hard to say, but probably most of it. Slick Percy might still feel some loyalty to me, but I suspect Doran is paying him a lot more. But neither of them know what happened at the motel, at least from me. I'm sure Doran knows I was looking for the two kids, but he doesn't know why. But he's not stupid, so he might have learned, or will learn, that the cops are looking into all of this. I doubt he knows about the feds, but you never know."

Frances Lincoln spoke up again. "I know why that girl hates her stepfather so much."

They all looked at her.

"He's been raping her. He's been forcing her into sex since she was a little child," she said in an angry, growling voice.

Bonaventure put a hand to his mouth.

"He's been beating her and whipping her and raping her, and he's been doing it for a long time. She opened up some to me last time we talked, and I spoke to another woman who knew even more and overheard a phone call between Gloria and her stepfather. It's terrible, *terrible* what's happened to her. When I first met her, I thought she was just a spoiled rich girl. Now she's out there, barely sixteen years old, no money and six months pregnant. That poor, poor girl. You men don't seem to appreciate that. She's afraid of you. She doesn't trust anyone and she has every reason not to trust anyone... especially men."

Bonaventure's face was wracked with pain and sorrow.

Carlton looked at him, wide-eyed.

Mrs. Lincoln said, "There's a woman by the name of Murphy that you should talk to. She lives on the west side and she takes in boarders. I'll give you her telephone number and address. That's where the girl was staying when her stepfather tried to kill her. Maybe there's some record of the incident because there was shooting. Happened back around Thanksgiving. And another thing... that girl said she got so mad that she took a shot at her stepfather."

"She's got a gun?" Checchi said. "Jesus! Where did a sixteen year old girl get a gun?"

"Just turned sixteen," Bonaventure said. "She had a .38 special that she stole from her stepfather. She also burned their house down in Grosse Pointe. When her father hired those guys who tried to shoot her, that same night, she went back to his house. It used to be her home too, and she burned the place down. Not only that, but the day she first ran away, she took his prized Corvette, drove to Belle Isle, and put it into the Detroit River."

Checchi was shaking his head.

Logan Carlton cleared his throat and looked at Checchi. "You need to think about what you're going to do when you get back to Beaubien. There's probably already a federal probe into what happened at the Cresthaven. That investigation will focus on the actions of the police. The feds already know the police killed an innocent woman and a child and tried to kill another one. The FBI won't let your department cover that up, and I believe they're likely to come down hard on police officers who lie to them.

"I too have my sources because I'm very interested in the Detroit Police Department. I'm told you're a homicide investigator who's not a hothead or a racist, and that you're not afraid to go your own way. You've never been associated with any of those racist good old boys, at least not that I could find out."

"Yeah, well I've put my fair share of colored people into cages," Checchi snapped. He shifted his attention to Bonaventure. "And I don't like the idea of a vigilante murdering two of my colleagues no matter how justified they think it is. And I'll tell you something else. The Detroit Police Department isn't gonna let the murder of two officers slide. They won't let the FBI let it slide either."

Carlton's nostrils flared as anger flashed across his face. "As it should be. Just remember, the feds won't let the murder of those two civilians slide either. And the Detroit PD shouldn't have either."

Checci nodded noncommittally. "Incidentally, the police were there in the first place because somebody shot a fireman and wounded him. The shots appeared to come from that motel." He snaked a finger underneath his shirt collar to scratch at his neck and his clip-on tie popped off his shirt. He didn't notice. "I never had any use for Erwin though. He's the inspector, the one in civilian clothes who got killed at the Cresthaven. He was one mean bastard who liked to hurt people, and he didn't like it if you weren't with his program. We were in the same precinct when I was on patrol."

Carlton had calmed himself. "As I said, Detective, you should think very carefully about what you'll do with what we've told you. I hope someday to be in a position to make changes in the police department. There'll be a lot of changes, more black officers for one thing. But that also means I'll want white officers that I can count on too."

"I'm Homicide," Checchi said. "No matter what you think, I want whoever killed Roscoe Lincoln. I want to nail Percy Dupree, if he did it. That's what I'm gonna work on. Probably be better if I found that girl before anyone else does. If you see her, tell her to talk to me. And I'll make sure she's safe. I talked to her that one time, and I liked her. Some of the officers at the rally liked her too." He took a sip of his wine and examined Carlton. "What do you mean by 'be in a position'?"

"I don't want to be a state senator forever," Carlton said with a light smile.

"You gonna run for mayor or something?" Checchi laughed. "I think Jerome Cavanaugh might have something to say about that."

"Forty-three people dead in a riot? Fuckin' busloads of white people moving out of the city every day? A fuckin' three-legged mangy dog could beat Cavanaugh in the next election," Carlton said.

Bonaventure grimaced, and Mrs. Lincoln covered a smile with her hand. "Oh dear."

January 25 – 28, Detroit

Later in the afternoon, Checchi was alone at home, still thinking about what he was going to do. He knew more about the Cresthaven than he had let on in the meeting with Bonaventure. Before the meeting, he'd talked with a detective who'd been working organized crime for several years. He'd learned that Bonaventure was involved in prostitution, gambling, labor racketeering, illegal after-hours clubs, and probably drugs. Basically, the Garganos had been letting him run things in the colored parts of Detroit for years. *Though the greedy bastards probably got a healthy slice of it.*

Also, Checchi, along with most of the other detectives in Homicide, knew all about the off-the-record investigation that was going on and what had really happened at the Cresthaven. No one in the department wanted the real story to get out. He also knew the feds were onto what had happened. If anything, he was surprised it had taken them so long. He thought Bonaventure and Carlton were more than a little naïve about the FBI. J. Edgar Hoover ran the FBI and he was no friend of colored people. Seemed unlikely to Checchi that anyone from the Detroit Police Department would ever officially be held accountable for killing the woman and her son. Not that he agreed with that, but it was the biggest urban riot in his lifetime and two cops were dead and the third was never coming back to work.

What he hadn't said at the meeting was that the inspector running the quiet investigation, Robert Edmunds, was Erwin's cousin, and Checchi disliked him even more than he had disliked Erwin. He knew he should tell Edmunds about Bonaventure and that the result would probably be Bonaventure's arrest within the hour. But Checchi believed Bonaventure had told him the truth, and that he might eventually have more to say. He also believed the police would never get the shooter's name out of him. Then Checchi would never get anything more from Bonaventure. *No, I'll do exactly what I told them at the meeting. I'll keep pushing on the Roscoe Lincoln murder. I need to talk to Percy Dupree.* "But how the hell am I going to do that?" he muttered. "He's probably in Vietnam."

Checchi was five foot one-inch tall, weighed less than a hundred pounds dripping wet, and looked like his mother still dressed him. But too many people, some serving long prison terms, had underestimated the diminutive sergeant. By almost any measure, he was the best homicide investigator in the Detroit Police Department. Some colleagues thought he should have been chief of Homicide but others scoffed at the idea of putting someone in charge who was the size of a fifth grader. Most homicide investigators had partners, but Checchi's current partner was out on sick leave with a hernia. Checchi preferred to work alone anyway.

After the long lunch, Checchi had dropped in on Mrs. Murphy on the way back from the restaurant. She confirmed everything that Mrs. Lincoln had said, even showing him the bullet holes beside the front door. When she confirmed the sexual abuse and added some details, he was saddened. He had been hoping that Frances Lincoln was either wrong or exaggerating. By the time he finished talking to her, it was late afternoon so he went home and spent the evening thinking about it all. He concluded that he had an opportunity to land bigger fish. He was setting his sights on Doran, and maybe he could also bag the Garganos. As far as Checchi knew, Bonaventure hadn't killed anyone.

The next morning, he went to have a cup of coffee with his friend Sergeant Antoine Lincicombe in Organized Crime and asked him about Matthew Doran. At six foot four and 230 pounds, Lincicombe was more than twice Checchi's size, but the two had been friends for a long time.

"Yeah, we know Doran does a lot of work for the Garganos," Lincicombe said. "We even had a tap on his phone a few years back when we had that task force with the feds. His name came up when we were listening to the Garganos, but we got nothing. We talked to him. He said his law firm just does tax work and provides legal services for them and that the Wop bastards are entitled to legal counsel like anyone else. They don't want to get caught on taxes like Al Capone. He makes a bundle from them."

"Okay, so what can you tell me about Percy Dupree?"

Lincicombe's lip curled up in a sneer. "Guy's bad news. I'd like to fricassee that bastard. Started out as a pimp for Clyde Bonaventure, but he's a bit on the rough side for Bonaventure, who's soft for the business he's in. Lately Percy's been freelancing for the Garganos, mostly Vinnie Ayala, and he's getting more violent. Get behind on the vig and Slick Percy will come calling. You might as well call an ambulance as soon as you see him. Seems to have acquired some nasty pals too. We think he's involved in at least three homicides."

"Well, I might have another one," Checchi said.

"That musician in the paper?"

Checchi nodded.

"And you think there's a connection with Doran?"

Checchi nodded again. He'd pulled the report of the shooting at Mrs. Murphy's house. He ran the descriptions by Lincicombe.

"That sounds like Slick Percy. He's a good-looking guy," Lincicombe said. "The big guy is probably Darnell Gates. He's more than three hundred pounds. Tried to play football at Central Michigan. Fucker's bigger than Bubba Smith, but he's borderline retarded. There's one more thing about Doran: he's a player who got caught a few times by Vice. They know him."

"Arrested?" asked Checchi.

"Nope. Never arrested, never charged. He's a friggin' lawyer and a big contributor to the Police Benevolent Association. Real pillar of the community and all that shit. No one's gonna bring in someone like him for gettin' blowjobs from under-age girls... or boys. Thing is, I can buy what he says as far as the Garganos are concerned, but he still makes my skin crawl. He's a real charmer when you talk to him, but the more you find out, the more you gotta wonder about the guy. You hear the story about when his wife died?"

Checchi shook his head.

"Some uniformed officers tracked him down to Greektown to notify him that his wife had been killed in an accident. He was having lunch with the Garganos. Doran insisted on finishing his lunch, and he even bought the two policemen lunch. Guy was absolutely stone cold. Slick Percy was there too. In fact, the uniforms said he walked in the same time they did. He was probably security."

***

In the afternoon, Checchi strolled over to the Traffic Division. It took him almost half an hour to locate the report of the accident in which Gina Doran had died, but he got lucky when he immediately found the young officer who had handled it. Angus McLeod was talking on a telephone at a desk not 20 feet away. Checchi learned that Gina Doran had been killed in the parking lot of a Catholic church, one she often attended. Although two witnesses reported seeing a large white truck in the lot, no one had actually seen the accident. Her injuries were consistent with being hit and run over by a truck.

A truck fitting the description had been found several miles away later the same day. There were traces of blood on the truck, but no fingerprints. It had been wiped clean. The truck belonged to a small delivery firm and the driver had called in sick the day of the accident. He had taken the truck home the previous night because he had to make an early morning pickup not far from where he lived. He'd told police that the truck had been stolen. It was gone when he woke up in the morning and he had called in sick because he was afraid to tell his boss the truck was gone. His wife and three kids verified that he had been at home the entire day of the accident.

Neither McLeod nor anyone else in Traffic had bothered to look up anything other than the trucker's traffic record, which Checchi thought was sloppy police work. Checchi did a little research on the driver. The man had been picked up three times on suspicion of transporting stolen property. He also had a juvenile record but Checchi couldn't find out for what. The stolen property involved goods taken from warehouses. A company called Falcon Storage owned both the warehouses.

It was late on a Friday and Checchi was still wondering about Falcon Storage. He called Lincicombe again and caught the sergeant as he was heading out the door. "I'll call you back if I find out anything," Lincicombe said.

Saturday morning Checchi called the Grosse Pointe Police. The lieutenant in charge of homicide, Dixon Webley, had been Checchi's partner longer than anyone else. Webley had gotten married and left the Detroit department for a more settled life with the Grosse Pointe PD. Webley couldn't immediately answer any of Checchi's questions about Doran, but he promised to check.

Half an hour later, Checchi's phone rang.

It was Lincicombe. "Falcon's owned by the Garganos. Doran drew up the papers, and he's listed as the controller. We could be looking at an insurance scam here. They've had quite a few thefts, made a lot of claims. Not just Falcon, but they have at least half a dozen other companies with warehouses. All of them have had thefts, but not enough so's you'd notice at any one company. Your driver worked for a couple of those companies. We think maybe the Garganos arrange the theft, then make an insurance claim. They also probably get most of whatever the thief gets when he fences the stuff. And they don't have a lot of risk."

Checchi and Lincicombe talked for another fifteen minutes. They agreed to keep each other posted and maybe have lunch the following week.

Checchi did a load of laundry and thought about going out and maybe buying himself a new suit. But it looked cold outside and buying a suit wasn't only difficult because the selection was so limited, but it was embarrassing as well. Sometimes it was easier to buy clothing off the rack in the boys section of department stores. He thought about calling Ellen, a woman he had been dating for the last six months, but decided to wait. Early Saturday afternoon, he settled in front of his TV and was watching an alpine downhill ski competition when Webley called back.

"Well, that fuckin' fire that burned Doran's house was definitely arson. Didn't look like an insurance job because it was underinsured and Doran's so loaded there's no way he needed the money. Insurance has already paid it off," said Webley. "We asked him who he thought did it, and he didn't give us anyone. Said nothin' about anyone shootin' at him either. That's news to us. By the way, he's never filed a missing persons report on his daughter either.

"I found out some about the wife when I asked around. Scuttlebutt is there were at least half a dozen incidents over the last ten or fifteen years, mostly reports from hospitals. She went to at least three different hospitals and they all remember her. Looks like he'd been beatin' the shit out of her for a long time. Same old shit every time, no charges ever filed. The guy's too connected. Really upset some of the nurses too, but he's golden with the hospital fundraisers. I found some reports; I'll mail you copies. Sounds like a real bastard."

It felt like a good day. Checchi went to bed a little early, mulling everything over. He got up early the next morning and took Ellen to an early Mass. By ten o'clock they were back at his Northwest Detroit home, making love. He didn't think about police work for the rest of the day.

CHAPTER 12

29 January, 1305 Hours, Nui Binh Base Camp

Major Jerry Shiffman, an intense, wiry man of medium stature, sucked hard on a Camel cigarette and stared as a Jeep being driven too fast slid to a dusty stop in front of the Nui Binh Base Camp Operations Bunker. First Sergeant Jubal Sypher from the 99th Assault Helicopter Company got out, causing the major to sigh as he pulled on his flak jacket and his olive drab helmet with the black major's insignia, and picked up his M16.

Two minutes later Sypher, now wearing a dirty and torn flak jacket, was standing inside the bunker in front of Shiffman's desk protesting the red alert that Colonel Hobbs had implemented at Shiffman's request. Red alert meant that each of the base camp perimeter bunkers was supposed to be manned with a minimum of six guards all night. Every unit in the base camp was responsible for staffing one or more of the perimeter bunkers. The 99th Assault Helicopter Company had an authorized strength of more than 300 men though most of the time it actually had fewer than 250 soldiers, many of them warrant officer pilots who wouldn't stand guard. The colonel had reduced their base camp defense responsibility to a single bunker.

"You have your orders, First Sergeant Sypher," Shiffman said, his voice gaining volume. "We are on red alert. I want six guards in that bunker before sundown. I can't make it any clearer than that!"

"Major, we're a fuckin' chopper company. We've only got seventy-five percent of our authorized strength. These poor bastards fly all day. You can't expect them to pull guard all night too." He glanced at his torn and dirty flak jacket. "Shit, even our field gear is under strength."

Shiffman studied the sweaty first sergeant as he stood stoically at attention. The first sergeant glanced to either side with his beady eyes to see whether anyone else in the bunker was paying attention to the conversation. No one was.

"Why not?" said Shiffman. "What do you think the grunts do? Check into a Holiday Inn at the end of the day? I know a couple of first sergeants out there who'd like to have your problems. Maybe you'd like to trade places?"

Sypher swallowed his anger, saluted, turned and left. He had been in the Army for 18 years, having joined after his job as a civilian contractor in China had ended with the fall of that country to the Communists. He was 46 years old and all he wanted now was to get his 20 years in so he could collect a pension and get health care. That, and to siphon off as much gravy as possible from the river of American money and goods pouring into Vietnam.

Furious, Sypher drove through the base camp until he pulled behind one of the hootches not far from a row of outhouses. He sat in the Jeep for nearly two minutes, carefully checking to see that no one was nearby, and then called to a shitburner. The wind shifted slightly, blowing the thick, rank black smoke from the burning feces toward him, making him nauseous. He put his sleeve to his face in a mostly futile attempt to stifle the sickening odor as a wretched, foul-smelling Vietnamese man approached the Jeep, furtively extending a sheaf of currency.

Sypher counted it and put it in his pocket. He got out of the Jeep and looked around once again. Then he reached in the back, took out a radio and handed it to the man.

The shitburner grinned, revealing major gaps from missing teeth, and began fiddling with the dials, unhooked the telephone, replaced it and looked at the antenna. He kept smiling and bowed slightly as he backed away.

Sypher sped off, spraying dirt on the shitburner who kept right on smiling.

1338 Hours, Northwest of Nui Binh Base Camp

Roughly 13 miles northwest of Nui Binh Base Camp two helicopter gunships were approaching a jungle clearing called LZ Puckett. The enemy had been there the day before. The whole area was a free-fire zone and both gunships were on their way home with unexpended ordinance. They hoped to catch some VC by surprise. Rivera leaned out the door of the Charlie model huey, savoring the wind whipping his face. He hefted the M60 machinegun against his shoulder and got ready to shoot up the tree line at the edge of the clearing. He loved it. Nothing in his life would probably ever come close to matching the exhilaration he felt while hanging out of the door of a gunship firing his machinegun. He would miss it when he went home in a week, and this might be the last time.

Quickly, things went wrong. There was a loud, quick rattle like marbles dropping into an empty steel washtub and Rivera knew they'd been hit. *Sounded like three or four hits.* There was an even louder, high-pitched snap. Suddenly, heavy vibrations were coming up through his feet. Terror erupted from a point behind his balls and ripped through his body like an electric shock. A shower of red splinters sprayed off the rear of the helicopter. The helicopter lurched so sharply that his left foot slipped out into thin air. For an instant he panicked because he thought he would fall, but that was foolish because his harness wouldn't let him fall. The machine lurched again, and then a third time, and one of the lurches enabled Rivera to replant his foot. "Tail rotor!" he shouted into the mike attached to his flight helmet. "We lost the goddamn tail rotor!"

The helicopter accelerated and stabilized, although in an awkward flying position. The ship was plowing diagonally into the wind, which was howling into the door on the other side. CW2 Walters was telling ops that they had a tail rotor failure and were receiving fire.

In the right door gun position, Hayes yelled, "Dinks, man! Groovy green tracers!" He opened up with his machinegun.

"Where are they?" Rivera and Walters shouted.

Hayes' machinegun stopped—"Ahh, 'bout four o'clock"—then started again.

The helicopter dipped into a wobbly turn.

"I see 'em," Walters said. "Ahh shit... can't hold it for a good shot with the rockets. Rivera, you're gonna get a chance before we have to blow this pop stand."

The helicopter started a slow turn, then dipped erratically. Suddenly it was all in front of Rivera. A dozen North Vietnamese soldiers in their tan uniforms, some with AK-47s, all foolishly standing up because they thought the erratic helicopter was going down, a big ugly black son of a bitch of a gun behind them with the gunner frantically trying to clear the weapon, all of them not more than 75 meters away when the ship reached the nearest point in the arc of its turn.

Rivera coolly squeezed the trigger, sending out a slightly curved stream of bullets in a perfect deflection shot that compensated for the motion of the turning helicopter. It was like shooting a water pistol out the window of a speeding car, but Rivera had done it so often that it was second nature to him. The tracers tore into enemy soldiers and, despite the unsteadiness of the helicopter, he was able to hold the fire on the enemy group for several seconds. Red patches appeared on the uniforms. A chunk of red flew off one head, the bodies jerked and danced like spastic puppets, the gunner on the big weapon slumped over the barrel. They were so close that he saw the last stark expression of terror on the face of one of the soldiers as he died. Only a few seconds later as they roared away, rockets from the second gunship detonated on the group.

1350 Hours, Nui Binh Base Camp

In the Orderly Room, First Sergeant Sypher sat at a gray metal desk talking on a black telephone. His fatigues were soaked with sweat and his face was flushed. He had taken a good stiff jolt of Jack Daniels when he'd returned—three big mouthfuls—just enough to take the edge off his irritation with Major Shiffman. He was talking to the brigade sergeant major, Brendan McAlister, an old and trusted friend. McAlister was one of the most influential senior noncommissioned officers in the entire U.S. Army, and one of the most corrupt.

"Jesus Top, you gotta get me outta here. It's hotter than Fort Polk in August," Sypher said. "The fuckin' colonel puts us on red alert every time he's got gas. Now I gotta have my fuckin' bunker manned with six fuckin' guards. I ain't got enough fuckin' men. These fuckin' shitbirds they're sendin' over... shit! They listen to godawful poundin' jungle music and smoke funny cigarettes. The VC attack and they're probably gonna kiss 'em, or worse. Jesus, what's this fuckin' Army come to?"

"I hear you loud and clear, Jubal. There might be something in the pipeline soon. We're gonna clean up. Better than Saigon two years ago." Sypher was having a hard time hearing over the staticky line that connected Nui Binh with Long

Binh where McAlister was stationed. He strained to pick up every word and nuance in Top's voice.

"Listen, you gotta look good, Jubal. You gotta give me a reason to go to bat for you. Court martials, that's what the brass wants. They're worried about the nigger unrest and Mary Jane."

Sypher burst out laughing although he was still puzzled over what Top meant. "Mary Jane who? Mary Jane Rottencrotch?" He laughed again.

"No," the sergeant major said, a little irritated. "Mary Jane Scrambleyerbrains. Marijuana, Jubal. Those funny cigarettes you're talking about. You need to court martial the bastards, but be careful how you handle the spearchuckers."

Static distorted the end of Top's last sentence, but Sypher understood him this time. He leaned back in his chair, a big grin spreading across his meaty, sweaty face as he glanced around the empty Orderly Room.

"Hell Top, we ain't got no nigger unrest around here. The problem is restin' niggers, and the problem can be solved by *ah*restin' niggers." He roared with laughter at his own joke. "How come I can't get more men? I could use some fuckin' grunts for my bunker. Are they all too busy gruntin'?"

"In the pipeline, Jubal," said Top. "It's in the pipeline. Remember your old buddy Rufus the Doofus? Private Rufus Roy? Turd you sent to Long Binh jail a month ago? Well he's out, and he'll be on the afternoon courier. They couldn't sell him to anybody else, so he's yours. Make a fine bunker guard." Top paused for effect. Even though Sypher was a friend, McAlister still liked to fuck with him. "Hear tell he's hell on wheels with a machinegun."

"Aww, shit. Thanks a lot, Top. Over and fuckin' out." He banged the phone down. When it was safely hung up, he muttered, "You know, Top, you can be a royal pain in the ass."

No sooner were the words spoken than he heard helicopters flying very low over the Orderly Room. His first thought was that Rufus the Doofus was coming early. He jumped up and headed out the door.

A huey gunship streaked low over the runway, another helicopter following above and behind. The first ship was wobbling a little and flying almost sideways. It made a jouncing turn over the runway, getting lower and slower, and more out of control. Finally, it touched down a long, shrieking landing on its skids, spraying a dense crescendo of sparks and filling the air with the excruciating, crackling screech of shredding metal. It slid off the runway and jolted to a stop a little over a hundred meters behind Bunker Three. Sypher and other soldiers began running toward the machine, but Sypher's run deteriorated into a moderately fast shuffle after a couple of dozen feet.

Rivera and Hayes jumped out and opened the front doors for the pilots. The two pilots were laughing. They shook hands with each other and slapped each of the crew on the shoulder.

Sypher approached the two warrant officer pilots, Walters and Comstock. They were both dressed in green flight suits and wearing flight helmets. Comstock was 19 and CW2 Walters was a few months past 20.

Comstock said, "Tail rotor got shot out, Sarge! Jesus, I thought we were goin' into the fuckin' bush! That was fuckin' close!" He'd been in Vietnam less than a month and this was the first time he'd been shot at.

Walters was looking at him and grinning. "You know the last thing that goes through a helicopter pilot's mind when he flies into the ground?"

Comstock thought about it and shook his head. "What?"

"His asshole, that's what."

"Jesus Christ," Comstock said, and laughed.

"Anybody hurt?" Sypher asked, worried about blank spaces on his roster.

"Naw, except maybe Rivera. His shit's gettin' flakier. Doesn't feel so hot. Wasted the dinks that got us, though. We're claiming twelve probable and six of them are confirmed. Hit those bastards good, probably got more of them than Prentiss did with the fucking rockets. That short-timer Rivera's ready to call it a war. We're gonna need another crew chief. Might be time for Purple Hayes to move up, though maybe he's pretty much up there already." Walters chuckled and turned back to Comstock. "That's not the way they handle a tail rotor failure at Rucker is it? Those training assholes don't take into account that when you lose your fuckin' tail rotor you might have to do something about Charlie if he's still tryin' to smoke your ass."

The two pilots began walking toward the company area.

Still giggling, Walters said, "How'd you like that landin'? Think I can get on with Pan Am?"

"I'm flyin' TWA if you do." Comstock was simultaneously relieved and proud. He had just passed into a lifetime brotherhood of pilots who had been under fire.

Rivera hung his head under the helicopter's tail boom and vomited. He had known that he was going to throw up within a minute of shooting the NVA soldiers. All the way back to Nui Binh, he'd fought against it by gulping deep breaths of air as it howled around him. Walters, Hayes and Comstock had been chattering like magpies out of relief once they'd determined the helicopter would continue to fly. There was no apparent damage other than the loss of the tail rotor, and Walters was more than capable of flying the crippled huey. He even let Comstock take the controls for a bit.

Finally, Hayes had asked the silent Rivera through the headset whether he was all right.

Rivera had flashed him a thumbs-up. "I'm okay. A little airsick is all."

Later, on the ground after he'd puked, Rivera raised his trembling hands and looked at them. *What's wrong with me?* He glanced over at Hayes, who was inhaling deeply on the remains of a cigarette—at least he hoped it was a cigarette. Hayes coughed out a cloud of cigarette smoke as he examined the stubby remains of the tail rotor, then flipped the butt away.

Rivera looked past Hayes and saw Sypher with three civilians walking back toward them. "Hey, cool it, here comes Sypher the Lifer."

Hayes took out another cigarette, lit it and jammed the plastic case in his shirt pocket.

"Lemme see those goddamn cigarettes, Private Hayes," Sypher said sharply. Hayes pulled the cigarette case from his pocket, opened it and offered a cigarette to Sypher. "Always got a cigarette for my first sergeant. Help yourself, Sarge," he said, smiling.

Sypher took the cigarette and sniffed it. "What kind of shit is this Hayes? Whaddya smokin' here?"

"Menthol, Sarge. Like, they're Kools, y'know?"

Sypher snarled and threw the cigarette to the ground. Hayes looked at it and decided it was too spoiled to pick up.

Three civilians, two men and a woman, with a big camera on a tripod had been standing at the side of the runway filming the scene as the helicopter had come in. They walked up, speaking among themselves in Castilian Spanish, not the Cuban dialect Rivera was familiar with in Miami, but he could understand it. The woman was telling the cameraman and the soundman that she wanted to talk to the soldiers from the helicopter.

Hayes looked at them and grinned. "Hi television guys. You gonna put me on TV?"

"Shut up private," Sypher said, then he turned to the two civilians. "You been authorized by the brigade PIO?"

The woman pulled a piece of paper from her pocket, unfolded it and handed it to Sypher.

The first sergeant read it carefully. "Y'all are from Spain, huh? Says here you can film outside in unrestricted areas." Sypher scratched his chin thoughtfully.

The woman turned to the cameraman and said in Spanish, "Don't waste film on this idiot. I want to get the two who were flying, but I have to talk to the idiot first." She looked at Sypher and smiled.

Rivera thought she was pretty, and she was displaying considerable cleavage although she looked like she had imbibed a little heavily from the cup of life. There was a hard edge to her face. He figured her to be at least five years older than him, and he was 22. Her perfume was nice. He wasn't sure he liked her, but he liked the way she looked and smelled. It had been six months since he'd been near an attractive woman. As she approached Sypher, Rivera sauntered a few steps past her so he could look at her ass. *Rear view's excellent too. Damn, I'm looking forward to going home.*

"Sir, what happen to this machine? Did the enemy attack it?"

The cameraman had set up his camera on a tripod and aimed it at Sypher. The soundman was plugging a microphone into the camera. The two men were much older than the woman.

Sypher smiled broadly. "Well hell, Charlie shot this here helicopter in the ass. Shot the goddamn tail rotor clean off." Sypher walked over to the tail rotor with the reporter and made sweeping gestures at the helicopter as he spoke.

The Spaniards exchanged puzzled looks.

The woman said to them in Spanish, "The sergeant's a fool. He doesn't know anything. He sits at a desk all day."

"Don't worry, the camera's not on," answered the cameraman in Spanish.

Rivera looked at Sypher and strained to keep from laughing.

"I don't think they understand anything you said, First Sergeant," said Rivera. "Their English is probably number ten. Want me to tell them what you said in Spanish?"

Frowning, Sypher scratched his ass and nodded, "Go ahead."

Rivera turned to the woman and began speaking Spanish, trying to eliminate his Cuban accent. "I speak Spanish. What do you want to know?"

"Spanish! And you were on the helicopter when it was shot down?" She turned quickly to the cameraman. "Get this," she said and held a microphone up to Rivera.

"You think our sergeant is an idiot. You've got lots of company," Rivera said, smiling at Sypher.

"Tell me what happened. How were you shot down?"

"Well, we didn't get all the way shot down. We were workin' an LZ over by Dau Tieng and on our way back, Charlie started shooting at us. Guess they didn't see we were gunships. They were NVA, North Vietnamese regulars, not VC. We could tell by the uniforms. Seems like a lot of NVA around the last couple of weeks. Anyway, this is a gunship. Mr. Walters tried to line them up for the rockets after we got hit. I think Charlie just got lucky. Nailed the tail rotor from damn near a thousand meters with their first burst. Then their big gun must have jammed. But we got lucky too." Rivera stopped for a second. It wasn't as easy to think in front of a camera as he thought it would be, and it had been a while since he had spoken Spanish.

"Tell me what you did. Did you shoot back?"

Rivera nodded, and continued in Spanish. "Yeah, we wasted them. Mr. Walters looks like he's about fifteen years old but he's been flying guns for six or seven months now and he's a great pilot. When we lost our tail rotor, the ship swung around sideways and he couldn't get a bead on them. Jesus, I thought we were going down. We all did, except maybe Walters. So he just goes with it instead of fighting it, and makes this beautiful turn. I think he was letting the loss of the tail rotor turn us. Anyway, we circled right toward them. Then he tilted down to my side and gave me a clear shot. We were close too. There was another gunship with us, but they were behind us and they hit them with their rockets. Happened real fast."

"How many did you kill?" she asked.

"At least half a dozen. That's what we're claiming, but probably more. Hard to tell how many I got before they got hit by the rockets too. I saw about a dozen of them but there were probably more that I didn't see. They had a crew-served .51 and I got a long burst right on them. I never got that close before when I was shooting at the enemy."

Rivera was still pumped up from the combat and gesturing wildly with his hands. Part of it was speaking Spanish again and part of it was talking to a sexy-looking woman. He had forgotten about getting sick.

"You enjoyed it? You don't feel bad about killing people?"

It was true, he didn't feel bad. He'd puked, so maybe some hidden part of him felt bad. At the moment he felt only a huge sense of exhilaration because he'd been in a fight to the death and he had won. Then, for some insane reason, he remembered going to the prom when he was a junior in high school, certain he was going to get laid, until Carmen, another Cuban refugee, a beautiful girl, had insisted on going straight home as soon as they had finished eating at the Holiday Inn after the prom. Her father was waiting on the front porch and all he got was kissed on the cheek. Now he shook his head and looked at the pretty reporter again, apprehension creeping into his consciousness and spoiling the alluring vision.

In Spanish, he said evenly, "Anytime somebody shoots at me and I don't get killed is okay with me. It's even better when I kill them because that means they won't shoot at me or my friends again. So yes, I enjoyed killing those bastards and I wish there'd been more!"

Sypher had been watching closely. Unable to understand what was being said, he was growing increasingly irritated. Finally he stepped between Rivera and the camera. "Enough of that beaner crap!" He turned to the woman. "You can go to the Base PIO for your fuckin' interview. G'wan, bugger off."

The journalists slowly began taking the camera off the tripod. They walked away without saying anything. Rivera figured they had gotten what they wanted. He didn't mind. The whole episode had shaken him out of his post-combat funk and sickness and had gotten him thinking about going home.

"Fuckin' beaners," said Sypher. "As if we don't have enough fuckin' problems with the fuckin' American press. Specialist Rivera, I don't want you talkin' to those fuckers again." Sypher watched the Spanish reporters leave and then he walked away.

Rivera and Hayes went over to the crashed helicopter and stared vacantly at the bullet holes. Hayes poked at one on the tail boom with his finger. "I wish I may, I wish I might. First tracer I see tonight... is gonna be groovy, man. Cause it ain't gonna be comin' toward me. Feelin' groovy... 'cause we ain't gonna be flyin' tomorrow, and that's cool."

That isn't likely, Rivera thought. Hayes would probably be flying another ship, or maybe even this one. It wouldn't take long to replace the tail rotor, and it didn't look like anything else was damaged. But Rivera had decided that he was done flying for good, done with the whole damn war. He wasn't going to let anyone make him go up again. He sighed and pulled his M16 out of the helicopter just as Hayes, still singing, lurched into him. In the background, Rivera saw that Sypher had stopped walking away and was watching.

Rivera wished Sypher would hurry up and leave. He was glad he had less than a week to be around him. The only thing he cared about was going home and what would happen then. He wanted to go home but he felt a sense of dread about it too. How would he get along with civilians? He put down the M16 and put his hand in his pocket where he kept a pistol, thinking he should give it to Hayes. "I've got to stop this shit. Six goddamn days and a wakeup," he announced loudly. "I won't fly anymore. The next time I get on something that flies, I better be headin' for the World. From now on I'm only shootin' people who try to make me fly," he said with a humorless laugh.

Suddenly, Sypher was beside him and grabbing at his pocket.

"What you got there, Sonny?"

Rivera pulled the pistol from his pocket, cocked it in one smooth motion and held it in front of Sypher's face. He didn't point it at him.

"It's a Tokarev, Sarge. Seven point six two millimeter... about a thirty two caliber." He slowly lowered the pistol and casually fired into the ground. The report was startling. "Makes a pretty big bang. Kill somebody dead real quick too."

Sypher's eyes were wide open, bigger than Rivera had ever seen them. He couldn't speak for several seconds. Rivera grinned, pulled the pistol slowly up to his lips and blew away the tiny amount of smoke coming out of the barrel.

"I could court martial you for that, Specialist," Sypher finally said. Then he turned and quickly walked away.

"Not if you're dead," Rivera said softly, grinning at his back.

1415 Hours

Sergeant Rusty Slobojan pulled the deuce and a half truck in the front of the motor pool adjacent to the Orderly Room and wasn't happy to see the first sergeant. Sypher had threatened to discipline Slobojan after his second infection with venereal disease in less than two months. Slobojan had been diagnosed with a third case that morning and had begged the flight surgeon not to tell anyone about it.

Slobojan was a curious blend of contradictions. He had an IQ in excess of 150 and had been a high school National Merit Scholar. He had designed an offense for his high school football team the year they were state champions. At 270 pounds, he should have been an outstanding lineman, but Slobojan was hopelessly uncoordinated. Although he had a keen grasp of how football should be played, he had no instincts for playing himself. Smaller opponents regularly blocked him or evaded his ungainly bulk. Similarly, his high IQ didn't mean he always did the smart thing, but he liked the Army and was hoping to make it a career.

Back from getting rid of the company's trash at a dump on the other side of Nui Binh village, a swell of military fervor had him humming Sousa marches and tapping the dashboard in time to the truck's clattering engine. He was taking the red alert seriously. It didn't seem unreasonable to him that they might be attacked. A prostitute named Lily at the dump had told him she had heard about a new Vietcong battalion in the province and there had been a lot of incoming rockets and mortars recently. So he was wearing a flak jacket and two bandoleers of M16 ammunition crisscrossed over his chest. He had a vest with pockets containing a dozen full magazines for his M16. A combat web belt with two canteens, two first aid kits, and an entrenching tool, was strapped around his big hips. A half-dozen fragmentation and smoke grenades hung on his suspenders. Stuck in the headband of his helmet was a tube of gun lubricant. He carried an M16 with one magazine taped end-to-end to two others, and a bayonet taped by the blade to the stock. A small hunting knife protruded from the top of one of his jungle boots. He was sweating heavily in the heat, and walking gingerly because of his infected and sore genitals, but he looked earnest and alert.

Sypher laughed. "Jesus Slobbo, You expectin' a human wave attack on the garbage detail? Who the fuck are you? John Slobbo Wayne?"

"Red alert, First Sergeant! Aren't we supposed to have our bunker gear on?"

Sypher grumbled, "Yeah, and as soon as the colonel farts, you can take it off."

Sypher began walking away and Slobojan sighed with relief. Then the first sergeant stopped, turned around and looked at him more carefully. "Slobbo, c'mere. I got an idea."

With a feeling of impending dread, Slobojan followed Sypher into the Orderly Room. The first sergeant sat down behind his desk. He looked ruefully at the chart depicting company strength and sighed. Slobojan stood warily, sweating in front of the desk and thinking about how his penis was hurting.

"Slobbo, you're a fuckin' problem. We got this fuckin' war, so the fuckin' Army's gonna pay you thousands to re-up?"

It was true. Slobojan was ready to re-enlist for six years, get promoted to staff sergeant E-6 and the Army would pay him a huge re-enlistment bonus. It had sounded like a good deal to him. If only he didn't have to deal with Sypher.

"Well, I think they're trying to retain skilled people, especially noncoms," said Slobojan. "You gonna re-enlist?"

"I re-upped before they started that goddamn program," Sypher said angrily. "A fuckin' burst of six and I get nothing' and you're gonna get ten fuckin' grand."

"Well, it isn't that much," Slobojan mumbled.

Sypher didn't hear him. He glowered at Slobojan. Then he smiled. "You'd like to be in charge of something, wouldn't you Sergeant Slobojan?"

"Uhh, yes First Sergeant. I'm a non-commissioned officer, a sergeant E-5." He paused. "Hope to be an E-6 soon."

"You really wanna be an E-6?"

"Ah, yes," Slobojan said. He sensed a trap.

"I need a permanent sergeant of the guard," Sypher said. "Base Camp Defense says we gotta keep six fuckin' guards in Bunker Three. I ain't got enough troops to do that. So I'm gonna put you and three other dirt ba—er, soldiers, in there. That's four. I figure the officer of the guard makes five."

"The officer of the guard only comes around 'bout twice a night at the most. Sometimes he doesn't come at all. It's usually a warrant who just sleeps with his clothes on half the time back in his hootch," Slobojan said.

"You know that and I know that, Slobbo, but that prick of a major back in Base Camp Defense doesn't have to know that."

"You said we gotta have six guards. Where's number six?"

Sypher got up and walked slowly across the Orderly room as he talked.

"Ah, number six... number six.... Sergeant Slobojan, number six is up to you. You gotta figure, at the most that fuckin' major is gonna come around maybe once a night. And it's darker than Uncle Ho's asshole out there. That fuckin' major ain't gonna be able to count noses, and if he does, I figure an enterprising potential senior non-commissioned officer like yourself ought to be able to help an officer count correctly."

Slobojan was beginning to get the drift. "Somebody out on a listening post maybe?"

"Very good, Slobbo. Perhaps I was wrong. You just might be E-6 material after all. If you're gonna be a senior non-commissioned officer, you have to learn to play the game. The Army has its rules, and you gotta know how to bend them."

"Yes, First Sergeant."

Sypher sat down behind his desk again, a frown pushing away the smile.

"I'm assigning Rivera and Hayes to you as permanent guards. Rivera's going home in six days. Neither one of them may last that long 'cause I'm gonna court martial them if I can." Sypher looked directly at Slobojan. "Slobbo?"

"Yes, First Sergeant."

"If you catch Hayes with any narcotics, I want him charged immediately. The brass has had just about enough of this Mary Jane shit."

Slobojan was puzzled. "Mary Jane who?"

"Drugs you shithead!"

"Oh, you mean marijuana."

"Exactly," Sypher said. "I want to make a fuckin' example of Hayes. On second thought, don't worry about it. I'll have the papers typed up tomorrow. And I'll court martial that cocksucker Rivera too. He's got an unauthorized firearm. He threatened me with it. But I'm gonna wait until the day he goes home. Then I'll keep him here for a while. See if I can bust his ass a couple of grades. Teach the bastard a lesson.

And, Slobbo, you're gonna be a witness. If you help me, I'll be in a position to help you with a promotion."

"Yes, First Sergeant," Slobojan said, thinking he'd figure out how to deal with this later. "Who's gonna be the other guard?"

Sypher looked at his watch, picked up and cranked the field phone on his desk.

"Ops? Yeah, this is the First Sergeant. When's the courier due in?" He listened for a few seconds.

"Fuckin' outstanding!"

He hung up the phone.

"Let's go meet him. He's on the courier. Be here in five minutes."

The first sergeant started out the door, then turned around and went back to his desk. He opened the bottom desk drawer, shoved aside the quart bottle of Jack Daniels and pulled out a .45 automatic. He strapped it on and led Slobojan out the door.

"Slobbo, you drive," Sypher said as he walked toward the deuce and a half. Slobojan dutifully obeyed and squeezed his bulk in behind the wheel. It took three attempts to close the truck door because it kept banging on his entrenching tool.

1430 Hours

Hayes, wearing his purple T-shirt and purple-tinted glasses, sat in the doorway of the crashed gunship, strumming a guitar, which was the Harmony that had been Ziegler's. Rivera was on the other side of the ship taking off the remains of the shattered tail rotor. Rivera's impending departure was one depressing thought. Another was not hearing from Gloria for so long. And he was unnerved by the whole harrowing tail rotor experience. He ran through the chords to "Feelin' Groovy," trying to sort out a lot of unpleasant thoughts and thinking about making a quick trip back to his hootch to get some marijuana, or maybe even the LSD pill that Gloria had sent him. Then again, if he dropped acid, he might have a bad trip. And acid would get him higher than grass. *What if we got hit?* Reluctantly, he dropped the acid plan for now and decided not to smoke any marijuana. Once again he recognized Rivera was right.

Hayes also recognized that his pre-draft peace-loving hippie persona had crumbled. Now his Purple Hayes nickname was a negative. It had been a long time since anyone had called him Jim or Jimmy. A lot of his peers didn't trust a gunner who got high. Instead of a killer guitar player in an acid band, he was a killer in the gun platoon. *Is that really me?* He thought about it. *It is now... and I'm not ashamed of it either. Six months in Vietnam, and another six months to go. Can I make it?* Smoking pot had been for survival, not fun, but he hadn't smoked since Christmas, with the exception of the day Abercrombie had died, so he was no longer sure any of that was true. More recently some of his thoughts had bordered on a religious experience. He thought about life and death and shuddered and missed a chord on his guitar.

Then there was Roscoe. Roscoe had been his best friend back in the World. He sang quietly, "Here I am in Vietnam," then went silent. *People trying to kill me every day and people around me getting killed, but back in the World where it's supposed to be safe, Roscoe's dead... murdered.* Roscoe's death hammered home the fragile nature of life, because Roscoe was so real. He was someone Hayes cared about and would miss for the rest of his life. Same with Lemaire. He would think about the others too, but Roscoe was supposed to have been safe.

And Roscoe had been more than just a friend. He had been Hayes' mentor, his future. He had thought a lot about him and Roscoe and Gloria playing together in a band. He'd never experienced a better or more natural musical fit. They'd clicked from that very first set in the blind pig. They were going to be a great band and Hayes was sure Roscoe and Gloria both sensed it too. He even thought about Roscoe's mother and wondered what would happen to her now. He had quietly cried for Roscoe, and for the big hole in his own heart that had opened.

Hayes pondered the nature of love. He was sure now that he loved Gloria, was surer of it every day when he woke up. With his band, he'd been wearing peace symbols and singing about love over a loud blare of guitars and drums, but it was all an act. The only things he and the band really cared about were getting paid and getting laid. Maybe that lack of sincerity was why his songs were so mediocre. Now he was in the middle of a war, and suddenly he cared for someone.

The 99th Assault Helicopter Company was full of violent men, some of them people he might have avoided in civilian life. Except, in civilian life, they were probably not much different from him. He cared about them, was willing to die for them, and they would do the same for him. *Isn't that a form of love? In fact, it must be a pretty high kind of love. Love....* He longed for Gloria. They hadn't even had two weeks and he had received only half a dozen letters from her. Was she okay? He knew so little about her. She played her guitar and she sang. Sang more than spoke. The songs they wrote together were magical, better by far than anything he had created by himself. He knew that her mother was dead and her father beat her. The memory of the marks he'd seen on her buttocks in the motel flashed into his mind. *Why didn't I ask her more about them?*

"I wish I knew who I was," she had whispered late their last night together as she clung to him. "I wish I knew where I came from."

"I wish I knew more about you too, Sunshine," he'd murmured. But he had been too consumed by lust to spend the time it took to get her to talk to him. And now he was scared shitless for a girl whose stepfather had whipped her hard enough to leave scars.

Off in the distance a helicopter lazily settled onto the side of the runway by the Operations Bunker. It was the courier from Long Binh and Cu Chi. A deuce-and-a-half was bouncing across the rough surface as someone got out of the courier. Then Sypher got out of the truck. The first sergeant began waving at the helicopter until the person who had gotten out dragged a duffel bag toward the truck and got in the back. The truck slowly turned around and started heading toward Hayes.

"Ahh shit, here comes the first sergeant again." He put down his guitar and lit a cigarette.

Rivera walked around the tail and looked. "What's the bastard want now?"

Like Hayes, Rivera had taken off his jungle fatigue shirt. Both of them put them back on, as well as their flak jackets.

The truck rolled to a stop about 20 feet away. There was a large black soldier in the back. He was just about the darkest-skinned black Hayes had ever seen. Then he remembered him from when he'd been sent to Long Binh Jail a month ago. He tried to remember the guy's name, but couldn't. He had only been with the company for a couple of days.

The soldier picked up a piece of rotten fruit from the truck bed and threw it away. "Place still stink," he said.

Sypher shouted, "Then get the hell out of the truck, dumbass!" Sypher unsnapped the flap of the holster.

The black soldier, looking startled, jumped out of the back of the truck dragging his duffel bag.

"Slobbo, get these shitbirds into some kind of formation," the first sergeant said.

Slobojan climbed out of the driver's seat.

Hayes was amazed at all of the gear he was wearing. He started to laugh, but stopped when he saw the concerned look on Rivera's face.

"Awright you guys," said Slobbo. "Let's see. Ah, form up on Rivera here."

Hayes, Rivera and the black guy, all grumbling loudly and guided lethargically by Slobbo, slowly formed a rudimentary line.

"Hey what's up, Slobbo? One hand grenade'll get us all," Hayes said.

"Shut up, Hayes," the first sergeant said.

"Certainly, First Sergeant. Need another cigarette?" Hayes said, still smiling, but his smile disappeared as irritation built in Sypher's face, one hand resting on the butt of his pistol.

"Hayes, your fuckin' college brain don't work no more, so keep your fuckin' mouth shut."

"Yes, Fir—"

"Shut the fuck up!" he snapped. "Slobbo, call these men to attention. I want to address them."

"Uhh, okay," said Slobbo. He looked confused for a second and uncomfortable. Then he shouted, "Ten *hut*!"

Simultaneous with the command, he farted. The men snapped to attention, more or less in unison.

A sickly sweet and very rank sulfurous odor assailed Hayes' nostrils and he jerked slightly, trying to contain the laugh that was building. His eyes started watering from the combined suppressed mirth and the smell. The odor hit Rivera too because he stifled a small high-pitched gasping cough.

Sypher looked at the two of them and then glared at Slobojan. "God almighty," he said, standing like he was paralyzed.

Finally, he walked in front of them and began inspecting each of the men. He stopped first in front of the new soldier who, to his credit, seemed oblivious to the fumes. When he spoke to him, he again rested one hand on the butt of his pistol. "You're lookin' pretty good, Private Roy. You might have gained some weight. They have lots of cold milk at Long Binh Jail?"

Roy made no movement to indicate that he had even heard the first sergeant. He was big and strong but everyone thought he was dumber than a post, though he was supposed to be a mechanic. He remained stock still as the first sergeant stared at him.

Roy, Rufus Roy... that's his name, Hayes thought. He recalled that the trouble had started when Roy had complained when the mess hall ran out of cold milk. A few days after he'd arrived, Roy had worked all day out in the heat helping build a bunker by the maintenance shed. He got to the mess hall just as the cold milk ran out. The first sergeant, who had put him on the bunker-building detail, had been calling him a doofus and a dumbass and Rufus had snapped. He grabbed an M60 machinegun from a passing door gunner and fired it into the empty cooler where the cold milk had been. He didn't hit anyone, but the tantrum had cost him four weeks in Long Binh Jail.

The first sergeant moved on to Rivera. "Specialist Rivera, you have a stain on your uniform," Sypher spat. "Looks like it might have come out of your mouth. Better get that cleaned. The VC see puke on you, they'll figure out that you don't have any goddamn balls."

Rivera didn't give Sypher the satisfaction of a reaction.

Then Sypher was in front of Hayes. Hayes tried to look him in the eye, but the first sergeant was looking at Hayes' neck. Sypher reached for the peace symbol hanging around Hayes' neck. "College boy, I want to know: What's the meaning of this shit?"

"Peace, love and firepower, First Ser—"

"Shut up, Hayes." Sypher ripped off the peace symbol. Then he grabbed the purple-tinted glasses and dropped them on the ground. "And these aren't part of the uniform of the day which, as I recall from eighteen fuckin' years in this fuckin' Army, has never included any fuckin' purple clothing. Get rid of the damn T-shirt!"

Sypher crunched the glasses with his boot and it was like Hayes had been kicked. He loved those glasses; they were from back in the World, and the last link to his hippie persona.

"Until further notice, you shitbirds are 24-hour-a-day guards, and you will live in Bunker Three. Sergeant Slobbo here is in charge." He focused on Hayes again. "Hayes, I suggest you have a long talk with Private Rufus Roy here. Find out all you can about Long Binh Jail, 'cause you're gonna be there real soon." He paused for a few seconds, thinking. "How long'd you go to college?"

"Two years, First Sergeant." That was a lie, the same one he'd told when he first entered the Army, and he wasn't about to own up to it now.

"That where you learned how to smoke narcotics? Or did you teach it?" Sypher scratched his chin.

Hayes decided that the first sergeant must be genuinely interested. "Marijuana isn't a narcotic, First Sergeant."

"That so?"

Rivera kicked Hayes as a warning, but Hayes plunged ahead. "I believe so, First Sergeant. Marijuana's milder than beer. Whiskey will mess you up a hell of a lot more."

Sypher paced back and forth. "Think you're real smart don't you? Well, we'll find out how smart you are after I enroll you in the university of Long Binh Jail. Tough fuckin' school." He glanced at Rufus Roy. "Ain't that right, Private Roy?"

Private Roy continued to stare straight ahead.

Hayes said, "What am I charged with?" He was beginning to think jail might not be so bad.

"Don't worry, I'll let you know soon enough. Meanwhile, you're part of this guard detail." Sypher looked at Rivera. "You've got what, a week left in-country? You don't want to fly, so you can be a bunker guard."

"Okay by me, First Sergeant."

"Just don't talk anymore of that beaner lingo around me."

"You got it, First Sergeant. No Spanish."

"And if I catch you with an unauthorized gun, I'll court martial you," Sypher said, once again resting his hand on the .45. "Understand?"

"Oh, I understand, First Sergeant. Guns are very dangerous. They kill people. You aim the gun at the somebody you want to kill, you pull the trigger and boom, they're gone. I know all about that, First Sergeant. I shot a bunch of VC dead earlier today." Rivera was smiling, staring right into Sypher's eyes. "Felt good too."

The two of them were nose to nose for several seconds. Slowly Sypher's face was overcome by the power in Rivera and he looked away. Hayes believed Rivera was stronger mentally than anyone he had ever known. He was certainly stronger than the first sergeant. Sypher backed away from Rivera and moved back to Roy.

"Private E-1 Rufus Roy, you must already know that I'm not bullshittin' about court martials. Tell me, how was Long Binh Jail?"

Roy remained motionless.

"At a loss for words, huh? Well ol' Rufus, you and me don't get along. The main reason I'm putting you out here is because this is as far away from me that I can put you. And the only reason you're back here at the 99th is that no one else will take your sorry ass. You know what that makes you?"

Roy blinked and his eyes momentarily shifted to Sypher and then back to the horizon.

"Means you're the worst piece of garbage in all of Three Corps, maybe all of Vietnam. And they had to stick me with you." Sypher finally moved away from Roy and approached Slobojan.

"Slobbo!

"Yes, First Sergeant."

"I want to make damn sure that if Rufus the Doofus here has a weapon in his hands, it's pointed away from the company area. If he tries to come into the company area with a weapon, you are authorized to shoot him," Sypher said.

"Shoot him... yes, First Sergeant."

"Slobbo, you are the sorriest excuse for a sergeant that I've ever seen. Somehow, you have achieved the rank of sergeant E-5. That means you should at least be able to take charge of one miserable bunker. Get this fuckin' place in shape. You're experienced in working with garbage. Remember what I told you about that major."

Slobojan looked a little puzzled and a little frightened and very uncomfortable. He put a hand by his crotch like his balls were itchy and he was going to try to surreptitiously give them a scratch. "Ah, First Sergeant?"

The first sergeant sighed. "What, Slobbo?"

"Rufus here is gonna need a rifle, and I don't think this bunker has much ammo in it. And what about chow, and showers, and changing clothes and stuff like that?"

Hayes thought they were good questions but the first sergeant was exasperated.

"Slobbo, you're supposed to be a goddamn sergeant. See to the welfare of your men. Take some fuckin' responsibility for once in your miserable fuckin' life. That's your fuckin' problem, not mine."

1615 Hours

Back in the Orderly Room, Sypher was feeling better than he had felt all day, better than he'd felt for weeks. He settled himself in his chair, slid open the desk drawer and knocked back a generous celebratory slug of his good friend Jack. He belched softly, savoring the pungent Jack Daniels fragrance that bubbled through his nose and mouth. He picked up the phone and was miraculously able to get through to Top in less than 30 seconds, although the connection was still howling with static.

"I got it all under my thumb, Top," he said when McAlister came on the line. "Under my fuckin' thumb. Took all the rotten eggs and stuck 'em in one basket, is what I did. Even ole Rufus is gonna like it 'cause he gets to play with a machinegun, though it's kind'a rusty. Ha!"

"That's good, Jubal, that's real good," McAlister said, his voice sounding like it was echoing off the walls of the Grand Canyon.

"And, Top, the court martials are gonna flow like the enlisted men's pissers on free beer night. When I put a certain PFC Hayes in Long Binh Jail, the Mary Jane business may go belly up from a lack a'customers."

"That's real good, Jubal, real good, though it doesn't matter now. Listen up. You're gonna love this. I got a slot for you that you won't believe. It's gonna be better than Saigon in '66.

"Tell me about it," Sypher said, suddenly excited. He awkwardly adjusted himself in his seat so he could snake his fingers down the front of his pants and scratch his sweaty balls.

"We're gonna clean up, Jubal. We're getting' into the drug business."

Disturbed, Sypher stopped his scratching. He withdrew his hand from his pants and scratched his head. "What the hell? Mary Jane? Fuckin' narcotics? I dunno 'bout that, Top. First you want me to court martial the bastards and then you want to get into the business? Jesus Christ... I mean, are you sure you know what you're doing?"

"Jubal, Jubal...." Bursts of static were drowning him out and then his voice was back on more clearly. "This stuff is very profitable... off in the future, and don't worry.... For now, I'm talking about real drugs. Pharmaceuticals. Hospital supplies. You know how valuable that stuff is in a war?"

"You mean pen'cillin, shit like that?" Sypher smiled and started picking his nose. His left nostril was loaded.

"That's it exactly, Jubal, and when you get to the 24th Evac, you and I are gonna start getting rich."

"The 24th Evac?"

"Yeah, it's the main evacuation hospital for Three Corps. You're gonna be in charge of supplies, though you'll have to keep a few officers in line."

"Can do," Sypher said, wiping his fingers on the back of his lower pant leg. He examined his fingers and started straightening up the papers on his desk. "Where is it?"

"Long Binh. Nice and close to Saigon, and there's gonna be some TDY in Japan too. You and me's gonna have to do some coordinatin' over there. And I've lined up a good supply of drugs comin' in from the States. Way more than you could ever divert from the hospital. I'll need your help with that too. You're gonna walk point on that one."

"Okay, Top. You're too good to me... too fuckin' good."

"Same split we had in Saigon," McAlister said. "A third of every dollar you make after it's converted to U.S. currency."

"Top, you're beautiful. You know you can depend on me."

"That's why I'm pulling major strings to get you there."

"And I 'preciate it," Sypher said.

A long burst of static drowned out the beginning of McAlister's next sentence. "...briefing half-hour ago. Said there might be some serious shit tonight. You sure you're gonna be okay? Don't get yourself hurt just when we're ready to go to the bank."

"It's all bullshit for the fuckin' press. We got a dolt for a colonel out here, thinks we're gonna get hit every other night. He's got us runnin' around like grunts, all dressed up for the big time. I keep my fuckin' ear to the ground. What this is, is a gook holiday. All the gooks have gone home. They ain't gonna do shit. They're too busy chasin' the fuckin' ghosts away with firecrackers. They call it Tet or somethin'. It's kind'a like New Year's Eve, 'cept they eat dogs and don't drink any fuckin' champagne."

There was a long pause and Sypher thought the connection had eroded so badly that he could no longer hear McAllister. Then the sergeant major's voice came on, echoing and phasing electronically like he was speaking in a wind tunnel. "Jubal, you're a piece of work, but be careful will ya?"

1720 Hours

Bunker Three was built out of martial matting, the same steel sheets used for the runways, plus sandbags and railway tie timbers. The walls were solid although monsoon rains had caused the sandbags to settle somewhat. A few of them had broken open. The dirt floor inside was littered with old, flattened air mattresses, empty ammo boxes, empty C ration tins, an ancient lawn chair and a single dusty folding cot. There was a firing port at the front of the bunker with an M60 machinegun on a platform of sandbags and boards. Three detonators hung by wires that led out through the firing port. A couple of field phones, one of them unconnected, lay on the floor. The inside of the bunker was almost completely dark. Only a small amount of gloomy light penetrated through the firing port and the entry in the rear, which was in the form of a hollow L to stop any shrapnel entering from explosions outside. It smelled dank and musty with a locker-room stench of old dirty sweat socks. Rivera and Slobojan were examining the machinegun with a flashlight

Rivera said, "Wow... I wonder if the fucker'll even fire?"

"Probably not now. Think we can we fix it?" asked Slobojan.

Rivera racked the bolt of the machinegun and blew into the receiver. "It's rusty and full of dirt. Bet it hasn't been cleaned for weeks. I'll get Hayes to strip and clean it. He's real good with them. There's less than half a box of ammo for it though. And the ammo's dirty too."

"Yeah, well, there's hardly been anyone on guard out here," Slobojan said.

Rivera took one of the clackers that detonated the mines and held the flashlight on it. "Think these are still attached to anything?"

"Squeeze them if you want to find out. I don't know if anything will happen. I wouldn't put it past Sypher to sell claymores to the VC. Anything for a buck."

"You kidding?" Rivera flew every day and paid little attention to what happened on the ground in the company. He had no friends outside of the Headhunters, even in the other flight platoons.

"Why do you think the chow has gotten so bad? Sypher and Horton are selling half our food in the village. I know they sell a lot of C rations there. One of the villagers told me."

"Son of a bitch! Must be why we're always having trouble coming up with Cs for lunch when we're flying. Half the time we're borrowing from the grunts or some other unit. Sometimes we don't eat. Word gets around about this, Sypher's likely to get blown away."

"Now who's kidding." Slobojan chuckled. He felt a little guilty about giving a case of C rations to Lily the whore, but only a little.

"Not me," said Rivera. "I almost blew him away this afternoon. Truly. Scares me that I came that close. I mean, it would have been so easy to do. Another week, I'm going home, so I got to stop that kind of shit. I mean, killing people isn't what normal people do back in the World, right?

"You would have killed Sypher?" Slobojan said, incredulous.

"In the blink of an eye. Bang!" said Rivera with a smile, but he wasn't sure he was serious.

"Jesus. That bastard told me about it, but I didn't believe him," Slobojan said. "He wants to court martial you."

Rivera shook his head. "Maybe I should have killed him,"

"He's gonna court martial Hayes for sure, or at least he's gonna try. He wants me to help him do it."

"So what are you gonna do?"

"Nothing. He doesn't need my help. I should have made staff sergeant by now, but he's persuaded the CO to hold it up for no reason at all. Maybe it was because he didn't want me inside the Senior NCO Club but he says it was because I got the clap, and I guess I did. Half those lifers are working black market angles. Well, maybe not half of them. Reyes and a few others are okay."

"Well, you re-upped," said Rivera smiling. "You're a lifer now."

"I guess I am. I want to stay in. There's nothing for me back home. I got two brothers and three sisters. My folks have a farm back in Iowa, but I hate farming. My brothers can have that life. I was in ROTC for a while in high school. Best shot on the rifle club too. I figure if I stay in the Green Machine, I can go to some tech schools, maybe even college, and the Army'll pay for it. I've thought of going to OCS, to become an officer, but I got this weight problem. Anyway, if I get twenty years in, I'll be thirty-eight with a nice pension, some education and experience. And most of the time it isn't such a bad life."

"Oh yeah, great experience," said Rivera. "With my experience, maybe I can be a hit man when I get home. Shit, I don't know what I'm gonna do."

"How long have you been here?"

"Twenty-two months, eighteen days, and...." He shone the flashlight on his watch. "About nine hours. But I been in the Army a little longer."

"Jesus! How come so long?"

"Well, you go home with less than a hundred and fifty days to serve, they just let you out. So I've spent almost an extra year in Vietnam to get that drop. A goddamn lifer screwed me when I was out humpin' the boonies. See, I came over here as a grunt. I thought I was signing a paper to extend three months in Vietnam in the rear. Fuckin' bush, I hated it. Ended up, I extended my enlistment in the goddamn Army for a fucking year. Same guy in personnel did it to four other guys in my company. He's dead now. Got French kissed by a Claymore one night when the bastard got up to take a leak. Somebody set it up with a trip wire right in front of the latrine he used. Fucker got smashed every night and always got up to take a leak so he was definitely the target. Blew both him and the latrine away. I'm sure one of those four guys did it. Maybe all of 'em. Shit, if I'd thought of it, I might have done it. Some night, Sypher the Lifer could get his too."

Slobojan hefted the machinegun off of its platform and looked through the port into the twilight. "So you were in the bush, huh? Tell me, if you were Charlie and you wanted to attack Nui Binh, how would you do it?"

"Hell, I don't know," said Rivera thinking about it. It had been a long time since he'd been in the bush and when he was out there, he'd never had to attack a VC camp. Most of the time, they seemed to wander through the jungle in a futile attempt to find the VC or to block VC fleeing from some other wandering unit. Sometimes they set up for ambushes. It was a challenging problem, but Rivera had a good sense of the layout of Nui Binh and the adjacent village, having flown over it every day for more than a year.

"Guess I'd try to take out one of these bunkers. Try to do it quick as possible before anybody could react. Get a whole bunch of people in here and kick the crap out of Nui Binh. Use satchel charges on the hootches and bunkers. I'd do that first, before blowing up the other stuff. Then I'd blow up the POL. When that jet fuel goes up it'll make a nice blaze. Then I'd blow up as many of our ships as I could and kill as many Americans as I could. You gotta figure the dinks know the layout of the camp. Probably got beaucoup spies in here. Getting in would be the hard part."

"Okay, but what bunker would you go after?" asked Slobojan.

"Well, this one's a pretty sorry-ass excuse for a bunker," said Rivera.

"Yeah, but you gotta figure the dinks, spies and all, probably don't know that. They know the layout of the camp and where everybody is, but none of the Vietnamese workers get to look inside the bunkers and they don't get very close to them. And all the dinks are out of the base camp by the time guards are posted," Slobojan said.

Rivera nodded. "Sounds like you already got it figured out."

"Yeah, maybe. Let me show you the way I think it could happen since I'm now sergeant of the guard. Let's go outside."

Rivera followed Slobojan through the doorway. He looked around and noted the long shadows. The light had started waning in just the few minutes the two had been inside the bunker. Rivera had gotten used to the sudden sunsets and sunrises, which, while short-lived, were often spectacular. Another thing he'd miss. Slobojan began climbing up a crude two by four ladder leaning against the back of the bunker. As he went up the ladder, he seemed to stumble and he groaned.

"You okay, Slobbo?"

"Yeah, yeah... give me a second." He sounded like he was in pain.

"What's the matter?"

"Got a bad dose of the clap or something," Slobojan said. "Doc stuck me with one of his horse needles this morning, but he wasn't sure if that was gonna do the trick."

"Jesus Slobbo, that doesn't sound so good."

"I know it. Doc wanted to send me to 24th Evac, but if I go there, Sypher'll probably get the CO to give me an article fifteen for sure. Said he'd send me to Long Binh Jail next time I got VD."

"Shit, I got the clap once in Saigon back when I was a grunt. Where the hell you been getting the clap, Slobbo?"

"Out at the dump," Slobojan said without offering further explanation.

Rivera wanted to know more. "There's whores at the dump? Jesus Christ."

"Well, there's some people living out there, including at least one whore," Slobojan said. "I mean, she's pretty and all you have to do for a short time is give her a pack a'cigarettes or some C rations. Actually, there's a couple of dozen people living out there, maybe more. Pretty damn sad, if you ask me."

"Great," said Rivera sarcastically. "Bet guys are just lined up for a garbage dump whore."

Slobojan hung his head a little and looked upset. "After the last time I got the clap, I wasn't gonna do that anymore. But I have to dump garbage every day and... well, that girl Lily likes me." He paused for a second. Rivera sensed a different kind of pain in his voice now. "Nobody else around here likes me. Not really. This gal Lily, she's real cute, and she says she's my girlfriend. I know it's bullshit. She usually doesn't charge me anything, though I give her some food and stuff. Okay, I kind'a like her too. Not her fault she has to be a whore. She ain't got much family left or anything. They mostly been killed, and by the VC too. She hates the VC." Slobojan straightened up and finished his climb. Rivera followed him and the two of them sat down on the roof. There was already some gloom at the edge of the village.

"I'm okay now," Slobojan said. "Let me tell you what I think the dinks are gonna do if they attack Nui Binh. You probably know this better than me 'cause you fly over it every day." He pointed. "Look at the village and the trees there. That's the closest the bunker line at Nui Binh Base Camp comes to the village. This is the least-open area in the whole damn bunker line. See the damn brush out there? Nothing grows in the first 75 yards or so. They dumped defoliant on that. But as soon as you get past that there's a lot of brush.

"Defoliant?" asked Rivera.

"Yeah, weed killer. Plants turn orange and die. Stay away from that shit. I know a couple of guys used to work with it and they got sick. Got evacked to Japan."

"Oh yeah," Rivera said. "Agent Orange is what we called it, but I thought it was because of the orange markings on the containers. You know, they're gonna evac *your* ass to Japan, you keep screwing Lily the dump whore."

"Yeah, you're probably right," Slobojan said. "Wish I could get her fixed up by the medics." He stopped and got out a cigarette, offered one to Rivera, and then lit them both. "Anyway, you can go all along the Nui Binh perimeter, look at every bunker and you won't find another place where the brush is closer than here. And it's closer by a lot, too. It's good concealment. Goes right up to the edge of the village. Most of the other units go out and cut it down, but not the 99th," Slobojan said. "Tomorrow, I think we should start cutting it if we're gonna be out here. And another thing, this damn bunker wasn't placed correctly. There's no bunker on that side," Slobojan said pointing to the left. "Just the front gate, and that's back from us. Then the bunker on the other side is too far away, and it's pointed too much to the right. I'll bet they can't see us very well and it would be hard to fire this way from their firing port."

They both smoked their cigarettes for a minute. Rivera remembered when he'd been in the bush as a grunt. When they dug in at night they placed fighting holes so they had interlocking fields of fire. It made sense that you would do the same thing with a base camp. Slobojan was right.

"There's too much confusion. Every unit in the base camp is responsible for one or more bunkers and every leader has his own ideas. Sypher's pissed at some major who's on his ass about how many people are on guard. He basically ordered me to lie about it. That major's likely to show up tonight, but I wonder if he or anyone else ever looks at the whole thing in daylight." He turned around and gestured at the base camp. "And then, look back there."

Rivera turned and looked off the rear side of the bunker. Hayes was there with his guitar, but not Roy. The crashed helicopter was facing the bunker almost directly. POL was behind the helicopter, the deep black rubber tanks of JP4 fuel looked ominous in the gathering darkness.

"This bunker's just a hop, skip and a jump from POL," Slobojan said. "And our revetments with the helicopters aren't much farther."

He's right, Rivera thought. He shivered and shook his head. "Jesus Christ."

"So if I was gonna hit this place, this is where I'd do it. I mean, it's so obvious, you'd think they'd reinforce this damn bunker, or even move it. Maybe that's why the major wants more men in it."

"You ought'a be a goddamn officer, Slobbo," Rivera said, and he meant it. "Lose some weight and stay away from whores."

"I wouldn't mind just being an E-6."

1655 Hours

Hayes and Rufus Roy were sitting in the doorway of the crashed gunship. Hayes had put down his guitar. He wasn't sure what to make of the big black man. All he knew was his name was Rufus Roy and he had been sent to LBJ for shooting up the mess hall. The guy was massive. His arms were as big as Hayes' thighs and he was well over six feet tall. Hayes thought he must run close to 250 pounds, and unlike Slobojan, it didn't appear that much of his bulk was fat. *Too big to fly,* Hayes figured. *Be like flying with two door gunners on one side.* Hayes picked up one of the two machineguns from the floor of the helicopter. He was thinking that he really should take them back to the armament hut, but he wasn't going to do it unless someone complained. And to do that, they'd have to find him first.

"Lemme show you how to clean a sixty," Hayes said.

"Sixty?"

"Yeah, a machinegun... an M60 machinegun." Hayes hoisted the weapon so it was at eye level. "This thing. Best goddamn weapon in the U.S. Army. Ain't that why that bastard Sypher sent you to LBJ?"

"So wha' 'tis LBJ?" His voice was expressive, almost like he was singing. It reminded Hayes a little of Gloria. "Me been Long Binh Jail. Boss mon sergeant be making me beaucoup angry. Me unhappy no cold milk in messing hall. Him making Rufus... what you say? Laffin' stock doofus nigra mon. Boss man wan' sen' you nex'. 'Tis bad 'ting him wan' do."

Hayes detached the ammo belt from the M60, put it back in, and took it out again. "This is easy. You just lift this cover up. See? There's a spring that holds the sucker up. Then you just plop the belt down. Lay it on the tray. The links go up, see?" Hayes fingers moved expertly as Roy watched closely. "If you leave one of the links empty, it's a little easier to get in position. But shit, it's easy anyway. Then you just snap the cover back down."

Hayes went through the whole procedure again. "Man, what kind'a accent you got? Like, it's bad, man."

"Wha' 'tis accent?" Roy asked. He reached out and touched the cover.

"Way you speak," Hayes said. "Man, you talk like some kind'a foreigner. To fire, you gotta take off the safety." He worked the safety and then let Roy do it. "Then all you gotta do is pull back on the bolt here, and you're ready to rock and roll." Hayes carefully removed the ammunition belt and ejected the chambered round.

"Me go USA... come from Haiti, mon, in a boat," Roy said. "Twelve, mebbe 'leven. But then, I live with Jamaicans."

"Cool, man. Sounds cool," Hayes said. "Grammar's like... fractured or something."

Hayes reached into the helicopter and picked up the other M60. He handed it to Roy. "We got to clean both these guns. I'll show you how. You just follow along with me and we'll have these suckers cleaned up in no time. M60's a real good weapon. Hardly ever jams. Some guys around here don't like cleaning 'em. But it only takes a couple of minutes. You ever get in a firefight and your gun jams, you're in a world of hurt."

"Wha' 'tis fractured?" asked Roy.

Hayes looked at him and smiled. "Means broken. But never mind. Ain't important. You have trouble understandin' folks?"

Hayes took the machinegun from Roy and removed a round from the chamber. "Gotta be careful. There was a round in the chamber."

Hayes held the bullet up in front of Roy's face. "Hold onto this. It's the only tool you'll need to take apart a sixty. How the hell did you get into the Army?"

"Judge seh me go Army or go t'corfew."

"Got busted, huh. What did you do?" Hayes picked up his M60 again. "Now watch this." He pulled back on the cocking lever and removed the operating rod. Roy watched intently and Hayes did it again.

"I shot boss mon, but no kill 'im. Him beated me wid gun stock."

Hayes shook his head. "Shit, it sounds like self-defense to me. They should'a let you off." Hayes started breaking the M60 down further. "See this little doohickey here? That's the firing pin. Hold on to it. You gotta be careful you don't let this thing in here fall out. You know, you seem to catch on pretty fast."

This time Roy smiled and Hayes saw that he had perfect, incredibly white teeth.

"Always wan' go t'school, mon. Can fix lots 'tings. See one time, can do. But no can read."

Hayes was incredulous. "You can't fucking read? You never went to school, even kindergarten?"

"Wha' 'tis kindergarten?" asked Roy.

Hayes noticed that he pronounced it perfectly.

"Me have no schoolin' in Haiti. No momma, no poppa. Live wid many peoples 'til I runned way to other side of the island and then to USA. Wan' mek beaucoup money. Me read own name. An' can write name Rufus Roy." He pronounced Roy, Wah. "Mos' peoples seh 'Roy,' like famous Rogers movie cowboy."

"Wah," Hayes said. "Wah."

Roy nodded enthusiastically, and Hayes turned his attention back to the machinegun. He started to remove the trigger assembly. "Watch this now. I'm gonna take out the trigger assembly. You try it too."

Hayes completed taking the trigger assembly out and then watched Roy do the same thing. "That's fucking amazing. I didn't learn that fast. You're supposed to be dumber than a stump, Rufus—Rufus the Doofus—but you ain't."

"Me be likin' gun machines," Roy said, his teeth glinting in the waning sunlight.

Hayes laid the weapon on his lap. "Next step is to take the barrel out. Like this, see?"

Roy took the barrel out of his gun.

"You can strip it down more, but this is further than you have to go when you're in a hurry anyway," Hayes said. "Now, we just clean up all these parts."

For several minutes the two of them cleaned the two weapons and reassembled them, Hayes watching Roy closely. Then Hayes went to the bunker and got that machinegun. He took it to the helicopter and let Roy clean it by himself. Hayes didn't have to correct anything, but he took some of the parts and scrubbed off dirt. He tried to scrape off the rust.

When they were done, the two climbed out of the helicopter and Hayes showed Roy one of the miniguns on the skid. "This here is the XM21 armament system."

"Wha' 'tis dat?"

"This one's a piece of shit is what it is. It's fucked up, man. Supposed to be a flex gun. Supposed to traverse, you know, go left and right, move up and down, but it keeps breakin' down. So I got them fixed in place for now, 'till we get some parts that work."

Roy bent over the minigun to look at it more closely "Dis look like six guns."

"Well, sort of." Hayes snickered. "See, they rotate. This sucker can pump out four thousand rounds a minute. That's sixty-six and two-thirds bullets every second.

"Hoooooeee! Shoot fast!" Roy said.

"Oh yeah. At night, the goddamn tracers look like a horse pissin' flames. Sounds like a great big fucking chain saw goin' through steel."

Hayes walked back to the helicopter and sat down on the deck, thinking he wanted to smoke a joint. Instead, he took out a cigarette and offered one to Roy, who took it and held it up and examined it. "No money, no cigarettes at Long Binh Jail."

"So you didn't much like Long Binh Jail, huh?" he said, fumbling for his cigarette lighter. He found it, lit his cigarette and lit Roy's.

"No, mon. 'Tis very bad place," Rufus said, inhaling deeply.

"Got any fuckin' VC shootin' at you in there?"

Rufus shook his head as he held the smoke in his lungs.

"Anybody gettin' smashed to mush in helicopter crashes?"

"No mon," he answered, smoke dribbling out his mouth and nose.

"You get your three squares every day?" Hayes asked as he watched Rufus inhaling the cigarette smoke like he was in a race. He looked like someone smoking a joint.

"Wha' 'tis squares?" Rufus emitted a cloud of smoke.

"You know, food. Did they feed you in Long Binh Jail?"

"Yes, mon," Rufus said enthusiastically in another cloud of smoke. "Is better than dis place."

"Well, there it is. Right on. Why should I fight it? If I gotta be in a fuckin' war in this dirtball country, I might as well be in Long Binh Jail. I mean, I don't care that much if I'm behind bars as long as I ain't gonna get my butt erased from the face of the earth and I don't starve. I mean, time is time, and I got six months to go. Might as well spend it there. Probably safer than here, anyway."

Rufus listened intently. He had smoked the cigarette down to a nub that was less than a quarter-inch. He dropped it on the ground. "No count. No counting da time in dat place."

"Whaddya mean, no count?" asked Hayes.

"Time in Long Binh Jail, no be countin'," Rufus said. "'Tis bad place. You no be countin' down to DEROS time while you in dat bad place. You still be havin' duh six months to go when you get out."

Hayes deciphered that and let it sink in. "Oh shit. I'm fucked."

1730 Hours

Hayes was sitting against the wall of the bunker beside the door. Rufus was on the roof trying to see the first visible stars. Hayes wanted to get stoned but the prospect of Long Binh Jail was looming larger. He didn't see how the first sergeant had any grounds to court martial him for any offense, yet he was sure it would happen.

As far as he was concerned, there was just about zero chance they would be attacked. Slobojan had gone to get them some chow and other supplies. Rivera had gone back to the company to take a shower. So Hayes was sitting with a rag rubbing the M60 that had been inside the bunker.

"I think this sucker might work," he told Rufus. "I'm thinking we should maybe fire a burst into the ground just to see."

Rufus looked at him, and then at the machinegun. Hayes could see he wanted to fire it. But Hayes could also see that they both could get in trouble.

"Operations would probably be pissed," Hayes said, thinking more about it. *Fuck it. We need to see if the gun works.* "Let 'em be pissed. They can kiss my rosy red ass. If they give a shit about us, they can fix the fuckin' field phone or give us a prick 25. There used to be one out here. Everyone knows the fucking field phone doesn't work half the time anyway."

Hayes began to put a belt in the machinegun. "Hey Rufus, come over here and do your thing," he said. "Man, you learned to strip 'n clean a sixty faster than anyone I've ever seen. You're fuckin' hell on wheels with a machinegun."

Rufus hopped off the roof and landed lightly on his feet beside Hayes. "Wha' 'tis hoppening, mon?"

"Sorry man. We ought to test this fucking gun. Thought you might like to try it. Just fire a burst into the ground about 20 feet out that way," Hayes said. He handed the machinegun and the belt of ammunition to Rufus.

A grin spread across Rufus' face. He slowly ran his fingers down the ammo belt. "Hokay. Like shootin'," he said. Quickly, Rufus flipped it open, dropped the belt on the receiver and racked a round into the chamber.

"Hold on a second, Bro'," Hayes said grabbing the gun. "It feeds better if you can keep the weight of the belt from dragging it down."

Hayes took the gun and showed him how to hold the ammunition belt. He wasn't sure Rufus would actually fire, especially since he'd just spent a month in jail for firing a machinegun. "We can feed it over a C rat can if Slobbo ever gets back with chow. Shit, there's probably a dirty one in the bunker, and it'll clamp right in there."

Hayes handed the M60 back to Rufus, then pointed. "Aim for that clump of dirt there. Let's see how good you are."

Rufus held the belt with his left hand and without hesitation fired a burst into the clump of dirt.

Hayes grabbed him to stop the firing.

"Ooooooeeee!" shouted Rufus.

"Good aim, Rufus," laughed Hayes.

"'Tis a fun 'ting, shootin' a sixty," Rufus said, his grin almost wider than his face.

Another machinegun began firing from the next bunker in the line followed quickly by another, and then by many other automatic weapons. Lines of tracers starkly visible in the gathering gloom streaked through the air. There were flashes and booms from heavier weapons too. The entire bunker line had erupted in an awesome display of firepower. A parachute flare popped in the sky though it was hardly dark enough to be needed.

Rufus raised the machinegun again and fired a burst, cut short when the weapon jammed.

Hayes screamed above the din of shooting, "We haven't got enough ammo for this crap!" The two of them looked at the dull orange tracers flying away from the bunker line. Almost as quickly as it began, the shooting subsided. As the shooting died down, a siren wailed in the distance. The parachute flare slowly drifted to the ground, illuminating the two soldiers in flickering light.

"I think we're gonna hear something about this," Hayes said. "Uh oh, here comes Slobbo." Hayes wrestled with the machinegun, trying to rack the jammed shell out of it. "It's all fucked up. It's probably the ammo," he said.

The two and a half ton truck with no headlights jolted slowly to a stop behind the bunker. The rumbling engine shut down and Slobojan jumped out and ran up to them, cocking his M16.

"Easy, Slobbo," Hayes said. "We were just testing this sixty."

"There's no attack?" he stammered.

"If somebody was attacking, would we be standing around out here jolly jacking and bullshitting?" asked Hayes. "If the fucking VC were attacking we'd be fucking dead by now."

"We're supposed to get clearance before firing," Slobojan said. He eased the cocking hammer down on his M16.

"How the hell we supposed to get fuckin' clearance?" Hayes said. "There's no fuckin' radio, the fuckin' field phones don't fuckin' work and it's a bit dark for goddamn semaphore."

"Semaphore?" asked Rivera who had also just appeared.

Slobojan snickered and shook his head. "Those sailors waving the flags on the ships," he said. "I learned it in Boy Scouts. Think operations could see me waving flags on top of the bunker?" He paused for a second. "I take it that the gun works."

"That is only semi-affirmative," Hayes said. "We've got two working machineguns from the gunship but this fucker jammed up. Probably dirty ammo."

Slobojan scratched his chin and thought for a few seconds, then snapped his fingers. "Got a letter for you, Hayes." He took an envelope out of his shirt pocket and handed it to Hayes, then turned his attention back to the machineguns. "We'll put one in the bunker and one on the roof. Rivera and Hayes on the roof, me and Rufus inside. We'll leave this one in the bunker as a spare. We don't have a good place to set it up or enough people to use it anyway. We'll split the good ammo half and half."

"Hokay," Rufus said. Rivera nodded. Hayes was holding his letter up to the fading light.

Rivera said, "Hayes and me got our M16s and you've got yours. And I've got my pistol. Did you get a rifle for Rufus?"

"No can do tonight. Couldn't find Reyes, and Horton's already drunk. Besides, Horton wouldn't release a weapon without Reyes' okay. Pisses me off... we could use another rifle."

"We need ammo for the machineguns more than anything," Rivera said. He indicated the heavy belt draped over his shoulders. "Got this from the armament hut, but that's all I could get. Hayes and me shot off a lot of bullets today, so we didn't get much from the ship. That ammo in the bunker looks cruddy. Hayes is right. That's got to be why that sixty jammed. If we don't count that, we've only got a couple hundred rounds for three guns. That's not much if we get into anything heavy."

Hayes stuffed his letter into his pocket. "I've got six magazines for my sixteen."

"Seven," Rivera said.

"I've got twenty five," Slobojan said.

For the second time, the sergeant impressed Rivera. It had taken him and Hayes some time to acquire the magazines for their M16s. Ammunition was normally issued in bandoleers and had to be loaded into the magazines. But the magazines fit nicely in the cotton bandoleers.

"Was there anything else in the bunker? Any more grenades? I've got four frags and a couple of smokes here," Slobojan said.

Rivera said, "Nothing but one flare."

"Shit, Slobbo. What good are you?" Hayes said. "Can't get a rifle for Rufus. Can't get a radio. Can't get any fuckin' ammo. Tell me, did you get us any chow or are we gonna starve to death before Charlie can shoot us."

"Chow? Of course, I got chow. Do I look like I'd let anybody starve? There's a couple of cases of Cs in the truck. I boosted them from Sypher's Jeep. They were probably headed for the village tomorrow. I got a cooler with cold sodas too, and some orange Kool-Aid. And Rufus, there's two quarts of cold milk in there."

1825 Hours

After drinking most of a quart of Courvoisier, the pleasantly high Walters and Comstock shuffled into the mess hall just as the cooks were closing it down.

Walters said, "Shit man, you gotta give us some chow. We got fuckin' shot down."

Apprehensively, Spec Four Brown looked at the two of them. He had to scoop half a dozen times before he got a few scraps of meat to go with the beef stew gravy and chunks of carrot and other unidentifiable vegetable matter. He found the remains of a loaf of bread.

"I was about to throw this shit out, so help yourselves. If you want more, get it now 'cause I'm closing this friggin' place down," Brown said.

Walters scooped more gravy into his bowl. Comstock took a can of beer out of his pocket and belched.

"There's a lot of mashed potatoes left," Brown said pointing to a pan "Didn't have any real potatoes to put in the stew, so we made mashed with the instant."

Walters went over and filled half a plate with a big mound of the mashed potatoes, which had the consistency and color of paste, and then drowned it with two scoops of the gravy.

"I'm hungry," he said as Comstock bent and sniffed the potatoes.

"Man, that Courvoisier is nice," said Comstock. "Never had it before. That was worth getting shot down."

Walters started to chuckle but belched instead. Then Major Lehman entered the mess hall. "Watch it," Walters whispered. "Here comes the XO."

The CO was now leading every mission because in addition to his poor flying, Lehman had demonstrated a knack for leading the 99th to disaster. A couple of days before he was about to lead them into a zone where they could have been hit by artillery. One of the platoon leaders had stopped them.

On the ground he was a stickler for running things by the book even when it led to problems. The difference was that on the ground, the problems usually couldn't kill anyone. It just pissed them off. But Lehman seemed oblivious to the low regard in which everyone held him. He adhered rigidly to all military courtesy protocols and seemed incapable of anger. He beamed a perpetual, eager friendliness, though he was quick to point out any sinful behavior that he noticed.

He smiled at Walters and Comstock as he approached their table. "Isn't the mess hall supposed to be closed?"

"We're just getting some chow to bring back to the hootch. We got shot down and missed supper," Walters said.

Lehman nodded. He seemed to be studying Walters' mashed potatoes. He could probably smell the Courvoisier, and Comstock's can of beer was on the table.

"Thought that was back in the afternoon, before the mess hall even opened," he said.

"Well, I don't know about you, Sir, but it took me some time to get rid of the adrenaline," Walters said. "I lost track of the fuckin' time, but Spec Four Brown still had some hot food left. Saves him from throwing it out."

Lehman nodded and seemed to be thinking about what to say. Walters figured Lehman was going to mention his profanity for he had recently begun a campaign against swearing, which was like trying to hold back Niagara Falls with a chain link fence.

Lehman finally looked at Comstock. "Aren't you officer of the guard?"

"Yes Sir, I am," Comstock replied, straightening his posture.

"You shouldn't drink on duty," said Lehman. "We're on red alert, and I understand chances of a ground attack are high."

"Well, we really were shaken up after that landing," Comstock said. "That was the first time I was ever under fire or experienced losing a tail rotor. I just had the one drink, Sir."

They both looked at the beer Comstock had placed on the table.

"Guess I'll pass on that beer too," he added.

Lehman nodded again and walked out of the mess hall.

Comstock chugged the beer.

2015 Hours

Rivera and Hayes scrabbled through the helicopter in the dark, looking for more ammunition. Rivera was trying to light a cigarette with a lighter that was out of fluid. He had been using it to illuminate the interior of the helicopter. He finally gave up but left the unlit cigarette in his mouth.

"Nothing. I think we got it all. Sometimes one of the pilots leaves a bandoleer up front. Nothing there though. Shit."

"Here," Hayes said, taking his lighter out of his pocket and lighting Rivera's cigarette.

"You been smoking any dope?" Rivera asked suspiciously.

"C'mon Rivera. We aren't flying and probably aren't gonna be flying tomorrow either. You're going home in a few days. Lighten up, you Cuban short timer. You're way too uptight. But no, I haven't smoked any since Christmas Eve, and I think I paid a high enough price for that."

"You don't tighten up some, Hayes, you might not go home," Rivera said evenly, not willing to let up.

"What do you mean? You want to help Sypher send me to LBJ?"

"No. I wouldn't do that. I'm talking about you getting your ass blown away. We get hit tonight, I don't want you stoned out of your mind."

"Hey, don't put me in a cage. A little weed just sharpens me up. But like I said, I haven't been smoking. I'm stone free! Besides, you know this red alert is bullshit. We aren't gonna get hit."

"I'm not so sure about that." Rivera leaned back against the pilots' compartment wall and began to scratch his belly. "You're a good gunner Hayes, especially for a stoner."

"I'm not a stoner, goddamn it!" Hayes snapped.

Rivera blinked and finally stopped. He swallowed air and nodded. "Sorry. I can't help it. Used to make me nervous to see you stoned all the time. I feel like you're getting ready to start again soon as I'm gone. One of these days it's gonna catch up with you. One mistake, just one little fucking mistake, and you can get your ass blown away."

Hayes thought for a long moment. "Hey, I don't get drunk and fly hung over like half of our pilots. I'm not poppin' the bennies like some guys are jacked up on. I never did anything stronger than marijuana. You know, I heard from a couple of grunts that a few of them have started smoking opium. That's just fucking crazy. I've smoked and I even dropped acid back in the World, but it didn't affect how I did my job 'cept to make it a little more fun. It kept me from lettin' this fuckin' war drive me nuts. What it does is it lets me put the bad shit somewhere else, somewhere behind a door that isn't gonna open till this bad fuckin' dream is over." Hayes closed his eyes and concentrated on thinking about the firefights he had been in, especially the first time. In his mind's eye, he saw the green tracers coming toward him, his orange-red tracers sailing back.

"The first time I took fire, when I was flying slicks, I wasn't stoned. I remember tracers comin' up on my side," he said. "Looked like fiery baseballs, even basketballs, almost beautiful, especially when they miss. I know it was a .51, but I didn't even know what a .51 was back then. I'd never seen anything like that before, but I always knew it was real, that it could kill me. I was scared shitless, but I was able to shove that aside. It's like the first time I played in front of a really big crowd, only a hundred times scarier. You just can't think about being scared and try to concentrate on what you do.

"But after it's over, when I'm back in Nui Binh, I couldn't be free from it unless I got high. I might have killed some of them that first time, and that bothered me too. And we lost White and McLean. Then I killed that ARVN, and I still think about him all the time. I've gotten stoned, and I'm sure I'll do it again, but I'm no stone killer. I wish I were. Thing that scares me the most is that someday I'm gonna have to open that door and let all that scary stuff out."

Rivera shook his head. "Again, I'm sorry. I'm just worried about you. We're on guard out here. It's like flying. We could get hit. It is going to happen one of these nights, and if we fuck up, we'll get killed. All of us. Hayes, you're okay, though sometimes I think Sypher might be right about your head not working. LBJ might be the ticket to keep you alive because I don't see how you can last another six months if you start getting stoned again. Sooner or later you're gonna fuck up."

Hayes smiled, leaned across the helicopter and re-lit Rivera's cigarette, which had gone out. "My head's workin' fine, Partner. Better than yours, I think, because I kept my brain lubricated."

"Thank you," Rivera said, relaxing a little and taking a drag on his cigarette.

"You're welcome, Specialist Rivera."

Neither said anything for several minutes. Then Rivera squeezed Hayes' arm, and flipped his cigarette butt away.

Hayes, sitting in the doorway of thc helicopter, looked at the night outside. The sky was clear and he could see a million stars. He let his vision wander across the sky. It was gorgeous and started him thinking again about getting stoned. Then he started thinking about Sypher. "I don't want to go to LBJ," Hayes said. "I'm just trying to get by the best I can. Jesus, you know the time you spend there doesn't even count as part of your tour?"

"Huh, I never thought about that," Rivera said. "Guess it makes sense."

"I didn't know it either. Rufus told me. Doesn't it worry you that Sypher said he was gonna put you in LBJ too?"

"No way," Rivera said. "No fucking way. First of all, I'm a Spec Five. Been here way too long. The CO would never let him do it, and a court martial or an Article 15 has to be signed by the CO. Shit, I'd go to Colonel Hobbs in brigade because he wouldn't let him do it either. Did you know that I crewed about a month for the colonel last fall? I doubt if Sypher could even get away with busting me a grade. He's just trying to blow smoke up my ass. But he's probably gonna try to get you. He's really got it in for you, and I don't know why."

Colonel Hobbs wasn't in their chain of command but he was a full bird colonel who knew Rivera. "It isn't fair," Hayes said. "It just isn't fuckin' fair. You know how I got here? Got my ass drafted is how. I had this great fuckin' band going. Universal Joint. Man, we were startin' to make a name for ourselves, psychedelic music. Shit, it was mostly surf music with bullshit love poetry, but don't tell anyone I said that. I was never actually enrolled at Michigan State. Just hung around sleepin' in my fuckin' car, stealin' food from the dorms, sneakin' into classes and crashin' on people's couches and floors. If I'd been enrolled, I'd have had a fuckin' draft deferment. I didn't try to get out of it. I didn't join the fuckin' National Guard. I didn't go to fuckin' Canada. Got relatives there too. I didn't pull some bullshit medical scam to flunk my physical." He paused for a second, scratching his head, and stood up. "I reported just like I was supposed to. What a fuckin' idiot. This whole goddamn war is shit, but I never ran away from it. I may not be a strack trooper like you, but I pull a hell of a lot more load around here than most of the goddamn lifers. I ain't gonna make it if I have to spend more than the six fuckin' months I got left to do. I just couldn't handle it."

Rivera had no sympathy. "Hayes, you better *start* handling it and worrying about not making it. You only have to fuck up once. You heard about Meadlo and Sturgis getting blown away by the B 40? Meadlo was a pothead. They got hit from his side. Maybe if he wasn't so fucked up, he would've seen Charlie in time. He and Sturgis would be alive, and Danziger and Madison wouldn't be Post Toasties in a burn ward back in the World. You know, I won't be here much longer to be your damn mother. You better get your act together."

Hayes opened his mouth for a retort, but settled for biting his lip.

"Sorry, Hayes. I—"

"Quit fucking apologizing when you don't fucking mean it," Hayes said.

The whole thing didn't mean a lot to Hayes because Meadlo and Sturgis had been killed on the smoke ship before he had come to the 99th. He grabbed his M16 and got up sullenly. "You know, there's about zero chance that we'll get hit tonight, but I promise I won't smoke any dope anyway," he said angrily.

Rivera regretted his outburst. Hayes was the best friend he had in the company. Rivera had always resisted friendship in Vietnam because friends could die on you. But his feelings for Hayes confused him. "I don't know... all the time I've been in-country, I've never been able to predict when I was gonna get shot at. It's always been a surprise, and then again, it's never been a surprise. Shit, maybe it's just because I'm short, but I'm nervous as hell. This place is gonna get hit one of these nights, sure as hell. With my luck, it'll happen before I can get the fuck outta Dodge."

As if on cue, a mortar round hit the runway, quickly joined by two more. They walked across the runway toward Hayes and Rivera in the helicopter, all three landing within a few seconds. By the time the third round hit about 50 meters away, Hayes and Rivera were prone. A siren began wailing again in the distance. A few machineguns and rifles opened up from bunkers. The two lay silently waiting for more incoming, but there was no more.

"Well, that answers your question. We've been hit," Hayes said.

"Nah... just keeping us awake, though they're kind of early. Probably trying to make us fire off some more ammo." He glanced at the impact craters in the runway. "Oh man... if there had been a fourth one it would have landed right on top of us."

"I don't like this shit," Hayes said. As he got up, right in front of him was one of the miniguns on the helicopter. He studied it. "You know, I wish there was a way we could use these things."

Rivera walked over to him and extended a hand to help him up. "I know how to fire them, but they aren't aimed at anything right now... except our bunker." Rivera slid his hand across the side of the helicopter. "You know, Mr. Walters has been showing me how to fly. He lets me take the controls sometimes on a test flight. He says I can hover better than some of the FNG pilots, for sure better than the fucking XO. Oh man! I never got the new tail rotor on! Shit, I'll do it tomorrow morning, soon as it's light."

Hayes looked at him. "You're pretty uptight about going home, aren't you?"

Rivera shrugged. "I guess. When I was back in the World six months ago, my old man said I had a dirty mouth. I've been getting shot at and killing people and he's bitching because I swear? My friends are growing their hair long and smoking dope... and I smoked it with them. See Hayes, I can loosen up when I want to. We all got ripped one night and saw Steppenwolf. Man, they are fucking great! That was about the only time I smoked that shit and I liked it, but shit, I don't fit in back there. Most young people hate soldiers. Fuckers kept asking me what it was like to kill somebody. I'm in the back seat of a car with this girl, getting ready to fuck her, and she asks me if I'd ever killed anyone. Can you believe that? I told her no, 'cause I knew that's what she wanted to hear, and she said, 'Good, 'cause I don't want to do it with anyone who has.' Guess that means she'll fuck about ninety nine point nine percent of the guys back there... what a slut. Shit, we were both drunk. I can't believe what girls are like now." He snorted to cover a sob. "I can't believe what *everyone* is like now. I can't believe what *I'm* like."

Hayes sensed Rivera's distress. He grinned and tried to push the conversation in a happier direction. "Well, did you fuck her or not?" It was the wrong thing to say. Rivera looked away in exasperation. Hayes gripped Rivera's arm, but the Cuban turned away. The two of them stood silently for a few minutes and then started walking back to the bunker.

Slobojan lumbered up panting when they were halfway back. "You guys alright?"

"No sweat. It's just Charlie's way of saying goodnight," Rivera said.

"We held our fire," Slobojan said. He seemed desperate for Rivera's approval.

"Good. Charles is just playing games."

"I got to get back. I don't want to leave Rufus there alone," he said, and lumbered quickly back toward the bunker. Rivera and Hayes walked slowly.

Hayes said, "Well, how 'bout if I go home in your place and you do my six months?"

"No way. I don't think I'd last another six months," Rivera said in a voice that rasped with fear. Hayes hadn't heard Rivera sound this way before. "I've been too lucky so far, and I think I used it all up. Got bad vibes about this place. I'm starting to have nightmares. Why are you so anxious to go home anyway? Your girl hardly ever writes."

"Shit," Hayes said. He felt the letter in his shirt pocket. He hadn't read it because he was afraid of what it might say. Gloria was capable of being a very angry person for someone who supposedly believed in peace and love. Generally, her anger was directed at her father and her father's associates with a little aimed at former teachers. She was a runaway, and he understood that. Hayes loved her, but he thought, *A beautiful girl like Gloria could do a hell of a lot better than a fucked-up army private stuck in this fucked-up war.*

"Like you say, girls today are unbelievable," Hayes said, starting to shade the truth. "Gloria has a lot of trouble writing and she's got... problems." He stopped and looked down, his hand on his pocket, feeling the letter in it.

"I'll meet you back at the bunker," he said. "I want to read this letter."

"You finally got another letter from her? That's great!"

"Maybe, maybe not," Hayes muttered. "I don't know what it says yet."

2105 Hours

Hayes waited until Rivera was gone before he opened the letter. He sat down cross-legged in the dirt halfway between the helicopter and the bunker, and took out his cigarette lighter for illumination.

My Dearest Jimmy,

I'm in the MSU steam tunnels! My stepfather and anyone else who's looking will never find me here. Except for some sniffles and the dirt, I've been doing okay. I've been here since Christmas. I left your car in the Shaw Hall parking garage during the holidays when school was out. Now I've put it in the far student lot. I just hope the police don't find it there. I stole a permit from another car too. It's a long walk when I go to it so I haven't been out there much. I don't think anyone else knows about the car.

My stepfather almost caught me twice. On Christmas Eve, I tried to get help from the church and a bad priest betrayed me. After that, I went with Roscoe's mother to meet some lawyers about the music we made in the garage. They want to put out a record. Can you believe that! But either the lawyers or the record company was trying to screw us. Roscoe's mother needs the money bad too, and so do I. Anyway, my stepfather showed up with a couple of big tough men. Someday I'll tell you how we escaped because it's funny, or at least it is now. I don't know what's going to happen with the record. Roscoe's mother said the record company has already given some of the songs to radio stations to play. I haven't heard any though.

Now for the big news. Jimmy, I am pregnant. I should have told you before but I was afraid to. I'll understand if you don't want to have anything to do with me anymore. The nurse at the clinic said she knew somebody who could rid of it, but I couldn't do that. My stepfather said he was going to do the same thing and that I'd soon forget all about it. That was before he tried to kill me. I'm going to have the baby.

Jimmy, I can feel our baby move. It's a real little person down there and I don't want to hurt him or her. My boobs hurt, though not as much lately. You should see how big they are! I worry all the time that something may go wrong. I want to see a doctor but I can't afford to, and they would probably tell my stepfather. I still have lots of vitamins that the nurse in the clinic gave me, and I'm eating okay. Sometimes it's hard to sleep when my back hurts or when I worry about you. I stole some couch cushions for a mattress, and blankets and pillows too, from a dorm during the holidays. At least I'm not getting sick much anymore. Most of the time, I feel good.

I know my stepfather has hired some private police to look for me so I'm afraid to go out. The real police are looking for me too. At least Clyde Bonaventure isn't after me because I spoke to him. Him and his politician friend, Logan Carlton. I've got some important news about Mr. Bonaventure, but it will have to wait.

I've been thinking about why my stepfather wants to kill me. He was always mean, but now he's afraid of me. I took some of his papers when I first ran away and he knows that I have them. Those German ones I sent to you—did you ever get them? If you did you should send them to your uncle. You told me he knows German, right? My stepfather also knows that I have a very good memory. I shouldn't have told him about all the things I overheard when I was a kid. They involve crooks and their money, things they could go to prison for. Some of those other crooks might be trying to find me too. I'm hiding the papers that I still have in a little black briefcase in the steam tunnels. Most of the German ones went to you.

I love you with all my heart, Jimmy, and I think about you all the time. Please be careful, extra careful. My stepfather threatened to kill you too, though I don't see how he could over there. But he mentioned it when he almost caught me.

This is my last stamp, my last envelope and my last piece of paper. I haven't written because I'm afraid to go to the post office when it's open. I only go out after dark, and even then, I don't go very far. It's been snowing and it's cold, so I can't play guitar to make any money. I'm afraid to play down here because it might attract attention. Not playing guitar is driving me nuts! I'm so glad you told me about these tunnels. Running out of room here. All my love, Gloria.

By the time he got to the end, he was frantic with worry. The last line curled up the right side of the letter. He punched the ground with his fist and stared at the letter for a long while, composing himself. He was angry, frustrated and completely helpless. He groaned, rocking back and forth, holding onto the letter with one hand and hitting the ground over and over with his fist. Finally, he jammed the letter back into his pocket and walked to the bunker.

He stopped beside Rivera who was sitting on the rickety lawn chair by the bunker entrance. Up on the roof, Rufus lay quietly watching the area in front of the bunker and sometimes looking down at Rivera and Hayes.

"Gimme a cigarette, I got to smoke something," Hayes said. He had given the rest of his cigarettes to Rufus. Rivera handed Hayes a cigarette and watched him light it and start to cough.

"This shit is worse than dope," he muttered, and put the cigarette out. Then he dropped it in his other shirt pocket. "I got this letter from Gloria. I almost didn't read it, 'cause she hasn't written anything since before Christmas. Figured it might be bad."

He took the letter out and looked at it again, confused because a sense of elation was building.

Oh Jesus!" he muttered. "Oh shit!"

He looked up at Rivera, an amazed look on his face.

"She loves me!" he said. "She fuckin' says she *loves* me, man, and she's gonna have a baby! *My* baby!"

Startled, Rivera looked at him. "Jesus Christ, Hayes! You're gonna be a *daddy*? Holy shit!"

Above them, Rufus' head appeared as he looked down from the roof of the bunker.

Hayes said, "Holy Christ! She loves me, and I love her. But shit, man. Her father's after her, the police are after her and Christ knows who else is after her. Her father's some kind of crook. Honest to god, the bastard tried to shoot her. She can't go to the police because.... Wow... she fuckin' *loves* me." Hayes glanced around and took the letter out again. "Oh man, what the fuck am I gonna do? How am I gonna take care of her?"

"Take care of her, yeah, but what about the kid?" asked Rivera. "What are you gonna do about that?"

"Yeah, there's that. But that's not what I meant. She's got this stepfather who's after her, and she says he tried to kill her. I thought I had enough problems worrying' about what happens to me... but the kid, I don't know. Maybe she should have it and let somebody else adopt it."

Rufus' voice cut into their conversation. "Me not be knowin' my poppa. 'Tis a bad 'ting to hoppen, never knowin' your mamma or your poppa."

"Thought you couldn't understand us Rufus," Hayes said, looking up, and he was surprised to see the set in Rufus' face

"Me unna'stan 'nuff. Not be doofus nigra, mon. No haff poppa. Momma be dyin' when I be little one. You not be real poppa mon, should be poppa to dis baby. Eva'body needs Momma and Poppa. Eva'body needs somebody to love 'em."

"The gospel according to Gracie Slick and Rufus Roy," Hayes said, nodding.

Rufus looked at him, burning with anger. He thought he had been insulted.

Hayes noticed. "No man, don't get upset. You're one hundred percent right. Gloria's crazy about finding out who her real dad and mom are, and I sort of have the same problem, though I don't care about it the way she does. My fuckin' mother took off when I was little and I don't know who my father was. I think my Uncle Sepp, who is my mother's brother, knows, but he won't say."

Trying to break the tension, Rivera laughed. "You can have my old man, either of you. All he cares about is Castro getting his ass kicked... as long as someone else is doing the kicking."

Rufus angry made everybody nervous. Nobody said anything for a long moment and he appeared to calm down. He went back to scanning the area in front of the bunker.

Hayes folded the letter carefully and put it back in his pocket.

2140 Hours

Slobojan ambled out of the bunker with the two field phones. He had found a roll of comm wire and connected them.

"You know, if we string this wire over to the next bunker, we can talk to them," Slobbo said.

Hayes asked, "What are we gonna talk about, Slobbo? Philosophy? Basketball scores? Pussy?" He started unbuttoning the flap on his shirt pocket to get the cigarette out.

"No, if we connect with them, they can relay anything they get from base camp defense to us." Just then there was the sound of a vehicle approaching. "Uh oh, we've got company."

Rivera said, "Sounds like a Jeep. It's probably that major from base camp defense. Christ, does anyone know the password?"

"Three nine," Slobojan said. "Sorry, I should have told you guys."

Hayes picked up a machinegun and cocked it. "Three nine. Okay. Well, I hope he knows it, or I can blow him away, right?

Gonna prove to ol' Rivera here that my head's on straight enough to shoot a fuckin' officer."

As they went back into the bunker, a Jeep door opened and closed, and footsteps were approaching. Slobojan began motioning frantically at Rivera, who didn't understand him. Finally, Rivera put his head next to Slobojan's.

"Take one of the field phones out the other side of the bunker and play along."

Rivera picked up one of the field phones and the roll of wire and dropped it out the firing port. The phone was connected to the other field phone in the bunker. He and Hayes quickly slipped out of the bunker, crept around the side and picked up the field phone that he had thrown out the port. Carefully playing out the thin electrical cord, he retreated into the darkness. He had hardly been gone 10 seconds when Shiffman, Comstock and a Spec Four named Klein entered the bunker. Klein, who had a pimply face, was holding a ballpoint pen poised over a clipboard. He must have been at least 19 years old, but he could have easily passed for 14.

Shiffman was thin and wiry, but his face was friendly enough. "Who's in charge here?"

"I am, Sir. Sergeant Rusty Slobojan," Slobojan said. He started to salute but Shiffman waved it off.

"Why did you start firing out here a couple of hours ago?"

"Sir, we didn't fire first. I think it started farther down the bunker line, that way." Slobojan pointed toward the bunker that had fired second.

"I see. They said it started over here. No one admits to firing first," Shiffman grumbled. He walked over to the firing port and looked at the machinegun.

"Someone probably thought they saw VC infiltrating," Slobojan said. "Better safe than sorry."

"Maybe," Shiffman said. He paced across the bunker, looking intently at the floor, his gaze flicking over to the M60 machinegun in the corner. He went back and examined the machinegun on the platform, scraping at the receiver with a finger. Comstock was slouched at the doorway, watching, and Klein was studying the floor. Finally Shiffman walked over and faced Slobojan. Slobojan thought he could smell alcohol faintly. But it wasn't coming from the major. "Sergeant, where do you have your men posted? Warrant Officer Comstock here isn't sure how many of you there are out here, though he says he's been out here."

"Sir, that's correct, he has," Slobojan said, nodding at Comstock. "We have two men inside the bunker and two men on the roof. There's another one dug into a listening post about fifty meters out the front and to the right."

"You have six men in addition to yourself, Sergeant? You're not bullshitting me are you? Specialist Klein here is making a list of people who have been bullshitting me."

A bullshit list, Slobojan thought, grinning inwardly.

"Yes Sir!" Klein said. He looked around eagerly with his ballpoint pen poised over the clipboard.

"Sir, that's six men *including me* and Mr. Comstock. Right now, I'm manning the bunker with Hayes. He and Rivera went back to that crashed ship to see if there's any more ammo in it that we can use," Slobojan said. "Roy and Rivera are on top. Mr. Comstock... well, he's wherever he feels he's needed."

Crouched outside and listening carefully, Hayes eased back toward the ship.

"I see. Who's in the listening post, and how do you communicate with him?"

"Specialist Carr, and he's got a field phone, but Carr's so crazy we'll probably know he sees something when he kills it.

You know, it's possible that Carr was the first one to shoot. I asked him, and he denied it. But in all honesty Sir...." Slobojan paused and shook his head. "That Carr's kind of nuts."

"What if the enemy gets Carr first?" Shiffman asked.

"Then God help us," Slobojan said. "But I would bet on Carr, Sir. Truth is, Carr volunteered to go out there and we were glad to see him go. Gets nervous around people and people are nervous around him."

"I'd like to meet this soldier," Shiffman said. It was impossible to tell whether he really meant it or was trying to call Slobojan's bluff, but it was too late for Slobojan to do anything except carry it through.

"I wouldn't recommend that, Sir. Carr sets up his own booby traps, and we've got a few of our own between here and the listening post. I can't guarantee your safety if you try to go out there in the dark. Carr's out there for the night," Slobojan said.

Shiffman picked up the field phone. "Okay, then let's talk to him."

Slobojan shook his head. "Sir, we don't ring the field phone," Slobojan took a step to one side so he was speaking directly at the open port in front of the machinegun. "If Carr sees something, he'll crank it and our field phone will ring. If we ring him, Sir, the noise of the ring could give away his position."

Shiffman nodded, begrudgingly. "What if the enemy cuts the wire?"

"Sir, every once in a while we give the wire a tug, and if all's clear, Carr tugs back a couple of times. Sir, what I'm more worried about is talking to base camp defense. We don't have a radio."

"No radio?" Shiffman said.

"No Sir."

"What happened to it?" asked Shiffman. "There was a radio here last night. There's supposed to be a radio in every bunker."

Comstock cleared his throat. "Sir? There are radios in the helicopter back there. And my crew chief Rivera's here. He knows how to operate them. Hayes probably does too."

Shiffman walked out of the bunker door and looked back toward the helicopter, thinking. While he stood there, still holding the field phone, he tugged the field phone wire. Almost immediately, the wire jerked twice in his hand. "Well, Carr seems to be alert. Good. Maybe Specialist Klein can find a spare prick 25 at base camp defense and run it out here.

"There isn't one, Sir," Klein said. "I'm sure, because somebody from the fourth of the twenty-third wanted one today."

"In that case, you'll have to use the radio in the helicopter. Where is this man Rivera?"

"Here, Sir," Rivera said appearing from the darkness at the side of the bunker. "I can operate the radio. We can call in a sitrep right now if you want."

Farther away, Hayes quickly trotted back toward the crashed gunship. Halfway there, he turned around and began ambling back to the bunker. As Rivera led the group with Shiffman back to the helicopter, they ran into Hayes.

"No more ammo," Hayes said, then turned around once again and joined the group.

When Rivera got to the ship, he picked up his flight helmet, put it on, and plugged in a cord. "Let's see, I've got to get on the base camp push," Rivera said, squinting at a knob on one of the radios. The ship was equipped with FM, VHF and UHF radios.

"Let me help." Comstock reached for the controls, but Rivera brushed him off.

"I can do it. The major here needs to see me do it. Why don't you help him transmit?" He turned a knob. "Got it. Okay, here we go.

"Headhunter Seven to Ramrod Charlie, come in."

A voice crackled in reply over the headphones in the helmet. "Where the hell are you, Headhunter Seven? Didn't know you were up, over."

"How do I transmit?" asked Shiffman

Comstock reached into the front and pressed a button on a control stick. "There you go. Just talk."

"Ramrod Charlie, this is Ramrod Seventeen. Disregard Headhunter Seven. Sitrep at Alpha Three is normal. Over and out," Shiffman said. He signaled to Comstock to cut and then turned to Rivera. "You've got the right idea, Specialist, but there's no point in playing twenty questions over the radio. I'll just explain it to them when we get back. Don't use this radio unless you've got an emergency. I want you in the bunker." Shiffman took off the helmet and got out of the helicopter, watching Comstock as he walked toward the company area. "Sergeant Slobojan!"

"Yes Sir."

"I'm really not sure how many men you've got out here, but if there aren't enough, I know it's not your fault. I want all of you awake and alert all night. I'm convinced there's a very high probability that we're going to get hit tonight."

"You can count on us, Sir," Slobojan said.

"As long as I don't count you," Shiffman muttered as he strode briskly toward the Jeep with Klein beside him.

30 January, 0255 Hours

Despite his orders from Major Shiffman, Slobojan decided that not everyone had to stay awake all night. He knew Rivera and Hayes were tired. He was worried that if they all tried to stay up, they all might fall asleep in the early morning, the period he was most worried about. He told Hayes and Rufus to be on guard until 0200 hours and then to wake him up and Rivera. The original plan was for one man to be awake inside the bunker and another on the roof. But the sighting was much better from the roof than looking through the firing port. With both men on the roof, they could keep each other alert. But by midnight, Rufus had fallen asleep on the roof and Hayes didn't bother waking him. He was having no trouble staying awake.

He was so desperate thinking about Gloria that it was making him physically ill. When he thought about Rivera leaving and Sypher's promise to court martial him, he got depressed. So he concentrated on guard duty. He concluded that worrying about things you can't control is a losing game. Sypher would either court martial him or he wouldn't. Rivera was going home. Gloria was on the other side of the world. There was nothing he could do about any of it, so he lay on his belly, scanning the darkened area where the brush was growing out from the village.

Sometimes he rolled over on his back for briefly to look at all of the stars, wishing he knew the names of the constellations. *Jimi Hendrix must have been looking at the stars when he wrote Purple Haze. There was a line... something about kissing the sky.* Thinking about the song and feeling Hendrix' guitar chords reverberating in his head slowly lifted him out of his funk. The song had come out when Universal Joint was at its peak at the East Lansing bar and it was one the band's most popular covers, one where they closely imitated the original. However, Hayes had been into the purple thing long before then. Purple was his favorite color and he owned several flashy purple dashiki shirts that he wore only when performing. He even had a pair of jeans that he had died purple. Before Universal Joint, he had briefly named his group the Purple Gang after hearing a band in Ohio called the James Gang. The Purple Gang had been famous Detroit outlaws.

He rolled back and scanned the shadows again. He had a strange desire that there be a ground attack because it was the dead of night and he was so awake now that it felt like his body was vibrating. With that feeling came a tremendous urge to get high. He scanned the shadowy world in front of the bunker for a long time, then rolled over again and looked up at the sky. The stars were gone, replaced by darkness, meaning clouds were moving in quickly. He looked at his watch, then rolled over again. He woke up Rufus, then slid down the ladder, entered the bunker and shook Slobojan. "I gotta take a crap, Sarge. I think I might have the runs from the fuckin' malaria pill. I'm gonna run to the crapper. I'll be right back."

He left before Slobojan could disagree and ran all the way to his hootch. Sleeping men occupied all the bunks except his and Rivera's. He quietly opened his footlocker, rummaged around until he found Gloria's letter with the little envelope containing the pill that was supposed to be Owsley acid. He popped it into in his mouth, closed his footlocker, took a swig of warm Coke that someone hadn't finished and disappeared out the door, already thinking he had just done something incredibly stupid. He drained another half-full can of Dr. Pepper that he found on the sandbag wall at the hootch entrance. Instead of racing directly back to the bunker, Hayes swung through the second Headhunters hootch looking for another unfinished can of soda. He didn't find a soda, but spotted two full M60 ammo boxes, each containing 200 rounds. Someone was probably trying to get a head start for the morning. Hayes picked them up.

0415 Hours

Comstock was hovering between hung over and still drunk, and he was very pissed off at himself. After his encounter with Lehman, he had vowed to take his officer-of-the-guard duty more seriously, but then he had drunk three more cans of beer. At least he had been able to go with Major Shiffman to inspect the bunker. He had planned on staying with the men, but then he decided checking on them every hour would suffice. As he lay down after finishing the last beer, he thought, *Maybe every hour and a half would work.* Then he fell asleep and didn't wake up until shortly after 0400 hours with a dull headache and his mouth drier than the Gobi Desert. He got up, drank a can of Coke, grabbed his M16 and began trudging toward the bunker. Halfway there, he stopped and urinated for a long time while looking up at the sky. It had been clear earlier, but the stars were gone. Darkness enveloped everything. *Clouds must have moved in,* he thought.

As he got closer to the bunker, it seemed to get darker and harder to see. Finally, he realized fog had moved in under cover of darkness. Gradually, he became aware of a darker shape. It was the crashed helicopter. He made a slight turn, hoping he was heading toward the bunker, and stopped when he thought he was close. He started walking the remaining few meters to the bunker very slowly. He felt lost. He could no longer see anything, and he was less sure what direction the bunker was. *Did I go too far? Am I heading into the mined area in front of the bunker?* He didn't think there were many mines, but he had heard there were some. *What about that crazy soldier out in the listening post? Did Slobojan make that up, or is there really a mentally unbalanced soldier out there?* Finally, he stopped and lay down on the ground, surrendering to the darkness.

* * *

Inside the bunker, Slobojan and Rufus were listening to a small transistor radio on low volume. Slobojan had tuned in a Vietnamese language station. Hayes was hunched over the M60, looking through the firing port of the bunker. Once he woke everyone up, no one wanted to go back to sleep. Slobojan was ecstatic about the ammo Hayes had brought back.

Hayes asked, "You listen to that dink crap very often?"

"Yeah... sometimes you can get Ho Chi Minh. I think this might be him now," the sergeant said. "This is one of the frequencies he uses to talk to people in the south, and this sounds like some kind of speech. I don't know enough Vietnamese to know what he's saying, but he's pretty fuckin' excited." Slobojan fiddled with the radio dial and tuned in another station that was a little clearer. "Wait a minute, here's somebody else is speaking... that's not Vietnamese anymore."

Rufus snorted and he smiled. "Francais."

"French?" Hayes asked.

"Oui monsieur. Him be speaking Francais," Rufus said. "Him have... accent tres strange."

"What's he saying?" asked Slobojan. He could speak more French than Vietnamese but he still couldn't understand most rapid conversation. It sounded like the French speaker was translating from Vietnamese.

"Me be tryin'a unna'stan... him say people risin' up... all people should be risin' up."

Hayes turned around from the machinegun and looked at Rufus. "General uprising?" Suddenly, his mind was coming unhinged. He'd thought the acid wasn't really acid and that nothing was happening, but his head was starting to spin. Literally. He had a sensation of observing himself from a vantage point outside of his head. The acid was just working a little bit and so far Hayes liked it. It was like when he first turned on the amplifiers to play a gig. There was an electric hum that penetrated all the conversations and other ambient noise, and you just knew that an awful lot of energy was about to be unleashed. It seemed like time had slowed down. He had to force himself back to the conversation. "Is this guy talking about a general uprising?"

"General uprisin'. Him say general uprisin'. How you know, Purple mon?"

"Jesus, general uprising. That's some serious shit."

"What's a general uprising?" asked Slobojan. "A commie revolution or something like that?

"No. It's more like a fight to the death for everyone," Hayes said. He tried to remember the Asian history class that he had sat in on. The professor had been an irritating little weasel of a man who liked to impress students with little-known counter-intuitive facts. "The last time the Vietnamese had a general uprising was when the Chinese invaded them about nine hundred years ago. They kicked the shit out of the Chinese. Vietnamese don't much care for foreigners."

"No be speaking French, now," Rufus said.

"Yeah, it's Uncle Ho again. He sure is wound up tonight," Slobojan said. Just then the field phone inside the bunker gave a short ring like someone had barely cranked it.

"Wait a sec. I think Rivera's trying to get us," Hayes said. He picked up the field phone and listened. "Rivera says shut up, he's got movement out there. Says he's got beaucoup movement."

Hayes lowered the phone from his face and looked at Slobojan and Rufus. He slowly raised the phone back up. "Is it a general uprising kind of movement?"

Hayes dropped the handset of the phone and loped silently out of the bunker with his M16. He scampered up the ladder onto the roof and slid down beside Rivera, who was prone with the M60 propped over the sandbags lining the top front edge of the bunker.

"Look out at the edge of the brush," Rivera whispered.

"Straight out?"

"Shhh! Straight out, both sides, everywhere. They're all over the fuckin' place."

"You sure you ain't been smokin' some of my cigarettes?" Hayes squinted and looked carefully in front of the bunker. He tried to will his eyes to see more, like he was opening the aperture of a camera. His eyes were two cameras and he was trying to change their settings. He was slithering into his thoughts, analyzing them and realizing suddenly that the acid was really starting to kick in.

Rivera hissed, "I wish."

Hayes couldn't remember what he'd just said. Then he remembered and marveled at himself. He examined the texture of the darkness, closed his eyes to see the difference, started to think about it. Then he pulled himself back to reality. After a few moments of peering into the darkness, he saw faint flashes of soldiers all along the edge of the brush in front of the bunker. It was like one of those puzzle pictures hidden in some kind of clever pattern. He had to stare at the patterns before the picture emerged. First, there was only brush, and then the brush widened from the way it had been earlier, and then there were shapes within the brush. *Helmets? No, soft caps.* He picked out the shadowy geometric straight lines of rifle barrels, barely discernible as slightly darker darkness. His heart stopped and a rush of cold, terrifying adrenaline swept through him. He wanted to run away as fast as he could. At the same time he glimpsed deeper inside himself and sensed a growing power. *I am a god... I can do no wrong.* "I see 'em. They're out there alright, and I am a god."

0420 Hours

Rivera glanced at Hayes. "Huh?"

Hayes was looking straight ahead with great intensity.

Rivera said, "Okay, we've got to tell that fucking major. Looks like they're massing. We're gonna get hit. Somebody's got to go back to the ship and use the radio. It's got to be either you or me. Slobojan and Rufus don't know how to operate it."

"Better be you. You got the rank and you talked to them before. They might not listen to me." It felt like it took him a week to say the sentence as each word peeled off and fluttered into the darkness.

Slobojan's head appeared behind them. He had climbed part of the way up the ladder. "See 'em? They're gonna come soon. It's darkest part of the night. Let's hold our fire till they're close. We still have to conserve ammo. Looks like a lot of 'em."

"I better go radio base camp defense," Rivera said. "It's gonna be interesting. We've already given them one false alarm tonight."

"Damn," Slobojan said. "Okay, get going, but get right back. Wish you could use those miniguns."

"He can, but they aren't gonna hit anything but the...." Hayes stopped whispering, lost in thought. Rivera was slithering to the back of the bunker to start down the ladder. Hayes took his place at the machinegun. He turned to face Rivera before he dropped to the ground. "You can get that machine up in the air, can't you? I mean, Mr. Walters let you do it a couple of times, right?" He was having a very interior vision of the helicopter like it was a model that he was holding in his hand. It was so real he could almost feel his fingers wrapped around the tail boom.

"With no tail rotor, it'll just spin around and probably crash again."

"What if somebody held the tail and kept it from rotating? Or at least controlled the spin some? I mean it's pointing right at the bunker right now."

Rivera thought about it and a smile creased his face. "Might be better with somebody's got some weight, and more muscle."

"Rufus," Slobojan said. "The guy's an ox."

Hayes said, "He's no doofus either. He's smart."

Slobojan followed Rivera down the ladder. He went into the bunker and a few seconds later Rufus came out. Rivera and Rufus disappeared into the darkness, heading toward the helicopter.

* * *

Outside, Comstock sensed someone close to him and awoke with a start. He couldn't believe he had fallen asleep again. He squinted and his eyes seemed to have adjusted to the darkness. The dark shape of the bunker was close to him, or the fog had lifted. He was only about 10 feet from the entrance. He turned his head and wondered whether someone, maybe two people, had passed by him heading in the general direction of the helicopter. He got up and walked quietly into the bunker. He startled Slobojan, who was hunched over the machinegun and peering through the firing port. The bulky sergeant lurched around and grabbed his M16.

"Easy," Comstock said. "It's me, Comstock. Guess I should have used the password."

"Jesus, I was gonna shoot you. Where the hell did you come from?"

"My hootch. Just came out to check on you guys. Should have come earlier."

"Shit, you're just in time," Slobojan said. "We're gonna get hit."

* * *

Rivera led Rufus at a fast trot up to the helicopter and grabbed the two flight helmets from the floor. He handed one to Rufus and plugged it in. The helmet had a longer cord that he'd rigged several months ago so he could walk around the helicopter and talk to the pilots on the intercom. "Put this on. You'll need it to hear me."

He put the other helmet on, plugged it in and flipped some switches.

"Can you hear me? Roger."

"Yaas baas, hear good. Who be Roger?"

"Uhh...never mind. Just don't talk anymore than you have to. Anything you say will be on the air. I'm gonna start the ship and I want you to hold onto the tail. You have to be on the other side from where the tail rotor used to be. The tail's gonna push against you. I'm not really sure how hard it'll push, but you have to hold it. Understand?"

Rufus nodded. "Me unna'stan."

"Keep your head down. Don't let your head get above the tail. As long as you keep your head below the top of the tail, the rotor won't hit you." While he spoke, Rivera was working more switches

"Mon, wha' 'tis dis?"

"Ramrod Charlie, this is Alpha Three. We are about to be attacked, over," Rivera said.

Rufus was more puzzled. He took a step toward the tail boom and tentatively got a grip on it.

"Ramrod Charlie, this is Alpha Three, come in."

Back in the operations bunker, Klein, the same spec four who had accompanied Shiffman on his visit to the bunkers was listening to the radios. He scratched his head. "Read you Alpha Three. Hold for Ramrod Seventeen, over."

Waking from a doze, Shiffman got up and walked quickly toward Klein. Before he could pick up the microphone, the radio crackled again. "Can't wait, Ramrod Charlie. We have beaucoup victor charlies here. Dozens, maybe hundreds. They're crawling up on Alpha Three. We're gonna try to use the miniguns on this ship. Can't talk anymore. Send the cavalry. Over and out."

Shiffman grabbed the mike and yelled, "Alpha Three, listen up! Come in!"

Nothing. Klein and Shiffman looked at each other.

"Okay Rufus, I'm gonna lift this ship off the ground and fire the miniguns. You're gonna hold onto the tail and aim this whole machine and the miniguns."

"Wha' 'tis miniguns?" Rufus said.

"They're like a whole bunch of machineguns. Shoot lots of bullets. See them on the skids there?"

Rufus leaned away from the tail to peer at the minigun on one skid.

"Purple mon say dis is gun flex. Say dis is crap piece Ecksem twenny one armed mons sizdem."

"Get ready," Rivera said. The helicopter engine started to whine and Rufus put his shoulder to the tail boom and wrapped one arm around it. The Lycoming engine's whine increased as the turbine blades whirled. The rotor made its first swing around, startling Rufus, who ducked lower. Then the engine died.

"Goddamnit. I fucked it up. God, I hope I can get this right! This fucker's not that easy to start."

0434 Hours

Slobojan was sweating although it was cool. He wiped his brow with his sleeve and turned to look through the firing port. He watched for nearly half a minute. Then his eyes grew wide and he urgently whispered, "Oh shit! We're really gonna get hit! Look at those motherfuckers out there!" He turned to

Comstock. "You better grab a rifle or get the hell out! Did you bring your sixteen?"

Comstock moved up to the port and looked out.

"Right along the brush line," Slobojan said, then groaned.

There were so many that it wasn't difficult to pick out the heads and rifles slowly moving. Then he realized that the reason he could pick out heads and rifles was because they were closer. They were camouflaged with pieces of brush and slowly crawling toward the bunker. But they were close enough for Slobojan and Comstock both to see that the brush was a living, moving mass of soldiers.

Comstock said, "Oh shit! Oh my God!"

"Where's your rifle?" Slobojan repeated. There was alcohol on Comstock's breath and Slobojan wondered how much he'd had to drink.

"Right here."

"Okay, good," Slobojan said. He struggled out of the bandoleers slung over his shoulders and took off his pocketed vest. "This is about twenty-five, maybe thirty magazines. You better go up on the roof with Hayes. I'll be hard for the two of us to fire out the port. Here, take the grenades too."

"Where's Rivera?" asked Comstock.

"He took Rufus back to the chopper. He's gonna try to get it in the air and fire the miniguns. Rufus is gonna be a human tail rotor."

Before Comstock could process what Slobojan was telling him, Hayes fired a burst from the M60 on the roof, shattering the quietness and illuminating Slobojan's sweaty, fearful face in a staccato rush of faint light flashes coming through the firing port.

Hayes screamed, "Rock and roll!" and then dragged out "Shotgunnnn!" in a loud scream that came right from his Universal Joint repertoire.

His voice sent a chill through Slobojan. It sounded to him like Hayes was singing. "Oh shit! Oh shit!" The big sergeant crouched down behind his M60 and fired a long burst. When he hunched down to aim, the machinegun knocked his helmet askew so when he ended the long burst, he reached up and tossed it across the bunker, sailing it just past Comstock's head.

Between bursts from his own machinegun, Hayes shouted, "Short bursts or you'll burn out the barrel!"

* * *

Comstock moved for the door, as much to get away from the noise as anything. The machinegun was deafening.

He lurched out the doorway with his M16 in one hand and the heavy vest full of magazines, the bandoleers and a pouch of grenades in the other. *How do I get on the roof? Must be a ladder. Must be in the back.* He found the ladder and struggled up awkwardly, his hands full and his mind racing. *This can't be happening to me. Shouldn't have drunk that Courvoisier. Does Rivera know how to start the engine? Why the hell didn't I put on a flak jacket? When was the last time I fired an M16? God, I'm thirsty. Wonder what Mom and Dad are doing right now? Hope Dad doesn't try to shovel the driveway by himself.* He scrambled onto the roof in a crouch and thought *Better get down* so he threw himself forward, aiming for a spot to the right of Hayes just as a sputtering of flashes started from the front of the bunker along with the distinctive, higher-pitched AK-47 gunshots. *Never heard that before. Wow, that was—* His mind snapped off as if a switch had been thrown. A jumble of half-completed thoughts froze in a blur and exploded into white nothingness like stuck film melting in a projector.

Just before he thumped onto the roof of the bunker, a 7.62mm slug from an AK-47 entered his open mouth, smashed through the base of his brain and severed his spinal cord before exploding out of the lower part of the back of his head. His heart reflexively convulsed a few more times.

* * *

Lying on the roof with one hand on the trigger of the M60 and the other feeding the ammunition belt, Hayes heard something land beside him. He glanced over between bursts. Comstock's face wore an expression of absolute shocked surprise, both eyes and his mouth wide open, a trickle of blood on the side of his chin.

"Short bursts! Short bursts!" Slobojan cried below him.

Hayes took in Comstock's frigid eyes and it didn't matter. He had eaten the LSD and now his mind had burst out of the confines of his consciousness into the vast, wide-open universe. Other than a slightly upset stomach he had noticed no change until the last few minutes. Now his mind was like an expensive and finely tuned sports car. The power, elegance and precision of his brain amazed him as it expanded and enveloped everything. Though he could discern what was real and what wasn't, the reality he was experiencing felt like a dream in which nothing could hurt him and everything he did would work perfectly. He would hit exactly what he aimed at while none of the enemy bullets could touch him.

Everyone else was functioning in slow motion while he was locked in a perfect high-speed groove. He knew the enemy soldiers were trying to kill him, but he also knew with absolute certainty they wouldn't succeed. Energy rippled and surged through his immaculately perfect body, coalescing into a dispassionate, methodical killing frenzy. It was similar to the instant when the ARVN had fired into the helicopter with the M79 and Hayes had reacted by shooting him. He wasn't thinking, just doing. But this reaction was open-ended rather than ending in an instant. It kept right on going.

He fired short bursts and long bursts from his M60. His all-seeing eyes picked out individuals and groups, but they were not people to him. He killed them carrying their machineguns. He killed them as they fired a rocket-propelled grenade that hit the bunker's sandbags and rocked him like he was on a helicopter. He killed them as they scrambled to outflank him on either side. He killed them as they ran screaming toward him. Dozens of bullets were hitting around him. Hayes felt them thudding into the triple row of sandbags along the top edge of the roof, and he heard them as they whizzed by on both sides, but he knew none would hit him. He also knew not to raise his head any higher than he had to. Once, he ducked just in time to feel the heat from a shot that almost hit the top of his head. He squeezed down and stopped firing momentarily to adjust the ammo belt, noting that the end of it was already in sight. He was suddenly aware that Slobojan wasn't firing.

"Claymores!" Hayes shouted.

Neither Slobojan nor Hayes was sure where the claymores had been placed, or even if they were still there, but the entire area in front of the bunker was alive with enemy. For two or three seconds, neither of them was firing and the enemy rose up like they were one big organism. Slobojan squeezed all three of the detonators. The first two did nothing, but on the third squeeze there was a loud cracking detonation as a white-hot flash sprayed outward, freezing the enemy soldiers like a hideous instant flash photograph. Then there was a writhing tangle of dead and wounded in front of the bunker. Farther back, an officer was motioning to another group to move around to the sides of the bunker.

Hayes aimed the M60 at them and fired a burst that consumed the rest of the ammunition in the belt. The officer went down and so did the soldiers beside him. Hayes was sure that he had killed the officer, but he wasn't sure about the others.

"I'm jammed! I'm jammed!" Slobojan yelled, his voice full of anguish and fear.

But Hayes had no time for him. The reactive frenzy was dissipating. He was starting to think again. He sensed the danger and fought to retain the feeling. He pushed the M60 aside and grabbed his M16. He started crawling to one side of the roof and spotted the pouch with grenades spilled out beside Comstock's body. He pulled the pin from a grenade, let the spoon spring off and threw it at one of the flanking groups of enemy soldiers. Bullets sang past him as he lay on his side checking his M16. There was a magazine in it and he chambered a round with the charging handle, then moved the selector to full automatic. He tried to stop thinking. He had pulled three full magazines out of Slobojan's vest before the grenade exploded amid the enemy soldiers. He fired bursts from the M16 and grabbed another grenade.

He rolled to the other side of the bunker, sliding over Comstock's body, bullets still whizzing past. He pulled the pin from a grenade and let the spoon flip off. He remembered when he was a kid that he would light the fuse on a big firecracker and not throw it until the burning fuse was about to disappear inside the firecracker. He looked at the grenade and thought, *I can't see a fuse.* He looked over the edge of the bunker, bullets tearing the top edges. A half-dozen enemy were trotting forward. He confidently heaved the grenade in a high, slow arc toward them, pulled his head down and imagined it exploding about six feet above the enemy group as he heard the explosion. And he laughed.

Now, he was popping bursts off with his M16, and he could see that the number of enemy soldiers had diminished. Slobojan had started firing sporadically with his M16. Only a few bullets were thudding into the bunker. Hayes squinted, and far back, maybe 100 meters away, it looked like a larger group was preparing another assault.

Slobojan said, "Oh my God! They're getting ready to come again! How are you guys for ammo?"

Hayes emptied an entire magazine into the large group and was satisfied to see them all go down, most of them ducking rather than being hit. When he ejected the empty magazine and reached for another, he was shocked to see half a dozen other empty magazines scattered around the roof and Comstock's body. He didn't remember reloading. He took more magazines out of the vest and gathered together the others that he and Rivera had brought, then took the magazine out of Comstock's rifle. All told, he still had about 30 magazines left. He shouted down to Slobojan, "I'm using my sixteen, Slobbo! I'm out for the sixty!"

"Me too. My M60's jammed," Slobojan said. "Wait a minute, I've still got the second box. No wonder you guys are out."

For a second Hayes studied expression on Comstock's face. *Is it getting lighter, or are his eyes burning in the dark?* Comstock looked even deader than he had before, but in Hayes semi-dreamlike state, Comstock's body was a small blip in his consciousness.

"Comstock is dead," he said matter of factly.

"Oh no. Are you sure?" Slobojan said.

Then they both heard the building whine of a turbine engine starting up through the diminishing din of the shooting.

"Slobbo, I'm gonna shoot off the flare. Okay?" asked Hayes. A vision of colorful fireworks exploding on the Fourth of July with everyone oohing and aahing came into his mind. He pondered his warped perception. He concluded that accurately assessing his changed perception with senses that still were under the influence of the mind-altering drug and still were changing wasn't to be trusted. That reminded him of that Kraut physicist Heisenberg who said it wasn't possible to determine both the velocity and the exact location of a very fast-moving subatomic particle. Neither can a warped mind assess its own warp factor.

He pulled out of the seductive, whirling loops of introspection. There was danger in letting his enhanced mental powers go to waste on meaningless paths of thought. He locked his concentration on the scene in front of the bunker. A hundred meters away, heads and shoulders were slowly rising in the gloom. Hayes fired several bursts, then cackled and gripped the flare. "Here they come again!"

* * *

The main rotor was spinning at full speed. Rufus braced against the tail boom and held it up off the ground. He had no trouble holding it as the skids were still on the ground. He looked over at the bunker just as two rocket propelled grenades exploded against the sides.

"Get ready, Rufus! Soon as it lifts that tail is gonna push against you! You've got to hold it! You're gonna steer this thing! You gotta aim it!"

"Yaas boss!" he shouted into the mike. The rotor wash felt like a hurricane blasting from above, but he understood what he was supposed to do.

Rivera pulled the collective up smoothly. The helicopter lifted off the ground and immediately turned about 45 degrees. Bullets started whizzing by the machine and there were clanks as some rounds hit the fuselage. The helicopter turned a little more but Rufus planted his feet, leaned up and into the tail, got it under control and then pushed it back around until the front was again pointed at the bunker. He groaned and dug his feet harder into the dirt to hold it there.

"That's it! That's it!" Rivera said.

But just then the helicopter windshield exploded, spraying Plexiglas into Rivera's face. He screamed and tried to hold the controls but the helicopter bounced onto the ground. Rufus fell down. As Rufus scrambled to his feet and grabbed the tail boom again, Rivera forced the panic in his gut to go away. He got control of himself and the helicopter. He wiped the blood out of this eyes with the back of his hand, then grabbed the collective again and pulled the ship up. He was having difficulty seeing. Into the headset he yelled, "I think we gotta raise the nose a little! When I start shooting, you aim using the tail! Watch where the tracers go!"

"Yaas boss!" Rufus said. He was struggling to get the helicopter pointed at the bunker again. It wobbled and bounced as Rivera pulled back on the cyclic to raise the nose. Just as Rufus was lining up on the bunker and the area in front of it again, there was a loud, hollow pop of a parachute flare igniting and everything was bathed in an unnatural, silver-white glare. The enemy soldiers, startled by the sudden light, momentarily stopped firing.

Rivera had already tripped the arming switch for the miniguns and as the enemy came into view, he fired. "Let it swing across!" he shouted.

Rufus shouted, "Shoot'em! We gonna git'em dis time!"

Rivera pulled back very slightly on the cyclic to raise the nose just enough as the stream of fire from the miniguns traversed the whole area around the bunker. It hit the bunker too and he prayed that Hayes and Slobojan had kept their heads down.

0441 Hours

As Hayes launched the flare, a cacophony of screams came from the enemy soldiers. It pierced the roiling, dreamy euphoria that had rendered him bulletproof and infallible. All of his invincibility vanished. He started to insert a magazine into his M16 but his hands were shaking so badly that he dropped it. He picked it up and tried again. It fluttered out of his shaking hands and tumbled over the edge of the roof. Just as he heard the pop of the flare he was stricken with panic as he realized he was above the sandbags lining the edge of the roof, in full view of the screaming enemy. He dropped flat on the roof and pushed his head hard into the sand bags. "I want to go home!" he moaned, absolutely certain he was about to die.

Then came the sound of the miniguns, a gigantic, deep-throated, grinding clatter. Inside, Slobojan was looking out of the firing port over the top of his M60, having cleared the jam, as he fired at the VC, who were suddenly so visible in the light. One second they were there, and the next they were falling with hundreds of bullets shredding their bodies. The bunker shuddered twice as the miniguns swept it.

Together the two miniguns were firing about 8,000 rounds of 7.62 millimeter ammo per minute, or almost 140 per second. In just a few seconds, they expended more than Hayes and Slobojan and the enemy had fired during the intense firefight that had preceded the addition of the helicopter to the mix. Slobojan and Hayes had killed a lot of enemy soldiers and more than surpassed anyone's standard for the effective use of their weapons. But Rivera, Rufus and the miniguns brought hell on earth to the attacking Viet Cong battalion. It was the end of the battalion. Never again would it fight as a unit.

The tragedy was compounded by the final order given by the battalion's commander. He had finally grasped that there were only a few soldiers opposing him in the bunker and that their firing had diminished. Only one machinegun continued shooting, and its bursts had grown increasingly short and then stopped. He ordered the entire battalion to charge so they could quickly overwhelm the bunker and enter the base camp before the Americans had a chance to reinforce. In fact, he hoped they would also surprise the reinforcements and catch them in the open. The colonel in command was highly respected by the men and women in the battalion, so virtually everyone had risen and was either running or walking forward when the helicopter opened fire.

Slobojan could see everything in the light of the flare. Silvery dust rose in gigantic swirls. Through it, he saw a few bodies twitch, or perhaps it was the last of the momentum imparted from the impact of hundreds of 7.62 millimeter slugs. Here and there flickers of light reflected off the metallic debris and clothing tatters propelled into the air. He thought everyone was dead, but as he watched, a head, then a head and shoulders holding an RPG popped up at the far edge of his range of vision through the firing port. He swung the M60 around but before he could fire, he heard the roar, saw the flame of the rocket, and almost immediately, an explosion behind him.

"No!" He fired a burst at the soldier with the RPG. The man went down fast and Slobojan wasn't sure he had hit him.

***

The rocket trail flashed for a split second in Rivera's peripheral vision, just long enough for his brain to take it in. He heard the explosion, felt the shock hit his body, felt the helicopter tipping forward and to the right, saw the rotor's disk approaching the ground. He reached to turn off the engine, thinking inanely that he might lessen the damage if he could stop the rotor from spinning. The machine bounced from one skid to the other as it tipped forward. Then the blades smacked the ground and the helicopter jerked and shook like a freshly caught fish. Rivera's vision was obscured by a swoosh of dust. *Why is the dust orange?* he wondered and the answer was clear when he felt the heat of burning jet fuel behind him. As soon as the thought formed, he unsnapped the safety harness.

He would never be sure exactly how he got out, but he found himself crouched on the center control console, looking between the tops of the two pilot seats. There was fire to the left and the open door to the right so he straightened his legs like a swimmer pushing off the wall of a swimming pool and launched himself diagonally between the seats. He sailed through the open door, smacking his shoulder, and then hit the ground rolling as if he had done it a thousand times before. He rolled over several times when he saw flames on his clothing. He started crawling away from the burning helicopter until he saw that most of the fire was on the other side. *Where's Rufus?* Rivera got up and scrambled around the wreck, stopping when he found him lying on the other side. Rufus was on his back, nearer the flames than Rivera, and the heat was almost more than Rivera could bear. Rivera scrambled forward and reached under Rufus' arms, trying to drag him away. Rufus screamed. He was stuck; his legs were pinned under one of the skids.

"Help! Cut me! Cut me! Be burnin'."

Rufus' voice was a shriek of agony, his screaming continual. Rivera saw that he had been sprayed with jet fuel. Some of the patches were still smoking and Rivera beat on them with his hands, making Rufus scream louder.

"I haven't got a knife," Rivera said. "Let me see if I can lift the skid."

He went to the front of the skid where it curved upward slightly and pulled on it. He got down into a crouch and put his back and legs into it. It didn't budge. Slobojan appeared at his side.

"Goddamn," he said as he grabbed the skid beside Rivera. The two of them pulled and this time there was a slight movement. Hayes walked up, glassy-eyed. He looked at Rufus, then at Slobojan and Rivera and then at the helicopter. The flames had almost died out. Hayes studied the helicopter for a moment like he was sizing up a vehicle in a used car lot. It was lying mostly on one side with the top skid about four feet from the steel revetment. "Why don't we push on the other skid and try to roll this fucker over?" He hopped up, planting his feet on the revetment and got one shoulder and his hands against the skid. Slobojan pulled himself up beside him in the same position. The skid was as hot as a car left out in the summer sun. The two groaned as they tried to straighten their bodies, feeling the helicopter move just a few inches. Rufus' screaming hit a new crescendo.

Rivera shouted, "Got him out!"

Hayes and Slobojan released the wreckage and it settled back with a soft bump. Hayes looked to see that both Rufus' legs were smashed to pulp where the skid had been.

Rufus was making fast, high-pitched noises like an out-of-balance tire about to spin off an axle.

Hayes hopped down and took Rufus' hand. He cradled his head in his lap.

Rivera, seemingly oblivious to the heat, leaned into the smoking wreckage and came out with the first aid kit. He fumbled out a morphine syrette and jammed it through Rufus' pants into his thigh.

Slobojan dribbled water from his canteen over the still-burning spots on him until he saw figures running toward them. "Medic!"

0511 Hours

An eerie grey fog slopped over Nui Binh Base Camp like a living entity trying to hide the horrific scene in front of Bunker Three. Each increase in light was accompanied by ever-thickening fog until it wasn't possible to see more than a few feet. But periodically, the fog ebbed and dead soldiers became grotesquely visible for a few minutes until the fog once again claimed them. Hayes sat cross-legged, leaning against the revetment beside the helicopter wreckage, strumming his guitar. He wore his purple T-shirt and fatigue trousers. Slobojan, with all his battle gear still on, was watching a spec five medic who was dabbing the cuts on Rivera's face with antiseptic and picking out pieces of Plexiglas with a pair of tweezers. Rivera's face and hands looked like they had been severely sunburned.

Hayes' random chords slowly found their way into "Jesus Loves Me," which he started singing.

Slobojan shook his head. "You are somethin' else."

Hayes kept on, but he was mostly humming because he couldn't remember any more than the first two lines. The medic and Slobojan laughed at him.

Rivera yelped as the medic pulled another plastic shard from his face. They were in the ecstatic state of soldiers who had narrowly escaped death.

Major Shiffman walked up. He shook his head and asked them what happened. Slobojan told him, and he and the major walked over to the bunker. Slobojan made no effort to explain the non-existent soldier he had lied about earlier, and Shiffman didn't ask.

About using the helicopter, he said, "That was a good idea, but you were damn lucky."

A three-quarter ton truck from the Mobile Army Surgical Hospital had picked up Rufus, and also Comstock's body. The medics weren't sure Rufus would survive because it looked like he had internal injuries in addition to his crushed legs. His burns looked very serious too. By the time the medics loaded him into the truck, he had passed out. The medics had wanted to take Rivera to the MASH, but Rivera insisted he was okay.

Two M113 tracks filled with soldiers rolled up and the major got into one. The two tracks followed the road behind the bunker line toward the main gate and disappeared into the fog.

"What the fuck is our fearless first sergeant doing out there?" asked Hayes. "Ain't nothing but a lot of dead dinks."

"Don't have a clue," Slobojan said. "He and a couple of others been out there with a deuce and a half in the fog almost since we stopped shooting."

Two shots reverberated through the mist.

"They sure as fuck ain't renderin' first aid," Hayes said. He sounded distant, disconnected from reality, but he kept strumming the guitar. Sometimes it sounded like "Jesus Loves Me," but mostly it had returned to random chords.

"Sounds like Sypher. This is probably the most action he's seen in two tours." Slobojan glanced at the medic, then gingerly reached into his pants to adjust his tender private parts. "I thought I heard the deuce and a half a little while ago. I remember the rattle in the cam. If you listen carefully you can sometimes hear stuff being loaded."

"Where'd the tracks go?" Rivera asked.

Slobojan said, "That skinny major said he was gonna make a sweep through the village. They won't find anything though."

"Why not?"

"Cause we 'bout killed them all and apparently Sypher's taking care of any survivors."

"There were still some of them left," Rivera said. "Quite a few got away, I think. How much you want to bet there's a tunnel out there?" Rivera pushed the medic away from him, turned to one side and vomited. "Every fucking time," he said. "Every fucking time I'm in a firefight."

"Well, you probably got some shock too," said the medic.

Hayes stopped playing and looked over at Rivera. "You ought'a smoke some dope," Hayes said. "Get you out of your head and mellow you out. That's what I'd do, but I'm not throwing up."

"What the hell, I don't care anymore," Rivera said.

"Actually, it does seem to get rid of nausea," said the medic. He looked around and then reached into his fatigue jacket pocket and produced a joint. He was a tall, long-legged black guy. He pulled a lighter out, lit it and took a drag. He passed it to Rivera who took a hit without hesitation, grinning at Hayes as he held his breath.

"Geez Rivera, you ought'a start smoking dope so you can extend another six months," Hayes said.

Slobojan touched the medic's arm. "You think Rufus is gonna make it?" It was the third time he'd asked.

The medic shrugged, took another hit from the joint and passed it to Slobojan. He looked at it, and finally took a small puff. The three of them continued to pass the joint around until it was nothing but a tiny stub that burned Rivera's finger as he flipped it away.

Hayes didn't smoke any of it. He was tripping from the acid, possibly more spaced out than he had been during the firefight. He was concentrating hard on maintaining his composure. It was strange. He knew he was flying on acid, but he was sure he could function if he concentrated. He was an outside observer in his own head, carefully watching everything he did. But his mind would spin off uncontrollably into a completely new line of thought if he didn't fight to keep it together. He had managed to stay on track most of the time but sometimes he slipped into a dreamlike state with hallucinations.

Presently, he was seeing all sorts of strange shapes bending, pulsating and swirling through the fog. They were spirits of the dead, but they didn't frighten Hayes. They were at peace with him, and he with them. He was a visitor in their realm, unsure whether he was welcome, but not afraid. He sensed the presence of White, McLean, Metcalf, Ziegler, Abercrombie and then strongly, Lemaire. He saw Roscoe smiling with his saxophone in one hand. It was too soon for Comstock to be there. And of course the ARVN was there, off to one side by himself, and he frightened Hayes enough to snap him out of the reverie. Had he fallen asleep? He wasn't sure but he was sure the spirits were real. He also was suddenly aware of how tired he was, but it was just his body that was tired. His mind was racing flat-out like a car on the Bonneville Salt Flats.

"If the shock don't get him, he might pull through," the medic said finally. "I think he'll lose his legs though. Crazy son of a bitch. Kept saying something about "miniguns beaucoup fun." He laughed.

"You know, I do feel a little better. I can't think straight but I'm not gonna throw up again," Rivera said. "Thanks."

Hayes looked over at Rivera again. "We'll make a hippie outta you yet, Rivera."

"Not sure exactly what a hippie is."

Again Hayes was silent for a few seconds. "You'll find out in another week," Hayes said. "Uh oh... this'll be interesting.

Here come the Spanish TV people. Sypher's gonna blow a gasket if he sees them."

Hayes, now sailing placidly along and completely out of his head, was contented as he watched and analyzed his own thought process. The ghosts of the dead receded back into the fog and the fog was turning into a surreal liquid canvas, displaying shapes like the artwork on posters for rock and roll shows. He strummed the guitar, moving through chords randomly.

The fog lazily thinned for a moment, and through the swirling wisps Sypher and two other men were tossing heavy objects into the back of the deuce and a half. Sypher seemed to scowl at the Jeep with the TV crew as it passed. He was barely visible as a shadow through the fog, but in Hayes mind he was as clear as if he were a foot away. Hayes spent what seemed like several hours examining and analyzing Sypher's scowl. Then Sypher and the other man climbed into the truck. Hayes stood and pulled off his purple T-shirt.

Slobojan said, "Will you look at that? They're gonna take off. What the hell are they up to?"

The Jeep pulled up and the three journalists jumped out.

"We are going to take pictures. Is it safe?" asked the woman. "I'm Josefina Madrid."

"Should be safe, Miss Madrid," Slobojan said. "Hayes and Rivera here can escort you. They'll be happy to shoot anyone who bothers you, provided they're not in the U.S. Army."

Rivera said, "Let Hayes do it. I'm wounded. Got brain damage."

"Yeah, you'd better at least come to the dispensary," the medic said, looking at him closely. "There's still glass in your face, and I want a doctor to look at the burns. I think your face is starting to blister."

Rivera shrugged, but he didn't move. Hayes put down the guitar and grabbed his M16, which felt like it weighed a hundred pounds.

"Be happy to tag along with you TV folks. My brain's in fantastic shape right now."

As they walked toward the bunker Madrid's eyes opened wide as the grotesque sight of the bodies came into view. "Tell me what happened."

Hayes slowed as he tried to organize the random thoughts that were colliding and competing to come to the fore. "Charlie attacked, and like, we kicked the shit out of him. Real turkey shoot. Rivera there flew that helicopter and just as they charged they got French-kissed by a couple of miniguns." Shaken, Hayes looked around. He had avoided looking at the bodies until now. He said softly, "Dawn's early light wasn't a good time for the bad guys."

As they walked through the bodies, Hayes tried not to look directly at the carnage. There was something not right about the bodies, but he didn't want to think about it. Instead he was sorting through "Jesus Loves Me," trying to write verses. Since he couldn't remember the words, he'd have to make up his own. It seemed really important.

Madrid didn't ask more questions, but she was looking at the bodies. She gasped and frantically directed the cameraman to keep shooting. At one point she carefully moved away from Hayes.

The cameraman got a shot of him walking through the tangle of bodies, his tired arms draped up and over his M16, balanced against the back of his bare shoulders. The mist was cold but Hayes' body temperature senses were not working right and he felt hot. He didn't notice that the woman was no longer next to him. His mind latched onto a powerful memory of Gloria and himself, naked and rolling around in the warm bed in the Cresthaven Motel. That image was quickly replaced by one of himself lying dead, surrounded by the dead he had just seen, with the ARVN watching from behind them. This time, the ARVN was grinning at Hayes' body. Hayes felt doomed. He would never come home and he would never see Gloria again. He sank to his knees. One hand became disengaged from the rifle and the weight of the other arm flipped it over his shoulder. It toppled to the ground beside him. Tears streamed down his face. He whispered, "Oh God, I love you Gloria... I love you." He didn't notice the camera whirring.

0645 Hours

Once more deep in a funk, Hayes walked back to the bunker behind the TV crew, noting that the fog had lessened considerably. He was concentrating on his ability to distinguish fantasy from reality, trying to regain his composure and most of all to make sense of what he had seen. But it was like someone had scrambled his brain. Slobojan, Rivera and the medic were still by the revetment. The TV crew peeled off and stayed at the bunker, the cameraman and the sound man setting up for a shot of the woman. She was leaning against the side of the bunker scribbling in her notebook, a microphone dangling over her arm.

"I know what Sypher the Lifer was doing," Hayes said.

Slobojan moaned. "Why do I think I'm not gonna like it?"

"Yeah Slobbo," Hayes said. "I don't think any of us are gonna like this. You neither, Rivera."

Rivera said, "Hold up a sec, Hayes, I want to hear what she says." He trotted over to corner of the bunker. The medic made a half-hearted effort to stop him, but then got up and went after him. Reluctantly, Slobojan and Hayes followed, and for the first time, Hayes noticed that the blackened patches on Rivera's clothing were actually holes, and the crusty black was his skin. Was it real, or a hallucination? Rivera got to the bunker just as the woman began speaking in Spanish.

"Late last night, some of the villagers told us that Americans fired into the village with rifles and machineguns for no apparent reason. And then early this morning American soldiers in this bunker massacred many dozens, perhaps more than a hundred, of unarmed Vietnamese here at Nui Binh. Walking through the horrific killing zone, this reporter could find no weapons."

In Spanish Rivera shouted, "No! No! That's not what happened. These were armed soldiers. You've got it all wrong!" Then he turned to the others and spoke in English. "Jesus Christ, she thinks these are dead civilians and that we murdered them. She says they don't have any weapons."

"That's what I'm trying to tell you guys," Hayes said. "They *don't* have any weapons. That's what Sypher was doing, collecting the weapons. They loaded that truck with them. They even took most of the web gear."

Slobojan said, "Jesus Christ! Commie weapons are worth quite a bit of money. I heard some swabbies'll pay a hundred bucks cash for an AK."

Rivera began speaking desperately in Spanish to Madrid and the other two in the group. "That idiot sergeant you spoke to yesterday and some others picked up all the weapons from the bodies. They're gonna sell them," Rivera said.

"I don't believe you, and nobody else will either," she said. "These were unarmed civilians. I saw women among them as well. If they were soldiers with guns, they would have killed you. There were far too many."

"We caught them with the miniguns on that helicopter," Rivera said pointing toward the wreckage.

"What helicopter?" she asked.

"That one! It got hit with a rocket during the fight," Rivera said. "But you saw it yesterday."

"The one that crashed?" she asked. "That proves it. That helicopter was disabled. It wouldn't work. It had no tail rotor and—"

He screamed, "You don't know what the fuck you're talking about! You weren't here! I was!"

The woman turned to the cameraman and in Spanish said, "Make sure you get this war criminal."

Rivera pulled the pistol from his pocket and started to pull back the slide to cock it. Hayes and Slobojan lunged for him.

"Cool it Rivera, there's nothing you can do."

"I can kill that bitch!" he said.

"No you can't," Slobojan said.

"Watch me!"

"Want to beat me to LBJ?" Hayes said

The cameraman continued filming the scene and Hayes and Slobojan held Rivera down. They heard another vehicle driving up.

"Holy shit," Slobojan said. "Put the gun away. It's the CO."

Rivera slipped the gun back into his pocket. The door of the Jeep slammed shut and Lieutenant Colonel Blair strode up accompanied by Major Lehman and CW2 Walters.

Walters embraced Rivera and then Hayes. "Glad you guys made it." Then he caught sight of Lehman glaring at him. Walters stood to one side and Rivera, Hayes and the medic saluted the three officers.

Blair and Lehman returned the salutes crisply and then Blair turned his attention to the camera crew. He was an imposing man with heavy lines of fatigue around his eyes that made him look older than his 30 years. He had been flying and leading the company every day in the air, and they had suffered a lot of casualties during the past month. Blair had the gift of being able to intimidate people just by looking at them. As he looked at the three Spanish journalists his lip curled slightly. He pointed his finger at the woman. "You all get out of here," he said softly, but the threat in his voice was strong. The cameraman picked up the camera and tripod and followed his companion toward their Jeep.

The colonel dismissed the medic, who looked with concern at Rivera, and then walked away.

"Now, I want to hear from each of you about exactly what happened here. We'll start with the lowest ranking person and work our way up. I believe that's you, PFC Hayes," said Blair. "The rest of you wait in the bunker because we're going to do this one at a time with no one hearing what anyone else has to say about it." Blair waited until Slobojan and Rivera had left, then looked at Hayes. "Okay, Private, let's have it."

"Well," Hayes said, "they hit us just before first light, probably about 0430 and—"

"Private, start at the beginning. How many men were on guard here?"

"Oh, there was Sergeant Slobojan, Rufus, Rivera and me."

"Just four of you?"

"Yes Sir, four of us. Well, and Mr. Comstock Sir. He showed up just as the fight started. I think he got killed before he fired a shot."

"But you told Major Shiffman from base camp defense that there were six of you."

"Yes Sir."

"Why?"

"Not sure, Sir, but I think Sergeant Slobojan was told to do that by the first sergeant."

"Okay, let's leave that until I talk to the sergeant. Now, tell me who fired first when everyone opened up last night," said Blair.

Hayes hung his head. He forced himself to ignore the spinning in his brain. *Speak slowly, one thing at a time.* "It was us, Sir. That machinegun in the bunker was rusty and hadn't been cleaned for a long time. The ammo was dirty too. So Rufus and I stripped it down and cleaned it. I wanted to see if it would work, so Rufus did a test fire. It jammed, but then everyone else started firing. Sergeant Slobojan wasn't here. He was getting us some chow. Rivera was taking a shower. So they had nothing to do with it. It was just me and Rufus."

"You didn't think to call base camp operations, or our own operations, to ask permission, or at least warn them?" asked Blair.

"Sir, we had no radio, and the field phone wasn't working to ops. We told that major when he came by last night that we had no radio. That skinny major said there was a radio here the night before, so I don't know what happened to it. The plan was to use the radio in that crashed helicopter if something happened."

Blair shook his head, but said nothing. He turned around to look at the wreckage of the helicopter and was silent, thinking. He looked skeptical. "So let me understand this. There were just four of you out here. You had no radio and the machinegun in the bunker wasn't operable, so you—"

"Sir, we had the two M60s from the gunship. I never brought them back to the armament hut. We put one on the roof and one inside. But we didn't have a lot of ammo for them. It was lucky that I was able to scrounge a little more last night from one of the Headhunter hootches.

"What about Warrant Officer Comstock? When did he get here?"

"Sir, like I said, Mr. Comstock got here just as we got hit. I didn't see him arrive. I heard—no, I *felt*—a thump as he landed beside me just as the enemy started firing, and when I looked over, he was dead."

"Tell me about the attack. Did you see them coming? Who fired first?

"Well, it was about 0430. Sergeant Slobojan, Rufus and me were inside the bunker listening to Ho Chi Minh on Slobbo's—I mean the sergeant's—transistor radio. Well, we thought it was Ho, but who knows? Rivera was on the roof and said he had beaucoup movement. Then we could see them too. They were crawling from the brush out there toward the bunker. It looked like there were hundreds of them. Rivera said he'd go back to the ship and radio base camp ops. That's when we got the idea of using the miniguns."

"Who's idea was that?" asked the colonel.

"Well, all of us. Some of it was me, some of it was Rivera and some of it was Slobbo. Rufus made it work 'cause he's so big. It just sort of came to us. Rivera knows how to operate the radios... well, I guess I do too, but he also knows how to start the helicopter and Mr. Walters taught him how to hover. And we figured Rufus was big and strong enough to hold the tail. So the two of them went back to the ship."

"That was before the shooting started?"

"Yes Sir," Hayes said. "I must have opened fire from the roof a minute or two after they left. They must have passed pretty close to Mr. Comstock, but if they saw him, Rivera never said anything about it. I think Mr. Comstock must have gone into the bunker first because he brought all of Slobbo's M16 magazines and grenades up here. And it's a good thing he did."

"Did Sergeant Slobojan order you to open fire?"

"No Sir, I started shooting first because they were getting too close. You can see how close the closest bodies are to the front of the bunker. Can't be more than 15 or 20 meters. I could see a lot better than Slobbo. I was up higher and he had to look through the firing port."

Blair nodded and walked around to the front of the bunker, followed by Hayes, Lehman and Walters. He stood in the front of the bunker for close to a full minute and then paced straight out, counting the paces until he came to the first bodies. He counted 17 paces. He turned to Hayes again. "So when the firefight started, there were only three of you here, and Comstock was killed right away, so there were actually only the two of you?"

Hayes nodded. "Yes Sir, but we were both firing machineguns."

"How long before the helicopter was able to fire the miniguns? It couldn't have been very long."

Hayes thought for several seconds, which seemed like hours. The firefight had seemed hours long too, but he knew it wasn't. "I'm not sure, Sir. It's hard to keep track of time in a firefight. Maybe a couple of minutes, probably less, but maybe more. I used all the ammo I had for the machinegun, which was a few hundred rounds. I counted eight empty magazines for my M16 after it was over, and I threw a couple of frags. And I fired that flare. How long does all that take? We were very busy but it's really hard to remember how long a firefight lasts. Maybe Sergeant Slobojan has a better idea than me."

"I'll get to him," said Blair. He looked at the bodies again, squinting. "What happened to their weapons?"

"The first sergeant had a truck out here early. I think he collected them," Hayes said even more carefully than he had been speaking before. He wondered whether he should volunteer that Sypher had probably shot several of the wounded as well, then decided that can of worms was best left unopened. At least for now.

"Major Lehman!"

"Yes Sir," said Lehman.

"I want you to go back to the company and look for that truck. When you find it, detail two warrant officers to make a complete inventory of the captured weapons. I want to know numbers and types of weapons. Perhaps the first sergeant already has some of that information. If so, make sure it's checked. Then order the first sergeant to report to me, right here, immediately."

Lehman turned and left, walking briskly toward the company area.

Blair turned to Hayes fully turning on his intimidating glare. "Private Hayes, are you aware that the first sergeant last night presented me with papers to court martial you for using drugs, specifically marijuana?"

Hayes decided to go down fighting. He met Blair's eyes. "I don't see how that can be possible, Sir."

"Private Hayes, do you smoke marijuana?" Blair snapped angrily and Hayes hesitated as his resolve slipped. The colonel said, "This is a war, and as your commanding officer I want to get to the bottom of what's going on around here. I'm responsible for this unit and for everyone in it. We can't risk lives because somebody's high on drugs. You will tell me the truth or so help me I'll have your ass in Long Binh Jail before lunch. Now, do you smoke marijuana?" he said again with an edge of command that broached no argument.

"Yes Sir, I have smoked marijuana," answered Hayes. "I was smoking on Christmas Eve and got an Article 15 for it. You signed it. That was the first time I'd smoked in more than a month. When I was flying slicks, I smoked it almost every night when we got back. But I quit when I went over to the Headhunters."

"Were you smoking it yesterday and last night before the firefight?"

"No Sir, I haven't smoked anything but tobacco since Christmas Eve," Hayes said, feeling anger coming on. "I know I have a bad reputation around here, but Rivera convinced me to stop. You know, there are a lot of pilots and crew chiefs and gunners and mechanics who regularly get drunk and fly hung over. And I've seen some of them fly drunk. You've got people popping bennies to stay awake. You've got people who don't do any of that and can't do their jobs. Major Lehman for instance. He's a teetotaler, but everybody's afraid to fly with him."

"That's enough, Private," Blair said quietly. "Go into the bunker and tell Specialist Rivera to come out here."

"Sir!" Walters said sharply. "I will support Private Hayes in everything he just said. He's one of the most competent door gunners in the Headhunters, and the other things he said are true as well."

Blair glared at Walters and nodded. "Duly noted." He watched Hayes disappear into the bunker.

"Walters, you go in there and make sure Hayes doesn't talk to the others." In a tone that was a little softer, he added, "And you keep *your* mouth shut as well."

Both Rivera and Slobojan had been called out for interviews, but neither lasted as long as Hayes' had. Ten minutes after Slobojan came back into the bunker, they had spotted Lehman outside with Sypher. Sypher looked pale and unhappy. No one spoke. Rivera dozed on the cot. About 15 more minutes passed and they could hear voices but not what was being said. Then, at Blair's order, they all filed out of the bunker. Without any instruction, they fell into a line standing at attention: Sypher, Slobojan, Rivera, Hayes, Walters and Lehman. Rivera was standing with his legs apart and slightly slumped over. He looked like he was in pain. In front of the bunker, Major Shiffman was supervising a detail of grunts who were arranging the bodies in a line and going through pockets.

"Men, stand at ease," Blair started. "I am pleased that your individual stories all agree with each other, and with what I've learned from Major Shiffman. I want to commend Sergeant Slobojan, Specialist Rivera, PFC Hayes, the absent Private Roy and the late Mr. Comstock for a job well done. Sergeant Slobojan!"

"Yes Sir?"

"Effective immediately, you will take over temporarily as supply sergeant," said Blair.

Sypher said, "Sir, that's an E-7 slot and Slobojan's only—"

"Sergeant Sypher, I don't believe I asked you to speak."

"Yes Sir," Sypher said.

Lt. Col. Blair looked at Slobojan. "You are dismissed."

Slobojan saluted the colonel and lumbered off toward the company area.

"Specialist Rivera!"

"Yes Sir," Rivera said.

"Effective immediately, you are grounded. You can help out in maintenance until you rotate home... unless they keep you at the hospital. You look like they might do that. Go over to the MASH unit right now," said Blair. "That is an order and you are dismissed."

"Yes Sir." Rivera saluted, turned and began walking slowly toward the company.

"Mr. Walters!"

"Yes Sir," Walters said.

"You won't be flying today so you will find time today to pack up Mr. Comstock's belongings. I would be grateful if you could draft a letter for me to send to his parents. I don't think he was married."

"No Sir, he wasn't," Walters said.

"You are dismissed," Blair said, and Walters saluted and left.

"PFC Hayes!"

"Yes Sir," Hayes said.

Blair looked at Hayes carefully, and Hayes tried to look him in the eye.

"You have been a problem, but I believe you are innocent of the charges made by the first sergeant. Furthermore you acquitted yourself well in this firefight."

"Thank you Sir. I—"

Blair held up his hand. "According to Specialist Rivera and Mr. Walters, you are a competent gunner and ready to take on the responsibilities of a crew chief, and God knows we're short of crew chiefs. Effective immediately, you will fly as a crew chief. You will not be court martialed. We're far too short-handed to lose competent people, whether it's to drugs, alcohol, VD or combat. But if you're caught smoking it again, you *will* receive an Article 15 at the very least, and a court martial for any subsequent offense, so I strongly suggest that you continue to avoid drugs. No, let me correct that. I am making that a direct order to stop. Will you follow that order?"

Hayes looked directly into Blair's eyes. "Yes Sir."

"Finally, effective immediately, you're promoted back to Specialist Fourth Class. You are dismissed."

"Yes Sir." He saluted, turned and began trotting toward the company area.

"First Sergeant Sypher!"

"Yes Sir," Sypher murmured.

"I was informed this morning that I will shortly receive paperwork to transfer you to the 24th Evacuation Hospital. I have to admit that solves a problem for me because in my opinion, you have failed to perform your duties as first sergeant adequately. I believe I have sufficient evidence to court martial you for disobeying a direct order from Major Shiffman to put six guards in this bunker, and I suspect that you gathered the enemy weapons this morning for your own profit. I do *not* believe you had any cause to try to court martial PFC Hayes. Furthermore, the chow in this unit has deteriorated since your arrival, and on some occasions, aircrews have gone hungry because they had no C-rations.

"I am not going to court martial you because court martialing a senior enlisted man is more trouble than I want right now. So I'll go along with your transfer. Sergeant Reyes, the supply sergeant who is the senior E-7, will take over your duties temporarily, and I want you to bring him up to speed before you leave. You are dismissed."

"Yes Sir," Sypher said. He grimly saluted and began plodding toward the company, leaving Blair and Lehman alone together.

"Walk with me," Blair said. He began slowly walking toward the company, his hands clasped behind his back, his expression troubled. Lehman fell in beside him. The colonel said, "This was almost a disaster. If it hadn't been for those four men, you and I might be dead now. We certainly would have lost more lives, some of our ships and who knows what else. The entire base camp could have been overrun. And it would have been my responsibility. I need your help to fix this."

"Sir, what's broken?" asked Lehman.

"Discipline for one thing," said Blair. "I've been flying almost every day and not paying attention to the discipline back here on the ground. We don't have enough men, for another. We are critically short of flight personnel. There isn't a pilot in this company who doesn't seriously exceed the maximum allowable flight hours, and by many, many hours. That's dangerous. And why are we so short on supplies? We shouldn't have to beg food from the infantry when we're flying." The colonel stopped and looked at Lehman. "Frank, you're the worst pilot I've ever known. How the hell did you make it through flight school?" asked Blair.

Lehman shrugged. "I don't know. I'm sure it's not from lack of trying. I wish I could practice more. I need more hours as a peter pilot," said Lehman.

"I agree, but it's more than just your flying skills. As soon as you're off the ground, you seem to lose your ability to think. I can't let you command the flight from the right seat because you don't know what you're doing in the air. I've never seen anything like it. So I need you to take more control of this unit on the ground. According to your records, you have been a competent administrator, but you have to be far more effective than you've been so far. I need that from you and you need to do it because your lack of flying skills is a major handicap for any further promotion. I don't believe you're cut out to command a combat assault helicopter company. You'll need my support if you're going to advance in some other area. I need you to do everything else."

Blair paused, then gestured. "Let's walk." As they started walking again, he said, "Okay, so I need you to fix the supply problem. Do whatever it takes to get us more men, especially flight personnel. Work on the discipline. The first sergeant isn't the only one not doing his job. I believe there are others who are drinking more than they should and who might be involved in illegal activities. Maybe the officers and the enlisted men's clubs should close earlier, or shut down completely. I don't necessarily want a campaign on drunkenness or even marijuana if the result is that we lose more men. We can't afford to lose anyone. Perhaps a few strategic Article 15s or even court martials wouldn't hurt, especially if they are aimed at men whose performance is questionable.

"I believed Hayes about what he said regarding marijuana, but something wasn't right despite what he said. He seemed a little strange, like he wasn't all there. Hard to tell with somebody after an action like that one. All three of them were severely shaken. But Sergeant Slobojan said it was mainly Hayes who repelled that attack initially, because the sergeant's machinegun jammed. As far as I can tell, Hayes is competent and has performed his duties as a gunner very well. He's a draftee too."

As they continued to walk Blair stopped talking for a long moment, then said, "Frank, we're walking a fine line here. This is a combat unit, and it has been a damn effective combat unit. Combat is our mission, our bottom line. We are not, and never will be, a parade ground outfit. So you need to exercise better judgment than you've exhibited so far." Blair stopped walking and looked past Lehman for a moment, thinking. "Frank, I know you're a preacher and perhaps you want to save some souls, but I need you to put that aside until you get home and out of this war. I need to know that you understand, pilots swearing is not a problem; pilots *flying hung over* is a problem. Dirty pictures are not a problem; *drinking on duty* is a problem. Major Shiffman told me he smelled alcohol on Comstock's breath last night. Sergeant Slobojan told me Comstock only came to the bunker that one time with Shiffman, and didn't return until just before he was killed. If he hadn't been killed, I'd probably be charging him with dereliction of duty."

"Yes Sir," Lehman said.

"I need you to fix these problems on the ground here. Can you do this, Frank?"

"Yes Sir. I will do the best job that I can Sir," Lehman said. "However, I really want to have the opportunity to continue working on my flying skills. I want to become a competent pilot."

Blair looked at him for a moment, then nodded. "Fair enough, but until you improve, I don't think you should be with the company on combat missions. Hone your skills on safe flights like the courier or some ash and trash missions. Perhaps while you're in Long Binh, you can make some contacts to crack those supply and personnel problems. I don't expect you to spend the rest of your tour in the company area here, but I do need you to solve the problems we've talked about."

"Thank you, and I'll try Sir," said Lehman. His hand brushed the bible in his pocket as he came to attention and saluted.

0950 Hours

Hayes, his mind chugging along placidly like an ocean liner easing toward a wharf, was standing in front of the Operations Bunker watching a helicopter come in. The Blackjack flight had left only five minutes before, a late start necessitated by the morning attack. All the ships had to be checked carefully for damage, and the CO had flatly refused to go until he finished his personal inquiries into his unit's performance. Hayes had taken a shower, changed into clean jungle fatigues and then hung around the Operations Bunker listening to the radio traffic for half an hour. He learned there had been several other attacks, but the one on Nui Binh was the biggest. However, NVA regulars had somehow gotten into another base camp, Cu Chi.

He was still spacey, still jazzed, but under control. That hadn't been easy. In the shower as the cool water ran over his skin, he drove away all thoughts of Gloria and his mind seemed to descend into some kind of mental sludge for a period. But his despair lifted and he became more aware of the hallucinations. Walls turned to rubber. Faces of people he met looked like Halloween masks. As he dressed in the clean clothes, savoring their intensely fresh smell, he realized the acid trip had turned entertaining. The fatigues were almost brand new, having only been worn and washed once. He hadn't had a chance to get a tailor to take them in to make them more form fitting, which wasn't only more in fashion but prevented them from flapping in the wind as much when he flew. Now he looked like the grunts in their baggy fatigues. Watching the helicopter come in, he closed his eyes and secretly levitated himself a few inches off the ground. He kept his eyes closed for a long moment, then drifted back to the ground. He remained convinced that no one could tell he was high.

Everyone he met clapped him on the back and wanted to hear about the firefight. He couldn't believe he wasn't going to be court martialed and that he was a spec four again. And now he was a crew chief. In the space of a couple of hours, his fortunes had dramatically reversed. He hadn't slept for more than 24 hours, but he wasn't tired. He'd half-expected, even hoped, that he would be asked to crew a ship in the flight that morning, but apparently he would get the day off. He knew that he ought to try to sleep before it got too hot, but he was still amped up, still enjoying the acid trip.

The helicopter landed and three replacements disembarked, dragging duffel bags toward the operations bunker.

"I'll take them to the Orderly Room if you like," Hayes said to the Operations clerk.

"Thanks," the clerk said.

The replacements were a warrant officer and two enlisted men. Their faces weren't masks and Hayes' levitation powers vanished. Hayes introduced himself and said he would take them to be checked in.

"You fly?" one of the replacements asked as he eyed Hayes.

"Yeah," Hayes said. "I'm a crew chief."

"How do I get flight status?" the replacement asked. "I'm avionics, but I'd rather fly as a gunner."

"Just tell 'em that," Hayes said. He looked at the nametag on the guy's shirt and saw his name was Hollister. He was a big good-looking black guy, a couple of inches taller than Hayes and muscular. Hayes figured he must be around 200 pounds. "You're pretty big, but we're short on flight personnel. I don't think we need help in avionics as badly. If you have any experience with machineguns that'll help, but unless you have a single digit IQ you can pretty much learn how to be a door gunner on the job... as long as you don't freeze up under fire that is."

"Shit, that'll be the day," Hollister said, looking with some disdain at Hayes. "And I know guns, even machineguns."

Hollister looked a little older than most new arrivals and was intimidating too, like he had a chip on his shoulder. His handsome face had turned into a mask with a sinister caste.

The warrant officer asked, "What about warrant officer pilots?" His nametag read *Maupin*. "Are you short of them too?"

"Yeah, if anything we need pilots even worse," Hayes said. "Flight crews around here hardly ever get a day off. This is the first day in six months that I haven't been flying. Well, I guess we all got Christmas Day off on account of the truce."

"How'd you get lucky?" asked Maupin.

"We crashed a helicopter yesterday," Hayes said. "You might have seen the wreck over beside the runway when you came in. Then I had guard duty last night and we got hit. It's a long fuckin' story."

As he opened the door to the Orderly Room it occurred to him that he might run into Sypher. That could be interesting. He had already heard that Sypher was leaving. But when he entered, Sergeant Reyes was talking to the company clerk who was hunched over a typewriter.

"Three replacements for you, Sarge," Hayes said. "A warrant officer, an avionics guy who wants to be a gunner and...." He looked at the third replacement, a very young looking white guy named Masterson. "Bat Masterson here."

"I'm a clerk." Masterson grinned. "And the name's Bobby, not Bat."

"Great!" said Cartwright, the company clerk. "I could use some help."

Hayes rapidly backed out of the door. He had only taken a few steps when Reyes came out the door of the Orderly Room. "Hayes, grab your stuff and get down to the flight line. They need you for a single ship mission. Ops just called looking for you."

"Okay," Hayes said. "Tell 'em I'll be there as soon as I can get my stuff."

He hurried to his hootch. He suddenly realized that as a crew chief, he didn't have to get the machineguns. Five minutes later he loped up the flight line to a lone helicopter where he could see Walters.

"Need a crew chief?" Hayes asked, saluting.

"And a gunner too, and a peter pilot," Walters said, returning the salute with a wave. "Glad you're here."

"Real sorry about Comstock," Hayes said.

Walters nodded. "Yeah. I should have stopped him from drinking so much." He put his hand on Hayes' shoulder and squeezed. "You did real well out there. I didn't know the first sergeant was trying to court martial you."

Hayes shrugged and looked at the helicopter. It was a nice, new-looking UH-1H, which wasn't a gunship. He hoped it wasn't going to be his ship because he didn't want to leave the Headhunters. He got out the logbook and saw that the ship didn't just look new but was actually brand new. It had arrived the day before. Hayes started the pre-flight inspection and Walters walked around with him. It took a few minutes and not surprisingly he found everything was in order. "Looks good to me," Hayes said.

"Me too," Walters said. "Now if we can get ourselves a couple of more bodies we'll be set."

"What's the mission?"

"We're taking over as courier today. We'll be going to Cu Chi and Long Binh, and taking our time," Walters said. "I'll sneak you into the officers' mess. They got ice cream."

"Sounds like fun." Hayes plugged in his helmet, which bore scorch marks, and discovered the headphones didn't work. "Sir, I have to go back and find another helmet. Mine must have burned up. I'll stop at Ops and see who's supposed to be our gunner. I'll try to get us some Cs too."

"Okay, but be quick," Walters said. He looked toward the Operations Bunker where a lone figure with a flight helmet was hurrying toward the ship. "Oh shit, I think it's Major Lehman, and I'll bet he's our peter pilot. He's always trying to get in flight time."

Hayes left at a trot. When he got to Lehman he paused to salute and explain what he was doing.

"They hadn't found a gunner when I left Ops," Lehman said. He looked at Hayes closely. "Are you okay now?"

Embarrassed, Hayes nodded. Lehman's face was melting and he knew he was still trippy. But he was used to it now. "I'm fine," he said. "A little tired, but otherwise okay."

"Well, it's just the courier, a milk run," said Lehman in a surprisingly friendly tone. "Kind of thing I need for practice and I'm going to try to see the First Aviation Brigade S 1."

When Hayes walked into the Operations Bunker, the captain in charge looked at him in surprise. "What are you doing here Hayes? I thought you were already out there."

"Looking for a helmet and a gunner," Hayes said. "Look, there was an FNG name of Hollister who came in this morning who said he wanted to fly as a gunner. He looked like he might be okay. Said he knew a little about guns."

"I don't know, but it's an idea," the captain said, thinking about it. "I guess if he's going to be a gunner, he might as well start now. We haven't found anyone else and we have to get this show on the road." The captain cranked a field phone and asked someone about a helmet. "Go over to supply. They got a brand new helmet for you."

"Thanks, Sir. If you get that FNG as a gunner, have him meet me at the armament hut. I'll help him with the guns 'cause he probably doesn't know shit about what he's supposed to do."

Hayes trotted out of the bunker. He was heading for the supply shed when he saw Rivera talking to the Spanish reporter woman. He couldn't believe Rivera hadn't gone to the MASH. Rivera waved at him and he trotted over. The two were rapidly conversing in Spanish and the woman's spectacular cleavage was on full display. Hayes could see a large swath of tits and a good deal of a very thin black lacy bra.

"I'm apologizing," Rivera said contritely. Hayes thought he looked terrible. In addition to dozens of small cuts on his face from the Plexiglas, he had blisters all over his face and the exposed skin on his arms. Hayes was hoping that it was the acid that was making them pulsate.

The woman walked away and when she was out of earshot Rivera said, "I might have gotten her straightened out on what happened in the firefight. She listened to what I said, but I don't know. Great tits though. Best I've seen since I've been over here."

"Big tits, small brain. I'm not sure about her," Hayes said. "I get the idea she doesn't like Americans."

"Jesus, I can't wait to get home," Rivera said. "Gonna find me a woman with big tits."

"Look Rivera, you got to go over to the MASH," Hayes said, taking him by the shoulders and pointing toward hospital. "You look awful. You probably scared her some more."

"Okay, you're right," he said. "I don't feel so good. It's really starting to hurt. You be careful, Hayes." He reached into his pocket and handed Hayes his Tokarev pistol. "Take this. I don't need it anymore. Go ahead and sell it if you want." He took a box of bullets for it from the other pocket and handed them over too. Then he started toward the MASH.

Slobojan was ready with the new helmet, a case of C-rations and a gallon cooler of cherry Kool-Aid. Hollister was standing outside armament hut with Cartwright. Hayes got two M60s, all the while explaining to Hollister what he was doing.

At the ship, Hayes showed Hollister how to mount the guns on the pedestal mount. He showed him how to load the first M60 and watched as he loaded the second one. Then he spent a couple of minutes telling him he had to watch out for anything the helicopter could hit on his side of the ship. He gave him a quick lesson on how the radio switch worked, showed him the seatbelt, and watched him put on his helmet.

Then engine started to whine and Hayes levitated himself onboard, or so he imagined.

"We been scrubbed as courier," Walters announced as the ship rose from the ground. "There's a special forces firebase, Camp Johnson, this side of Long Binh that's been under attack all night. They want us to fly in a load of ammo. It could be a hot one, but probably not."

1233 Hours

Camp Johnson was on top of a rocky hill several hundred meters high. There was a small river running through a valley on the west side of the hill and on the other three sides triple-canopy jungle grew right up to its base. Even from a thousand meters up, Hayes could see bodies on all sides of the hill. Two Cobra gunships were firing rockets at the jungle on the north side of the hill and raking it with their 40-millimeter cannons. From the radio chatter, it sounded like they were trying to take out a .51, which no one had actually seen. Each gunship fired two rockets and then made a run toward the explosions where they pummeled the area with miniguns and cannon fire. A few tracers were coming up toward the gunships, but none of them looked like they were from a .51. When they were picking up the ammo, he'd heard that the camp was manned with half a dozen Green Berets, two dozen Montagnards and a platoon of ARVN Rangers. They'd been hit hard the night before, and were receiving periodic mortar fire, but they were holding their own. There hadn't been a ground attack since the sun came up.

Both of the Cobra aircraft commanders were telling them that the area might be too hot for them to go in. They were pretty sure they hadn't gotten the .51, but Hayes wondered whether it was really there. The Cobras only had fuel for another 10 minutes. The Green Beret commander, a lieutenant, said they were almost out of ammo and had three critically wounded.

"Okay, we're going in. Sounds like they need what we got," Walters said.

Hayes had an involuntary intake of breath as a rush of fear passed over him. He regretted getting Hollister because no one should get a mission like this on his first day.

Lehman switched the radios to private so no one else could hear the conversation.

"We'll approach from the south, and we'll go in low, below the level of the top of the hill," Walters said. "That'll put the hill between us and the .51, if it's there, but it also means we'll be exposed to anyone in the jungle. It looks like triple canopy so they can probably only see us from the tree line.

"Hayes and Hollister, you guys start shooting up the tree line as soon you can. When we get to the camp, you let those guys on the ground pull the ammo off and load the wounded. You guys keep shooting, especially you, Hayes, because if the .51's there, it'll most likely be on your side. Let's be fast, before we lose the snakes."

But the Cobras were already gone. Walters banked around to the south side while talking on the radio to the camp. He hadn't been kidding when he said he was going to go in low. They were only a few feet off the ground. Hayes watched the leaves on the trees vibrating like the strings on Dick Dale's guitar and melting into the ground in the rush of the rotor wash. He wasn't sure whether it was hallucination or real, but he didn't care.

As they approached the hill, the helicopter started up like a fast-moving elevator. It was sheer joy to be flying like this in a new helicopter that hadn't yet been worn down by heat and dust and too many maneuvers that pilots had been warned not to try in their flight training. Helicopters could just break, and of course, there was no shortage of maintenance snafus. A picture of a stoned mechanic flashed through Hayes' brain and he renewed his promise to stop getting high.

Hayes and Hollister were firing at the tree line, and Hayes was able to push his fear aside, not thinking about anything but how cool the leaves and the bushes looked. It was a little psychedelic, with the jungle and tracers moving in time to the music in his head, but the acid seemed to be wearing off. None of the tracers came close to them. He was feeling confident, but not the irrational confidence he'd experienced on top of the bunker. It looked like they had caught the enemy by surprise.

Suddenly, they were at the top of the hill. Walters flared the ship and hovered less than a foot above the ground. He had turned the helicopter so Hayes was facing north, which had him looking right where the .51 caliber anti-aircraft gun was supposed to be located though it would below the lip of the mountain. There were no twinkles but he kept firing. Then tracers were coming toward him from a little to one side and he moved his M60 to bear on them. But the tracers weren't big enough to be a .51. He was only vaguely aware of the boxes of ammunition flying off the ship. He didn't notice anyone pulling them; his concentration was fully on his own fire. The tracers stopped, but he kept firing. Now wounded soldiers were being shoved onto the ship. He had a flash of a black man holding his own guts, visible on both sides of a bloody bandage. He saw a face. It was Asian: narrow, slanted eyes, a flat nose and a hideous overbite. His mind finally completed the picture. The top teeth seemed to be sticking out because most of the man's lower jaw was gone, his tongue flapping where the chin should have been, with no lower teeth or lip. Blood was running over his bandaged neck.

1237 Hours, Cu Chi Operations Bunker

First Sergeant Jubal Sypher was seething over the loss of all the NVA weapons and other paraphernalia. It eventually would have brought more money than he had made so far in his tour. But even worse was the dressing down he'd received from the 99th's CO. Aside from the humiliation, he was now worried that it might follow him to his new assignment at the evacuation hospital. It could conceivably get him bounced out of the assignment or more likely, make him the subject of closer scrutiny, and that was the last thing he needed. He would have to be exceedingly careful. It hadn't been easy for McAllister to get him the assignment and there was the potential in this new position to make them both a lot of money. If he screwed it up, that could destroy what had been a long and productive association with McAlister. *And it's all the fault of that fuckin' college boy drug addict, Hayes.* Sypher had been sitting outside the aviation Ops bunker in Cu Chi waiting for a helicopter ride to Long Binh for most of the morning with over a dozen others, all wanting to go somewhere, and was watching yet another huey disgorging a load of passengers. He slammed his fist into his palm at the thought of Hayes.

Just then, another irritating sight came into view. *That fuckin' Spanish TV bitch.* Her cameraman and soundman were dragging heavy cases of equipment through the rotor wash while she held a floppy hat on her head with both hands, the roaring air pressing her clothing tightly against her body. *Christ, she has a nice set of tits,* Sypher thought. The little sexual flash quickly entered the roiling mix of anger, frustration and exasperation in his feverish brain where it catalyzed an idea that blossomed into full fruition as quickly as an exploding flashbulb. He produced a wet, snorting, high-pitched laugh at the sheer audacity of it.

He waited until the Spanish woman was clear of the helicopter, which was already taking off with another load of passengers. As the sound of the engine faded, he walked up to her. She didn't look happy to see him, but he would change that. "Did you by chance hear about what happened at Nui Binh early this morning?" he asked her. He knew she had because he had seen her, but he was pretty sure she hadn't seen him.

"I believe those were Vietnamese civilians—unarmed civilians—who were murdered by you Americans," she said. She had her hands on her hips and her jaw thrust forward, daring him to deny it.

Even better than I hoped. Sypher hung his head and tried to look ashamed. "Could I talk to you off the record?" he asked carefully. He'd also been around PIO operations enough to know a little about the press. "I can give you some good information, but if the Army finds out it came from me, I'll get in a hell of lot of trouble."

She considered it for a few seconds. The two men in her crew were ambling toward the Ops bunker. "Okay, off the record. I won't mention your name or even your rank."

Sypher nodded. "That Hayes kid, the one with the blonde hair, is the worst drug addict I've ever come across. That's why he's a PFC. I busted him for smoking pot and I was getting ready to court martial him. I think he was higher than a kite, and maybe the others were too, when they shot all those people."

"Drugs! I never thought of that! He did seem to be out of it, but I don't think that big fat sergeant was on drugs."

"You mean Slobbo? His name's Russell Slobojan," Sypher said. He quickly spelled the name. "No, he's not taking drugs as far as I know, unless it's penicillin. He's just incompetent. Real stupid, though you wouldn't know he's stupid until you've been around him for a little while. Catches VD all the time. I heard he sees prostitutes working at the garbage dump."

"Prostitutes at a garbage dump!"

"And that big nig— I mean the colored soldier who was wounded, Rufus Roy. He just got out of Long Binh Jail," Sypher said.

"Jail," she muttered as she took out her notebook. "What about the Cuban soldier, the one who speaks Spanish?"

Sypher shrugged as he tried to think of something bad about Rivera. "Name's Rivera... Francisco Rivera. He's been in Vietnam a long time. Maybe too long. I caught him with an unauthorized weapon."

"What do you mean, an unauthorized weapon?"

"He had a pistol. I think it was Communist manufacture," Sypher said, desperately trying to go somewhere with this thread. "This is a war zone, Ma'am, and there's a lot of guns around. All sorts of guns. That pilot—the one flying that helicopter that crashed when it lost the tail rotor—he has a Chinese submachine gun."

"Why would Americans carry enemy weapons?"

"I don't know," he said slowly. "I'm just an old sergeant who's been in the Army a long time. Where do all the weapons go from the battles? All I know is that I've seen a lot of Americans who have enemy weapons."

"Do you think they would plant them on civilians to make it look like they were soldiers?"

He shrugged. "I don't know about that."

"That Spanish-speaking one told me you and some others gathered a lot of weapons from the battlefield, that you were going to sell them," she said.

"What? You don't believe that stupid fuckin' son of a bitch, do you?" He paused for effect, let himself appear to be calming down. "Sorry about the language, Ma'am, but I don't like being accused of something like that."

He didn't say anything as she wrote in her notebook.

She didn't seem to notice that he hadn't denied the accusation. "Well Sergeant, you have given me some interesting facts. I'm going to check on them as best I can."

"Well, there's one more thing about that Hayes kid that you might want to look into."

"What's that?" she asked.

"He killed an ARVN, a South Vietnamese soldier. I heard about it because everyone was talkin' about it. He machine-gunned the poor bastard when he got off the helicopter. Wasn't any accident either," Sypher said.

Madrid gasped. "He killed a South Vietnamese soldier?"

"Yes, Ma'am, that's exactly what he did. And right after that, they put him in the Headhunters. Guess he likes killin', especially little yellow people. Don't let the peace symbol he wears fool you either. And from what I hear, that Cuban son of a bitch is even worse. He *loves* the killin'."

She looked up from her notebook. "Why are you telling me this?"

He mustered all the false sincerity he could. "Well, to tell the truth, I felt a little bad about cuttin' off your interview yesterday. Hayes and Rivera are just not the kind of soldiers who should be representin' the United States Army. They're two of the worst I've ever come across. I just got transferred out of the 99th and I'm not sorry. I did the best I could while I was there, but that unit's an undisciplined mess, a lot of drugs and drinkin' and whorin'. They're outta control. I sure hope you don't use my name, Ma'am, because if it ever gets out I told you this stuff, my career is over."

"Don't worry, Sergeant. And thank you."

Only 10 minutes later, Madrid and Sypher both managed to get on a helicopter to Long Binh. The Spanish reporter made a quick trip to Long Binh Jail and confirmed that Rufus Roy had been released just as Sypher had said and that he had been jailed for shooting up a mess hall. She was also able to confirm that Francisco Rivera had been in Vietnam for almost two years, though there were no blots on his record that she could find. She thought about him. He had talked to her and seemed earnest. He hadn't seemed stupid and he was an enlisted man, not one of the military PR types. But he had almost killed her too. He had been too cool, too nonchalant, as he described how he and the black man had slaughtered the Vietnamese with the miniguns. It didn't seem credible to her.

By telephone, which was almost a miracle given the growing chaos in Vietnam, she talked to a Sergeant Reyes at the 99th, who confirmed that Jimmy Hayes had received an Article 15 for using marijuana and that he had a reputation as a drug user. The sergeant also told her that it was true that Slobojan had caught VD at least twice. He didn't seem to care for Slobojan. The sergeant said he didn't know much about Hayes shooting the ARVN, but it was clear that he'd heard about it. She was appalled at his attitude.

"So what if he did?" Reyes said. "Most of those ARVNs are worthless shits. Can't trust the gook bastards at all."

Madrid concluded that Sergeant Sypher had told her the truth, or at least mostly the truth. She had a good story, a real scoop, about American soldiers murdering Vietnamese civilians. She had film of the weaponless bodies; she had Rivera on camera talking about killing Vietnamese, though he claimed it was enemy soldiers and he had been talking about an incident that occurred the day before. Still, he had sounded particularly cold blooded. She had great film. Now she would confront the

American brass with her facts. They would deny and lie, and that might make the story better.

She stopped at the Long Binh PIO office and spent an hour waiting for someone to talk to her, someone she could confront. Everyone was caught up in the growing enemy attacks. She felt a fleeting twinge of apprehension about her story, then clenched her teeth. *No, I have the story.* She left, heading for the airport where her luck continued. She was able to hitch a ride to Tokyo on an Air Force C130.

1239 Hours

"Only got two wounded," Hayes said into the mike. "Otherwise we're clear."

"Okay," Walters said.

The helicopter lifted, tilted and started quickly forward.

They cleared the edge of Camp Johnson and were rapidly gathering speed as Walters hugged the downslope of the small mountain. It was like a rollercoaster, a little push up and over as they accelerated into translational lift and then near weightlessness as they roared down the mountain. Then their luck ran out. Flashes and tracers were coming from the tree line that was only a hundred or so meters away.

Hayes had to swing the machinegun as far as he could toward the front of the aircraft to return fire, but before he could shoot, bullets were clanking into the ship. It sounded like pieces of metal smacking together in an echo chamber. It was much louder than when they'd lost the tail rotor the day before. And he felt the shocks. Something exploded beside his head and he instinctively ducked. The helicopter wobbled, turned slightly and began to vibrate, and the sound of metal ripping gave way to a new high-pitched shriek and the smell of burning rubber and plastic. Walters was on the radio. Hayes got a better view of the area where the tracers were coming from. He began firing back. They rocketed over the tree line and the incoming fire stopped. He glanced back and saw black smoke pouring out behind them. "We're on fire!"

"Losing hydraulics. Maybe the fluid's cooking off," Walters said calmly, and after a slight pause, "We're going in." He was on the radio again giving their location while the lieutenant at Camp Johnson suggested they come back.

"No can do," Walters said, his voice slightly higher, but still sounding calm.

Hayes leaned as far as he could out the side of the helicopter, undoing his seatbelt and holding onto it. Fuel was streaming back on the side of the machine in the slipstream. It was hot and steaming where it was near the engine exhaust. There was also black smoke but he couldn't see any flame. He realized they might burst into flames at any moment. "Big fuel leak on this side," he said. "It's hitting the exhaust."

"Shit," Walters said. "I was hoping it was the gauge."

The engine shriek went lower. It was quitting.

"Brace yourselves," Walters said.

"Little clearing on the right!" Lehman shouted.

"See it," Walters said.

With horror, Hayes remembered he'd taken off his seatbelt. The helicopter tilted right, which put Hayes up in the air. He grabbed the bottom of the seat with both hands. For a second, the turbine whines and shrieks increased and the helicopter leveled as Walters tried to land. Then the noise abruptly stopped, and a split second later they hit the ground.

They hit hard, but it was better than Hayes had expected. He slammed into the partition behind the pilots but didn't lose consciousness or feel anything break. Then he smelled JP4. "Get the fuck out of here!" he yelled, but the radio and intercom were dead. He tried to rip off his seatbelt, momentarily forgetting it was unattached. He ran to the front of the helicopter and wrenched open the door for Walters. The windshield had shattered, maybe from Walters helmet. Walters looked dazed with a half-smile on his face, but he was taking his harness off, slowly though. Hayes ran around the nose and opened Lehman's door. He helped Lehman get out. Lehman looked okay.

He went back to the side to grab the Vietnamese Ranger who was missing his lower jaw, but the man was dead. He had to climb back into the helicopter to reach the black man with abdominal wounds. He grabbed him under the arms and dragged him out of the helicopter. The man groaned as his legs bumped on the ground but Hayes kept dragging him until they were about 25 meters from the helicopter where he could longer smell the fuel. He went back and got the machinegun and a box of ammo. He looked at the Vietnamese Ranger again to make sure he hadn't made a mistake, but the man was dead, his eyes fixed open, staring lifelessly. Now Hayes saw that in addition to losing his jaw, head wounds had exposed his brain. He felt himself getting ready to throw up and looked away only to see Walters.

Walters was nonchalantly poking his gloved fingers into the holes in the Plexiglas and glancing back at the steaming vapor coming off the exhaust. Black smoke was billowing into the air. Walters still seemed dazed as he ambled over to the door Hayes had just left. He picked up Hayes' M16. "Hey, you want your M16, Hayes?" Walters had his Chicom submachine gun slung over his shoulder.

Hayes put down the machinegun and ammo box and ran back to Walters. He grabbed the M16, then quickly reached into the helicopter and took the bandoleer of ammunition and the cooler of Kool-Aid. "This fucker's gonna blow," Hayes said. "Let's get out of here."

"Naw," Walters said. "It's already cooling off. If it was gonna blow, it would'a already blown."

Then there was a soft liquid pop and flames sprang up around the engine exhaust. They looked at each other. Hayes grabbed Walters by the arm to pull him away but Walters didn't need pulling anymore. Heat at their backs, they stumbled back to where Hayes had left the wounded soldier. The heat was intensifying and at the same moment, they both flopped on the ground.

The helicopter didn't actually explode but it burned quickly. Within a minute the roaring flames had begun to subside and the machine was reduced to smoldering, twisted wreckage. There was an explosion of ammunition like a big string of firecrackers all going off at once. Hayes guessed that Hollister hadn't saved his machinegun.

Walters asked, "Lehman and the FNG—where are they?"

"Major Lehman!" Hayes shouted. "Major Lehman!"

"Over here," came a faint reply. A few minutes later, Lehman and Hollister found them. As Hayes had expected, Hollister didn't have the machinegun. Strangely, he was holding a big knife down the side of his thigh, almost like he was trying to hide it. After dragging the machinegun over to them, Hayes took the Tokarev pistol out of his pocket.

"Here," he said, handing it to Hollister. "I'll trade you. This'll be better than nothing or that knife." Almost reluctantly, Hollister took the pistol and handed him the knife.

Lehman was looking at the pistol, and at Walters' submachine gun. He looked like he was going to say something but didn't.

"We'd better get away from this thing," Walters said, looking at the wreckage. A column of black smoke was still rising into the air. "That smoke's gonna lead the gooks right to us. "

"We head for Camp Johnson," Lehman said decisively. Now that they were no longer flying he was assuming complete command. "What do we have here? One M60, a rifle, whatever that thing is you have Walters—"

"Chicom SKS submachine gun... basically a shortened AK-47," Walters said. "Only got the one magazine though."

"You don't have your thirty-eight?" asked Lehman. "I ran out so fast when I heard they needed a peter pilot that I forgot mine."

Walters raised the Chicom. "Just this."

Hayes was kneeling beside the black man. "I think he's dead." His eyes were open and Hayes could detect no breathing. Lehman bent down to look.

"I forgot about them," said Lehman. "Wasn't there another one?"

Hayes pointed at the wreckage. "I didn't have a chance to pull him out. He was dead. I didn't think he was gonna make it when they put him on. His entire jaw was gone."

Lehman bowed his head. At first Hayes thought he was looking at the dead black man, and he was, but he was also praying, speaking so quietly that no one could hear the words. Then he reached down and closed the man's eyes. "We can't take him with us," he said, looking around at the rest of them.

Walters nodded.

"Well, this ammo box is about half-full," Hayes said, "and there's six or seven magazines for the M16 in that bandoleer. And I've got one smoke grenade." He held up the grenade, examining it. "Ah, purple," he said with satisfaction. "Hollister's Tokarev just has the one magazine as well, but I've got a few extra bullets."

"Okay, Hollister, you take the M16 and its ammo. Hayes, can you carry the M60 and the ammo box, at least for a little while?" Lehman asked.

Hayes nodded. "For a little while."

"Walters, you take the point because you probably have the best idea of which way to go. Hayes, you go second, then me. Hollister, you take the rear."

They were all thirsty and passed around the Kool-Aid until it was completely drained. His belly full of the ice-cold cherry drink, Hayes tossed the empty jug onto the wreckage. Suddenly realizing that he had both hands free, Lehman took the ammo box from Hayes who nodded his thanks. Then Walters reached over and took the ammo box from Lehman.

"Makes more sense that I carry it if I'm gonna be next to Hayes and his machinegun. If we get tired, we can maybe switch the machinegun and ammo to you two," Walters said. "You want to take the Chicom?"

Lehman considered it, and nodded. "That's good," he said, and took the weapon from Walters.

"Let me go first with the machinegun," Hayes said to Walters. "In case we run into the gooks. Just tell me which way to go."

For the next half-hour, they walked slowly and carefully, worried that they were going to run into enemy soldiers at any time. It wasn't triple canopy jungle as Hayes had thought, but the bush was too dense to see more than a few feet ahead. They had to walk around thick tangles of brush and climb over big hillocks of grass. They struggled through one stretch of saw grass that was over Hayes' head. Trees towered over them. Nowhere did they see anything that resembled a trail. Hayes soon had scratches and cuts on his exposed skin. He wasn't sure they'd covered more than a few hundred meters when Walters stopped Hayes so they could rest. They had pulled away from Lehman and Hollister. Walters figured they were 50 feet or less back, but they didn't want to get separated. The sweat had completely soaked through Hayes' jungle fatigue shirt and rivulets were running down Walters' face into his flight suit. Walters would be even hotter in the flight suit. Hayes was already thirsty again.

"Christ," Walters muttered, looking at a small compass. "I wish I knew exactly what direction to go."

"We must be heading in the right direction, or close," Hayes said. "We're going up and Johnson's up a mountain."

Suddenly, there was a loud crack from the direction they'd just come.

Hayes' head whipped around and he whispered, "That's a gunshot! Sounded like the Tokarev!"

***

Slick Percy Dupree was thinking that he was due a big bonus from Doran. *I didn't sign up for this much shit. Thought I was gonna die in that helicopter crash, and now I might die in the fuckin' jungle.* He should have waited for an opportunity at Nui Binh instead of trying to get the job done quickly. *I shouldn't'a believed that fuckin' asshole captain who said this was just gonna be a milk run.* But he'd jumped at it when he found out Hayes would be along. The longer this went on, the deeper he was getting sucked in. *How long before someone figures out I ain't Hollister? What if I end up in the fuckin' hospital?* He had noticed Hollister's dog tags said his blood type was AB. He couldn't remember what his blood type was, but he didn't think he was AB. *What the fuck? I'm in the middle of the fuckin' jungle after getting shot out of the fuckin' sky and I'm getting' more pissed off by the second. I don't remember ever bein' this pissed off.* "Mother*fucker*!" he said loudly.

The major stopped and turned to glower at him.

I don't like that by-the-book bastard either.

Dupree had never been big on thinking things through. He much preferred action. He was good at action, good at following his instincts, which usually served him well. Without thinking, he dropped the M16, pulled the pistol out of his pocket, cocked it and shot the major in the head.

"Goddamn tight-ass motherfucker," he said quietly. The major's mouth popped open in surprise, blood gushed across his face and he crumpled to the ground. He fell forward, landing on top of the Chicom submachine gun.

Dupree stepped over him and began walking toward where he'd last seen Hayes and Walters. He slowed, taking a wider arc so he would not approach them from the same direction they had just taken and where they would probably be looking. Every fiber of his being was on high alert. *There they are... less than 10 yards....* He had come up on them from the side. He raised the pistol and took a bead on Hayes, then hesitated. *Got to get this right the first time.* He rehearsed what he was going to do. Shoot Hayes in the head and then as quickly as he could, but still taking the time to aim, he would shoot the pilot in the head. Despite the fact that the two soldiers had seen intense combat, Dupree was confident that he was more ruthless and quicker when it came to outright murder. He concentrated on Hayes' head and began to squeeze the trigger.

There was a loud burst of gunshots, and Hayes recognized the sound of an AK-47. He turned just in time to see blood flying off of Hollister's face as he jerked toward Hayes and collapsed. Hayes had the machinegun up and his finger on the trigger when Major Lehman, blood all over his face, stepped from the brush behind where Hollister had been. Hayes thought, *The gooks have got us and I don't know where they are! Why's Lehman aiming the Chicom at Hollister?* He decided it must be the acid and that he was hallucinating again. He didn't know what to do.

"That fellow shot me," Lehman said calmly. "Got me in the head, but I'm okay."

There were no more shots. Hayes, still confused, couldn't move, but Walters walked over to the bloody Lehman and took him by the arm. He sat the major down against a tree and took the Chicom.

Lehman looked at Hayes. "He was going to shoot you." Blood was still flowing out of a hole in his forehead. "I don't know why, but he was definitely going to shoot you. Do you know why? I think he was a very bad man. He was using foul language and I was going to ask him to stop. He shot me in the head, but I don't even have a headache. I'm very thirsty though."

They had no water.

"I'm going to be okay because I pray to Jesus Christ every day. Did you know that I'm an ordained minister? You men should pray to Jesus because He will save you. He has already saved you once. This fellow shot me right in the head, but Jesus let me live so I could stop him from shooting you. And I don't even have a headache. I'm feeling a little strange though and it's getting dark. Is it night already? And I'm so very, very thirsty. Goodness gracious, would I ever like a cool clear drink of water! I've never drunk alcohol in my life, and neither has my wife Dolores. Oh dear... she's going to be upset, but she'll be okay. She'll know I'm with Jesus and that someday we'll be together with Jesus. I'm sure there's cool, clear water for me in heav...." Lehman closed his eyes.

Walters took his hand, then looked at Hayes. "He's dead. Holy shit." Then he looked at the major and quietly said, "Sorry."

29 and 30 January, Long Binh

Staff Sergeant Jimmy Ray Suggs was an Army CID investigator. The major in charge of the Long Binh detachment thought Suggs was the best investigator he had ever worked with and was trying to get him promoted to warrant officer. Suggs was 25 years old and had spent almost three years as a dispatcher for the police department in Gulfport, Alabama. He was familiar with police procedure, he was smart and he was a young man who wanted to get ahead. After he had been drafted, he had re-enlisted for an extra year to guarantee an assignment to the military police. With his civilian experience, promotions came rapidly so that after 18 months in the Army, he was already an E-6 staff sergeant on his way to becoming a warrant officer. And he had managed to get himself a job in the Criminal Investigation Division, which was what he wanted to do. He had told his major that he wanted to make the Army a career.

When an incoming rocket had exploded at the 79th Replacement Depot—the Repo Depot—in Long Binh and killed a soldier who couldn't be immediately identified, the matter had been assigned to Suggs. Suggs had gotten there about two hours after the explosion. He had insisted that an autopsy be done although everyone said it was obvious that a rocket had killed the poor fellow. Suggs got a doctor from 24th Evac who had some real-world pathology experience to look at the body. That doctor had found marks from a garrote on the victim's neck and surmised that he had been strangled before his head had been turned into a pulpy mess. It probably wasn't a rocket, said the doctor, who had seen many shrapnel victims. He was about 75 percent certain that an American grenade had caused the explosion. At first light Suggs had organized a detail of FNGs—Fucking New Guys—to inspect every square inch of ground within a hundred yards of the explosion. It took less than 15 minutes to find the pin.

Suggs concluded that he was now investigating a murder. Murder wasn't unheard of in Vietnam. It wasn't even the first time Suggs had investigated one. He had failed to solve the case of an infantry lieutenant who had apparently been shot in the back by one of his own men. He hadn't found the murderer, but an autopsy had found a bullet from an M16 in the lieutenant.

Several roll calls and careful examination of records at the Repo Depot didn't reveal any soldiers who were missing. However, soldiers were leaving steadily and Suggs knew he should not stop the process of sending badly needed replacements to their units. So he got a list of every soldier who had been at the Depot at the time of the murder. There were 136 names on that list, including the soldiers who were assigned as cadre to the Depot. After checking with the commanding officer, an anal retentive slightly chubby captain by the name of Willard Malmsby, to make sure all of his cadre were accounted for, he concluded the victim had been among the replacements. Suggs asked Captain Malmsby if he could give him the race and age of all the remaining soldiers.

"Oh yes!" The captain beamed and then beckoned for his clerk, who gave Suggs his list of names with race and age. The victim had clearly been black and according to the pathologist, probably less than 25 years old. Suggs' list of possible victims was now down to 35 individuals who were black. He eliminated seven men who were over 30, reducing the list to 28. The grenade had exploded behind the Enlisted Men's Club so Suggs was betting that the victim had been an enlisted man. He prioritized the list into four groups: enlisted men under 25, enlisted men over 25, officers and warrant officers under 25 and officers and warrant officers over 25. There were 19 in the first group, which in Suggs' mind was by far the most promising group. He went back to the captain and asked if he kept records on height and weight.

Sadly, the captain shook his head. "If you give me a little time, I think I could get some of that information. They all get new clothing, so our supply shed will have their sizes. We can make a reasonable guess on height and weight. Also, they all hand carry their 201 personnel files to their units and I can ask for them to be sent here. I can get the files from anyone who's still here."

"Okay," Suggs said. "Work on that for the black soldiers."

As soon as he could, Suggs brought the fingerprints that the autopsy doctor had taken off the victim to his major. His major had warned him that it would take Washington many weeks, perhaps months, to check the fingerprints against existing records, but nevertheless had sent them to the Washington CID office by both telex and courier. Now Suggs went back to his major with his lists. "I'm pretty sure that we'll find our victim in the first nineteen." He explained his reasoning and what he had done. Once again, the major was impressed and immediately telexed the list to his contact in Washington CID. Washington had begun to follow the case with some interest. A murder in Vietnam that appeared to be a real whodunit was unusual. So was the fact that a young staff sergeant was the lead investigator. Two hours after the major's telex went out, a reply came back that the prints matched one of the names on the list: Specialist Fourth Class Marvin Hollister. Suggs, however, wasn't in the CID office when that telex arrived. Actually, no one was checking telexes. Every available man was responding to what was looking like a major enemy offensive.

After a couple of hours, Suggs went back to see Captain Malmsby at the Repo Depot. He was thinking about why he had a body while no one was missing. And why had a murderer taken the trouble to hide the identity of the victim? One reason might be that the murderer wanted to assume the victim's identity. If that were the case, it seemed possible that the murderer had gotten some help from someone at the Repo Depot. Suggs was pretty good at reading people, and he didn't think the captain would have helped. But he thought the captain would know the most likely candidates.

"Captain Malmsby, if I wanted some inside information on replacements—who they are and where they're going, that sort of thing—who in the 79th might be inclined to help, especially if I was willing to compensate them for their trouble?" Suggs asked. "It'd have to be someone with full access to records."

The captain grimaced. He didn't like the question but he replied almost immediately. "Sergeant Collins," he said. "He's a sergeant first class who does his job, but just barely. He drinks too much and I'm suspicious that he might have been changing some assignments for senior NCOs. Collins has been in the Army more than 20 years, and that's a pretty clubby group. They take care of themselves."

"Mind if I have little talk with him?" asked Suggs.

The captain shrugged. "Okay, but I'd better tag along."

"Let's go then, but I'd appreciate it if you let me talk to him without interrupting, Sir," Suggs said.

The captain led him to Collins' office.

Not waiting for the captain to introduce him, Suggs said, "I'm Jimmy Ray Suggs from Army CID and I'm investigating the murder that took place here on Monday." CID investigators normally didn't use their rank when conducting investigations but he knew that Malmsby might have learned his rank through his connections. He took out his wallet and showed Collins his identification.

"What murder?" Collins asked. "Are you talking about the kid killed by the incoming rocket?" He was a tall, lean and craggy man close to 50 with dark circles under his eyes and prematurely wrinkled. He wore a sour but surprised expression on a face dominated by a nose reddened from too much whiskey. When he seemed to shrink away, Suggs was sure he had him.

He slapped his list on the desk so Collins could read it. "I have reason to believe the murder victim was one of these men and that you helped someone, who is almost certainly the murderer, identify the victim. The autopsy shows that the man was strangled before a grenade exploded beside his head. You can talk to me and cooperate here and now, or you can talk to me over at Long Binh Jail as a suspect." Suggs had no intention of bringing him to the jail, at least not yet, but he thought Collins knew something.

Collins looked at the captain hopefully, but the captain remained silent. He looked down at the list. "I think it might be either Hollister or Masterson," he said. "I had a guy talk to me a few days ago. He was interested in people going to the 99th Assault Helicopter Company. There was one other guy going there, a warrant officer, but I don't see him here."

"Who talked to you? What was his name?"

"Never gave me a name," said Collins. "And I don't think he had a nametag on his fatigues either. I remember that now."

"How much money did he give you?"

"What makes you think—"

Suggs leaned closer and glared at him.

Collins shrugged. "A hundred bucks. I didn't see any harm in it. He asked me to delay sending them there for a couple of days, so I did."

"What did this guy look like? Describe him for me," said Suggs.

"He was a nig— He was colored, about twenty-five, maybe older. Hard for me to tell with the colored. Big buck, little over six feet, and tough."

"Light skinned or dark?"

"I just told you he was a nigger," said Collins indignantly.

"There's different shades of black," said Suggs patiently.

"Yeah, I guess there are. Okay, he was a little lighter than most. His hair was short, but it looked to me like he'd just got it cut. Most guys arrive in-country with a little more hair. He knew the military better than most replacements do. I had the feeling that he'd been in the Army for a while. Thought at first he was a transfer from Germany."

"Why?" asked Suggs.

Collins spread his hands. "I'm not sure... he just seemed like he knew the Army way. He knew at least enough so that he wasn't out of place in uniform. He was also scary. I mean, he gave me money, and I shouldn't have took it, but the way he looked at me I think he would have done me some harm if I didn't do what he wanted."

"How did he know to ask you for help?"

Collins shook his head warily. He didn't speak for a long time and Suggs was about to go back to the suspect's description. Then Collins said, "Brendan McAlister. He's a senior sergeant major. Known him for a long time, ten years or more. He called me and asked me to do him a favor, but no favor's worth getting involved in a murder."

Suggs questioned Collins for another 20 minutes but didn't learn much more except that Hollister had been black and Masterson white, and he already had that from Malmsby. That meant Hollister was most likely the victim.

Suggs warned Collins not to talk to McAlister. Then he got on one of the 79th Replacement Depot's telephones and tried calling the 99th Assault Helicopter Company. Because of the fighting that had broken out all over Vietnam, the phone system was overwhelmed. For the first time Suggs became aware of what was going on around him. Now that he thought about it, there had been a lot of activity: outgoing artillery, helicopters and aircraft flying overhead and taking off and landing and even some distant small arms fire. He had been so focused on his investigation that he had shut all of that out. On his second attempt, he connected with a familiar operator and a few minutes later he was talking to the 99th Assault Helicopter Company's operations sergeant.

"Hollister? That guy just got here this morning and he's already flying. Gung ho son of a bitch volunteered to fly the courier, which turned into an ash and trash. They were going to a special forces camp over by Long Binh but I don't know how long they'll be there. Christ, I thought it was gonna be a milk run, but we heard they might have caught some shit already and the CO's got the ass about it. Listen, I gotta go. We have lot going on here."

"Who else is on the chopper?" Suggs asked.

"Well, Major Lehman, Mr. Walters, PFC Hayes and your man Hollister. Wait, Hayes just got promoted back to Spec Four. He's the crew chief and Hollister's the door gunner. Walters is the A/C and Lehman's the peter pilot, but he's also our XO. The CO is upset because he wanted Lehman on the ground here. Hayes too, for that matter, so if you see 'em, tell 'em to get their asses back here as soon as they can. Sorry, I gotta go."

Suggs sat at the desk smoking a cigarette and thinking for a few minutes. Then he got up and walked briskly to his Jeep, stopping first to thank Malmsby.

"What do I do with Collins?" the captain asked morosely.

"Nothing for now," replied Suggs. "We'll probably want to charge him regarding the bribe, but I still don't know enough about what's going on here. For now, just make sure he doesn't get in touch with that Sergeant Major McAlister. Restrict him to quarters."

The captain nodded glumly.

Suggs came to attention and saluted.

The captain stood and returned the salute. "It's been interesting and I wish you luck, Sergeant," he said, revealing that he did indeed know Suggs' rank. "Let me know if I can be of further assistance."

Suggs drove a Jeep to the Long Binh Operations bunker. He had often gone there to hitch helicopter rides when he needed to go to another base, and he'd decided he had enough to go to Nui Binh and arrest Hollister, except Hollister wasn't there right now. He was hoping he could get the helicopter with Hollister on it to come to Long Binh, because apparently they were close. That would be a little tricky.

Outside the Operations bunker, he discovered one of the stranger sights he had ever seen in Vietnam. Two men in full suits and ties and wearing sunglasses were standing next to the entrance. One of them was a heavy, sweating six-footer with a red face and reddish hair streaked with gray. He looked to be late forties or early fifties. The other one was a couple of decades younger, smaller, with black hair and handling the heat better. From their body language, Suggs had a feeling they didn't care for each other. Part of the puzzle was why they were outside in the heat when the bunker was air-conditioned to keep the fancy communications gear cool. They looked hopefully at him, but Suggs walked past them into bunker. The operations personnel were busy, but he managed to corner the operations sergeant, with whom he was casually acquainted.

"99th Assault Helicopter Company ship? How the hell would I know... oh yeah. Those guys are bringing a load of ammo to Camp Johnson and taking out wounded. Sounded like it might be trouble because there's supposed to be a .51 in there. There were a couple of Cobras working it."

The sergeant led Suggs past the counter to where several soldiers were on the radios. There was so much chatter that he couldn't discern any of the several simultaneous exchanges, but it sounded like there was a firefight going on.

A spec five turned to the sergeant. "You leave for a minute and now we got a major fucking firefight and a bird going down," he said excitedly.

Where?" asked the sergeant.

"Johnson again."

"Aw shit," the sergeant said. "What happened?"

"They got the ammo in and they must have gotten out. Then something started at Johnson and the helo got hit. The pilot said they were going in. Those were the exact words he used—'We're going in'—and we haven't heard anything else from them. I think he tried to radio a location but it was garbled." The spec five listened to his radio for a moment. "Meanwhile, Johnson's getting hit from two sides. That's what you're hearing now. Not that easy to follow, but I think they're givin' Charles hell."

Suggs said, "What about the helicopter? Can you—"

The sergeant held his hand up. "Not now. Let my boys do their job."

"Sure." Suggs went back around the counter as a captain scurried by. Suggs recognized him as one of the operations commanders. About 10 minutes had passed when the two men in suits burst through the door. They were both hot and angry.

The big, older one said, "I demand that you get someone to take us to the Army military police immediately!" His suit had once been a resplendent glen plaid but was now wrinkled and heavy with sweat. Sweat was beaded on his forehead and running down both temples and cheeks. He reached into his breast pocket and pulled out a leather identification wallet and let it flop open to show a shiny gold badge. "I'm Special Agent Bradbury of the FBI and this is Special Agent Ovenden." They started around the counter.

Suggs put out his arm to stop them. "You can't go in there. They're busy."

Bradbury turned to him, still holding his badge. "Maybe you didn't hear me, Sonny, but I'm Special Agent Bradbury from the FBI and I *will* go back there!" He started to push on Suggs' arm.

"Well, you have no jurisdiction in Long Binh." Suggs stepped into Bradbury to stop him. "This is Vietnam."

"And just who the fuck are you?" asked Bradbury.

"Name's Jimmy Ray Suggs. I'm an investigator with Army CID." He took out his own identification and held it up so both Bradbury and Ovenden could see it.

"Were you sent here to pick us up?" Bradbury asked indignantly.

"No Sir. I'm on the trail of a murder suspect. Now, how can CID be of service to you gentlemen?"

Bradbury put his badge away and Ovenden followed suit. "We're from the FBI's Detroit office. We've come here to interview a Michigan soldier by the name of James Hayes and take him back to Detroit," Ovenden said, speaking for the first time.

Suggs didn't react to the name. Out of the corner of his eye, he saw the operations sergeant lean out from behind a table and a shelf heavy with radios. The sergeant gestured. Suggs wasn't sure whether it was because of the commotion from the FBI agents or whether the sergeant wanted to talk to him.

"Hold on a sec. I might be able to help you," he said and walked over to the sergeant. "Got something?"

The sergeant shook his head and gestured with his head toward the FBI agents on the other side of the wall. "I kicked those assholes out once already." He shook his head. "Johnson's kickin' the shit out of Charlie and I think they'll be okay. Seems to be tapering off. Got a couple of casualties that they'd like medevacked and I don't know if we can get anyone in there right away. We haven't heard anything from that 99th ship. Nothin'. Not a peep. Looks bad. Johnson didn't actually see them hit the ground, but they saw a lot of smoke. Looks like they crashed and burned at least a mile out. Hope those guys got out. They had a couple of badly wounded guys from Johnson with them too. We're having a hard time finding anyone to look for them. There's just too much shit going on."

Suggs shook out a cigarette and offered it to the sergeant before taking one himself. The sergeant lit them. "Try calling the 99th," Suggs said. "It's their ship and the peter pilot is their XO, so they might find a way to help."

"Shit, good idea!" the sergeant said. "Thanks."

"Just let me know as quick as you can if you find them. I'm looking for someone on that ship, and so are our federal guests." He inclined his head toward Bradbury and Ovenden.

30 January, 1505 Hours, Vicinity of Camp Johnson

General William Westmoreland was trying to squeeze in one more task. He had spent the day flying almost the length of Vietnam to meet with the Marines about Khe Sanh, and then he had gone to Cu Chi by helicopter. Now he was listening to the radios on the way back. It was a little awkward for him because his adjutant usually worked the radios but he had left his adjutant with the Marines to make sure they had a good contingency plan if the North Vietnamese stepped up their attack. They were attacking everywhere else and Westmoreland was convinced that it was a diversion to get him to pull troops out of Khe Sanh. He was having none of it. He already thought the Marines were too thin in Khe Sanh. He was halfway convinced to reinforce them with some Army troops but that would leave other areas critically thin.

Meanwhile, he had been following the chatter about the Camp Johnson, which was nearby. After all, he had pioneered the whole idea of fire support bases. It sounded to him like the base was winning their fight. They had casualties to evacuate and he was considering picking them up, but a helicopter had apparently gone down. He told the pilot to change course slightly so they could at least pass over the area near Johnson where the helicopter was thought to have crashed. Then he heard a transmission from the 99th Assault Helicopter Company that it was their bird and that their executive officer was on board.

"Get lower," he told the pilot.

"Sir, that's not—"

"Lower," Westmoreland said, and the ship dropped. Not half a minute later, either the crew chief or the gunner shouted, "Purple smoke!"

"Let's take a look," the general said. The helicopter circled the purple smoke, staying a few hundred feet above a tiny clearing.

"There's two of them," said the gunner. "They're Americans. One of them's in a flight suit and the other guy is as blonde as Jayne Mansfield."

"Go get them," the general ordered.

"Okay Sir. It'll be tight, but I can do it."

The helicopter threaded its way down among the trees like a Frisbee settling to earth after a long, high flight, the rotor blades shearing off branches at the end.

The two soldiers ran up to the open door. The one in the flight suit was a warrant officer, a CW2, and Westmoreland saw that he had taken in his rank right away. Nevertheless, the warrant officer leaned in shouted something to the gunner.

Then the gunner said, "They've got two KIAs. Do we have room for two bodies?"

"Of course. Bring them in," said the general. The gunner unstrapped his seat belt and went with the two soldiers. When they returned, the warrant officer and the gunner were dragging the body of the black man and the blonde soldier was carrying another body slung over his shoulder. The blonde soldier laid the body he was carrying almost reverently on the floor. Westmoreland could see it was a major who had been shot in the head. The gunner dumped the second body on the floor.

On the way back, the general listened to the radios again, learning that two FBI agents were anxious to talk to James Hayes, who had been the crew chief on the downed 99th ship. Westmoreland noticed the tiny black PFC chevrons on the blonde soldier and wondered about that. *There can't be too many PFCs in Vietnam who were crew chiefs and who had attracted the attention of the FBI, so he's probably in trouble... big trouble.* Then he heard a CID investigator was waiting as well. The general sighed and studied the PFC. He was sitting with his head down, apparently asleep. The general reached over and woke him, causing him to sit up with a start. Now he could read the soldier's nametag: Hayes. Westmoreland told the pilot to head for Long Binh Operations first.

When they landed, the general walked with the two soldiers into the cool bunker. "At ease!" he shouted before anyone could call them all to attention. He took in the two sweaty men in suits and a competent looking soldier who wore no rank. *That would be the CID man.*

The larger civilian man was studying nametags. He stepped forward and grabbed Hayes by the shoulder and flipped open a badge in a leather case. "You must be James Hayes. You'll have to come with us. We're from the FBI."

Westmoreland stopped him with an icy glare. "I need to know what's going on here, and we'll start by identifying ourselves."

"I'm Special Agent—"

"We'll start with the PFC here, and the rest of you will hold your tongues until I ask you a question."

The FBI waved his badge again. "General, I—"

Suggs raised one arm and firmly pushed the FBI agent back one step.

Westmoreland nodded at him and turned to Hayes. "Private?"

"Actually I'm a spec four again since a few hours ago. Spec Four Jimmy Hayes," he said, and then added with just a hint of pride in his voice: "I'm a crew chief, since this morning too."

"Could you explain that?" the general asked. Hayes peered at him, just realizing that he was talking to a general, and General Westmoreland no less.

"Ah, it's a long story, Sir, and not a good one. I screwed up and got busted. But I got promoted back to spec four and forgot about these, Sir." He started taking off the PFC chevrons.

"Okay," Westmoreland said. He turned to Walters.

"CW2 Arnie Walters, Sir. I was A/C of the ship that went down. We're from the Blackjacks, the 99th Assault Helicopter Company. And may I add that Spec Four Hayes is one of the finest crew with whom I have served."

Westmoreland looked back at Hayes, who seemed to be on the verge of falling over. The warrant officer also looked unsteady. He spoke to Hayes. "You look shaky, Son. Are you hurt?"

"No Sir," Hayes said, straightening up. "I'm just tired and thirsty... really thirsty. Been a long time since I slept."

Walters said, "Sir, Hayes was in a firefight last night and we've been flying—"

Westmoreland turned to the sergeant behind the operations counter. "Get these men some water and some chairs." He turned back to Walters and indicated he should continue.

"Well, Hayes was flying when our gunship got shot down yesterday. Lost a tail rotor. Then Hayes had guard duty last night and there was a ground attack at Nui Binh. Happened in the morning. My peter pilot from yesterday was killed and another soldier was badly wounded, but Hayes and three others repelled the attack. Just the four of them killed about a hundred VC. He deserves a medal for that Sir."

"Nui Binh?" the general asked. "I saw a report."

Walters nodded. "Then today we were assigned a single ship mission to resupply Camp Johnson and take out some wounded. We took some fire and got hit just as we were getting out of there. We went down and the ship burned up."

"Who are the two KIAs?" asked the general.

"One of them is Major Frank Lehman, our XO. He was peter pilot. He's been trying to improve his flying and—"

"And the other one?"

"Oh, he's an FNG—sorry, Sir—he's a new guy who just came in today by the name of Hollister. He was a spec four."

"Killed when you went down?" asked Westmoreland.

"No Sir. We survived the crash okay, but the two wounded guys we picked up at Johnson didn't. We had to leave the bodies there," Walters said. "The rest of us got out before the ship exploded and we high-tailed it away from there. Figured the bad guys would find us quick if we stayed next to that burning ship."

"What happened?" the general asked.

Walters' face screwed up and he glanced at Hayes. They looked at each other. Then Walters said, "It's hard to believe,

Sir, but apparently Hollister shot Major Lehman in the head. We didn't see it happen. Hollister was gonna shoot Hayes and probably me too. Lehman didn't die right away and he had a weapon, a Chicom submachine gun. He emptied it on Hollister. Then Lehman sat down and talked to us for a minute before he died."

The sergeant brought two folding chairs and a canteen of water, which he handed to Hayes. Hayes gulped down several mouthfuls and handed it to Walters, who also drank quickly.

The sergeant looked at Westmoreland. "Sir, we're getting some urgent calls for you."

Westmoreland glanced at his watch. "I need a few more minutes here. Put them off."

Walters and Hayes had finished the canteen and sat down.

"I'll fill it again," the sergeant said.

Westmoreland turned to Suggs.

"Let's hear from you next. Are you the CID investigator?"

"Yes Sir, Jimmy Ray Suggs, Sir."

Westmoreland's gaze flicked over to the two impatient FBI men and then back to Suggs.

Suggs quickly told the general about his investigation.

Westmoreland listened with growing interest. For the first time, the two FBI agents looked interested in something other than themselves.

"So it would appear that someone showed up at the replacement depot and murdered Specialist Hollister in order to assume his identity. And the murderer was interested in the 99th Assault Helicopter Company," Westmoreland said. He turned to the two FBI agents. "Now, let's hear your story." He looked at his watch.

"I'm Special Agent Austin Bradbury and this is Special Agent William Ovenden. We're from the Detroit FBI Office.

Actually, I'm from headquarters in Washington on loan to Detroit. We're part of a task force investigating the murder of two Detroit police officers and the wounding of a third. We have reason to believe that James Hayes here, and possibly a girl by the name of Gloria, last name unknown, witnessed what happened. This occurred during last July's urban riot in Detroit. We'd like to question Mr. Hayes at length and most likely bring him back to Detroit to talk to others on the task force.

"Is Spec Four Hayes a suspect?" asked Westmoreland.

The two agents looked at each other. Ovenden said, "No, but we need to interview him. If he saw what we think he saw, we'd like to know why he didn't report it to the proper authorities."

Hayes was shaking his head and wanted to speak, but remarkably, he remembered the general's admonition to speak only when spoken to. He looked at the general and the general looked back.

"I have to go," Westmoreland said. "I have a war to fight." He turned to Walters. "Mr. Walters, I'm going to appoint you to act as counsel for Specialist Hayes here. I'm not sure he needs counsel, but if he does, that will be your responsibility. Normally, that's a job for a commissioned officer, but you'll have to make do. Remember he is innocent and has not been proven or even suspected of being guilty of anything. Furthermore, he is in the military and subject to the military judicial system, not civilian authority. I am ordering you to be present whenever he is questioned." He turned to the FBI agents. "Agents Bradbury and Ovenden, you will not question Private Hayes until tomorrow after both he and Mr. Walters have had a chance to recover from what has been an ordeal. I suggest you get together with Mr. Suggs here first. You will not under any circumstances interview Specialist Hayes unless Mr. Walters is present, and you will not take him back the U.S. unless you first get written permission from the U.S. Army. Is that clear?"

Bradbury nodded.

Westmoreland said, "I'll tell you right now, you are not likely to get permission to take him back. The enemy has launched an offensive and we need every soldier we have." The general turned to Suggs. "Mr. Suggs, I strongly suggest that you cooperate with the FBI and continue your investigation. It could be related to the FBI's mission. You and they have more to gain by working together than by being at odds with each other. Frankly, I'm hoping that you and the FBI can clear this up tomorrow so Specialist Hayes and CW2 Walters can get back to their company, and Mr. Bradbury and Mr. Ovenden can go home."

He turned to Hayes. "I want you to cooperate with the FBI, but remember that you are a soldier and subject to Army discipline. The FBI has no authority over you. That belongs to the Army, the CID and specifically Mr. Suggs here."

31 January, 0200 Hours, Long Binh Bachelor Officer Quarters

Hayes didn't go to sleep for what seemed like hours. He was so tired that he couldn't be sure he was fatigued or experiencing the lingering effects of the LSD. He couldn't sleep and he couldn't hold onto any single thought for long.

Walters said he had a bad headache, but he fell asleep right away. In fact, Hayes wondered whether Walters had passed out. He and Walters were sharing a tiny room with just enough room for two cots, and he listened to Walters sleeping soundly as his mind chewed on Bunker Three, Camp Johnson, Long Binh, Gloria, Rivera, Slobojan, Rufus, the two badly wounded from Camp Johnson, Westmoreland and Walters and then descended into a jumble of dead people: Lehman, Hollister, Comstock, Roscoe, faceless bodies of the Vietcong, and as always, the ARVN holding the M79 grenade launcher. He couldn't see the ARVN's face, though he sometimes saw the bullet holes. His face always seemed to be in shadow, but he always knew him. He wasn't sure he was dreaming when he heard small arms fire and artillery, but none of the dead people fell. Then he understood it was a dream. He was finally asleep, but it wasn't restful. In the dream he understood that the gunfire he was hearing was real. He wanted to wake up and became afraid that he couldn't. Then, with a start, he did wake up to see Walters lying a few feet away and looking at him. He seemed a little better, like he had rested, and Hayes was jealous.

"It's not that close," Walters said, "but there sure is a lot of it."

They listened for a few minutes until there was a knock on the door, which opened immediately. Bradbury said, "Didn't think you could sleep through that. Maybe we could get started early. We can't sleep through this racket either."

"I think we could sleep. We're used it," Walters said.

Ovenden was behind Bradbury and looking uncomfortable.

"No, you guys are awake. Look at you," Bradbury said and Walters turned to see Hayes sitting up.

Hayes said, "Why don't we just get this done?"

It sounded like the firefight was getting more intense. It wasn't close, but near enough to draw Hayes' interest and it had been going on for some time.

"Let's get this over with so we can get the hell out of here. I'm sure you gentlemen would like to get back to your business too," Bradbury said.

"I gotta take a leak," Hayes said.

"Out the front door and to your right," Walters said. He looked at Bradbury and Ovenden, and then back at Hayes. "Coffee?"

"Yeah," Hayes said.

"I'll see what I can do," Walters said. He was back 10 minutes later with a big Thermos and four china cups, which Hayes thought was a miracle. He looked at his watch. It was a little after 0200 hours.

They were all crowded into the small room that Hayes and Walters had been sharing. Ovenden looked at Hayes. "Why don't you start by telling us exactly what you saw at the motel? Go completely through it once, and then we'll probably have some questions."

"Okay," Hayes said. He reached for the Thermos and refilled his coffee cup.

"Where's Suggs?" Walters asked. "Shouldn't he be here?"

"Screw Suggs," Bradbury said. "He's probably sacked out somewhere quieter."

So Hayes told them about the motel in as much detail as he could remember, though not the details of the sex. But he admitted that he and Gloria had booked the motel under the pretense that they were brother and sister. When he got to Bonaventure, he didn't identify him and described him simply as a short fat black man. He had given a lot of thought about what Bonaventure had done and concluded that he might have done the same thing if he'd had a gun. He thought that Gloria might agree with him.

Ovenden asked, "Why didn't you tell all this to the police?"

"Because we'd just seen the cops kill two innocent people, a woman and a kid, and they'd beat up the hotel desk clerk. We didn't want to be next."

The two agents looked at each other. Ovenden said, "Well, maybe, but why would you think they would do anything to you? You'd be helping them find the man who killed their officers. Weren't you afraid of the guy who shot the cops? Wasn't he a threat to you? You and your girlfriend saw him kill two policemen."

Hayes shrugged. "We didn't have time to think about it. He shot the cops and was on us right away. He could have killed us right then and there. I thought he was gonna shoot us for a second. Maybe that was another reason we didn't tell the police, because he didn't kill us, and he could have. He had a shotgun and we didn't have squat," Hayes said. "But he didn't do anything to us. Anyway, all three of us were more afraid of the fuckin' National Guard than anything else because some idiot cut loose with a fifty cal. I didn't know a fifty-caliber machinegun from a water pistol back then, but it scared the shit out of all three of us. A fifty cal will do that. We didi'd out of there as fast as we could. My girl and I didn't have much time to even think about talking to the police."

"Didi'd?" Bradbury asked with a puzzled look.

Walters said, "Short for *didi mau*. It's Vietnamese for get the fuck out of Dodge," He grinned at Hayes.

"After we left and had time to think about it some more, we were still afraid to go to the cops. We just wanted to forget about it."

Bradbury looked at him a little contemptuously.

"What is your girlfriend's full name?"

"Gloria Doran," Hayes said.

Bradbury asked, "What's her address? Where can we find her?"

"I don't know," Hayes said. "She's on the run."

"What do you mean, 'on the run?' What's she running from?"

"Her stepfather. He tried to kill her, or at least that's what she told me in her letters, and I believe it," Hayes said. "He's been trying to find her ever since she ran away from home last summer. He's some kind of crooked lawyer or accountant, something like that. At least he works for bad guys. That's what she told me in the letters she wrote. She said he works for the Gargano family. That's another reason we didn't want to go to the police. She was afraid they'd just send her back to her stepfather."

"The Garganos?" Ovenden said. "They're the Mafia in Detroit. What's her father's name?"

Hayes shook his head slowly. "It's probably Doran, don't you think?" Hayes smirked.

"No other names?" Bradbury asked.

"You know, like I said, he's not really her father. He's her stepfather. She said his name used to be Dorrinian, and that he changed it a long time ago. She has this thing about finding out where she came from. She was adopted and doesn't know who her real parents are."

"Didn't she send you some papers that were in a foreign language?" Bradbury asked. "German? Don't you have an uncle who knows German? Did you send those papers to him?"

"No," Hayes said. "She told me she sent me something like that, but I never got anything. She must have mailed it before she had my address. I never got any of the letters that she said she sent when I first got here. I didn't hear from her for so long that I thought she'd dumped me."

Just then there was a loud knock at the door. Ovenden moved out of the way and opened the door. It was Suggs. He looked around carefully. "Started without me, huh?"

"You shouldn't waste your life sleeping," Bradbury said.

"I haven't been asleep. I've been working," Suggs said angrily. "And the next time you try to question Private Hayes without me being present, I will have you on the next big bird back to the fucking World. So gentlemen, either we start cooperating, or you'll be on your way home."

"Take it easy," Bradbury said. "We just had Hayes go through what he saw at the Cresthaven Motel in Detroit. I don't think it has anything to do with your investigation."

"I'll be the judge of that," Suggs said, looking at Walters.

"Yeah, that's mostly what Hayes talked about. And he's a spec four now," Walters said. "Pretty interesting. Hayes and his girlfriend saw some Detroit cops shoot a woman and a teenage boy and try to shoot another one. Then they saw someone shoot the cops. He was just saying that someone's trying to kill his girl, right?"

Hayes nodded. "She wrote me that her stepfather and a couple of hoods shot at her," His voice took on a desperate edge. "I'm really worried about it and I don't know what to do."

Bradbury said, "I need to know about those papers in the foreign language. If you didn't get them, where are they?"

Suggs held up his hand. "Wait a minute." He turned to Hayes. "What papers?"

"He was asking me about some papers that Gloria said she sent to me. She found a bunch of her stepfather's papers and she said she sent some of them to me. She didn't know what they were because they were in another language. She thought it was German and she wanted me to send them to my uncle because he understands German pretty good. I never got anything like that, but I never got any of the early letters she sent because she didn't have my address. She said she sent them to me in Vietnam and wrote "please forward" on them. Shit, they probably never got here."

"Okay," Suggs said. He looked at Bradbury and Ovenden. "I've been back to CID HQ and 12th Group Ops. There's a lot of shit going on right now. The VC have been attacking all around us. That's what you've been hearing out there. They're worried about a ground attack here."

"Oh shit," Hayes said, "not again."

Just then there was a series of very loud sharp bangs, with the last one making the entire building shudder. Walters and Hayes both instinctively hit the floor followed by Suggs. The two FBI agents both jumped up and ran out the door, then stopped, unsure of where to go.

Hayes grabbed his M16 and the bandoleer.

Walters shouted, "One twenty-twos!" as they both headed through the door.

"Where's the bunker?" Hayes shouted as they ran.

"Left and across the street!" Suggs yelled.

They spent the next 25 minutes in a crowded bunker listening to rockets and mortars coming in.

Then a lean sergeant first class stuck his head in the bunker. "Gentlemen, out to the perimeter, right now!" he said. "We've got a ground attack."

So with a dozen others, most of them officers who had been in the bunker, they trotted over to a sandbagged wall along Highway 1. Many of them didn't have rifles, but a sergeant came by with rifles for those who lacked them and ammunition for everyone.

Walters put down his Chicom and took an M16 instead. "Only got about three bullets left for it," he said about his Chicom. "I wonder if they have any enemy ammo? I've never actually fired it and I'd love to give it a spin."

"*You* are a fucking cannibal," Hayes said, making Walters smile. When Walters had been temporarily in command of the Headhunters, Hayes had started calling him Cannibal, as in Cannibal and the Headhunters, and the nickname had started to catch on.

Somewhere between the room and the bunker, the two FBI agents had disappeared.

They did a lot of disorganized firing in the next half-hour. Hayes expended a lot of ammunition, of which there seemed to be an unlimited supply. It wasn't like the previous night's ground attack. He didn't feel much danger. They watched gunships making rocket and minigun runs, presumably at the sites where the 122s and mortars were being launched. The incoming rockets and mortars stopped not long after they got to the perimeter.

"Wonder where those FBI guys went," Walters said during a lull. "Probably still in a fuckin' bunker somewhere. Maybe someone will get 'em with a satchel charge. That Bradbury's an asswipe."

"Don't you have to be an accountant or a lawyer or something to be an FBI agent?" Suggs asked. "Maybe that explains it. I got no use for lawyers. I don't know about accountants. Don't know any."

Hayes had almost forgotten about him. He looked at Suggs curiously. "How come you were looking for me?" he asked. "I've been in some trouble, but I didn't think it had spread to Long Binh."

"No trouble," said Suggs. "I'm sure the guy you knew as Hollister wasn't Hollister, and that he murdered the real Hollister. And it sounds like he murdered your executive officer. So now I'm investigating two murders."

Walters looked at Suggs. "I don't get it," Walters said. "A lot of guys in the 99th didn't like Lehman, but not enough to kill him. Besides, Hollister just got here. Why would he want to kill the major?"

Suggs said, "We don't know who he really was, but it looks like he killed the real Hollister so he could go to the 99th Assault Helicopter Company. I don't know why he wanted to do that, but it sure is interesting that the FBI showed up at the same time looking for Hayes." He turned to Hayes. "Tell me, you know anyone who might want to kill you?"

"Yeah, all those commie motherfuckers out there." He laughed. "But it's nothing personal, if you know what I mean." Then he remembered what Gloria had written and a frown replaced the smile. "Wait... like I said, my girl's stepfather tried to shoot her. Now that I'm thinking about it, she also wrote that he wanted to get me too, but she didn't see how he could do that since I'm in Vietnam and—"

"And you said her stepfather works for the Mafia in Detroit," said Suggs. "What's he do?"

Hayes shrugged, trying to think. He was tired and maybe still a little spaced out. For a second he wondered whether he had fallen asleep and the conversation was a dream. "I'm not sure. It was something to do with money. She was a rich girl. I remember she told me she taught herself to drive going up and down her driveway in her stepfather's Corvette." He stopped and started fumbling through his pockets looking for cigarettes. A cigarette might wake him up. He found the plastic box with the cigarettes but he dropped it. He bent over, and then got down on his hands and knees looking for it, still talking. "I only knew her for about two weeks. We were in love and—"

A deafening explosion, louder than anything that Hayes had heard in his entire life, cracked above him. The shock hit his body like he'd run full speed into a wall. Walters and Suggs came down hard on top of him. Hayes just flattened out and was trying to will is body to sink farther into the dirt. He felt them hit him, then more explosions, but all he could hear was ringing in his ears.

Later he learned that the ammo dump had exploded, or more accurately had started exploding, for the eruptions were continuous. Hayes would never be sure how long it kept exploding, but he was so tired, he almost fell asleep even while the concussions were ringing through his body as if he were inside a giant bell. His hearing came back a couple of times and when it did, the explosions were louder by far than the loudest amplifiers at the loudest rock concerts he'd ever played or been to. Despite the noise, he could feel himself sliding toward sleep. He had his hands over his head, fingers in his ears, face shoved into the dirt with just enough space to breath. The others were on top of him, like a heavy blanket that vibrated with the detonations. He wasn't afraid; in fact, he felt safe. He thought he might be dying, and if so, dying wasn't unpleasant but strangely peaceful despite the detonations that kept going on, sometimes fast and sometimes slow, and he thought it would end when his death was complete. And he didn't care. He was content. But then it finally ended and he had to wriggle out from under Walters and Suggs.

The medics took both of them away. Walters was unconscious with blood coming out of his ears. Suggs was semiconscious, but barely. One of the medics told Hayes that he thought both of them would be okay. "Concussions, but they'll recover," he said confidently. "Probably just be out a day or two. You were all lucky. You were as close as anyone on the line to the explosions." A spec four who was farther away had been killed, and several others had been taken out on stretchers.

Hayes realized that Walters and Suggs had been standing up when the dump went off while he had been down in the trench. He had indeed been lucky. However, his luck ran out about half an hour later when Bradbury and Ovenden showed up just as he was getting ready to sack out on top of the sandbagged wall. Remarkably, both of them were clean-shaven and looked like they had just showered, though their suits were wrinkled.

"Fuck," Hayes said, "not you guys again."

"We're glad to see you too," Bradbury said with sneering insincerity. Hayes' hearing hadn't fully returned and Bradbury sounded far away. "You're coming with us, and I think you'll like where we're going."

"You want to tell me where we're going?" asked Hayes. "Or at least where you think we're going?"

Bradbury motioned. "This way."

Hayes didn't move. He was remembering Westmoreland's orders.

"Okay," Bradbury said. "We'll do it the hard way." He reached behind his back under his suit jacket and came out with a set of handcuffs. He snapped one cuff on Hayes' right wrist in a smooth motion. Then he snapped the other cuff on Hayes' left wrist so both hands were behind his back. He wrenched Hayes arms, dragging him off the sandbags.

"You're coming with us, Sonny." Bradbury sneered. "The general will have to fight his fucking war without you. Don't get upset. The cuffs are only temporary."

With Bradbury on one arm and Ovenden on the other, the two FBI agents dragged him across the open expanse of the base camp toward a road. Bradbury was holding his FBI badge up with one hand.

"What the fuck are you doing to me?" Hayes said loudly. All around, soldiers gaped at them, but no one said anything, including a full-bird colonel with a major and two lieutenants. At the road, they piled Hayes into a civilian car, a dirty light-blue Ford Falcon driven by a blonde-haired man wearing jeans, a loud sport shirt and sunglasses. A stubby submachine gun lay on the front passenger seat.

Bradbury caught Hayes looking at it as he and Ovenden pushed him into the back seat. "Don't even think about it."

They drove quickly out of the base camp, passing Army grunts and groups of ARVNS. They pulled over to let two M113 armored personnel carriers coming from the opposite direction clatter by. Soon, they stopped at a gate to a big airfield. The driver held out his wallet with credentials and the guard waved them through. They seemed to be expected. It was the same place where he had arrived in Vietnam six months ago. The car drove across the tarmac to a Boeing 707 with stairs pushed against it. Bradbury got out, pulled Hayes out by the handcuffs and prodded him up the stairs. Ovenden followed. As soon as they entered the plane and the door closed behind them, a ragged cheer went up. The plane was full of soldiers.

Hayes thought, *It's the Freedom Bird! Holy shit!* They went all the way to the front of the aircraft where Bradbury shoved Hayes into a window seat. Ovenden got into the seat beside him as the plane starting to move.

A young stewardess looked over from the seat across the aisle. "You bastard! Baby killer!"

"I haven't killed any babies," Hayes said.

"Shut the fuck up," Bradbury said. He looked at the stewardess. "Excuse me, Ma'am, but they all say they're innocent."

"Seat belt," said Ovenden. He unlocked the handcuffs, relocked them around his hands in front this time, and helped the Hayes fasten the seatbelt.

Hayes asked Ovenden, "What's with the baby killer shit?"

Ovenden whispered, "We had to tell them we were taking a criminal back to the U.S. to get on this flight. I guess he must have told them you were gonna be tried for war crimes, for killing women and children. Don't worry about it. It was just to get us on this flight. You're going home. Cheeseburgers and blonde pussy."

The plane took off with the stewardess glaring hatefully at him, and when it reached altitude Ovenden spoke to him again, still in a whisper. "Gonna be a long trip, but we have to keep the cuffs on. It's the only way Bradbury could get us on. We told them you were dangerous. We're taking you back to Detroit. That can't be all bad, right?"

Hayes said, "The general said you couldn't do this." He tried to think for a few minutes, but he decided he was too tired to think. He had picked up that they were going to Detroit, so Gloria would be closer. He reclined the back of the seat as far as he could, not caring if he pissed off the guy behind him, got as comfortable as he could, and was asleep in less than a minute.

CHAPTER 13

January 30, 11:35 p.m., Detroit

Gloria had gone back to Mrs. Murphy, who had sent her to a niece who had a spare bedroom in her home. From the corner of the bedroom window with all of her lights turned off, she'd been watching a grey Chevrolet with two men in it idling outside of the house for about 45 minutes. Maybe they had followed her, or maybe the niece's husband had called someone. He had been unfriendly and didn't like having Gloria there. He had stopped his wife from making dinner for her when she arrived. She was very hungry.

Out on the street, another car, a Ford, joined the grey Chevrolet, parking right beside it in the middle of the street. Four men, all of them big, got out and walked toward the house. Gloria was already putting on her parka when she heard the knock at the front door. She grabbed the suitcase and her big handbag, scampered into the hallway and down the back stairs of the old house.

"Gloria, there's some policemen here want to see you," the man called. He had answered the door so quickly that Gloria thought he must have been waiting right beside it.

She quietly slipped out the back door. She had parked the Rambler in the alley that ran behind the houses. For a moment, she considered turning herself in to the police, but she was afraid of them. They wouldn't help her and would eventually turn her over to her stepfather. She had thought about going back to her real father, Clyde Bonaventure, but he and his friend Logan Carlton wanted to put her in juvenile hall. That might be a last resort. She didn't want to go to Roscoe's mother. The woman would help, but the police and her stepfather were probably watching her. There were always the tunnels, but she had fled them after one of the maintenance workers had found her and threatened to turn her in. He had correctly guessed that she had stolen the cushions she was lying on from a dormitory. And she was almost out of money.

So she drove through Detroit and stopped at the Biff's on Grand River Avenue. She counted her money and then ordered coffee and pancakes. She'd found that if she didn't keep something in her stomach she might not only get sick, but also faint. She estimated that she was six months pregnant, and it was quite noticeable when she wasn't wearing her coat. Anyone who had known her before could have seen right away that she was pregnant. She could pass as chunky to strangers. And now she could feel the baby moving, tiny little kicks and other movements. It seemed that the baby had sleep periods and wake periods.

She had written several letters in the past two days and was getting better at it, but so far she hadn't been able to mail them. Her letters were several pages long. She told Jimmy again that she didn't want him to feel obligated just because she was pregnant. He might have other dreams and she didn't expect him to give them up. She finished her pancakes and went out to the car. She started it and let it idle and warm up again. The temperature had dropped below zero.

While she was waiting for heat, she took stock. She had $8.35 in cash and at least three-quarters of a tank of gas. She looked through the glove compartment of the car and found the registration. She had never looked at it before. To her surprise, the car wasn't registered to Jimmy, but to Sepp Hayha.

Hayha.... She stared at the name on the slip of paper for a long time and swallowed hard. *Didn't Clyde Bonaventure say my mom's name was Hayha?* It was an uncommon name, one she'd never heard before Bonaventure had said it. Then she remembered that Jimmy had told her that his uncle had given him the car. *This must be his uncle. Are Jimmy and I related?* She tried to drive the thought from her head, but it wouldn't go away.

The address on the registration was Sault Ste. Marie, Sugar Island, Michigan. She pulled a map of Michigan from the glove compartment. It took her a few minutes, by which time the car was warm, but she found Sault Ste. Marie all the way up at the top of the state. It was a long way. *Will Jimmy's Uncle Sepp help me?* Jimmy had told her that his uncle was a bosun on a lake freighter, but she was pretty sure the boats didn't operate in the winter. Jimmy had spoken fondly of his uncle so it was worth a try. *And I'll be returning his car. That has to count for something.* She looked at the map again. Sugar Island was next to Sault Ste. Marie, which was almost straight north, and once she got out of Lansing it appeared that the road was freeway all the way. She was a little worried about driving that distance, but it couldn't be any harder than driving around East Lansing, Ann Arbor and Detroit in the winter had been.

It was almost five in the morning when she pulled into a gas station with a restaurant at Gaylord. She wasn't sure where she was or how much farther she had to go. The gas tank was almost empty and she asked the attendant to put in five dollars of regular or fill it up, whatever came first. The five dollars got her a little over ten gallons and the gauge was right on the F. *That should get me to Sault Ste. Marie,* she thought. In the restaurant, after a bowl of soup, a hot turkey sandwich, french fries, milk, and a couple of candy bars that she would save for later, she had 91 cents left. She debated leaving a tip, decided against it and then apologized to the woman behind the counter who had served her.

"Yeah, I know, you need it for the bridge toll," sighed the waitress.

"What bridge toll?" Gloria asked.

"The Mackinac Bridge," said the woman. "It's $3.75 each way. Everyone's complaining that it's too high and it's hurting the tourist industry. They're talking about lowering it, but don't hold your breath."

Gloria had shed her parka.

"When you due, Honey?" the waitress asked.

Gloria barely heard her. She went out and opened up the map again. *Maybe there's another route....* But there wasn't. The only other way was to drive completely around Lake Michigan or Lake Huron, and she'd need several tanks of gas to do either. She sat in the car trying not to cry until she finally started feeling the cold. Then she started the car.

"I can't be the first person who doesn't have the money," she said as she pulled back onto the freeway.

Just as she got to the bridge, the clouds cleared and the sun came up. It was a spectacular sight, the biggest bridge she'd ever seen. Her fatigue evaporated and her spirits soared. The deep blue lake water gleamed below her, stretching to shorelines that were cloaked in sparkling white ice and snow. There were no boats in the water and only a few other cars on the bridge. As she came to the first tower, she saw a large snowy white bird that looked like it had ears perched high above her. It was a beautiful creature and she took it as a good omen. The tollbooth was at the far end of the bridge so she would already be across the bridge before she told them she didn't have the money. *Will they send me back when they find out I can't pay? Maybe they'll just let me go on my way.*

The bridge attendant was an unshaven man in his fifties. She opened her window, leaned out, smiled and said, "I don't have enough money to pay. All I've got is 91 cents."

She proffered the money and attendant looked at her for a long time. He scratched the stubble on his chin. "Identification. Let me see your driver's license."

"Ahh, I don't have it with me. I lost my purse. That's why I don't have the money."

He eyed her again for even longer than the last time. He asked her to pull forward a few feet, then leaned out the window and wrote down her license plate number. "Okay, there's a restaurant on the left when you take the exit. Pull in there and wait. If you don't wait, you'll be evading arrest and that'll just make it worse." He shut the window of his booth and picked up a telephone. When she kept looking at him, he pointed down the road. She drove down to the restaurant and pulled in. After idling for half a minute, she turned the engine off to save gas. Fifteen minutes later, a fast moving police car appeared and pulled into the parking space beside her. A big mean-looking sheriff's deputy with red hair got out and slowly walked up to her window. She rolled it down. A nametag on his coat read *Page*.

"Driver's license and registration," he said. She repeated her story about the lost purse. The deputy, who appeared to be no more than 30 years old, looked skeptical. He was looking past her at the inside of the car. He didn't look friendly.

"What's your name?" he asked.

"Gloria," she said, and when she saw he was waiting for a last name, she said, "Gloria Hayes."

"Do you have any drugs in there?"

"No," she said.

She hadn't wanted to tell him Doran because that could send her back to her stepfather.

"Most people keep their registration in the car, not on their person," said the deputy.

"Oh," she said remembering the registration she'd looked at earlier. She quickly fumbled in the glove compartment until she found it.

When she turned back to the window, the trooper had stepped back and was holding a revolver with both hands, pointing it at her head. "I want to see both of your hands! Now!"

She froze and slowly raised both of her hands up to the window where he could see them. The registration was in one of her shaking hands.

"Get out of the car and turn and face the car," he said.

"Please, I'm—"

"Move it!"

She got out and he pushed her firmly toward the back of the car.

"Put both of your hands on the car," he said.

She did it. The car was frigid. "Now spread your legs, put your hands behind you and lean against the car."

She put her hands behind her, trying to lean sideways. She fell against the car, hitting her head and one shoulder as handcuffs snapped around her wrists.

The officer pulled the registration slip out of her hand.

"It's my boyfriend—my husband's uncle," she said. She sniffed loudly and was on the verge of tears. She felt sick to her stomach, still tasting the slick french fry grease coating the inside of her mouth. And she suddenly needed to pee. "I'm pregnant and my boyfrie—husband is in Vietnam. I don't feel very good and I really need to use a bathroom."

"Shut up, and don't move."

There were footfalls as he walked away and then the sound of his car door opening. After a minute or so, she took a chance and turned her head. He was talking into his radio microphone. She turned a little more and saw several people in the window of the restaurant looking at her. She turned back to the car. She was very uncomfortable, and she was embarrassed. After hours of sitting behind the wheel, her legs were cramping in the awkward posture. She concentrated on not peeing her pants.

The deputy finally came back. He pulled her painfully upright by her arms and marched her into the restaurant. He looked at the waitress behind the counter. "Agnes, give me a coffee."

Agnes glared at him and then turned to Gloria.

"What would you like?"

"Uhh, hot chocolate, thanks."

He led her to the ladies' room and then unlocked the handcuffs. "Go ahead. I'll wait out here for you."

She went inside, used the toilet and then took a long time washing her hands and face. It was warm inside so she took off one sweatshirt. She rinsed out her mouth, wishing she had a toothbrush. Finally she came back out to see the trooper standing in the same place, still holding the handcuffs.

He snapped them back on, but this time with her hands in front. "You better not try to run on me. You wouldn't get far anyways."

He pushed her roughly into a booth by the window just as the waitress arrived with cups containing coffee and hot chocolate. She plopped a blueberry muffin down in front of Gloria.

"Hey, where's mine?" asked the deputy.

The waitress said, "You ain't pregnant, and you don't deserve one, the way you're treating her. You ought to be ashamed of yourself, treating people like that just because they can't pay that unfair toll."

"You mind your own damn business, Agnes, or I'll run you in. And you tell Alvin that the next time he calls the police and nobody else." He paused for a beat to adjust his gun belt. "She ain't no more pregnant than I am."

The waitress was a plump thirtyish woman with streaks of premature grey in her black hair. She looked at Gloria. "Stand up, Honey. I'm Agnes, by the way, and I don't take any crap from these guys." Gloria stood up and Agnes ran her hand across Gloria's swollen abdomen. "Definitely pregnant," said Agnes. "I can always tell. I'd say at least five months, maybe six."

Gloria nodded and sat down. She took a sip of the hot chocolate and a bite of the muffin.

The trooper gulped most of his coffee and then got up. "I have to use the pay phone. I'm gonna call your husband's uncle."

Looking out the window, Gloria could see her car door still open. She got up and went to the counter where Agnes was wiping the counter. The deputy had been about to dial a number and put the phone down to watch her.

"Could you do me a big favor and go out to my car and get my guitar? The door's open and I don't want it to get too cold," she said.

"Okay," she said. "Maybe you can play us a tune?"

"Well, I can't play with these," she said holding her handcuffed hands. "Otherwise, sure, I'd love to play."

There were two men in plaid shirts and denim coveralls eating at the counter. One of them turned to look at her, but the other kept shoveling pancakes into his mouth.

Gloria smiled for the first time, stole a glance at the deputy and saw him scribbling in his notebook in the phone booth. Only three of the booths and tables were occupied, with two couples and a group of four men who looked like local businessmen. Agnes came back with her guitar and said something to the deputy.

The deputy looked at Gloria again. It looked like he was swearing, but he motioned for her to come over. Without a word, he unlocked the handcuffs.

She rubbed her wrists, fiddled with her guitar for a minute because the cold had messed up the tuning, and then started strumming chords, not knowing what she was going to play. She'd had little chance to play her guitar recently. She closed her eyes and eventually her meandering chords worked their way into "Somebody to Love," one of her favorite songs and one of the covers she and Jimmy and Roscoe had recorded. They had changed it and put their own creative stamp on it.

She started slowly, getting used to playing again, then increased the power and the tempo as she went along. Between verses she picked out runs, remembering how Jimmy had played. She could hear his Stratocaster's wet, echoey reverb with the feedback licking at the edges. She had always been good at using her guitar to mimic whatever she heard. She doubled-picked on the two heaviest gauge bass strings high up on the neck of the guitar and then zoomed all the way down using a little tin ashtray that she'd snatched from the table. Her fingers danced through delicate, sprightly runs, mimicking Roscoe's piano. Then she battered her guitar with power chords as she sang. Once it had been a song of hope for her but now it was sad. Jimmy called it psychedelic blues. What could be worse than not having someone to love or to love you?

And that was the story of her life. Her stepfather was trying to kill her. *Did my real mother ever love me? Did my father? He never knew I existed so how could he love me? Does Jimmy love me? I love him, but does he know it? He might die in the war and then he would never know it.* She still couldn't remember ever saying to him that she loved him. *Will he believe it when he sees it in my letters? Did he actually receive any of them?*

She slowed again for the last verse. Gina was dead. Roscoe was dead. And Jimmy might die in the war. Her stepfather was after her and wanted to kill their baby, the little baby that was kicking in her. She was on the verge crying. Finally, she just let the song end in a series of fading chords because she had to stop. Her eyes were watery but she was determined not to let the deputy have satisfaction of seeing her cry.

The two farmers at the counter and then the others in the restaurant all started clapping.

"Wow!" Agnes said. "You're *amazing*!"

Gloria smiled. She wanted to wipe her watery eyes with her sleeve but instead she blinked and shook her head. "Thanks," she said, loudly enough to acknowledge the applause.

One of the farmers from the counter, a young guy with long hair whose overalls were particularly dirty, came over to her. "I swear I heard a song a lot like that on the radio yesterday."

"Yeah well, it's a Jefferson Airplane song."

"Yeah, I know that, but the one I heard was supposed to be some band from down below. Singer sounded like you. Had some really cool electric guitar in it, kind of the way you were playing, except it was electric. Anyway, I really liked it on the radio, and the way you just did it."

"Thanks," she said again, and smiled at him.

Then the deputy grabbed her arm and pulled her back toward the booth.

Agnes brought another coffee and hot chocolate. This time she had muffins for both of them though she slapped the one down in front of the trooper in a far from friendly manner. "You don't deserve it."

"I'm just being careful," he said, sounding a little defensive. "We got notice from Detroit cops that they were looking for that Rambler. They said it was in connection with the shooting of two police officers. They say they want to question a young woman looks like this gal, and a young man." He looked at Gloria. "Whom I presume is your husband. They're trying to keep the whole thing quiet and my supervisor doesn't think they're playing straight with us. There's no warrant so he won't let me bring you in. He's making a big mistake in my book."

He didn't sound happy about it and Gloria got the idea that he wasn't saying everything. He drank some coffee and they both munched on their blueberry muffins. He tore a page out of his notebook and tossed it onto the table.

"Your husband's uncle said he knew you had the car. Son of a bitch is kind of squirrely." He shook his head. "But he said he knew about it. Sounded surprised like he wasn't expecting you. Wanted to be sure you knew how to find the house. The directions to the house are on the paper." He tapped the page he'd torn out of the notebook with his finger. He was talking in a stern, almost threatening tone. "We'll forget about the toll. Like Agnes says, it's not too popular around here. I'm gonna give you a ticket for not having a license. Detroit would prefer that we locked you up, but my supervisor doesn't want to do that. Says holding a pregnant woman for failing to pay the bridge toll might get into the papers, especially since we've already got Agnes riled up. I'm still not convinced you're pregnant. I think you might just be fat." He glared at the waitress and Agnes glared back. He wrote out the ticket and had Gloria sign it. Then he asked, "You ever met your husband's uncle?"

She shook her head.

"You have enough gas? It's about fifty miles."

"I filled up in Gaylord," she said.

He nodded and looked around the restaurant. People were avoiding looking at them. "You'll need money for the Sugar Island ferry."

"How much is it?" she asked.

"I don't know, and it's not my damn problem." He sat there for a minute, looking unhappily at her but said no more. He seemed frustrated and angry. He didn't want to let her go. He looked around at the people in the restaurant, all of whom were looking away except for Agnes. Then he got up and left. Gloria watched him through the window as he got into his patrol car. He didn't look back. Everyone in the restaurant was watching him now. Agnes came over as the car drove off.

"He's a mean bastard, and a bully too," she said. "My brother and I went to the same high school as him. Nobody liked Page. I don't know how he ever got hired into that department. I thought they had some standards."

"He said I'd need to pay for the Sugar Island Ferry," Gloria said. "All I've got is 91 cents."

Agnes smiled. "Really? Well girl, why don't you play us another tune?"

Gloria did, and collected a little over $10. She took her time and played her guitar off and on for a couple of hours, the music improving her spirits and settling her down.

11:15 p.m., Sugar Island

The Sugar Island directions led her into a driveway next to an old wooden frame cabin. It had been painted light blue a long time ago and the paint was peeling off the boards. It had a roof of gray shingles with a large section that had been patched with tarpaper. Beyond the cabin through the barren Maple trees about a hundred yards down a gentle slope, was the frozen St. Mary's River where it widened into Lake

George. There were several little huts out on the ice. A couple of feet of snow covered the ground, but the driveway was packed ice on top of frozen dirt and it was slippery. Gloria had just slid the Rambler to a stop when the front door of the house opened.

The man who came out looked to be in his forties and had thinning brown hair. He was studying her carefully, not smiling, but not threatening either. He was a little shorter than Jimmy but more heavily built, muscular and not fat. He was wearing faded blue work pants, worn work boots, a white T-shirt and a red flannel plaid shirt that was unbuttoned. He looked like he hadn't shaved for several days. His eyes caught her attention; they seemed familiar. They didn't look like Jimmy's eyes because they were more hazel than blue, but they held the same openly curious look. As she got out of the car, he smiled, and it was the same way Jimmy smiled.

"You must be my Jimmy's Gloria," he said in a strong Finnish accent. She nodded and he continued right up to her and wrapped her in a bear hug that seemed like the most natural thing in the world. "Jimmy has written to me about you. Come in, come in. Get warm." He opened the back of the Rambler and started grabbing everything. When Gloria moved to pick something up, he said, "No, no... go inside. Get warm." So she followed him into the cabin, carrying her large handbag. He had the two guitar cases and her large suitcase, and he had her Army blanket folded under one arm. He appeared to be very strong. He laid everything down carefully and appraised her again, then went back out and got Jimmy's amplifier.

She looked around. There was a stone fireplace with a wood-burning stove inside it, and it was obviously working because it was warm inside. The cabin looked like it had been hastily cleaned up. There was a stack of newspapers and magazines in one corner and a big collection of dirty dishes by the sink, which had water in it. All horizontal surfaces were stacked with dishes, tools, books, cans and boxes of food, and a wide range of items were leaning against the walls: a broom, fishing poles, a pair of skis and ski poles, snowshoes and curtain rods. She didn't know what half the things were.

He said, "You must be tired."

She nodded.

"Come." He led her to a short hallway and gestured toward the door at the end. "That's the bathroom. There's a shower if you want to use it." He opened one of the doors in the hallway to reveal a small bedroom with an old single bed that had been freshly made up. "You can stay here. This was Jimmy's room," he said. "You can lock the door if you're afraid."

She wasn't afraid, but she was tired. She went into the room and then took a shower. Afterwards, she got dressed, mostly in some of Jimmy's old clothes that she'd found in the room. She smelled something cooking. It was whitefish, and it was delicious. Sepp had prepared it along with boiled potatoes and a salad. Gloria made them some coffee. They ate mostly in silence, neither of them sure of how to speak to the other. But it wasn't an uncomfortable silence. Not speaking was normal for Gloria, and she recognized the same trait in him. When they finished eating, she helped him wash the dishes.

Finally she said, "We need to talk." The meal had revived her and she was anxious to see where she stood with him.

"It's good to have someone here who Jimmy cares about," he said. "I'm glad he found you."

She thought that was an interesting way to phrase it. He sat down at the kitchen table again but she remained standing, leaning against the counter by the sink. She'd been sitting so long in the car that her legs felt better when she stood. Finally she said, "You know, don't you?"

That caught him by surprise, but maybe not completely. He didn't answer for a long time, which was fine with her. She wasn't sure how to talk about it either.

"Well, you look a lot like your mother, a little darker and a little heavier," he finally said. "But when Jimmy sent me your picture, it still took me weeks to figure out why you looked so familiar."

She thought, *He doesn't want to come right out and say it.* "You should see the picture of my great grandmother. I'm the spitting image of her."

His brow furrowed in confusion. "Your great grandmother?"

"You don't know who my father is, do you?" she said. "His name's Clyde Bonaventure. You know who that is?"

"Clyde Bonaventure?" He shook his head, looking puzzled but very interested.

"I'm darker because he's a black man in Detroit." She paused to let that sink all the way in.

He didn't say anything but he seemed to be studying her. It hadn't shocked him the way she had expected and he looked uncertain.

"And I look heavier because I'm pregnant..."

He continued inspecting her, his head starting to nod.

Finally she said, "He runs after hours night clubs with prostitutes in Detroit. He did the same thing in Germany a long time ago."

"Oh," he said, and seemed to be thinking about it.

"My stepfather, who was Matthias Dorrinian then, brought my mother to him to work as a prostitute. That was how she was gonna pay for her and you to come here."

Pain crossed his face. "Dorrinian," he said, then muttered something that sounded like a curse in Finnish. "I know who he is."

"I had a lot of time to think about it while I was driving up here. The main thing is that I love Jimmy. It happened right away. I saw him playing blues guitar and I couldn't take my eyes off him. There's this thing I have, usually when I feel good, that I see shimmering colors, and when I saw Jimmy playing there was a purple glow around him. I wanted to be close to him. Later, I felt safe with him. I could talk to him, and I have a hard time talking to people. He probably thinks I don't talk much, because back then, I didn't, but with him I was a regular chatterbox compared to the way I usually was. Funny, it's the same with you. Anyway, I knew from the start that I loved him, and it changed everything. I think he loves me too. I hope so. We didn't even have two weeks together but we were never apart for all of that time. Of course, I didn't know he was my half-brother then."

"You think Jimmy's your half-brother?" He started to say something, then stopped himself. He didn't seem to know what to say.

She looked at him, suddenly less sure. "I learned my mother's name was Saija Hayha, and your name is Hayha, and Jimmy said his mother was your sister, so—"

"No, no, you have it wrong." He ran both hands through his hair. "Saija is my sister and she's your mother, but she's not Jimmy's mother."

"What? Then who's Jimmy's mother?"

His expression grew more easy, like he was relieved. "It was a woman Saija knew from the war. I think she was Norwegian and after the war she was living in the same DP camp as us. She died of meningitis when Jimmy was just a few months old. We took care of Jimmy."

"Oh! I... I didn't know any of that... thank you...." She grew quiet and started whispering the rosary as a tear rolled down her cheek.

Sepp got up and put his arms around her.

She whispered. "I'm sorry. I'm so mixed up about everything. I just love Jimmy so much, and driving up here, I finally decided that I didn't care if he was my half-brother. I'm so afraid he'll get killed in the war and I'll never see him again... and our baby will never know his father."

"It's okay," he said. He tightened his embrace and patted her back. "He isn't your half-brother and there isn't anything you can do about that war now. I worry about Jimmy too, because he's like a son. I know he loves you because he told me when he wrote. He's crazy for you."

Finally they were over the hump and could talk.

She told him almost everything, all about the Cresthaven, Roscoe's murder, her stepfather's attempts to find her and kill her, and how she had managed to elude him. He knew some of it already from the FBI. The only thing she didn't talk about was what her stepfather had done to her. She was beginning to suspect that he had done the same thing to her mother, and she needed time to think about that.

They talked about leaving as soon as they could. But they couldn't decide where to go. At first Sepp wanted to go to Canada to his cousin. But Gloria had no identification, and they both concluded there was a good chance the border patrol was already looking for her. Neither of them wanted to risk going south over the Mackinac Bridge. That left heading west through the Upper Peninsula. Sepp said maybe they could hide in Escanaba or Gladstone or Wisconsin. Or maybe they could go to Chicago.

Fatigue finally caught up with Gloria. "Can we decide later? I need to sleep." She yawned.

Sepp nodded.

She crawled into Jimmy's old bed in her clothes and went right to sleep.

January 31, 1:05 p.m., Detroit Police Headquarters (Beaubian Street)

Al Checchi was sitting in Homicide eating a hot dog and fries that another detective had picked up but couldn't eat because he had been called out to a homicide. It was a Coney Dog, a hot dog smothered with hot chili and onions. Checchi didn't really want it—he didn't care for onions and preferred his chili in a bowl instead of slopped over a hotdog—but he didn't feel like going out into the cold to get something else. So he was working on the dog, reading files and listening to the radio news about Vietnam when the phone rang. It was someone from Washington in the U.S. Army Criminal Investigation Division looking for help identifying a body in Vietnam. Checchi wasn't paying a lot of attention until he heard the name James Hayes.

"What's that name again?" Checchi mumbled, his mouth full of onions and chili. He had the caller go over the story again.

"We have the body of a young Negro male that a CID investigator in Vietnam believes was responsible for two murders there and who may have been trying to kill an Army soldier by the name of James Hayes, who's from Michigan. The investigator in Vietnam sent us prints and a picture and said we should try the larger police departments in Michigan."

Checchi gave the man the TWX number and was waiting at the machine when the prints and picture came over. The picture was a blurry shot of a dead man's face, but Checchi thought it was Slick Percy Dupree. He had never met Dupree, but he had been looking at pictures. Within half an hour, after he had interrupted several people eating lunch at their desks, all of it looking more appetizing than the Coney dog, he had a positive match for Dupree on the prints. He immediately called Army CID back and told them to whom the prints belonged and said he would telex Dupree's record to them. He asked if there was any way he could speak to the investigator in Vietnam.

"Not likely," the CID man said. "Communications are overloaded right now with the attacks. It's total chaos over there. No one here's actually talked to him. Name's Jimmy Ray Suggs. He doesn't have a phone and most of the time we can't get anyone to answer at the office he uses."

"Well, I really think we can help each other," Checchi said.

"All I can do is ask him to call you. We've been getting through to him by telex."

Checchi gave him both his office and home numbers. After the call, he sat at his desk for almost 10 minutes, contemplating the situation. Finally, he decided he'd better keep pushing while his luck held. Hungry, he ate the remainder of the cold hotdog while thinking maybe he could shake something loose by talking to Doran. He was starting to believe he had a shot at taking down the Garganos. He got a number for Doran from the phone book and dialed it.

Doran picked up the phone before the first ring had ended. "Yeah?"

"Detective Sergeant Al Checchi, Detroit Police Department here. I'd like to talk to you." There was a long pause. "I have some news about Percy Dupree."

After another long pause, Doran said, "Okay. Why don't you come to my office? Thirty-second floor of the Guardian Building. But it'll have to wait until six. No, make it six-thirty. I was about to leave but I'll be back by then."

As the afternoon wore on, Checchi was in the grip of serious heartburn and regretting his lunch, but he was feeling better and better about talking to Doran. He had pulled together a good circumstantial case against him for murder. He was confident he could persuade the truck driver to cooperate with testimony about the murder of Doran's wife. He almost certainly had made the truck available to Dupree. He had a wife and kids, and he wouldn't want to go to prison for Percy Dupree, who was dead and no longer a threat.

If the teletype was correct, Doran might be tied to two murders in Vietnam that directly related to two more that had occurred in Detroit. As a homicide investigator, he had sometimes confronted suspects early, before they had a chance to hire lawyers and think and before he had all of his own evidence nailed down. Doran was a big-shot Grosse Pointe attorney and Checchi was thinking he might panic and want to cut a deal if Checchi caught him by surprise. He was hoping to persuade Doran to start ratting out the Garganos. If he brought Doran down to Beaubien, he'd have a lawyer, maybe an army of them, and probably say nothing. But if he just met Doran for a chat, who knows what he might let slip when the shock of being a suspect in four murders hit him? He was actually pleased that Doran wanted to wait a few hours. It gave him time to pull it all together and think through exactly what he would say.

Late in the afternoon, a series of enormous belches relieved the heartburn and triggered another idea. He called Lincicombe, thinking the two of them could go and see Doran together. After all, he believed Doran was involved in four murders, so having some backup was prudent. More important, Lincicombe knew a great deal about the Garganos, and Checchi could trust Lincicombe. The last thing he wanted was to see his investigation taken over by some of his politically ambitious supervisors. Lincicombe, however, was out, and not expected back that day.

He would go alone. *I'll punch the bastard in the balls if he gives me any trouble.*

January 31, 1:55 p.m., Travis Air Force Base

The flight from Tan Son Nhut to Travis took a little over 20 hours, but Hayes was barely aware of the passage of time because he slept through most of it. In the middle of the trip, he stayed awake with his eyes closed for a couple of hours, going over everything he knew, considering all the possibilities that occurred to him, surreptitiously taking inventory of everything on his person, never letting on that he was awake. He came to some conclusions and made a few promises, including another renewal of his vow to stop getting high. Rivera was right. He couldn't afford to make even a small mistake. Finished thinking, he went back to sleep.

Eventually, there was an announcement and the cheer that erupted in the plane woke him up completely. He sat up and snapped the seatback up. A blue ocean was outside the window and the plane felt like it was descending.

"We'll be on the ground in Travis in less than half an hour," said Ovenden. "You must have been tired. I've never seen anyone sleep so much on a plane."

He sounded sympathetic, but Hayes ignored him. The plane landed and he watched everyone file off except Bradbury, Ovenden and himself. The stewardess gave him a last hateful look as she departed.

"Gonna take these off now?" Hayes asked holding up his hands.

"Naw, I think we'll leave them on. Don't want you getting any ideas now that we're Stateside," Bradbury said.

"I thought I was just a witness," Hayes said.

"You are, but you're not telling us everything we'd like to know. You aren't exactly cooperating in my book."

"I haven't done anything wrong," Hayes said. "I answered your questions."

"Got lots more questions. Need to know about those German documents," Bradbury said. "Now that you haven't got those military fuckwads Suggs and Walters, maybe we'll get better answers. Besides, I'm getting to like this prisoner thing and we'll have to fly straight civilian now."

He stepped back and nonchalantly opened his jacket so Hayes could see the pistol on his hip. "Just don't get any ideas, Sonny. We're on my turf now, and I *do* have jurisdiction."

With the handcuffs on, Hayes tried to stretch the kinks out of his body as he and Ovenden stood by a shed beside the runway. About 20 minutes later Bradbury appeared driving a blue Chevrolet. As they got into the car, Bradbury pushed Hayes so his head smacked the roof of the car.

"Hey, that wasn't necessary," Ovenden said.

"Yeah it was," Bradbury snapped. "Fuckwad here needs reminding who's in charge now."

They drove for almost an hour in traffic, crossing a large bridge. Hayes got hungry looking at a hamburger stand. He studied the street signs, the restaurants and the people he saw, trying to figure out what time of day it was. He had lost his watch and he didn't know either the time or what day it was. Even though the view from the plane had been sunny, it was foggy and cool on the ground. But on balance, being back in America felt better.

The inside of the car was dirty and littered with the discards of an office worker. Bradbury was driving and Ovenden was in the passenger seat, leaving him alone and handcuffed in the back seat. The car was a two-door so he couldn't just jump out. He looked around at the detritus in the car and spotted a big paper clip holding a sheaf of papers together. He picked the papers up and removed the paper clip from the papers, holding it in his hand.

They parked the car beside a terminal at a big airport. As they were walking into the terminal Hayes turned to the two agents. "Look, I really have to go to the bathroom. It's been a long time."

The agents looked at each other. "I'll take him," Ovenden said.

"No, I'll do it," Bradbury replied, seeming to imply that he didn't trust Ovenden.

Bradbury escorted Hayes into the first men's room they came to. Bradbury used his badge to roust out a teenage boy who was inside.

"I have to take a crap," Hayes said, holding up his hands. "Gonna be hard to wipe my ass with these on."

"Well Sonny, you're just gonna have to figure it out because those bracelets are staying on," Bradbury said.

Hayes felt a flash of anger and watched as Bradbury took out a pack of Lucky Strikes and lit one. Now he was sure he wasn't just a witness. He shrugged, looked around at the empty bathroom. He snatched Bradbury's lit cigarette and went into one of the stalls.

"You shit," Bradbury said, but he didn't do anything except reach for his cigarette pack again. Hayes unbuttoned and dropped his pants. He sat down and began voiding his bowels, slowly. Meanwhile, he straightened the paperclip and then bent it into an S shape. He picked the handcuff locks in less than 30 seconds. He'd learned how during his weekend in jail after the dispute with the Lemaire's. He carefully put the cuffs in his fatigue jacket pocket, making sure they didn't clink. Then he finished up in the bathroom, taking his time, squaring away his clothing. Finally, he took the Tokarev automatic from the jungle fatigue jacket pocket where it had been since he had taken it from the dead Hollister. It was loaded with a full magazine, but the rest of the bullets were gone. He was about to flush the toilet with his foot, and then changed his mind. He backed out of the stall so that Bradbury couldn't see his hands. He turned around holding the Tokarev just as Bradbury looked up from a magazine he had been reading as he leaned on a sink. "Both hands behind your head," Hayes said.

"Jesus H. fuckin' Christ!" The agent complied and Hayes took the big automatic from Bradbury's belt along with an extra magazine that he found clipped beside it. "For a supposedly crack fuckin' FBI special agent, you're an absolute moron for not searching me. Especially when you consider that soldiers are generally armed. Now, keep your fuckin' mouth shut."

Hayes prodded him toward the stall and through the door.

"On your knees," he said. Bradbury got down on his knees.

"You're making a big mistake, Sonny," he said.

"I told you no talking," Hayes replied. "I want you to do exactly what I say, and don't try anything. Keep in mind that I kill people for a living. Now, take your left hand away from your head," he said, then waited. "A little bit farther." Hayes snapped the handcuff on it.

"Now place that hand against the wall at the back right beside the pipe," he said. "Now slowly, put your other hand on the wall on the other side or the pipe."

Holding the Tokarev against Bradbury's temple with his left hand, he reached under the pipe for the dangling open handcuff and snapped it on Bradbury's other hand. It left Bradbury on his knees, his face over the unflushed toilet, his hands cuffed around the pipe that went from the back of the toilet into the wall. Hayes patted the agent's pockets, removing his wallet and the leather case with his badge. A quick glance revealed about a hundred dollars in the wallet. He thought about taking the agent's pants off and wearing them. But he'd need to get the shirt and the coat too. To do that, he'd have to uncuff him again. It would be a lot of trouble, and the agent was much thicker around the middle.

But it gave Hayes another idea. He quickly took off Bradbury's shoes, then his pants and his underwear.

"I don't want to hear a word out of you," Hayes said. "I'll be here a few more minutes."

He let the lit cigarette drop out of his mouth onto Bradbury's back hoping it would land on his bare ass. But it rolled off onto the floor. Hayes went to the sinks and washed his hands and face. In the mirror, he looked at his jungle fatigues. There was dried blood on one sleeve and one side of his chest. There were remains of mud stains all over. But most of the mud had turned to dust and dirt and it had come off during the long flight. Using the agent's pants as a damp rag, he spent five minutes brushing off as much of the remaining dirt and dried blood as he could. He was concerned about the clothing. Soldiers weren't supposed to wear fatigues in public, and no one wore jungle fatigues Stateside, so he felt very conspicuous. However, he didn't think most civilians knew that soldiers weren't supposed to wear fatigues.

He slipped quietly out of the bathroom and spotted Ovenden looking at a newspaper in the newsstand across from the bathroom. The agent had his back to him. Hayes turned and started walking as quickly as he could farther into the terminal. He stuffed Bradbury's pants and underwear, in which he had wrapped the agent's gun, into the first trash receptacle that he came to. Soon he was in a more crowded area where a flight was boarding. He walked up to the woman at the counter beside the gate, glancing up at the sign to see that the flight was going to Chicago.

"Ma'am, are there any standby seats for this flight?" He reached into his back pocket for his own wallet, took out his military ID and showed it to her.

"Oh yes, it's only about half full," she said. She looked at Hayes closer. He was thinking that he didn't smell very good. "Haven't seen that uniform before."

"What we wear in Vietnam, Ma'am," he said, trying to sound cheerful. He was wondering how much a standby ticket would cost. "Yesterday I was in the jungle. Sorry, but I'm still a little raggedy."

He smiled and she smiled back. She copied some information from his ID.

"How much is a ticket going to be?" he asked.

"Soldiers in uniform fly free on standby." She handed him his ticket. "Better hurry, they're trying to close the gate now."

It wasn't until the plane had taken off and he had listened to the conversations around him for 10 minutes that he learned it was mid-afternoon. Half an hour after they took off, a stewardess served a meal. When he scarfed it down before she was out of sight, she gave him another one. He ate that one more slowly and pondered what to do when he got to Chicago.

CHAPTER 14

1 February, 0420 Hours, Long Binh

Suggs woke up with a fierce headache in a long room full of soldiers on cots. He vaguely remembered coming into the hospital, and a long period when he was nauseated and in a fog. He remembered talking to people but couldn't remember what he'd talked about or who they were. He thought he had been lying on the cot for a long time without sleeping, and then he finally did sleep. Now, other than the headache, he felt better. He was sitting on the side of a cot wondering where he might find his clothes when a medic walking by noticed him.

"You'd better lie down," the medic said.

"I'm okay. Just got a headache," said Suggs. "What happened? I can't remember how I got here."

"What's the last thing you remember before coming here?"

Suggs thought it over.

"I was out by Highway One with a Spec Four Hayes and a CW2 Walters, and there had been a ground attack. I think there was an explosion."

The medic nodded. "The ammo dump blew up." He examined a clipboard hanging at the end of the cot. "You were semi-conscious when they brought you in. You feel all right now?"

"Yeah, just a headache." He looked at his watch and at the medic. "What day is it?"

"Thursday morning," the medic replied. "You been in dreamland the last couple of hours, but they told me you were awake before that."

"Jesus Christ, I got to get out of here," said Suggs.

"Well, we could use the bed," said the medic. "Got beaucoup guys coming in."

"I'm looking for those two guys I was with."

"I remember Walters. He got sent to 12th Evac in Cu Chi," said the medic. "Don't remember anyone by the name of Hayes around here." The medic watched as Suggs stood up. "Dizzy? Any double vision?"

"Feel okay, considering." Suggs shook his head. "Except for the headache. But it might be starting to feel a little better already."

Half an hour later, Suggs was eating breakfast with Lieutenant Fosdick in an officers' mess near the Repo Depot. He had been planning on going around to both officers' and enlisted men's messes asking whether anyone had seen Hayes, Walters or two FBI agents and he'd found Fosdick right away. That was good because he didn't feel like he had the energy to run around. It was early, but there was a lot of activity. Fosdick was on the staff of a 25th Infantry Division colonel and had seen a blonde soldier in handcuffs being led away by two men in civilian clothes. From his description, Suggs was sure it was the FBI men.

"Thought it was strange. We all did, even the colonel," he said. "They got into a Ford Falcon driven by some guy in sunglasses wearing a bright sport shirt. I saw shirts like that in Hawaii when I was on R and R."

Suggs thought the loud shirt, the sunglasses and the Ford Falcon added up to the CIA. He had seen the Falcon before and someone had told him it belonged to the CIA. He knew where their compound was but had never been inside and never had spoken with anyone in the CIA. Suggs decided he had better talk to his major before approaching them.

However, back at the military police compound, the major wasn't there. Hardly anyone was there. A sergeant told him that most of the unit was in Saigon, and there were half a dozen or more casualties. He'd heard that people had been killed and he was trying to find out how many and who they were. Suggs felt sick, wondering how many of them he knew. He went to the desk he shared with another investigator and sat down. There was a manila envelope on the desk and someone had scrawled *Suggs* on it. It looked like his commanding officer's handwriting. Inside he found a note from the major:

This telex came in from a Detroit PD homicide detective via Pentagon CID. Looks like it might help you. One of General Westmoreland's aides, Major Kucharski, called about you. You need to let me know when you contact generals! It's okay, but get hold of him ASAP. Your case is top priority. Stay on it. Catch me up when you can. Your promotion should come through any day.

The major had written his first name, "Ernie," at the bottom, which he had never done before when communicating with Suggs.

Suggs took the material out of the envelope. There was a recognizable picture of Hollister except that he was identified as Percival Alois Dupree. There also was a note detailing that he was the prime suspect in the murder of Roscoe Lincoln in Detroit, plus a list summarizing his arrest record in Detroit, mostly for assault but with no convictions. There was a copy of a military document relating to Dupree's dishonorable discharge from the U.S. Army in 1962. He had beaten up prostitutes in Germany. Finally there was a typewritten letter, with several typos, from the Detroit homicide cop, Detective Sergeant Al Checchi. He believed Dupree had been sent to Vietnam by Matthew Doran to kill James "Jimmy" Hayes. Checchi said he didn't know the motive for the killing, but that he was sure it was related to the Lincoln homicide that he was investigating and to the possible homicide of Doran's wife, Gina Doran. Hayes and a girlfriend were believed to have witnessed several homicides that had occurred during the Detroit riots, specifically the killings of two police officers and the wounding of a third. Detroit Police were anxious to know whether Hayes could identify whomever had shot the policemen.

"Shit," Suggs muttered. He picked up the phone to call the number he had for Westmoreland's headquarters. He found out that Major Kucharski most likely could be found a short walk away from him in the Long Binh PIO office. A few minutes later Suggs was there, standing in front of Kucharski.

"Hey, am I glad to see you," Kucharski said and returned his salute with a wave. "I need PFC Hayes and I'm told you know where he is."

"He got promoted back to spec four, but I don't where he is," said Suggs. "Two FBI agents took him away. Not only that, but they apparently got help from the CIA to do it."

"Are you shitting me? The fucking CIA?"

He quickly filled the major in on what had happened after the ammo dump blew up. Kucharski listened patiently, took out his notebook and looked up a number. Suggs listened as Kucharski skillfully talked his way through two different people from the CIA who were obviously trying to blow him off. The major identified himself as a member of Westmoreland's staff, dropped the name of a full bird colonel who was presumably known to the CIA and issued a couple of veiled threats. He was a major who acted like a general, one skilled in the nuances of the military power structure. *Impressive,* Suggs thought.

Finally, a third person came on the line and Kucharski listened for a couple of minutes, interrupting with two questions: "When did this happen?" and "Where did they land?" And after another minute he said "Thank you" and hung up. Then he sat down on the desk and indicated for Suggs to sit in the chair. "They took him back to the States, in handcuffs. An hour after they landed at Travis, Hayes escaped their custody. That just happened. That's all they'll say, and I had to threaten them with Westmoreland to get that much."

Suggs rubbed his head. The headache was waning, but it was still there. "He's gonna go for his girl," said Suggs. "He said her stepfather tried to kill her. Said her stepfather threatened to send someone to kill him. I don't think he even believed it at first, but I believe it now. What's going on? Why is General Westmoreland interested in Hayes?"

"There's a Spanish TV network about to run a story that says American soldiers massacred almost a hundred Vietnamese civilians, and Hayes is right in the middle of it."

"At Nui Binh?" asked Suggs.

"Yeah, how'd you know?"

"Heard Hayes and his pilot, a CW2 by the name of Walters, talking about a big VC ground attack. Walters seemed to think Hayes deserved a medal."

"No shit. We have no indication of any massacre of civilians. It was a VC battalion, or at least a good part of one. We got two independent detailed reports, one from the CO of the 99th and another from a major who's the brigade S2 in Nui Binh. They're both solid officers, in fact I know Shiffman personally. We were at the Point together." Kucharski said that the Spanish TV reporter tried to talk to someone at the PIO office but they were all too busy. Now they had learned that she was also trying to peddle the story to an American network, and the network was interested, which could be very bad. "Her story's probably going to be aired on Spanish TV soon. We're kicking the crap out of Charlie, but that's not what people are seeing on TV at home. We're winning the war on the battlefield, but we're losing the propaganda war. If this story blows up it could be very bad. Besides, Westmoreland is apparently very interested in your case."

Suggs nodded. "Well, I'm interested in it too."

Kucharski got on the phone again and told someone at the other end about what had happened to Hayes. From the way he was speaking, Suggs knew it was a senior officer. Kucharski listened for several minutes, saying only "Yes, Sir" and "I like that idea, Sir" and "I'll get going on it, Sir," as he hung up. He looked at Suggs. "We're gonna get you priority on military transportation. We want to try to get Hayes to New York, to that American network. It's CBS. That's the first thing. We've got to convince them that the Spanish TV story is wrong. Hayes made an impression, and so did you. Westmoreland seems to think the kid's credible and he doesn't think much of the Pentagon's PIO people. Washington has already got someone talking to the network, stalling them, so now they're gonna say we have a soldier who was there who can tell them the truth. That ought to shake them up. We're trying to get CBS to hold off as long as possible. We can get a few days, but probably less than a week."

"You said you've got me priority transportation," Suggs said. "Aren't you going too?"

"I want you to find this Hayes kid. He's the eyewitness and he's already Stateside. We're looking for another soldier who was there who may have derosed home, or he might be in a hospital. Anyway, if he's gone back, that could give us two people who were actually there. The general sees that as a better move than the usual Pentagon song and dance, and he's insisting. But no, much as I'd like to, I'm not going with you. They apparently have a platoon of PIO officers at the Pentagon ready to handle this. Besides, I'm not PIO, though I've done it before. I'm on Westmoreland's staff. I'm a fireman, and this is only one of the fires I'm trying to put out right now."

Suggs thought about it. "Seems like a long shot to me. By the time you get this together, the media will have moved on to something else."

"Maybe, but a long shot is better than no shot at all. We're at a tipping point in this war. A lot of young men are dying out there. We have to fight battles with words as well as bullets, and we need to fight the propaganda war as hard as we're fighting the one in the field. There's another thing too. The fucking CIA. They're up to something here. Why would they help the FBI? I got the idea this was a big deal for the CIA."

"I meant that me being able to find Hayes in time is probably a long shot." Suggs shook his head. "You know, there was something not right about those two FBI guys. They didn't like each other, and the older guy didn't even seem like a cop to me. No cop in him at all. The younger one might have been the real thing, but he was green."

"Well, nobody's gonna find Hayes unless they look, and you have more reasons to find him than anyone else. The general seemed to think you were pretty smart, and he had me check you out. I have to agree with him, so work on it. I'll give you paper from Westmoreland that'll unstick any military roadblocks. The civilian ones are up to you. Now you tell me where you need to go and be ready to leave on an hour's notice, maybe less. Keep checking in with me so I know where you are all the time."

"Detroit," said Suggs. "He'll head for Michigan and his girl."

"Okay, where are you gonna be?"

"The post office."

Suggs had only walked past the post office in Long Binh. He'd never been inside. He flashed his badge to a spec five who was the highest-ranking person there. "What do you do with letters that show up here undeliverable?"

"Return to sender." The spec five was humming an Elvis tune.

"What if there's no return address?"

"Well, that's the case more than you'd think. People are lazy," he said. "We have sort of a dead letter section back there. Some of us want to throw all that stuff out and some of us want to ship it back to the World. All of us would like to get rid of it but it's been sitting there for as long as I've been here. Must be three or four bags of the stuff."

"Can I go through it?"

"Help yourself. Hell of a way to fight a war."

"Hell of a way to investigate a murder," said Suggs.

"Murder? You're investigating a murder?"

"Yup. Several of them."

Suggs was looking for something larger than an ordinary letter, but probably not a parcel. So when he dumped a bag of mail out he concentrated on oversized envelopes and small packages. He found it in the third bag.

"Found it," said Suggs, a note of triumph in his voice. The spec five looked at him with renewed interest. Suggs showed him the eight-and-a-half by eleven, inch-thick manila envelope.

"How in hell did it even get here? All it says is PFC Jimmy Hayes, Vietnam, please forward, and it's got maybe twice as much postage on it as it needs. Whoever mailed this just slapped stamps on it and probably stuffed it in a mailbox. Looks pretty cuffed up. It should have gone into the dead letter file in...." The spec five looked at the cancellation stamp. "Ann Arbor. They should have never sent it over here."

"Well, do you think they want dead letters anymore than you do?"

"Fuck no."

Suggs headed immediately back to the PIO office where he found Kucharski.

Kucharski looked at his watch. "I was just looking for you. Can you be ready to go in an hour?"

"Sure," said Suggs. "But I need to get some copies of this stuff first. It could be important."

"What is it?" asked Kucharski.

"I found these papers that the FBI asked Hayes about. Hayes' girlfriend sent them to him, but she didn't have his address. They were in undeliverable mail at the post office."

He held up the envelope and the papers it contained. He had opened it while walking to PIO. There were a couple of dozen pages.

"We got a machine here can do that. Just leave them," said Kucharski. "Why's it important?"

"You're worried about a TV story, but I started out investigating an unidentified body, which turned into a murder, which turned into two murders. According to a telex that I got from a detective in Detroit, there are two more over there. Then the FBI shows up here to talk to Hayes because they say he and his girl saw someone kill two Detroit police officers. But Hayes said they also saw the cops kill two other people. That's eight dead bodies, nine if you count the alleged murderer here, because he's also dead. That FBI agent, who doesn't seem like a cop, was asking Hayes about these papers. My gut feeling is that agent knew about the papers before he got here. These papers seemed damned important to that screwy agent. You're right. Something's going on here that we don't know. Plus, how do two FBI agents who have been here one day have the juice to enlist the help of our local CIA and get Hayes on an airplane back to the USA?"

Kucharski looked past him and bellowed, "Specialist Crutchfield!" A burly black spec four rose from a corner desk in the back and hurried up to them. "Make a copy of this stuff."

"Make that two copies please," said Suggs. "One for CID here and one for me. I'm gonna send these originals to the Pentagon CID office. And I better come with you. I'm betting this will end up being classified. It's old and a little fragile, so please be careful. Looks like it dates from World War II. Most of it's German. I see some swastikas, but there's some Asian script too."

"Let's have three copies," Kucharski said, rising to join them. "One for Westmoreland's office."

"Okay," Suggs said.

CHAPTER 15

January 31, 6:55 p.m., Chicago

After the stewardess collected his dishes, Hayes took out Bradbury's wallet. First, he emptied the money on the seat next to the window. There were four twenties, a ten, a five and three ones: $98. He noticed the wallet seemed thick. He peeled up a thin leather lining and found five $100 bills. He pulled the driver's license out of the plastic window. The agent's full name was Austin O. Bradbury and the license listed an address in McLean, Virginia. He went through the rest of the plastic windows taking everything out and found a Social Security card, a Virginia fishing license and some green stamps. In one side of the wallet were credit cards for Shell, Texaco, and Sears and a MasterCard. In the other side he found three business cards, all of them for FBI agents, including Ovenden's card. It still felt like there was more in the wallet. After fiddling with it for a minute, he found another hidden pocket and in it was a California license and more cards. Except this time, there was another name: Robert D. James III. There was a second MasterCard, a Diner's Club card and a second Shell card, all in James' name. And there were a dozen business cards bearing the name Robert D. James along with a telephone number and an address for a San Francisco postal box. Hayes put everything back in the wallet where it had been except the cash. He put that in his own wallet.

After awhile, he dozed again but he woke up with a start when he heard the announcement that the plane was coming into Chicago. Suddenly he was homesick. He looked around, taking in the nylons on the shapely legs of a woman, a vague scent of peppermint in the air and the female voices in the buzz of conversation. He wanted to talk to Gloria. He closed his eyes and tried to will her into the airplane, only to be disrupted from his vision by the sharp clunk of the airplane's wheels hitting the runway. "Jesus, I love you," he whispered.

The plane landed and Hayes was relieved that there were no police waiting for him as he got off the aircraft. Acutely conscious of being dressed in jungle fatigues, he walked quickly through the terminal. Then he saw a phone booth and stopped. He went into a nearby bar, ordered a Coke, and gave the bartender the $10 bill. He asked for the change in silver. "I have to make some phone calls."

It took the bartender more than a minute to count out the change. He had to break open a new roll of quarters and a new roll of dimes. A strikingly handsome man with long hair and a beard, and dressed in a full-length leather coat was waiting impatiently at the bar beside Hayes. The coat was open, revealing an expensive suit and a bolo tie with a silver rattlesnake clasp. He was wearing polished snakeskin boots and there was liquor on his breath. He had an empty glass in his hand. Hayes thought at first the guy was young, his own age, but when he turned to look at him more closely while he waited for his change, he could see he was closer to 40. His long hair looked expensively barbered and Hayes thought it was colored because it was so much lighter than his eyebrows.

"You look like one of those Vietnam soldiers I seen on TV," he said in an unfriendly tone. He sounded drunk, and belligerently drunk at that. "You know, that ain't a cool look. You ought'a get more appropriate attire."

Hayes started picking up his change and the guy persisted.

"Like the Beatles say, all you need is love. Peace is the only answer," he said in a hostile tone that was far from peaceful.

The bartender looked at him, concern in his eyes.

"Anyone who supports the fuckin' war is part of the fuckin' problem, nothin' but scum. What are you? Some kind of soldier? Or one of them flag-waving patriotic Bircher assholes? My country right or wrong? Well you're fucking wrong, buddy!"

His temper rising, Hayes put the change in his pants pocket, his hand brushing against the gun in the fatigue jacket pocket. Then he shook his head trying to hold down the emotional reaction. *The guy's obviously drunk.* "I just want to make a phone call. Sorry you had to wait," he said evenly. He pressed a couple of dollars into the man's hand. "Have another drink on me."

He walked quickly toward the phone booth across the walkway, the man following. There was no actual booth, just a metal partition that went around most of the phone and only extended down to Hayes' waist. The man looked at him and then at the two dollars. He took one more step toward the phone booth, then turned around, a little unsteady on his feet, and walked back into the bar. He sat down at the bar, swiveled his seat around and looked across the walkway directly at Hayes. He held up the two dollar bills, tore them in half and dropped them on the floor. Then he lurched up again and started walking slowly toward the phone booth. He was holding his arms out from his sides flexing his fingers like he had a gun belt on.

Furious, but still under control, Hayes put down the phone and started to walk away.

"Yeah, you get out of here, you goddamn warmonger!" the man said loudly.

Something in Hayes snapped. He spun around and glared at the man, who stopped just short of Hayes. Hayes snarled, "You are one hundred percent right! I *am* a warmonger, and you better fuckin' believe it!" His hands were balled into fists at his sides as he faced the man. "Take one more step, fucker!"

The man looked at Hayes for a long moment and then turned and walked back into the bar. The whole time, Hayes was thinking, *Yes, I'm a warmonger. I'm a gunner in the 99th Assault Helicopter Company. I'm a fucking Headhunter!* He reached one hand up and felt the Headhunter patch on his jungle shirt pocket. He had been making war and he wasn't ashamed of it. He had been taken prisoner for reasons he didn't understand, but he had broken free. He was back in the World, but that didn't mean he was home free. He couldn't let his guard down and relax. He also understood that he had just made a critical error. He couldn't afford to lose his temper and do something stupid, not if he was going to find Gloria and help her.

For the first time since shaking the two FBI agents, he had a clear idea of what he was trying to do. He was in a different war, one that he didn't fully understand, but at least this was a war where the stakes were clear because they were personal. He couldn't afford to lose.

Hayes kept walking until he got to the baggage claim area where he slowed and looked around. He spotted some unattended suitcases, including one that looked like a small tool bag. He picked up the tool bag and a suit bag, walked outside and jumped on a shuttle bus. It was going to a parking lot. There were about a dozen people on the bus. After three of them got off, he got up with the bags and walked to the front door.

"Anywhere along here is fine, I'm in this row," Hayes said to the driver. The driver stopped and Hayes got off.

When the bus was gone, he looked in the suit bag. It contained women's clothing. He grabbed a wire coat hanger and tossed the suit bag between two cars. He looked in the tool bag and sure enough, there were tools in it. He walked through the parking lot looking at the cars. He finally stopped at a dark green Plymouth Barracuda that appeared new. It took him almost five minutes to work the coat hanger through the edge of the window and release the door lock. It was another half-hour before he finally got the car started. A professional car thief probably could have done it all in minutes, but Hayes had never hot-wired a car before and he was very cold in the light jungle fatigues.

The Barracuda's driver had left the parking stub in the glove compartment and Hayes was encouraged that the car had been left there only a few hours earlier. Hopefully, the driver was on a long trip. As soon as he drove out of the airport, he pulled into a shopping center and drove around until he found a phone booth. He called his uncle's number. He had no idea how to reach Gloria and his uncle was the only person he could ask for help.

A voice he didn't recognize answered.

"Who's this?" asked Hayes. "I'm trying to reach Sepp Hayha."

"Identify yourself. I'm a police officer," answered the voice.

"Jimmy Hayes, his nephew." He wondered whether his uncle was in trouble.

"Jimmy Hayes," repeated the voice.

There was a long pause. Hayes thought there was a hand over the receiver. He could hear faint talking but couldn't make out any words.

"Well I'll be damned, Mister Jimmy Hayes! We were just thinking about you. You don't know me but I know you real well," said a new voice that was higher pitched. "I'm somebody with a with a gun pointed at your uncle and someone else you know. I'm gonna let you talk to her."

There were muffled voices again.

"Jimmy?" asked a voice, and he knew it right away. He just couldn't believe it.

"Oh my God!" he said, his voice catching even as he stammered, "I... I love you Gloria."

"Oh Jimmy, I love you too!" Gloria said. Then she shouted. "Jimmy, there are men here with guns. They beat up your uncle. Don't come—"

He heard the slap clearly through the phone lines.

"That's enough, bitch!"

There was another long pause. This time Hayes could hear some muffled shouting that sounded like his uncle. Then there was a loud bang and the shouting stopped. For a few seconds he heard nothing and then the second voice was back on the line.

"Hope you heard that, Kid. Had to put a bullet in your uncle. Just winged the Nazi bastard. I'm gonna kill him if you don't do exactly as you're told. First, I want you to get your ass here as fast as you can. Where are you?"

"I'm in San Francisco," Hayes said. "How the hell am I supposed to get there? I don't have any money."

Just then the operator came on the line asking for more money to continue the call. Hayes dropped more quarters into the phone.

"Funny, Kid, but I don't believe you," the man said laughing. "Nice try though. Thought you were smart. I'm guessing you're in Chicago. That's where Bradbury thinks you went. And he says he had a few hundred in his wallet so you got the means to get here. Best you try to get here before Bradbury does because he's seriously pissed at you. And it wouldn't surprise me if Doran comes up here. With me, you and the girl got a chance. Let me put it this way. I got no beef with either of you unless you cause me trouble. So we need to talk, man to man, come to an understanding."

"Okay, but it's still gonna take me awhile to get there. I'll probably have to take a bus or maybe hitchhike. I think I have something you want, something in German, and if you harm my girl or my uncle, you'll never get it." He hung up, and then after thinking about it for half a minute, he called back. To whomever answered, he said very quietly, "I just want you to know, you hurt my girl or do anything more to my uncle, I'll kill you." He hung up.

A couple of minutes later, Hayes was rocketing onto the freeway and had the car up to 100 miles an hour before he backed off. It was a nice car, but he couldn't afford to get stopped for speeding or have an accident. He brought it back down to 65. There was snow on the sides of the freeway, but the road was dry and clear. The car had less than a quarter tank of gas so Hayes stopped to fill up and bought a heavy jacket, a map, a Coke, and some chocolate cupcakes and was back on the freeway in minutes.

10:10 p.m., Sugar Island

There were four of them. One was Vinnie, a man who had often visited Gloria's stepfather when she was young. When she was little, he had been nice to her but that stopped around the time she was nine or ten. Now he seemed indifferent.

Page, the deputy who had detained her when she couldn't pay the bridge toll, seethed with open hostility and had handcuffed her again. He was the one who had slapped her when she had been on the phone with Jimmy. He wasn't wearing a uniform now. She could taste blood from a cut on the inside of her mouth. He said, "You try to run, and you'll get smacked even harder." He shoved her down on the floor beside Sepp in front of the wood-burning stove. Sepp had been shot in the upper arm and repeatedly kicked in the ribs. He was in considerable pain. Half an hour after the phone calls, two men came in from the outside. They were the same two large black men who had been with her stepfather when she and Mrs. Lincoln met the lawyers and also at Mrs. Murphy's house. They both looked at Gloria but neither said anything. The smaller of them sat on the couch beside Page while the other sat in a chair. They turned on the TV set and started watching a basketball game. The front door had been open for a long time and now the fireplace stove was slowly warming the cabin again.

After awhile, Vinnie went into the kitchen and made a telephone call, talking softly. Gloria was positive he was talking to her stepfather, but she couldn't hear anything he said. Finally, he got off the phone. When he came back into the room he seemed more hyped up than he had been. "Doran's not coming up," Vinnie announced. "Says he has too much business to take care of down there, but he said this guy Bradbury's on his way. We can expect him early tomorrow morning. The Hayes kid might arrive any time, so we better be ready for that. He'll have to take the ferry, so I want one of you guys—Leonard, you do it—take the Ford across to the other side and wait for him. When you see him, you call and then get on the ferry and tail him. There's a hamburger stand over there. There should be a phone there. If it's closed, you might need to find another phone. There must be one around there somewhere. The best thing would be to call us if you can do that without losing him or letting him see you. Then we can all get him. But if you think you have to take him down yourself, do it. Just be sure you take him alive."

He stopped to light a cigarette. "I want him alive 'cause Doran wants to talk to him. Don't nobody kill him," Vinnie said. "Bradbury says he's got a gun, so be careful. But he's a kid, only nineteen, and he's probably never had a gun pointed at him in his life. And shit, there's four of us. He got the jump on that Bradbury, but Bradbury sounds like a pussy."

Leonard said, "Well, he's in the Army, so he must know something about guns."

"Yeah, and when he called back that second time, he said he was gonna kill us if we harmed his girl or his uncle," Page added. Then he sneered, "Not that I'm fuckin' worried."

Vinnie looked at the two of them and muttered something about a couple of pussies. "He's full of shit. He's just a fuckin' helicopter mechanic," Vinnie said. "Doran told me the Army taught him to fix rotor blades. He got somebody to look up the Army records. And before the Army, he was a fucking hippie guitar player in a band. He's just one of those fuckin' peace-lovin' hippies."

Gloria smiled. *They don't know Jimmy was a door gunner.*

Leonard shrugged but Page colored and then looked at Gloria. "Hey, can I kill the girl?"

"No," Vinnie said.

"Why not?" Page asked.

"Same reason. We need to talk to her. She and her boyfriend got something Doran wants," Vinnie said. "Why do you want to kill her?"

"General principles," Page said. "I don't like that cunt. Besides, your brother-in-law said he'd pay me ten grand to do it."

"Pietro really said that?" asked Vinnie.

"Well... yeah, he did."

"When?" Vinnie asked.

"A few days ago," Page said. "He was thinkin' she might come up north, so he called me. Anyway, your brother-in-law told me if I saw her, he'd give me ten grand to take her out. I could use the money. I wanted to do it when she couldn't pay the fucking bridge toll, but there were too many witnesses."

"Huh," Vinnie said. He was looking at Gloria now, scratching his chin, and then his eyes shifted back to Page. "Offer's off the table now. Doran wants her alive. Tell you what though," Vinnie said. "You can finish off the uncle, but later, after we're done here. Take him out into the woods and whack him."

"How much is that worth?" Page asked.

"I don't know, not ten grand, maybe a thousand or two," Vinnie said impatiently. "You ever killed anyone before?"

When Page didn't answer right away, Vinnie said, "I didn't think so. You can whack the uncle. That way I see if you got the balls for this kind of work. Do that and I'll find more work for you."

Page nodded, then got up and kicked Sepp hard in the ribs. "I got the balls, and a heart of stone too." Then he sat down again.

Leonard asked, "So what's this kid look like?"

"Good question," Vinnie said, and he turned to Sepp. "You must have a picture."

"What do I need a picture for." Sepp moaned. "I know what he looks like."

Page got up and kicked him again in the lower abdomen. Then he and Vinnie made a quick search of the cabin and didn't find a picture.

"Maybe he's telling the truth," Vinnie said. There were no pictures of any kind on the walls. Gloria was thinking she had pictures of Jimmy in her purse and thought Sepp might have one in his wallet. That's where men kept pictures. But that didn't occur to them. She was beginning to think they weren't very smart and that raised her hopes.

"Okay, like I said, he's nineteen years old. He has very blonde hair and it will be short because he's in the Army. He's six feet and skinny. I saw a picture of him from before he was in the Army. Not many fat soldiers in Vietnam. You might look especially close at any car with Illinois plates. Chances are he'll rent one."

"Shit, can you rent a car when you're nineteen?" Leonard asked.

No one answered.

Vinnie said, "Well, he'll get here eventually 'cause he'll want to get to the girl and his uncle. Probably take him awhile though."

Leonard left after writing down the cabin's telephone number. Vinnie paced around the cabin and Page stayed on the couch beside the big black man, who had moved out of the hard chair. The two of them didn't say much to each other but continued to watch the basketball game. The game soon ended and the local TV news, which originated from Traverse City, came on. There was a long story about the big Communist offensive in Vietnam. This time it didn't scare Gloria. She watched a Vietnamese military officer shoot a captured a Viet Cong in the head. There were soldiers climbing into trucks and close-ups of soldiers shooting their rifles and another of someone firing a machinegun on top of a big tracked vehicle. She watched closely when there were helicopters. She wasn't hearing most of what the announcer was saying because the sound was low and the two men on the couch were still talking about thc basketball gamc.

Gloria closed her eyes and did her best to pray for Jimmy. He was facing new dangers now.

February 1, 7:58 a.m., Sault Ste. Marie, Michigan

It was still dark by the time Hayes got to Sault Ste. Marie, and wind-blown snow had further reduced visibility, but he sensed that morning was near. He stopped the Barracuda a few hundred feet from the corner of the road that led down to the Sugar Island Ferry. He spent a couple of minutes focusing, just like he'd do before playing a gig. He was still wearing some of his Vietnam clothing, jungle fatigue trousers and jungle boots. However, he had purchased a flannel shirt, a fur-lined jacket and wool gloves. The Tokarev was in the side pants pocket. He still had his Vietnam mindset. He had never been trained for what he was about to do, but he had never been trained as a door gunner either. He had to get it right the first time. He took the pistol out of his pocket, ejected the magazine, checked it, put it back in and racked a round into the chamber. He was ready.

The wind was blowing hard icy snow particles almost horizontally, and it stung Hayes' cheeks when he got out of the car. The drive-in restaurant by the ferry was closed. A man was sitting inside a Ford parked and idling beside the drive-in. When he walked by, Hayes saw that the man was black, which in Sault Ste. Marie was unusual. There were very few blacks in the Upper Peninsula of Michigan and the few blacks around Sault Ste. Marie were usually airmen from Kincheloe Air Force Base. Hayes walked onto the docked ferry and climbed up to the wheelhouse. He was about to rap on the door when it opened and there stood Claude Lemaire, the oldest and biggest of the Lemaire brothers. Growing up, he'd always thought of Claude as a big strong guy, someone he feared, but now he looked diminished. He was about the same height as Hayes and he had a roll of fat on his waist, but his shoulders were still impressive.

"I'm really sorry about Pierre," Hayes began, but before he could continue, the Indian enveloped him in a bear hug. Hayes patted him on the back and when he let go, he could see Lemaire's eyes were moist.

"We got two letters from Pierre. First one said he'd seen you in the field just before he went out on his first operation. He was real excited about seeing you. Said you looked good, that you were flying helicopter gunships." He studied Hayes. "Said you were different. 'Hard' was the word he used. Said we'd never try taking that deer from you the way you were. Now I see what he meant. Then the next one, which was the last letter we got, and it was real short, he said your gunships saved them, that he and his squad owed their lives to you. His exact words were, 'Jimmy Hayes and the Headhunters saved our asses, and I'll never forget it."

Hayes was thinking that it was Pierre Lemaire's first combat and that it probably seemed worse than it was. But it had gotten as bad as it could for Pierre. "Well, close air support, that's what we do. We were just doing our job," Hayes said. "I sure was glad I got to see Pierre. We had a good talk. Tore me up when I found out he was KIA a few days later."

"Army's not telling us much about what happened," said Lemaire. "Said he was killed in an explosion during the battle. That's all. But it seems like they could give us some more details. You know anything?"

Hayes was wondering whether he could get in trouble for telling Lemaire what he had heard, but he was already in a lot of trouble. "Well, what we heard was that it was a short round," Hayes said.

"Short round? What's that?" Lemaire asked.

"It was an American artillery round that landed short of where it was supposed to go. Back in our company, I heard that a soldier had been killed by a short round, and the next day, I found out it was Pierre. One of our slicks took the body out. They call it friendly fire."

Lemaire looked out over the floating chunks of ice clogging the dark water of the river, his eyes growing moist.

Hayes put his arm around him and squeezed him again. "Fuckin' war."

Lemaire stepped back toward the controls. "Got to get this ship moving."

"Listen, can you wait a minute or two? I got my car parked out on Riverside and I'll be real interested to see if that guy in the blue Ford follows me onto the ferry," Hayes said.

Lemaire looked over at the Ford.

"He's been out there since before midnight. Seen him every time I tied up," Lemaire said.

Hayes pressed money into his hand for the fare, which Lemaire tried to refuse. "Money, I got," Hayes said.

"You in trouble?" asked Lemaire.

Hayes nodded. "Got that too."

"Need help?"

"Thanks, but you'd better steer clear. It's gonna get very ugly and it's not your trouble."

When Hayes drove onto the ferry, the blue Ford followed him. It was a short ferry ride and Hayes stayed in the car, focusing again, getting back into his Headhunters mindset. The Ford followed him off the ferry. Hayes drove toward his uncle's cabin but stopped on the road a little over a quarter-mile from the turnoff. The Ford rolled by slowly, then stopped five or six car lengths in front of him. He watched as the man got out of the car. He kept his back turned to Hayes and it looked like he was getting something out of his pocket. So Hayes took out the Tokarev, cocked it and held it on his lap in his right hand. The man from the Ford walked slowly toward him. He was holding something in his hand, keeping it hidden behind his leg. As the man reached the front of the Barracuda, Hayes cranked the window down with his left hand. The man was just starting to raise a large revolver when Hayes shot him in the chest and then again in the forehead, the gunshots so loud in the confined space that they hurt his ears.

He got out quickly. He picked up the man's revolver and slipped it into his jacket pocket, but he couldn't bring himself to look at the man right away. Instead, he listened until a series of wet gasps stopped. When he looked down, dead eyes were looking up at him in the middle of a bloody face. He shuddered, then grabbed the man by one ankle, dragged the body around the car and up the bank of snow that had been piled up by snowplows. He pushed body down the other side of the piled-up snow. There was a bloody patch on the snowy road, so he went back and scooped big double handfuls of snow from the snow bank till he had covered the blood. A thought occurred to him, and he retrieved the tire iron from the trunk of the Barracuda.

He walked slowly along the side of the dark road about half the remaining distance to the cabin, then went into the woods. It wasn't snowing hard, but the wind had picked up and was blowing both the falling snow and some of what was on the ground. It stung his face, but he barely noticed. It was getting light. Hayes worked his way down to the river on the assumption that anyone who was outside watching would more likely be watching the road. The wind blowing off the river howled through the trees. The sound of the two shots wouldn't have carried and he hoped the wind would muffle the sound of his approach. It was very slow going because he sank up to his calves, and sometimes deeper, in the snow. His feet were cold, but he was sweating.

Then another black man appeared less than 75 meters away. He was wearing a duffel coat, a fur hat, galoshes and big mittens. He was a lot larger than the first one. Hayes studied him. *Carrying a rifle but he'll have to take off those big mittens to fire it.* As Hayes watched, the man stamped his feet. Hayes got down on his hands and knees, and then on his belly, and took 20 minutes to cover the next 70 meters. It was cold but not difficult. It was like stalking deer though usually not this cold.

The man heard or sensed something and started to turn, but Hayes was close enough and rising out of the snow. He swung the tire iron, smashing it into side of the black man's head just below the fur cap. The man didn't go down but he dropped the rifle and wobbled sideways. Hayes hit him again, this time on the bridge of his nose. His hands came up to his face as his knees buckled and he ended up on his knees and elbows. Hayes raised the tire iron and hit him on the back of the neck. The man went slack and toppled onto his side. Hayes glanced at him. *Even if he isn't dead, he won't get up anytime soon.* He picked up the rifle, looked at it, then propped it between the two main branches of a split tree trunk a few feet away.

For the next half-hour, he carefully circled the cabin but saw no one else. Finally he snuck up to a side window and looked in. He could see across the kitchen area into the living room. A red-haired man was sitting on the couch with a black semiautomatic pistol in his hand on his lap. He wasn't moving and had his eyes closed. Someone was lying on the floor in front of him with his hands tied behind his back. His feet were also tied. The hands were moving, as if the man was trying work the ropes loose. He couldn't see the man's face, but he thought it was his uncle. There was no sign of Gloria.

He crept around the cabin and looked through another side window into his old bedroom. The room was dark but the door was partly open, allowing some light to filter in. The bed looked slept in, but it was empty. He put his ear up against the glass but couldn't hear anything. He continued around the cabin past the back door and looked through his uncle's bedroom window. There were curtains but the room was pitch black and he could see nothing through the tiny space in the middle between the two curtains. He returned to the back door. He put down the tire iron and the big revolver he'd taken from the first man and carefully took off his fleece-lined suede jacket. He took out the Tokarev and cocked it.

As he had hoped, the door wasn't locked. He opened it as quietly as he could, straining to hear the slightest sound. The cold air might wake the man dozing on the couch. The cabin had always had creaky floors but they seemed even worse than he remembered.

Someone in the main room called, "Gates, is that you?" Someone got up and there was a muffled thump. "Out of the way, you Nazi cocksucker."

Hayes dropped to his knees and scrambled the last few feet down the hall. The red-haired man came into view and managed to fire first but it went over Hayes' head. Then Hayes fired the next five shots and none of them missed: two to the chest, one to the forehead, two more to the chest. The man dropped, his gun clattering across the floor until it stopped at Hayes' foot. Hayes scrambled into the living room and started cutting the ropes from his uncle's hands and feet with the Gerber knife he'd gotten from Hollister. His uncle was also gagged with a piece of rope and a rag wadded in his mouth. His uncle was trying frantically to take the gag off with one hand and making noises. Hayes sliced the rope holding gag with the knife and his uncle pulled a wad of cloth out of his mouth.

"There's another one!" his uncle rasped, but it was too late.

"Drop the gun," someone said from behind him.

Hayes turned to see a man standing just outside the door to his uncle's bedroom with a pistol leveled at him.

Hayes dropped the gun.

"Turn around."

Hayes turned around.

Footsteps approached and then something hit him hard on the back of the head and he hit the floor.

Hayes didn't think he'd lost consciousness, but he couldn't move for some time and he was suddenly aware that his hands were tied in front of him with nylon rope. His feet were hobbled with his shoelaces. His uncle was lying unconscious beside the dead red-haired man, and his arm was bloody. He didn't know the man who had hit him in the back of the head but he was speaking non-stop as Hayes' awareness returned.

"...get you tied into the car. Shit, wait a minute, I'll toss you in the trunk like Bradbury did with the girl. Then I'll come back and shoot the Nazi with Page's gun. Leave that pistol you used in your uncle's hand. Pretty fuckin' smart if I do say so myself." He spoke matter of factly, almost cheerfully. He was a loquacious Italian about Hayes' size with greasy light brown hair and a cigarette hanging out of his mouth. He offered one to Hayes, who nodded. Then he lit it and put it in Hayes mouth.

"When the cops find this, they'll figure the two killed each other in a gunfight," Vinnie said as he puttered around, placing the guns. He kept the gun in his hand loosely trained on Hayes. Despite that, he seemed almost friendly. "Bet you didn't know Page was a St. Ignace deputy sheriff, did you? I don't have time to look for Gates out there. Too fuckin' cold. I'm gonna assume you got him. Did you get Leonard too? Must have. Found a fuckin' tire iron with blood on it out back and that big fuckin' revolver Leonard had."

Hayes started thinking about it and remembered he'd been wearing gloves when he used it.

"I need'a get my fuckin' Ford back too. Might be hard to explain why I'm driving Page's piece-of-shit truck. Jesus, I gotta hand it to you, Kid, you got some serious balls. Fuckin' surprises me. Kind'a proud'a you. But I have to give you up to Fat Matt. He's my lawyer an' I don't wanna go down for any of this stuff up here. Shit, I don't want to go down for the ones in Detroit either. I don't understand how you got him so pissed off at you. Says he's gonna make you an' the girl talk. Tough break, Kid. I had no reason to see you or the girl get hurt. We might'a worked somethin' out. Your uncle's another thing though. I never liked that fuckin' Nazi cocksucker.

"That Bradbury's an asshole, an' a fuckin' coward to boot. We let him take the girl but only after Fat Matt and me threatened to kill him if he don't deliver her intact. Son of a bitch is anxious to get her back there. Fat Matt's really torqued about Slick Percy too. Jesus, Kid, did you take that son of a bitch down? He's some serious fuckin' muscle. An' you're what, fuckin' nineteen? Jesus Christ!" He laughed enough so that the cigarette fell out of his mouth and landed in the puddle of blood around the dead deputy. He stepped carefully to avoid the blood. He waved his gun around recklessly but was still mostly pointing it at Hayes. "Shit, you almost pulled it off too. Lucky for me you didn't see me sleeping in there."

Walking backwards, he led Hayes toward the door, holding the gun carefully, his gaze darting left and right. Hayes hadn't said a word as he took the small shuffling steps with his hobbled feet. He was trying to act as non-threatening as possible, like he was still woozy, and he thought the Italian's guard might be down just a little. He would have to make his move quickly. His uncle had only minutes to live, and it sounded like he and Gloria wouldn't last long once her stepfather got them. *Bradbury must have arrived at the cabin earlier and taken Gloria.* The only thing that he and Gloria could have that her stepfather wanted were the German papers, which he had never seen. However, he knew from her letters where she had hidden the ones she'd held onto.

He kept his head down but was carefully looking everywhere in the cabin. There was a coat rack in the corner to the right where the hall to the back door began. Sepp had hung his ancient dirty green nylon jacket and a woolen watch cap on it. Behind the coat was his ice fishing spear. Only the wooden end with the attached rope was visible. Sepp wore the jacket and cap when he went ice fishing, which he did most nights in the winter.

The spear was a five-foot pole about as thick as a broomstick with a nylon rope attached to one end. The business end was stainless steel with seven very sharp barbed tines, each four inches long. Sepp had made the spear himself and Hayes had fished with it many times. He raised both his hands up to his chest as if to scratch himself. When the Italian turned to glance down the hallway at the back door, Hayes snatched the spear with both hands, planted his feet and drove it hard into the side of the Italian's neck. Trying to drive hard with his legs but able to take only short steps, he still pushed the man almost to the back door before he dropped. Before that his gun clattered to the floor. He kept pressure on the spear even after the tines scraped the floor, and the man kicked a few times.

Hayes bent down and looked at him. He wasn't quite dead. His eyes were still moving. An expression of stark terror indicated he could still see and he was trying to form words. But no sound came. One of the tines had severed his spinal cord. There was almost no blood. Slowly, the life seeped out of the eyes and Hayes let go. He slumped onto the floor to catch his breath.

Claude Lemaire knocked on the front door. "Hayes, you okay?"

"Back door! Maybe I *could* use some help."

Hayes left Claude Lemaire with most of a big mess to clean up. They decided to drop the bodies through the ice hole in Sepp's ice-fishing shack. The current would move them a good distance before they were found, which probably wouldn't be until the ice broke up in the spring. That would be at least six or eight weeks. Hayes stayed long enough to help Lemaire retrieve the body from the road and the three bodies from the cabin, drag them out to the ice shack and shove them through the hole in the ice. The Indian said he would drive Sepp to War Memorial Hospital in Sault Ste. Marie. He'd tell them that he had heard a gunshot and found Sepp unconscious in his cabin. Since Sepp had a reputation for drinking to excess, no one would be particularly surprised. Even a gunshot wound in his arm might not surprise them. Sepp was going to claim that he'd accidentally shot himself. The next day, Lemaire would drive the Ford over to Canada where he could sell it without papers to another Indian he knew. A few days later, the car would be sold again, somewhere in southern Ontario. He wasn't sure if he would do the same thing with Page's truck, which was a rusty Dodge and not worth much, but he'd get rid of it. Lemaire thought he'd keep the rifle that Hayes had stashed in the forest. It was an almost brand new .30-.30 Model 94 Winchester. Hayes also gave him the large revolver and the deputy's automatic. Hayes kept the Italian's .45 caliber automatic. He gave the Tokarev to Lemaire and asked him to keep it for him. He would have taken it with him but there was only a single bullet left for it.

Ninety minutes after Claude Lemaire had arrived Hayes was on his way south in the Barracuda. His only chance was that Gloria would go to where she had hidden the papers. He prayed that she would go there and that he could catch up. He kept the Barracuda 10 miles per hour over the speed limit. He was tired and hungry so he stopped in St. Ignace for coffee and a pastie, a tasty meat and vegetable pie sold in Michigan's Upper Peninsula. He stopped again for gas and more coffee in Gaylord.

"Miles to go before I sleep," he said yawning as he pulled out of the Gaylord gas station.

8:25 a.m., I-75 South

Bradbury had stopped and taken Gloria out of the trunk just south of Mackinac Bridge. As he drove down I-75 outside of Grayling, her hands still were tied in front of her with yellow nylon rope. Sudden awareness that her bladder was full snapped her out of the trance-like state she had been in. She started moving her hands on her chest.

Bradbury was startled by the sudden movement. "What are you doing?"

"Crossing myself," she said. "I was trying to pray."

"Praying?" he said glancing at her, and then he snickered. "For what? God ain't gonna help you, Girlie."

"I was praying for a bathroom," she said. "I'm gonna need a stop soon."

"Well, you better just cross your legs and hold it because I'm not stoppin'. I had a bad experience with your boyfriend over a bathroom break."

"Suit yourself," she said. "But I'm pregnant, so I have to pee a lot. And I haven't had anything to eat for a long time, which means I'll probably throw up soon too. I'll just let it all come out right here."

"Goddamnit," he muttered.

Not long afterwards, they saw a sign for a rest area and Bradbury pulled in. He untied her hands and let her go in the women's restroom. "You ain't out in five minutes, I'm comin' in to get you." The rest stop was deserted. As soon as she was back in the car, he tied her hands again. A little later, he got off the freeway at a small town. He drove around for a little while and then parked behind a big crumbling brick building with broken windows on the outskirts of the town. There was no one around. He took her out of the car and put her back in the trunk. It sounded like he pulled into a gas station and then the car was parked for 10 or 15 minutes. He drove another five minutes before stopping, and then he opened the trunk again. They were behind the same crumbling building. He untied her hands and put her in the back seat of the car. He got in the front and handed her a cardboard container with a bacon, lettuce and tomato sandwich and French fries. He gave her a pint of milk. He took out his pistol, showed it to her and placed it on the dashboard of the car. "Eat," he said. She was hungry and she ate. He also had a BLT and started eating. "Let me tell you about some of this, because you probably don't understand," he said, his mouth full of sandwich. "Matthias, I guess he calls himself Matthew now, your father is—"

"He's not my father. He's my stepfather."

"That's interesting," Bradbury said thoughtfully. "Might explain some behavior. Anyway, Matthias is gonna torture you to find out where those papers are, and then he's probably gonna kill you. Even if you don't talk, which seems very, very unlikely, he'll still kill you. He's gonna do the same to your boyfriend unless those retards up there kill him first, which they might. There's just one chance, Girlie, for you and your little bastard, and that's to tell *me* where those papers are. Once I have them, I've got no reason to do you any harm. I'll let you go."

Gloria didn't believe him, but she didn't say anything. She just ate and listened.

He took a cigarette out of a silver case in his jacket pocket and tapped it on the case, but he didn't light it. He put it down and ate most of his sandwich before speaking again.

"Let me tell you a little more about Matthias. I want you to understand why these papers are important. He worked for the Nazis, for the Gestapo. He was the worst of the worst, and he should have been executed. Hell, he deserved to be tortured *before* he was executed. I don't know everything he did, but what I know is enough. I think he hid money for them. I know he found skilled specialists in the death camps, and I'm sure he killed children, probably a lot of children. And I don't think I know half of what he did.

"At the end of the war, he had a list of where a lot of the Nazi big shots had hidden their money. He traded that list to the Americans for his life. I worked for the OSS then, so I'm one of the good guys. I wasn't a spy; I mostly worked behind the scenes. But I was the one who handled Matthias Dorrinian so we could get that list. Except Matthias is exceedingly smart. He didn't give us everything. He held a lot of it back because he knew once we had that stuff, we'd probably try him as war criminal. Whenever he gets in trouble, he calls me and dribbles more stuff out. That's how he got into this country.

"Now let me tell you more about me. I'm a freelancer now. I work for myself. I have to scramble to eat. Those papers are worth serious money to me. I do stuff for the CIA that they don't want to do themselves, and I need to keep them happy. They'll pay enough for those papers to keep me happy for the rest of my life. Even if they won't, I could sell them to somebody else like maybe the Israelis or even the Russians for a lot more. Matthias helped me with a very profitable little operation for the CIA. Except it kind of pisses me off that I'm not getting' a cut of those profits.

"Matthias is more than a little pissed off at me right now because he found out I went to Vietnam and tried to get the papers you sent to your boyfriend. I figure he must have another copy of them. It looks to me like his goal is to make sure nobody else gets them. If the CIA gets them, it's all over for him. When you told him you were gonna give them to the cops, he went nuts. And when he found out the cops were looking for you, that was even worse. Now he's worried about the Garganos finding you too. He needs those papers and he wants you and the boyfriend dead, the sooner the better. Even if he doesn't get the papers back, he'll kill the two of you.

"Me? I just want to fund my retirement. I have no reason to kill you. So what do you say, Girlie? You gonna help me out, or you wanna take your chances with Matthias? You probably know him better than I do. I'll give you a few minutes to think about it. Let's say until I finish this cigarette."

Bradbury lit his cigarette and began smoking it as if he had just discovered smoking was the latest artistic fad. He'd take small puffs and examine the cigarette like it was something he'd never seen before.

Gloria said nothing. She didn't trust anyone, and that included him. But if Jimmy was going to have a chance to help her, she needed to give him as much time as possible. She didn't think Bradbury would kill her, but he might hurt her if he got angry. *And I'm going to make him very angry.* "Okay, the papers are in a safety deposit box in a bank in Kalamazoo."

A look of skepticism crossed his face. "And do you have the key?"

"No," she said. "I hid it in the basement of a boarding house where I was staying. It's out in the country south of Kalamazoo."

He thought about it for a long moment. "You better not be lying." Then he started tying her hands again.

8:45 a.m., Detroit

Clyde Bonaventure awoke to his doorbell and then a pounding on his front door. He grabbed his robe and put it on as he stumbled down two flights of stairs and opened the door to find an angry Logan Carlton.

"We need to talk, Clyde," Carlton said, pushing through the doorway. "Put on some fuckin' coffee. This shit I have is gettin' cold." He dropped a copy of the *Detroit Free Press* on Bonaventure's kitchen table along with a bag of donuts and two cardboard cups of coffee. "I heard yesterday that little shit Checchi had been talkin' to the organized crime people in Beaubian, Grosse Pointe cops and God knows who else. I think he wants to put away the fuckin' Garganos."

Bonaventure thought about it. "So what's wrong with that?" He could think of quite a lot that was wrong, but he wasn't going to admit it to Carlton.

"What's wrong? I'll tell you what's wrong, Clyde. I know you have a lot of after-hours clubs with a lot of chippies who are available for extra-curricular activities. I know you don't have a license to sell booze and I know folks can get somethin' extra at your clubs. And I know if somebody's credit's in the shitter and they want a loan, you're the man to see, and if they pay it back late they could be seein' stars. And that's probably not half of it. You've spread a lot of money around, and people like you. Shit Clyde, even I like you. We've been friends for a long time. But now I'm hearin' that you're peddlin' smack so strong that it'll kill you if you aren't careful. And I hear that if you piss off Clyde Bonaventure, Slick Percy Dupree might kill you. And now there's this!"

He picked up and then slapped the paper back down on the kitchen table, poking his finger at a story that was stripped down the left side of the front page. A picture of Al Checchi took up almost as much space as the story.

Veteran Detroit Detective, 2 Crime Bosses Dead

Late Wednesday afternoon, the body of Sergeant Albert Checchi, 43, a longtime homicide detective, was found in a parking lot near Griswold Street beside the Guardian Building. The subsequent investigation led police to two more bodies in an office on the 32nd floor of the same building.

Police sources later said those two bodies were Pietro Gargano Sr., 67, and his son Pietro Gargano, Jr., 45. Police said both men had been shot to death.

"We believe the three deaths are related, but we will have no further comment for now," said Lt. Robert Carnegie, a homicide detective. "This investigation has just begun."

Shortly before 7 p.m., a witness who refused to give his name was walking to his car. He said he heard a scream just before Checchi's body landed in the parking lot less than 30 feet from him.

"It was awful and I'm going to be hearing that scream for a long time," said the man. He said he had just come from a meeting with an attorney who has an office in the Guardian Building.

Police have long suspected that both Garganos were Mafia bosses in Detroit. Three years ago, a joint FBI-Detroit Police Department task force targeted the Gargano crime family, but no indictments were ever handed down.

Checchi had recently been investigating the murder of Roscoe Lincoln, a local musician who had played on several record albums and toured with musical acts in Midwestern area concerts. Carnegie would not say whether Checchi's death was related to that murder, or to any other investigation. Carnegie also said he had no reason to believe that Checchi might have taken his own life.

"We don't think he jumped. He had been working all day and was still on duty when he died," Carnegie said. "He was one of our top homicide investigators and a fine police officer who served the people of Detroit for almost 19 years."

"Jesus Christ," Bonaventure said when he had read the story. "I wonder if it was Vinnie."

"Vinnie?" Carlton shoved a donut into his mouth.

"Vincent Ayala," Bonaventure said. "He's married to Pietro's daughter. Everyone assumed when the old man stepped down, and most of us thought it would be soon, that his son would take over. Vinnie and Junior mostly got along, but this probably means Vinnie will take over. I have to believe he'll be suspect number one."

Carlton said, "The cops are gonna know that fuckin' pissant midget talked to us. I'm a state senator for Chrissakes, and if the papers get hold of this I wouldn't be able to beat Elmer Fudd in an election for dogcatcher. I don't need this shit, Clyde!"

"Doran! You know, it could have been Doran!" Bonaventure said, studying the paper. "But why?"

"You mean *Matthew* Doran?" Carlton asked, small wet chunks of donut falling out one side of his mouth as he spoke. He coughed and gulped some of the coffee, which made him cough more. He got up from the kitchen table and bent over the sink, where he hacked up more donut pieces.

"C'mon Logan, get a grip. Help me think this through," Bonaventure said. "Remember what the girl said about her stepfather taking a shot at her? I didn't really believe that, thought maybe she was exaggerating. You know, teenage runaway... pissed off... pregnant."

Carlton shuffled back to his chair, eyeing the gurgling percolator. He noted Bonaventure had used "that girl" and not referred to her as his daughter.

"Shit, I've had to deal with a lot of pissed off girls in my time. She's not even the first one who ever pulled a gun on me. I don't take it seriously. Usually best to let them vent," Bonaventure said. "And we were a little drunk when she knocked on the door."

Carlton nodded, got up and poured two cups of coffee into china mugs that he took from a cupboard. He brought them back, opened the donut bag, peered inside for a long time and finally selected a chocolate coconut one. He sipped some coffee and alternated between studying the donut and looking at Bonaventure.

Bonaventure sat rock-still staring out the window for a long time before turning to Carlton. "Look, Logan, there's a chance I could be next. I need some help. I'm dealing with very dangerous people here, and I guess it's time for me to do something that's going to piss them off. This is not integrating the officers' club and being told you're an uppity nigger. This is flying into enemy territory against experienced opponents. I don't understand everything yet, but it's starting look scary as shit. Now I'm the one in danger here, not you, but I need your help if I'm gonna do the right thing."

Carlton didn't hesitate. "I'm in! Ain't I just about the uppitiest motherfuckin' nigger you know?"

2:55 p.m., Detroit

When Suggs got off the Delta flight in Detroit, he was stiff and tired. From Vietnam all the way to Travis in California, he had been on military transport aircraft. Most of the time he had been able to stretch out on the floor but he had hardly slept. He still had a headache and he'd slept too long before starting the trip. In Travis, and again in San Francisco, he had tried to call the Detroit detective. The first time, he got a run around. He was passed from a desk sergeant to a homicide detective to another homicide detective and finally to a Lieutenant Bob Carnegie in homicide who asked him how he knew Checchi. Suggs identified himself as an Army CID investigator and gave him the Washington number for someone in CID who knew about the investigation, but Carnegie kept asking him questions and not letting him talk to Checchi.

"I don't know who you are, Bud, and until I do, I'll ask the questions," Carnegie said.

"Why don't you call Army CID in Washington?" Suggs said as politely as he could bring himself to speak. "I'll call back when I get to the airport in San Francisco."

But when he called from the San Francisco airport, Carnegie wasn't in and they still wouldn't let him talk to Checchi. But this time, the homicide detective who had answered the phone was more polite. He said that Carnegie wanted to talk to Suggs, and that he was expected back soon. So Suggs waited on the phone for almost 15 minutes shoveling in quarters every minute or so. He hung up when his Detroit flight started boarding.

In Detroit as he was walking through the terminal and wondering where he could pick up a heavier coat in a hurry, he grabbed a *Detroit Free Press* at a newsstand because he spotted a story on a police murder. Even before he had paid for the paper, he knew that Checchi was dead. "Holy shit," he said.

Half an hour and a snowy taxi ride later, Suggs was finally talking to Lieutenant Carnegie and quickly wished he hadn't bothered. Carnegie had called Washington, but he made no apology and in fact, seemed to be treating Suggs more like a suspect than a fellow police officer. An Inspector Edmunds, who neither offered to shake hands nor gave his first name, joined Carnegie, and the two of them grilled Suggs for an hour. They were anxious to find Jimmy Hayes and since Suggs was in the Army, they were suspicious when he wouldn't produce Hayes. Suggs did learn that Hayes' uncle had been dropped off at the hospital in Sault Ste. Marie, which was up north somewhere. He had apparently been in a drunken fight. Sepp Hayha had suffered a minor gunshot wound and been fairly seriously beaten up. The Detroit detectives were furious that he had been released from the hospital. No one knew where he had gone.

Suggs didn't like the two Detroit policemen. He answered their questions, but if it didn't relate to Jimmy Hayes' whereabouts, they weren't interested in answering any of his questions. When Suggs gave them Hayes' version of what he had seen at the Cresthaven, they listened but were upset when he told them that Hayes hadn't identified the man who shot the policemen. The business concerning what Hayes had said about his girlfriend, her stepfather or the murder of the musician that Checchi was investigating never came up, and Suggs was so unhappy about the way he was being grilled that he didn't volunteer it. Actually, he didn't get much of a chance to volunteer anything. He thought the questioning was a waste of time for both him and the Detroit Police.

Suggs was anxious to call Washington CID to see what they had learned about the documents that he had sent, and he wanted to talk to the local FBI, especially Special Agent Ovenden, if he was there. He had a feeling he wouldn't find

Bradbury there. And he needed a jacket and other heavier clothes. It was snowing and just a few degrees above zero outside. He was wearing tennis shoes, light slacks, a short-sleeved shirt and a light windbreaker. He had some papers relating to the case, a change of underwear and a .45 automatic in small flight bag. He wanted to get out of Detroit police headquarters as soon as he could. He hadn't even asked them for the use of a phone. He thought it best to bag out in a hotel where he would have a phone and a chance to think.

As he walked toward the elevator on the third floor of the police building after he had been dismissed by the two Detroit cops, a tall plain-clothes policeman approached him. "Are you Suggs?" He seemed friendly enough.

"Jimmy Ray Suggs, Army CID," Suggs said, extending his hand.

The man took it. "I'm Sergeant Antoine Lincicombe, organized crime. Al Checchi was a good friend."

"I'm sorry about what happened to him," Suggs said. "We never had a chance to meet and I suspect that was my loss."

Lincicombe finally released his grip. "Thanks. Listen, we should talk, but not here. Edmunds is an asshole, but he's also an inspector," said Lincicombe. "Have you eaten?"

"Airplane food a couple of hours ago. I've been on airplanes forever. In fact, I'm not sure what day it is," Suggs said. "I need to get a hotel and I need some warmer clothes, but at least no one's shooting at me here, not even Edmunds... at least not yet."

Lincicombe grinned and looked him up and down, taking in the light clothes. "Okay, wait by the door where you came in. My good friend Sergeant Dombrowski is on the desk. Look for a dirty blue Chevy."

An hour later, Suggs was settled in a room in the Pick Fort Shelby. Lincicombe had taken Suggs to a department store called Hudson's and helped him get some winter clothes. "I know you must be tired, but I think time is of the essence. Let's you and I and Dixon Webley—he's a homicide detective in Grosse Point, and another Al Checchi friend—meet in the hotel coffee shop in an hour. In fact, I can call you when we get there."

Suggs nodded. "You know anyone in the local FBI? I'd especially like to talk to an agent by the name of Ovenden. He might be the last reliable person who saw Jimmy Hayes, and who talked to him."

"You know, it crossed my mind to call the FBI myself," said Lincicombe. "I got to know a few of them when I was on a task force with the feds a couple of years ago. Dix and I are pretty sure Al was onto something big. The problem is Edmunds. He wants to get Hayes and his girlfriend first because he still thinks he can control the direction of the investigation into what happened at the Cresthaven. He's a hard charger but not a very bright one. He seems to think Hayes might be involved in Checchi's murder, though that makes no sense at all."

An hour later, Suggs was sitting in a restaurant that had been chosen specifically because it wasn't a cop hangout and because it had a room in the back where they could talk privately. In the room with him were Lincicombe, Webley, Ovenden and Jeff Mosley-Williams, special agent in charge of the Detroit FBI office. Ovenden had just gotten in from the West Coast. He had been with the FBI for less than a year and was already on Mosley-Williams' shit list. It turned out that neither the Washington FBI Office nor anyone else in the FBI had ever heard of Austin Bradbury.

Mosley-Williams' upset was tempered by the fact that several other agents in the Detroit office had interacted with Bradbury and no one had been suspicious, though no one had liked him either. "Par for the course for those DC jerks," said Mosley-Williams.

The fact that Bradbury had known details about the closely held investigation into the Cresthaven Motel incident and had managed to travel all the way to Vietnam had the Washington FBI seriously pissed so that Mosley-Williams was now occupying a prominent place on their shit list. He didn't seem to care, and Suggs liked him. In fact, he liked all the cops at the table.

Mosley-Williams didn't stay long. "I'm leaving this to Ovenden. He can brief me later. Despite everything, he's still the one person in my office who's on top of this." He got up. "I have to go talk to a potty-mouthed state senator by the name of Logan Carlton."

At Suggs' suggestion they had gone around the table and each policeman related what he knew. They had a good laugh when Ovenden told them about finding Bradbury handcuffed over a smelly toilet without any pants. *Chalk one up for Jimmy Hayes,* Suggs thought. He listened with fascination as Lincicombe and Webley told them about their conversations with Al Checchi. Checchi had built a solid case to arrest Slick Percy Dupree for killing Roscoe Lincoln. And Checchi had been sure that Dupree had killed Gina Doran at the behest of Matthew Doran. Lincicombe and Webley were both convinced Checchi had been right.

Suggs asked, "Do Carnegie and Edmunds know about this?"

Lincicombe said, "Well yeah, they know now because I told them, but with Edmunds, it went in one ear and out the other. All he wants to do is nail whoever shot three policemen at the Cresthaven, maybe because one of them was his cousin. Edmunds knows Al Checchi was looking for Jimmy Hayes and his girlfriend. If he had his way, every swinging dick in the department would be looking for those two. But Edmunds and his cousin Erwin never cared for Al Checchi on account of his small stature and his big success. Erwin tried to bounce him out when he was a rookie, but Al had a waiver on the minimum height requirement.

"I think Carnegie was more interested in what I had to say, and he's a decent homicide cop, but he's a career ass kisser and he won't buck Edmunds. I know he had a couple of his detectives check on Doran and he has an alibi. He was banging a whore in the Book Cadillac, and he's been banging whores daily over there for weeks. He was trying to be discrete about it, but you can't hide something like that from the hotel staff."

Webley looked at him like he was going to say something, but he didn't speak.

Suggs told them Checchi had probably seen his telex about Dupree being the prime suspect in the murders of Hollister and Lehman because he had received a return telex identifying Dupree and containing his background. Suggs told them every detail he could about what Jimmy Hayes had said when Bradbury and Ovenden were questioning him. Ovenden confirmed it and added a few more details. Then Suggs told them about the documents he'd found in the Long Binh Post Office. "I just called the CID office in the Pentagon. They have mostly finished translating that stuff. Most of it's in German, Nazi papers. Seems to be bank records from several different countries, Switzerland and South America, with the names of high-ranking Nazis. It looked like their nest eggs, money they were putting away because they knew the war was going to end badly. There were a lot of very bad people on the list and some of them have not been accounted for since the end of the war. CID got some information from old Army Intelligence records.

"Matthew Dorrinian—he usually went by the more Germanic Matthias—changed his name to Matthew Doran when he came to the States. Claims to be Armenian. There's classified information on him that we can't get. We really don't know where he came from originally, but he was in Germany at the end of the war, and my best guess, not confirmed by anything, is that he was part of the Nazi regime. He lived in Germany as Matthias Dorrinian for several years after the war. He was thought to be involved in smuggling people from Europe to Canada and America for profit. The details of how he got here are not clear. Most of the Army Intelligence about Dorrinian is classified, and very highly classified at that. The old OSS—the Office of Strategic Services—was actually running some kind of project with him. As you may know, the OSS morphed into the CIA. The CIA isn't telling us much of anything, but they want us to turn over the documents to them."

"Damn," Ovenden said. "We haven't been able to get anything out of the CIA either, and we suspect Bradbury is tied to the CIA. I mean, how else could he have gotten their help getting Hayes out of Vietnam? He got out of San Francisco damn quick too. One phone call, and he was gone."

Suggs told them there were a couple of documents that were in Armenian and another in Thai. Army CID had a Thai Army officer who was on an exchange program and he had translated the document right away. "It was paperwork for a new airline that Matthew Doran had set up. It had one small aircraft and operated out of a remote Thai town near the Golden Triangle. There's one sheet of handwritten notes, probably made by Doran. It describes a process for purifying heroin."

"That's interesting," said Lincicombe. "Detroit's been flooded with high-grade heroin the last few months.

Suggs nodded. "But what do we have regarding Al Checchi, and where do we go from here?"

"Well, it looks like Al had connected Doran to four murders," said Webley. "When we were partners, he sometimes liked to get real ballsy with suspects. He'd try to shake something loose, and it worked more often than not. He liked to make the busts himself. Something about being five feet tall made him want to be the big man. He was, in fact, pretty damn tough."

Lincicombe said, "Yeah, he was, but why would he go see the Garganos?"

Webley asked, "What makes you think he was gonna see the Garganos?"

"Because they were shot dead with Al's gun," Lincicombe said sarcastically.

"Yeah, but doesn't Doran have an office in the same building?" asked Webley. "Isn't his office on the same floor?"

"I think so, but he also has an alibi."

"When I'm working a homicide, I don't see alibis from whores as rock solid," Webley said. "How about if Al went to see Doran to try to shake something loose? And the something most likely would involve the Garganos. Maybe he thought he could get Doran to rat them out."

Lincicombe looked around, drumming his fingers on the table. He slowly nodded. "Yeah, I can see that. Al was getting interested in the Garganos last time I spoke to him, and he called my office looking for me the day he died. With the old man and his son gone, that probably means Vinnie Ayala takes over. Vinnie was closer to Doran than the two Garganos were. He was the nastiest of the three too, but he was also the son-in-law. The old man was gonna pass everything to Junior. Al Checchi and the two Garganos dead would be a big help to both Doran and Vinnie Ayala. I remember when we were monitoring calls and tailing those bastards, Doran talked to Vinnie a lot more than he talked to either of the Garganos. And Vinnie's disappeared. No one can find him. His wife says he left town the same day as the murders, but well before they happened. We got to be careful though. Doran's a big shot in the community and well-connected even in the department. Gives a lot of money to the PBA." He looked at Suggs. "Police Benevolent Association."

Suggs lit a cigarette. "I need to concentrate on finding Jimmy Hayes. The Army needs Hayes badly for another problem that has nothing to do with this case. The media's about to hit us with story that we slaughtered civilians in a firefight. It's not true and Jimmy Hayes was there. I'm supposed to find him and get him to New York. I like Hayes. Seems like a good soldier, though maybe not perfect, which is pretty normal. Likes his marijuana and got busted for it. He'll be looking for his girlfriend, who's Doran's runaway stepdaughter. He says she told him that her stepfather is trying to kill her. Hard to believe, until you think about Al Checchi looking at Doran for four murders and the fact that Doran was probably a Nazi and might be connected to the heroin trade. According to Jimmy Hayes, she remembers a lot of stuff she overheard when she was growing up."

11:40 p.m., Pick Fort Shelby Hotel

Suggs didn't care for his room in the Pick Fort Shelby. It was too warm, except when it was too cold, and it was too dry except when it was too damp. Outside it was snowing but hot dry air blasted out of a vent in the room. Suggs cracked open the window before he went to sleep and that created a cold draft. When the wind blew hard enough some snow reached his face. Despite that, he went right to sleep. He slept approximately 20 minutes before the phone rang.

"Good morning! It's Ovie... Bill Ovenden. Did I wake you?"

"Maybe," Suggs said yawning. He looked at this watch. "It isn't morning."

"It's morning somewhere," Ovenden said. "Isn't it morning in Vietnam?"

"I don't know," Suggs grumbled, sitting up. "What's up?"

"Mosley-Williams just called me with something very interesting: seems that state senator he talked to, Logan Carlton, is a friend of Clyde Bonaventure's. Clyde Bonaventure runs most of the Negro rackets in Detroit: prostitution, drugs, gambling, a little loan sharking. Bonaventure and Carlton are both Negroes, and they were in the Air Force together in World War II. Bonaventure was a damn good P51 pilot. Shot down four Germans. Then he got court martialed after the war when he and Carlton and some others were trying to get served in an officers' club that was whites only. Anyway, according to Mosley-Williams, Bonaventure and Carlton had lunch with Al Checchi right before Al started asking questions about Doran and the Garganos. Seems that Bonaventure told Checchi he knows who shot those cops at the Cresthaven, but he wouldn't tell Checchi who it was. But now Bonaventure wants to come clean and spill his guts, but to the FBI, not Detroit PD. And get this—both Bonaventure *and* Carlton have been talking to the girlfriend."

"Huh." Suggs was thinking that he had definitely been asleep. "Did you call Lincicombe?"

"Well, Mosley-Williams and I talked about that. If Bonaventure told Checchi that he knew who killed those cops, and Checchi didn't tell anyone in the department, namely Edmunds, he probably had a reason," Ovenden said. "But now Checchi's dead and if we pass that tidbit on to Lincicombe, he might think this is too much to hold back from Edmunds. I mean, it would put a serious hurt on Lincicombe's career if

Edmunds found out he'd been holding out on something like that. Mosley-Williams doesn't want Detroit to snatch Bonaventure before we get him. Carlton's gonna bring Bonaventure to the FBI office tomorrow morning, and once that process starts, I kind of think finding Jimmy Hayes will be back burner."

"Shit, you're probably right," Suggs said.

"Carlton's an ambitious politician. Mosley-Williams thinks Carlton has his eye on being mayor someday. But he's also concerned about his friend Bonaventure. Claims Bonaventure's not really that bad, that he makes most of his money from 'victimless crimes,' is how he put it. Then he puts a lot of money back into the community. In other words, he's probably a major campaign contributor to Carlton, though it would be hard to prove that. Mosley-Williams says there's some truth to Carlton's description of Bonaventure though. He's not as bad as most in his business. So what I thought is that you and I might want to go over and talk to Clyde Bonaventure," Ovenden said.

"Is that what Mosley-Williams suggested?"

"Not exactly," Ovenden said. "But why did he tell me all of this? It was also Mosley-Williams who pointed out that once Bonaventure comes clean, it's possible that the only one who'll be interested in finding Jimmy Hayes is you. There's one other thing too: Bonaventure doesn't want the girl to get hurt, or her boyfriend, but especially the girl. He's real worried about her, and so is Carlton. So do you want to go see Bonaventure tonight?"

"How long will it take you to get here?" Suggs said.

"I'm in the lobby right now."

February 2, 12:22 a.m., Detroit

When someone knocked on the door just after midnight, Bonaventure was expecting either the FBI or the Detroit Police, or maybe both. He was ready. He knew Logan was meeting with the FBI and he had agreed with Logan that it was best to come clean and tell them everything. He expected to be arrested. He expected to go to prison but he hoped it wouldn't be for the rest of his life. And maybe he wouldn't go at all. There were, after all, witnesses to the provocation at the Cresthaven and he was a war hero. Black people were starting to be treated better. He could afford good lawyers. He would have some support from the community. He could count on Logan. He wondered what his family would think of him. How much would they support him?

Most of all, he wondered about his daughter. What would she think? She didn't think much of him so far. She had gotten a shit sandwich from almost everyone in her life, including him. He'd thought a lot about her in recent days and he was afraid for her. *It's gonna be hard,* he thought as he went to open the door. Things could hardly have turned out worse, but he had a fighter pilot's confidence that he could turn some of it around. He had beaten difficult odds before. But when he opened the door, he knew right away that he would not be going to prison. He was receiving a death letter.

Matthew Doran shoved Gloria through the door with the gun in his hand. She stumbled, tripping over the threshold and then sprawled onto the floor twisting onto her side. Her hands were tied in front and she had an ugly cut over a big bruise on her cheek that was scabbed over with dried blood. Then Doran stepped in followed by a chunky man with wispy red hair and wearing a nylon parka over a suit.

Doran said, "Clyde, I understand you were looking for my daughter. Here she is. And this is Austin Bradbury, my not very intelligent intelligence contact."

"She's not your daughter," Bonaventure said. "She's mine."

"Well, she could have been yours. Might have been better if she had been yours, but the stupid cunt decided to run away and cause all this trouble instead."

"No, I mean she's my daughter. I am her father. And I'll thank you not to use that kind of language in my house." He reached down to help her up, and in doing so he stepped between her and Doran.

Doran shoved his gun in Bonaventure's face. "Isn't that interesting? No wonder she's so dark. Probably why she plays that goddamn nigger music on her guitar. A nigger daddy makes her a nigger too." Doran kept poking Bonaventure in the face with the gun, forcing him to sit on the floor next to Gloria. "Let me tell you both how it's gonna be. Young lady, I'm gonna cause you a great deal of pain until you tell me where those papers are."

Gloria showed no reaction.

He gestured toward Bradbury. "My intelligence colleague here says you told this tubby little turd about those papers."

Bradbury was nodding. "She told him all about what you do for the Garganos too after she led me on a fucking wild goose chase."

She glanced at Bonaventure, who looked back at her. He caught the guilt in her eyes. "It's okay girl," Bonaventure said. He touched her cheek near the bruise, causing her to wince a little.

"You were always one smart nigger, Clyde. That's one reason I liked doing business with you," Doran said.

Gloria said, "I never showed them to him. He—"

Doran hit her in the side of the head with the gun, just hard enough to hurt. "Shut up."

Moving with surprising quickness, Bonaventure grabbed for Doran's arm, but Doran slammed the barrel hard against his mouth, snapping his head back.

Bonaventure gasped and spat out a piece of tooth, blood running down his chin from cuts on both lips. He spoke slowly because of his damaged mouth. "I've understood for a long time that you rape children. One of the worst mistakes I ever made was deciding that was none of my business." He glanced at Gloria, then back at Doran. "I never saw any Nazi papers but you must have been a Nazi. It's probably financial records. I'd guess that you were doing some of the same things for the Nazis that you do for the Garganos." He paused and looked at Gloria again. "And for me."

"You're smart, but you never had the balls," Doran said. "That's why you're on the floor and I'm standing here with the gun." He turned to Gloria and pointed his gun at her belly.

Gloria moved both her arms to protect her baby. She pulled her knees up until she was in a fetal position.

"Relax," he said. "Maybe we'll play football with the squiggler later."

He turned back to Bonaventure.

"Now Clyde, I want you to answer this next question correctly because if you don't, Gloria's pain will start right now. I'm talking about the kind of pain that comes with flames and second degree burns. You have to be careful when you play with fire that you don't burn too much. When you kill the nerves, you kill the pain." He bent over Bonaventure to get closer. "Now Clyde, you must have a gun in the house. Tell me where it is."

Bonaventure looked relieved. "Sure... upstairs, first room on the left, in the bottom desk drawer," Bonaventure said.

"Well, we'll all have to go up there and get it," Doran said. All four of them trudged upstairs, Doran opened the drawer and took out Bonaventure's .38 special revolver. As he looked around the office at the pictures on the walls, he snapped the cylinder open and saw that it was loaded.

"I didn't know you had all this family, Clyde." He looked at Bonaventure for a few seconds. "Sit down in the chair."

Bonaventure sat on the chair by the desk and Doran turned to Gloria.

"Now young lady, you tell me where those papers are or say 'bye-'bye to Daddy," Doran said. She recognized the danger in his tone.

"I hid them in some tunnels under the campus at MSU in East Lansing," she said quickly. "That's where I've been hiding."

Doran looked at Bonaventure and sighed. He had a gun in each hand, with Bonaventure's in his right. He turned to Bradbury. "You got a gun?" he asked.

Bradbury unbuttoned his coat and then the suit jacket underneath, awkwardly pulling out an automatic. "You're not gonna kill him are you?" he asked. "I don't want to have anything to do with killing."

"That's too bad," Doran said, "because *you're* gonna kill him."

"What?"

"Time you did a little more than slow things down," Doran said. "You took your time getting the girl here."

"I told you, she said she'd hidden the papers in Kalamazoo. I was trying to get them for us."

"You took off for Vietnam without telling me too," Doran said.

"Same thing. I was trying to get those papers for us, and you didn't tell me that you'd sent somebody else."

"Look, if we're in this together, you have to step up. I'm not gonna do it all," Doran said in a tone that was deadly serious. "Now shoot him."

Resigned, Bradbury racked the slide on his pistol and aimed at Bonaventure. Then he closed his eyes and fired once into Bonaventure's chest. Gloria screamed. Doran immediately shot Bradbury in the middle of the forehead with Bonaventure's gun.

Doran bent over, wiped Bonaventure's gun with Bonaventure's shirt and placed the gun in his hand. "Gunfight," he said as he jerked Gloria up. "I guess we have to go to East Lansing. You better not be playing games with me because I'm done fucking around."

* * *

Ovenden pointed out Bonaventure's home as he and Suggs cruised by in Ovenden's Chevy Blazer. It was snowing again, but not hard and the wind had died down. There were lights on in the house so it looked like he was up. The truck was big, the street was narrow and full of parked cars so they went around the block and parked on a cross street by the corner. They had gotten out of the truck and were walking along the dark street when they heard two shots. Moments later Bonaventure's front door opened. Suggs pulled Ovenden into a driveway where they crouched behind a hedge. A man and a woman came out. The man was squat and powerful, dressed in a dark nylon parka and a fur hat. He was looking carefully up and down the street, one hand holding a gun, pointed at the woman.

Suggs and Ovenden froze. The woman was wearing a dirty sweatshirt and sweatpants. Her head was bowed with her hands tied in front of her. She stumbled as the squat man prodded her down the front walk where he pushed her into the back of a cream Oldsmobile station wagon. Suggs and Ovenden drew their guns.

Ovenden asked, "Shall we try to take him?"

"Better not. The girl might get shot. I think that might be Hayes' girlfriend. She looks young."

"And that's probably Doran. He fits the description."

The station wagon started.

"See if you can tail him," Suggs said. "I'll see what happened inside the house."

Ovenden sprinted down the street as the Olds pulled out. He was behind the Olds and running in the opposite direction it was heading so he thought his chances of being seen were slim. But by the time he got the Blazer going and fishtailed around the corner, the station wagon was out of sight. He sped down the street, trying to think of the most likely route that Doran would take to get on a freeway.

Meanwhile, Suggs walked to the front door, stopped to listen and, hearing nothing, drew his pistol and pushed the door open with the toe of his new boot. He stopped to listen again, then began searching the house. He found nothing on the first floor. Again, he stopped at the bottom of the stairs to listen. Nothing, but now he smelled gunpowder. He went up the stairs quickly and found a bloody man he presumed to be Bonaventure sitting in a chair in the first room he entered. Bradbury was lying on the floor, a bullet hole in his head. He searched for a pulse on Bonaventure and thought there might be a flutter. There was a phone on the desk. He dialed zero and got an operator. "Two people have been shot here. I think one of them might still be alive," Suggs said. He tried to remember the address, but couldn't. But he remembered the cross streets where they had parked the Blazer and gave the street names to the operator. "I believe the man who might still be alive is Clyde Bonaventure and this is his home."

Suggs hung up. He got out the business cards he had collected earlier in the evening and found where Mosley-Williams had written his home number. He called it.

"Jimmy Ray Suggs here," he said when Mosley-Williams answered. "I'm at Clyde Bonaventure's house. Bradbury and Bonaventure have been shot and Bradbury's dead. Bonaventure might still be alive. Ovenden's in pursuit of the shooter, who's driving a cream-colored late-model Oldsmobile station wagon. It looked like Doran and he's got the girl. Detroit PD is on the way. You better get here quick."

He hung up as Mosley-Williams started to say something. There were sirens in the distance. He put his gun in his back pocket, took out his badge and held it open in his left hand. Then he picked up the phone with his right hand and dialed the number for the Pentagon CID Office. He had just reached the duty officer when heard policemen coming through the front door. He gave his name to the duty officer and said he was going to need help dealing with the Detroit police. That was as far as he got.

"Drop the phone!" said the first officer who had raced up the stairs when he heard Suggs talking. Suggs placed it back on the table. The second officer reached for his badge and examined it.

"I'm an investigator with the United States Army. I'm the one who called the police," Suggs said. The other policeman spotted Suggs' pistol in his back pocket and snatched it. The two cops turned Suggs around and handcuffed his hands behind his back. Suggs made no attempt to resist. Within 10 minutes there were a dozen uniformed cops on the scene and an ambulance. Bonaventure was still alive, so the medics loaded him on a stretcher and rushed out of the house.

Just then Ovenden walked in, his badge hooked in the front pocket of his coat. The FBI agent shook his head dejectedly when he saw Suggs. Seeing a long, unpleasant night ahead, Suggs sat down on the floor.

12:47 a.m., I-96 West Between Detroit and East Lansing

The big Oldsmobile station wagon hurtled through darkness, the only sound a soft rushing of air and a muted hum of the tires, but Gloria heard nothing. Her death would end the pain soon and she was preparing. She prayed.

She prayed for Jimmy's soul. She had thought he would find her, but all hope vanished when she saw her stepfather kill her father and Bradbury. She would never see Jimmy in this life again. He might already be dead. But perhaps he wasn't. Since leaving home, she had learned that many people became worse when facing adversity. So she prayed that Jimmy would stay Jimmy, that he would remain the boy she loved despite all that was happening. She prayed that he would not be destroyed by the evil around him: the war, her stepfather, the Detroit Police. The Jimmy she knew was full of love for her and for life. That was the Jimmy she loved, and she wanted God to save him but she knew He might not.

She prayed for Gina's soul, for Roscoe's soul and for her father's soul too. She prayed that God would grant them peace. Since she had left home, she had learned why Gina had prayed. Prayer had brought peace to Gina, just as it was now bringing peace to Gloria. She'd learned that on Christmas Eve. Before that revelation, Gloria thought you prayed to God to ask for something. But God didn't grant wishes. Wishes might come true, or they might not. God didn't have anything to do with it. People made the bad things happen and you couldn't do anything about it. All God could do is help her cope with it.

She prayed for her own soul. Whatever happened to her and Jimmy and their baby, she wanted peace. Since she had left home, she'd learned that some people broke when bad things happened. Gina had been broken, Uncle Sepp had almost been broken, and the war might break Jimmy. She loved Jimmy. She loved their baby, she loved life, and she loved God. And because of that love, she was at peace. So she prayed she could hold on to the love and the peace no matter what happened. She and her baby would sleep in heavenly peace. In her mind, she sang the words of "Silent Night." The music flowed through her body as her fingers twitched on the guitar chords.

1:35 a.m., Michigan State University Campus

At Michigan State University, Jimmy Hayes was waiting in an alley behind some trashcans. He'd been there for a long time, having built himself a crude blind by stacking cardboard boxes of trash. He was in the darkest part of the alley. The cardboard boxes were brown and his new suede jacket was brown, so he hoped he blended in. The steam rising from the tunnel entrance provided more concealment. He didn't know what time it was or how long he had been there, but he had a good view of the tunnel entrance. It was the only entrance he'd told Gloria about, so he was betting it was the one she had been using.

But as time passed he felt colder and more discouraged. Had he been too late? Was she somewhere else? Was she alive? He was afraid to walk around. If he came out from behind the trashcans, he'd be in full view of anyone who came into the alley. He wasn't just concerned about whomever might have Gloria; he was worried about the campus police, university employees or students. It was Friday night and there had been people walking past on the street at the end of the alley. How could he explain why he was lurking in a dark alley with a gun?

No one had entered the alley except a student couple who had kissed and fondled each other for a few minutes, but it was too cold for them to stay longer. He had a fresh pack of cigarettes and wanted to smoke. But if he did, anyone coming into the alley might smell the smoke. He had started to stamp his feet to keep warm, but that made too much noise. Periodically, he opened the front of his coat and put a hand in his armpit for a few minutes. He was tired so he tried sitting down, but it was difficult to see around the trashcans. However, getting up and down kept him awake, so he crouched every few minutes.

Before long, he started falling asleep despite his efforts and he lurched noisily into a trashcan, which woke him. *That won't do.* He stood up, playing rock and roll songs in his head, moving his lips to the words and his fingers through the chords as if he were playing them. He was going through the Universal Joint set list, thinking about the proper order for songs. The band had played certain songs together that worked with the same settings on his guitar and amps. As he was in the middle of "Moanin' the Blues," they came.

Gloria rounded the corner first, her head down as she stumbled slowly up the alley toward him. Her burnished golden hair flashed for an instant in the streetlight, and his heart jumped. He crouched down just a little as her head came up. There was a man behind her. The man prodded her with a gun when she slowed, and Hayes thought he said something. The man's powerful shoulders were evident despite the parka he was wearing. He had a face like a block of stone and his bearing was methodical and threatening. His head moved like a gun turret as he inspected the alley.

Hayes didn't move an inch.

***

Gloria, still numbly at peace, still preparing for her death, had stopped thinking about God. Now she was thinking about her life. Sixteen years old, she loved someone and that somebody loved her. It was a joyful miracle because not long ago she had thought no one would ever love her. She had heard Jimmy say "I love you" and she had told him "I love you." She believed him and was sure he believed her. That was all that mattered now. Her life was complete. Some people lived their whole lives without ever loving or being loved. And for a little while, she had touched people as Sunshine. Some people never touched anyone. She was content to die as Gloria. But here she was, still alive and clinging to peace. And so was her baby, fluttering inside her as she walked up the alley. *Take it easy, little guy,* she thought. *It's gonna be okay. We'll be in heaven soon.*

Looking for the tunnel entrance, Gloria slowed. Her stepfather jabbed her in the back with his gun. She ignored it as she saw the grate. But that's not all she saw. At the very back of the alley, she saw Jimmy, the top and side of his head going down and then peeking out from behind a box on a trashcan, almost obscured by the steam rising from the grate. He looked like something in the trash, but Gloria had recognized the hair instantly. Adrenaline and love surged through her and it was just like the church on Christmas Eve when she had been sure that her stepfather was going to capture her. It wasn't over yet. Perhaps God did grant wishes. But perhaps she should try to help. She walked slowly around the grate, her stepfather following closely with the gun. When she stopped, her stepfather stopped, and his back was to Jimmy. She had no idea what Jimmy would do, but she thought it best to get out of the way, so she crouched down to examine the grate. Then she got lower, on her knees, to peer through it.

* * *

Doran had decided that he would leave the United States as soon as he got the documents from the girl and killed her, which would be a genuine pleasure. He had already taken care of the goddamn Italians and Bonaventure and that cowardly Bradbury. He had taken care of them all. Out on the Guardian balcony by the Garganos' offices, the shrimp detective had tried to punch him in the balls. Doran had picked up the wriggling little bastard, grabbed his gun and thrown him over the parapet. Doran thought Pietro Gargano pathetic as he ambled around his gloomy offices, and Pietro Jr. seemed to embrace the same dull existence. Doran treasured the shocked expression on their faces as he'd shot them with the detective's gun. *At least Vinnie Ayala has a little more life in him,* Doran thought, *though damn little ambition.* They were still ostensibly friends, but Vinnie would have to take care of himself now.

As Gloria crouched, Doran tried to look through the acrid, foul-smelling steam emanating through the grate. He could see the top of a metal ladder but not the bottom.

Then Gloria lay down beside the grate. She said, "Do you believe in hell and eternal damnation? Can you smell it?"

What a stupid question! He sneered just as something slammed hard into his back. He thought he had been hit with a rock or a club. And it hurt. He couldn't remember ever feeling pain that intense, like fire on both his back and his chest. A terrible weakness enveloped him and he fought to keep his knees from giving way. Worse, he couldn't breathe. The gun was dropping from his hand. He tried to look down at Gloria beside the opening and saw a big bloody point was sticking out through his coat. Then something else slammed into his back, high up, almost on his neck, and he was falling forward. The pain disappeared, and then everything disappeared. He didn't even see the pavement as his face hit it.

4:05 a.m., East Lansing

Hayes and Gloria were in a Holiday Inn in East Lansing talking about what to do. Should they turn themselves in to the police or should they keep running? They hadn't succeeded in getting any sleep. They were both sick with exhaustion, but too jacked up to sleep.

Gloria said, "We have to talk about some things. We have to talk about us. I've found out some things that you need to know."

"Okay," he said, feeling like he might throw up. *Is she gonna dump me?*

First she told him about Bonaventure being her father, and what had happened to him.

"So you saw your father murdered?" Hayes said. She nodded and he wrapped his arms around her.

"It means I'm half-black."

He tightened his hug and nuzzled her cheek. "Doesn't matter. You're still one hundred percent beautiful." He was relieved because he thought that was all. "I love you."

She looked into his eyes. "There's more... a lot more."

Jimmy said, "I'm right here. Let's get it out."

Looking down, she nodded. Then she told him that she thought Vinnie Ayala might be his father, that Ayala had still been at the cabin when Bradbury took her away, and she wondered what might have happened to him.

He looked at her and shook his head. "Nothing I can do to bring him back. I don't think I'd want to anyway. He was gonna kill Uncle Sepp for sure, and I think he was gonna kill me. I don't really want to talk about the rest of what happened up there. Not yet. I've done a lot things, terrible things and I don't know what to think about it. I don't know how to talk about it... someday maybe."

She kissed his cheek and held him tight. "I have things like that too, what my stepfather did to me, worse than what you know."

He looked at her and saw the pain in her face. "I love you, Gloria. We have the rest of our lives to talk about that stuff."

She nodded and took a deep breath. "This next one is ah...strange, and it might be the toughest one for you." She looked at him for a long moment. "I thought for awhile that we had the same mother, Saija Hayha... that we were brother and sister."

"What made you think that?" He was smiling when he said it but stopped when he saw she was serious.

"Turns out that Saija Hayha is my mother, but she's not yours. And Uncle Sepp is my uncle and not yours," she said. His mouth gaped open and she quietly told him everything, taking her time. "Uncle Sepp never told you who your mother was. He said she died when you were only a few months old. If he knows her name, he didn't tell me. He let you think his sister was your mother maybe because you probably remember her."

Hayes lay back on the bed and didn't say anything. He was silent for so long that Gloria thought he might have fallen asleep, but his eyes were wide open.

"Are you okay?" she asked.

"Yeah, I'm fine," he answered. "It's strange, but it doesn't change anything. I'm gonna keep calling him Uncle Sepp. I thought I remembered a mother, but it was vague and I never remembered any attachment. She wasn't my mother. Only Uncle Sepp was always there."

"He said you're like a son to him," she said.

"Yeah, he was more a father than an uncle, but he's still gonna be my Uncle Sepp."

"My Uncle Sepp too." She laughed and began kissing him.

* * *

A little while later, they drove to Detroit and Grand River Avenue. Hayes wiped down everything he thought he'd touched in the car and they walked four blocks to Frances Lincoln's the house. He was apprehensive, but they couldn't think of anyplace else to go where they felt safe. The woman invited them in, then hugged Gloria and inspected Hayes for a few seconds. Finally, she grasped him and gave him a tentative hug. He told her how sorry he was about Roscoe, and hugged her back.

Five minutes later she was making pancakes. Logan Carlton had called her to see if Gloria had been there. He had left his telephone number. Then "a nice man from the FBI by the name of Special Agent Ovenden" had called her and left his number. "He also left a number for a hotel where an Army policeman by the name of Jimmy Ray Suggs was staying. He said to call Mr. Suggs if I couldn't reach him." She looked at Gloria. "They're all very worried about you, Gloria, and I was too. You heard about Mr. Bonaventure? It's been on the radio."

They both nodded. Bonaventure had died at the hospital. They had been listening to the radio driving into Detroit, but they'd heard nothing about Doran.

After they ate breakfast, Hayes called the hotel and asked for Suggs.

CHAPTER 16

February 5, 8:45 a.m., New York

Hayes had always wanted to see New York but he didn't get to see much. Lady Liberty was standing tall through a break in the swirling clouds as their flight descended. He was surprised at the thrill it triggered. He smiled at her. The cold, wind-driven sleet over New York was bad, but the glimpse of the statue made it worthwhile.

Suggs had booked them on a red-eye out of Detroit that landed at La Guardia a little after 9 a.m. Before leaving, they both got brand new dress green uniforms, including overcoats, at Fort Wayne. Hayes shined his shoes and polished his brass, and both he and Suggs looked sharp.

Gloria was on the flight because the FBI and Army CID wanted to interview both her and Hayes, and she had insisted on bringing Frances Lincoln along. They had money to pay for it. Logan Carlton had met them at the airport in Detroit and gave them $5,000 cash that Bonaventure had given to him for Gloria when he decided to turn himself in to the FBI. Carlton also told them that Bonaventure had changed his will to make Gloria his sole heir.

A full colonel and a lieutenant were waiting at the gate for them. The colonel's name was Albert Wiedyke and the lieutenant was Charles Fisher. Both scrutinized Hayes closely and quickly returned his salute. The colonel was slightly built but ramrod straight, about 40 years old with a thin mustache and a crew cut. "You're Hayes? I thought you were a PFC?"

Hayes was suddenly glad he and Suggs had spent the time getting their uniforms in order because he felt like he was back in basic training standing inspection. "Sir, I'm Spec Four Hayes now."

"The report I read said you were a PFC."

"My commanding officer promoted me."

"As well he should if those reports are even halfway accurate," the colonel said. He eyed Gloria and Mrs. Lincoln. "Who are these people?"

"Sir, this is my girlfriend, Gloria Doran, and her friend, Mrs. Lincoln."

Mrs. Lincoln extended her hand. "I'm Frances Lincoln, and I'm pleased to meet you."

The colonel took her hand and nodded. But he was looking at the scabbed over cut on Gloria's cheek that was still surrounded by an ugly bruise. "What happened to you?"

Gloria swallowed and issued a little grunt, trying to answer.

Hayes put his arm around her and squeezed her shoulder, then looked at the colonel. "Far too much to explain, Sir."

"This is supposed to be official Army business," the colonel said gently. "They shouldn't really be here."

Dragging two suitcases, Suggs came up. "Sir, I'm Jimmy Ray Suggs, an investigator with Army CID." He took out his badge and showed it to the colonel. Then he handed him the paper that Major Kucharski had given him.

The colonel scanned it. "Okay," he said. "I wasn't expecting that Hayes would be accompanied by military police."

"I'm following orders, Sir. I've been investigating two murders that occurred in Vietnam, which appear to be connected to some Stateside murders. In addition to my investigation, I was asked to bring Spec Four Hayes here, so I have brought him. When we're done with CBS, I'm planning to talk to the FBI and to some CID officers. We're going directly to the FBI offices from CBS."

The colonel looked at Suggs and nodded. He turned to Lieutenant Fisher.

"You'll have to find something for Specialist Hayes and his friends to do when Sergeant Suggs goes to the FBI."

Suggs said, "Begging the colonel's pardon, Sir, Hayes and Miss Doran are coming with me. The FBI and CID want to talk to both of them as well,"

The colonel's eyes widened. "Could you brief me about this investigation?" He looked at his watch. "We've spent considerable time at the Pentagon preparing the briefing for CBS and this is a surprise. Can you do it quickly?"

Suggs shook his head slowly. "With respect, I don't think that's a good idea, Colonel. It's complicated and it would take some time to explain. Some of the issues are classified and shouldn't get into the media. It might be better if you don't know. Let me assure you that the incident that is the purpose of your visit to CBS is not what I am investigating. Let me further assure you that neither Specialist Hayes nor Miss Doran are suspected of any crimes. In fact, they were both intended to be, and have been, the victims. Attempts were to murder both of them. Miss Doran has been through an ordeal and Mrs. Lincoln's son was a murder victim. Maybe we should talk about what we're gonna do at CBS."

Glancing at his watch again, the colonel agreed. He shook hands gently with Gloria and again with Mrs. Lincoln, who then left in a taxi for a hotel. Hayes, Suggs, the colonel and the lieutenant were in another taxi for a long time, with the colonel talking almost constantly. His main concern was that he do the talking at CBS and that Hayes speak as little as possible.

That was okay with Hayes, but Suggs told him that General Westmoreland had insisted that someone present at the firefight talk to the network.

Finally they stopped in front of a big building and ran through the rain to get inside. The colonel looked at a little notebook as they rode the elevator up and he appeared to grow nervous. A friendly, plump woman led them down a hall to a room with a big table. She turned on a coffee percolator in the room and told them to help themselves when it was ready. Then she left.

A TV set in the room was tuned to an interview show. Right away, Hayes recognized the man from the airport in Chicago who had called him a warmonger. He was an actor from a TV show that Hayes had never seen. The actor was going on about an anti-war rally where he had spoken on the previous weekend in Chicago and one where he was going to speak in Boston.

Hayes pointed at the television. "I saw that guy at the airport. He called me a warmonger."

"Really? He's an actor in one of those cowboy TV series. One I don't watch," the colonel said. "He shows up at a lot of anti-war rallies. Real bullshit artist." The colonel gestured for the lieutenant to turn off the TV and turned to Hayes. "I want you to tell me about the action in Nui Binh. I've read the reports, but I should hear firsthand what you saw."

So Hayes told him everything and the colonel listened carefully, even taking a few notes.

"That's very interesting. I don't know what they'll ask you, Specialist, but answer any question truthfully and try to keep it short. Let me do the talking unless they ask you something. They will definitely ask you questions though. As long as no civilians were killed, no women and children, that's the main thing. And that's true, right?"

"Yes Sir. We didn't kill any civilians. They were Viet Cong, in those black pajama uniforms, and they were trying to kill us. Thing is, they don't look that much like uniforms because a lot of Vietnamese wear similar clothing. But they had web gear and weapons. But some of the VC who were killed were women. You sometimes see female VC."

The colonel looked a little puzzled, but he nodded. "I wouldn't volunteer that, but don't deny it either." he said.

"What do you want me to do if they say things that I know aren't true?" Hayes asked.

"Tell them it isn't true," said the colonel. "Try to be respectful. Don't lose your cool. Don't interrupt them. You should write down anything you think should be challenged. Do you have a pen and paper?"

Lieutenant Fisher opened a briefcase and pushed a pad of paper over to Hayes and then slid over a ballpoint pen.

Then they sat in silence for a bit with the colonel looking at his watch again. Then he asked Hayes how long he had been in Vietnam and if he liked the Army. When he found out Hayes was a draftee, he asked him what he'd done as a civilian. When Hayes told him he'd been a guitar player in a rock and roll band, the colonel asked him who he liked best, the Beatles or the Rolling Stones.

Hayes was beginning to like him just a little when the door opened and four people entered. One of them was the Spanish reporter, her cleavage on full blazing display in a low-cut scoop-necked green sweater. She seemed surprised to see Hayes. He kept his gaze fixed on her as introductions were made. She was accusing him of mass murder and he suddenly realized he was angry. Her story had already run once on a Spanish TV network and he, Suggs and Gloria had gone to a little UHF TV station in Detroit to see it. A Spanish-speaking woman at the station had translated some of it, and it was bad.

There had also been a small wire-service story in the *Detroit News*, and Gloria had seen it. He had told her it wasn't true, but he wondered whether she had doubts about it, and about him. What would happen if the same story ran on TV all over the country? More and more people seemed to be speaking out against the war. He remembered the stewardess on the flight out of Vietnam and what Gloria had told him about a big teach-in rally in Detroit where she had sung.

The last man in the group was introducing himself. He looked familiar, someone Hayes thought he'd met before. He was about 50 with a little moustache and a busy scruffiness like he had already put in a full day. He was dressed in a grey suit, his tie loosened, and he had an unlit pipe in one hand. He had a comfortable friendliness and was looking at Hayes with his hand out just as Hayes snapped out of his funk.

"I'm Walter Cronkite," he said in the voice that Hayes had heard many times before. "I'm pleased to meet one of the soldiers at the center of this, and I hope we can straighten it out. I'm going to let our producer, Bill Sutliffe, and perhaps Josefina here ask the questions, but I may jump in. Take your time. We want to hear all of your side. The film Miss Madrid has shown us is both compelling and disturbing, and the allegations in her story are grave. But perhaps you have an explanation. We are starting to get a lot of very compelling film out of Saigon."

The colonel said, "We hoped to have another soldier who was present, Specialist Francisco Rivera, but unfortunately, he's in the hospital. I might be able to bring him by later this week."

Hayes was startled. *How badly is Rivera hurt?*

"Well, let's try to settle this today," said Cronkite, his unlit pipe bobbing up and down in one hand. "Let's try to do that."

Sutliffe asked Hayes how long he had been in the Army and in Vietnam. Hayes started to answer but the colonel answered for him. Then he immediately launched into a description of the firefight, looking down at a sheaf of papers. The lieutenant had distributed three copies of the papers, and Hayes was a little unhappy that he hadn't gotten one.

The colonel related an exact timeline of the entire incident down to the minute, an exact number for the dead Vietnamese, including their ranks, and an exact listing of all of the different kinds of captured weapons. He rattled off a kill ratio based on there being five people in the bunker. He didn't mention the helicopter miniguns or any other details. He made Comstock out to be a hero, and also Rufus. He barely mentioned Rivera or Slobojan, and ended his description of the attack by giving Hayes more credit than anyone else for repelling the enemy. Without hesitation, the colonel segued into other recent actions, calling it all an enemy offensive, "the Tet Offensive." He talked about the strategic importance of the current fighting winding all the way to the Domino Theory. "Make no mistake, gentlemen, this is a major play by the Communists for all of Southeast Asia."

Everyone in the room listened politely. A young man whose introduction Hayes had missed seemed to be some kind of stenographer, mainly there to take notes, and he was scribbling furiously as the colonel spoke. But Hayes noticed there was also a tape recorder with a microphone recording everything.

Hayes didn't think the colonel had made the story about the firefight very clear or believable, though he was impressed with how he presented the larger battlefield issues. The colonel never came right out and said it, but he certainly implied that television wasn't being fair. From the little TV he'd watched since he'd been back, Hayes had to agree. Now the colonel was talking about Khe Sanh perhaps being the key, comparing it to Dien Bien Phu and the French. He was complaining about inaccuracies in a specific story he'd seen on CBS when Sutliffe interrupted him.

Sutliffe looked right at Hayes. "Private Hayes, Miss Madrid told us that she believes you and the other American soldiers were using marijuana during this action. Is that true?"

"I don't think that's relevant and Private Hayes has a right not to incriminate himself," said the colonel, but he stopped under a withering glare from Cronkite.

Sutliffe said, "This is not a court. We're trying to get to the truth of the matter here. I was a B-17 navigator in World War II, so I know a thing or two about how men deal with the stresses of war."

Hayes had been looking at Cronkite, but he turned to Sutliffe. He was an almost painfully thin man with a hard, boney face, circles under bright hazel eyes and dark-brown slightly greasy hair. Despite a world-weary demeanor, he exuded the confidence of someone who already knew the answers to his questions. He was friendly, at least superficially so, but Hayes thought he was just waiting to trip him up. "No Sir, I didn't smoke any marijuana and neither did anyone else. And I am a specialist fourth class, not a PFC. I did receive an Article Fifteen for smoking marijuana back on Christmas Day," Hayes said, and the colonel hung his head and shook it slightly. Hayes remembered the advice about answering the question and keeping it short, but now felt he had no other choice but to explain further. "I got in trouble for smoking pot on Christmas Eve. I got busted from spec four to PFC for smoking it, and I was promoted back to spec four right after this firefight. But I swear, I haven't smoked any marijuana since Christmas Eve."

Immediately, he realized he'd forgotten about the joint he smoked when Abercrombie had been killed. Then he remembered the medic passing the joint around after the firefight. *Tough shit,* he thought. *Time to shut up.*

"Okay," Sutliffe said. "I'd like to hear your version of what happened,"

Hayes looked at the colonel whose lips were pursed tightly but picked up an almost imperceptible nod. He figured that Sutliffe was hoping to get him to contradict something the colonel had said. "I didn't think anything was gonna happen that night, but my friend Rivera did. He was on guard with me. And so did Sergeant Slobojan, who was in charge of the bunker. A major came around to check on us after dark and he warned us that he thought the chances of a ground attack were great. So we were all on high alert. I was wide awake all night.

"They hit us early in the morning, just before sunrise. Some fog had started to come up. Rivera saw them first, but once he spotted them, we all saw them despite their camouflage. It was like the brush was slowly moving toward us. You know, like Birnam Wood in Shakespeare."

A look of surprise crossed Cronkite's and Sutliffe's faces. Hayes stopped and sipped from a glass of water. He was thinking that all the TV people had probably looked at the Spanish film and maybe the colonel hadn't. But none of them had been there either. Everyone was silent.

Hayes glanced at the colonel. "With respect, Sir," then turned his attention back to Sutliffe. "The colonel didn't explain how we were able to kill all those enemy soldiers. And they weren't civilians, they were all Viet Cong regulars, most of them wearing uniforms, the black pajama uniforms that you see in that Spanish TV lady's film. A few of them didn't have uniforms. That's just the way the VC are. Most of 'em are guerrillas. They might be farmers during the day. But this was the biggest group of VC any of us had ever seen. They had web gear and they all had weapons. They were trying to kill us and get into Nui Binh Base Camp. If they were unarmed civilians, how do you explain Mr. Comstock getting killed and Rivera and Rufus Roy getting wounded when the VC hit the helicopter with a rocket?

"The day before, Rivera and I and Mr. Comstock were flying a mission. Our helicopter was hit by ground fire and we lost the tail rotor. That time, it was the North Vietnamese with a big crew-served fifty-one—that's a .51 caliber antiaircraft gun. Mr. Walters was the A/C—sorry, that's aircraft commander, which is the main pilot—anyway, he was able to keep enough control of the ship so that Rivera got a clear shot and took out that NVA crew. Then another gunship hit them with rockets. After our gunship crash-landed back in Nui Binh, it ended up right behind that bunker." He glanced at the Spanish reporter. "Miss Madrid was there taking pictures when we crash-landed, and she interviewed Rivera in Spanish after it happened. He was the only one around who could speak the language. So that part in her story where Rivera's talking... well, he was talking about the incident where our tail rotor got shot off, not the firefight that happened the next morning, and she knows it. After the firefight, Rivera's face was all cut up with glass from when the helicopter windshield exploded and he had burns on his face, and you don't see that in the film. Anyway, those NVA almost shot us down, but we ended up getting them. So yes, he was all jacked up and happy about it. We all were because we'd just been in a big gunfight and we came back alive.

"The morning of the ground attack, just before the VC attacked, Rivera and Rufus ran back to that helicopter. We didn't have a radio in the bunker, and the field phone wasn't working. The two of them used the radio in the helicopter to call base camp operations and warn them that we were about to be attacked. However, Rivera's been a crew chief for a long time, and he can fly a helicopter just a little. He knew how to start the ship and get it off the ground. And Rufus is a big strong guy so he held onto the tail. He was a human tail rotor. Rivera and Rufus used that gunship to spray the VC with a burst from its miniguns. They caught the VC just as they were about to overwhelm Slobbo and me... that's Sergeant Slobojan."

Hayes stopped to catch his breath, thinking about Rufus, wondering how badly he had been wounded. He drained the rest of his water and cleared his throat. "We got lucky. I can't believe how lucky I was. I should have died. And you know what? That would have been okay. Better me than Comstock. The colonel made him out to be a hero. I don't know about that because he got killed before he had a chance to do much, but he was a good guy. Me, I'm just a draftee who got busted for smoking pot. I never was good soldier material. I was a guitar player in a rock and roll band. Mr. Comstock had officer of the guard that night, and the day before he was the copilot on our gunship when we almost got shot down. That was the first time he'd ever been under fire. Everybody liked him, but now he's dead. Rufus is probably gonna lose his legs. I'm not even sure he's still alive. Rivera got a face full of Plexiglas and got burned pretty bad. I was right in the middle of everything and didn't get a scratch, and neither did Sergeant Slobojan."

He looked around the room. Josefina Madrid was looking down at the table. The colonel looked like he wanted to tell Hayes to shut up, but nobody said anything.

Hayes said, "I saw Miss Madrid's story, the one that was on Spanish TV. I don't understand Spanish but somebody told me what she said. Near the end, it shows me going down to my knees and dropping my rifle, and she implies that I'm feeling remorse for killing civilians, that I may have been crying."

Cronkite was looking directly at Hayes.

Hayes looked right back into his eyes. "I was crying alright, but I was thinking of my girlfriend. I'd just found out the night before that she was pregnant. I was thinking of her and the baby. I was thinking that I should have been dead, and that I would probably be dead soon enough and that I would never see her again, or the baby." He coughed, and then let anger push back the despair that had been building. It was something Gloria had told him she did.

"You can take this war. I didn't start it and I don't want to be fighting it. The VC and the NVA and all those Communists never did anything to me until I got drafted and sent over there. You say you want the truth, so why are you so ready to believe a TV reporter from Spain who was only in Nui Binh for 24 hours before you'll believe an American soldier like me who's been in the war every day since last August?

"Is it because of the pictures? Right after the fight was over, some lifers... excuse me, a sergeant in our company, and some others, went out there and picked up the weapons. They took away that web gear and stuff like belt buckles. Then Miss Madrid showed up with her camera. When Rivera, who speaks Spanish, heard her saying we'd killed civilians, he talked to her. He tried to tell her what happened but she didn't want to hear anything we had to say. I don't think she likes Americans.

"We never did anything like what she says in that film. I swear. I have never seen an American deliberately kill a civilian, and I'm a gunner on helicopter gunships. I've been there since August. There are rules—rules of engagement—and sometimes we don't like the rules, but we follow them. We go into free-fire zones where there aren't supposed to be any civilians, but you see people who sure look like civilians. We don't fire on them, at least not that I ever saw. Maybe people do shoot at them but I haven't witnessed it. We're fighting a war and there are civilians all over the place. It's terrible. You can't imagine how bad it is. Do you think we like it? Why does TV have to make it worse? We killed more than a hundred VC in that firefight. Isn't that bad enough? They were soldiers, but not long ago, they were just like me before I got drafted. They had girlfriends and wives and mothers and brothers and sisters and babies."

Hayes paused again, thinking he was getting off the subject. And though he'd told the truth about civilians, he had heard stories about Americans killing civilians. He just hadn't seen it.

"You sound like you feel sorry for yourself," Sutliffe said, jumping into the void. There was a trace of contempt in his voice. "You've got what, another six months to go? Don't you soldiers serve a year and then you get to go home? World War II, we were in it for the duration, and none of us knew how long it would last."

Hayes looked at him, not sure what to say.

The colonel cleared his throat. "A year of war is more than enough for anyone, and this is a different war than the one you fought in."

Hayes said, "With respect, Mr. Sutliffe, you said you flew on bombers. How many missions did you fly? I read *Catch 22*, and I know it's fiction, but there's a recurring theme in it about how the bomber crews had to fly 20 or 25 missions before they didn't have to do it anymore. In the book, they keep raising the number. Well, in our unit, the 99th Assault Helicopter Company, I flew every single day in the six months I've been there. The only day I didn't fly was Christmas when there was a truce, and even then we were on standby. Most days we went from sunrise to sunset and sometimes we flew night missions too. We fly seven days a week. We are short on flight crews, especially pilots.

"All of our pilots are way over the maximum hours that regulations say they're supposed to fly. I'll bet we put in more flight time in a year than you guys did in the whole war. And you didn't have TV second-guessing you along the way. I wonder what kind of story Miss Madrid might have done on the firebombing of Dresden or Tokyo. I don't mean to disparage your service because it was defeating Hitler and Tojo. It was a great thing. But why is my service less than yours? Is it because you don't like this war? Do you think I do? I'm fighting for my country just like you were. Damn right it's a different war. I don't really know why my friends are fighting and dying in Vietnam. Congress has never declared war. The VC aren't gonna bomb Pearl Harbor or invade New York.

"But this is all about a lie, that we killed civilians. I swear we didn't kill any civilians. But we killed a lot of enemy and right now, I don't feel good about it. I felt good when it happened because they were trying to kill me. The colonel here's right. We're kicking the crap out of Charlie. If you don't like that, please bring us home, but don't tell lies about us."

Sounding rattled, Sutliffe said, "It's pretty common for people to blame the messenger when they don't like the message." Hayes wasn't sure the comment was relevant.

"Well, Miss Madrid's message is a lie so why would we like it?" Hayes said. "Or her for that matter?" He looked over at her.

She glared at him, but didn't say anything.

"I was a door gunner, then a crew chief, a specialist fourth class, and I don't know much about all that strategic stuff the colonel was talking about, but I do wonder about your messages. A stewardess on the plane out of Vietnam called me a baby killer, and that actor that was on the TV here just before you came in called me a warmonger when I ran into him in the airport in Chicago. I think he was drunk. My girlfriend was at a teach-in in Detroit a couple of months ago, and she said the speaker there kept saying soldiers in Vietnam were pigs, and every time he called us pigs, everyone cheered.

"Why do people despise soldiers like me? They didn't do that in World War II. Why are we different? Why are we not treated honorably? Sometimes I think TV wants to destroy our honor with lies. Maybe it's not what you are saying to people as much as what you are showing them. I read a little Marshall McLuhan—you know, the medium is the message guy. You think the pictures you show don't lie? Well, Miss Madrid's pictures lie because those were not dead civilians like she says."

He looked at Cronkite. "Mr. Cronkite, you call the pictures from Vietnam compelling and disturbing. But are they telling the truth? Is it okay to show people disturbing pictures that compel them to come to the wrong conclusion?"

Hayes stopped because he had run out of things to say. He had thought the colonel would interrupt him, but the colonel had kept his mouth shut. The colonel, in fact, looked stunned. His mouth hung open as he stared at Hayes, but he didn't look angry.

Josefina Madrid pursed her lips tightly, her mouth moving like she was trying to swallow something sour. Her eyes bore into Hayes but still she didn't speak.

Hayes got up and slowly walked the length of the room to pour himself a cup of coffee. Cronkite followed him with his eyes, interested and patient. As Hayes took a sip of his coffee and started back, Cronkite lit his pipe. As if on cue, Sutliffe and the stenographer both lit cigarettes and inhaled deeply.

Hayes wanted a cigarette, but he had sensed that Gloria didn't like him smoking.

"Please, another question," Sutliffe said, smoke coming out his mouth as he spoke. He looked at Madrid, then Hayes, and Hayes was suddenly on edge again. "Miss Madrid says that you shot and killed a soldier in the South Vietnamese Army, and she says that she confirmed this with the U.S. Army in Vietnam and with someone in your own unit, in fact."

The colonel said, "That's not pertin—"

"No secret about it, that's true," Hayes said, relieved to have something he could answer. He told them the story about the ARVN shooting out the chin bubble with an M79 grenade launcher and injuring the peter pilot. "I reacted without thinking and shot him," Hayes said. "He was the first person I ever killed. I felt terrible. Still do. I dream about it all the time."

"That incident was thoroughly investigated," Suggs said, speaking for the first time. "It was documented by several witnesses, including the victim's Vietnamese commanding officer. Specialist Hayes was completely exonerated. No charges were filed and the Army compensated the victim's family even though he was at fault."

Cronkite said, "I've been curious about why you're here. What did you say your unit was?"

"Military Police," Suggs said. "I'm with Army CID—Criminal Investigation Division."

Cronkite nodded and drew on his pipe. Sutliffe sucked on his cigarette like a condemned man awaiting execution. Hayes thought again about asking him for one, but he wanted no favors. The colonel was looking at Hayes and nodded slightly when their eyes met.

Cronkite looked at Suggs expectantly. "You came all the way over here to talk about the South Vietnamese soldier?"

"No Sir, I came over here for a murder investigation," Suggs said, realizing instantly that he'd made a mistake.

"Really?" asked Cronkite. "That sounds like an important bit of information. Is Specialist Hayes here involved in a murder? What is he accused of?"

"Nothing. He's not accused of anything. My investigation is not related to what happened in Nui Binh, but I have had to investigate Hayes. There was an attempt to murder him. I can tell you that he's mostly been a good soldier. In fact, except for smoking marijuana, which a lot of soldiers in Vietnam are doing and for which he was reduced in rank from specialist fourth class to private first class, his military record is outstanding. Specialist Hayes was apparently intended to be the victim of a complex murder plot by a now-deceased assailant who murdered two other U.S. soldiers in Vietnam, and perhaps more victims in the States. My investigation is not complete, so I can't talk about it further. You can verify this with Army CID in Washington, though they probably will be upset that I've mentioned it at all."

"Sounds like it could be a story," Cronkite said.

"Could be," Suggs said. He smiled a little. "But not until we complete the investigation, and maybe not then either. There are some classified issues."

Cronkite got up and walked to the coffee pot, but it was empty. Hayes had taken the last cup. Cronkite stopped and looked out the window, staring at the rain. The room was suddenly silent and they all listened to the rain pattering on the window. Cronkite turned around. "We won't be using your story, Miss Madrid." He looked as if he was going to say more, but then he clamped his teeth on his pipe, which was now out, and shook his head. He turned to the colonel. "Colonel, I wish you senior military PR people were as forthcoming as Specialist Hayes has been. This was a brilliant move, bringing him. He acquitted himself well against Bill here. If you don't like what you see on TV or read in the newspapers, it's because too many of you colonels and generals and too many other government people have not been forthcoming with the truth. Not you, Colonel Wiedyke. You have always played it straight with us, but I'm afraid some of your colleagues are dishonorable men. Frankly, some of them have been lying to us for years. They think they're lying to reporters, but they're lying to the nation, and people know it."

The colonel pursed his lips but said nothing.

Cronkite turned to Hayes. "Son, I believe you. I think you've been let down by the same lies. It's those liars who have stolen your honor, not television. The only thing I can think of to say to you is thank you. Thank you for telling the truth, including admitting to your mistakes. And thank you for serving your country. You are absolutely right. You didn't ask to go to Vietnam and you deserve better." He shook Hayes' hand and patted him on the back. The he addressed the group. "Let me warn all of you that this is going to get a lot worse. This war is at a turning point, both on the battlefield and here at home. I fear we are heading for a stalemate, or that we could lose." Cronkite turned toward the door.

Exasperated, the colonel said, "But we're *not* losing. As Specialist Hayes put it so bluntly, we are kicking the crap out of the enemy. Another six months and we'll run them all the way back to Hanoi. Any competent reporter should be able to figure that out."

Cronkite paused, turned around and took his pipe out of his mouth. "Well, I'm about to leave and go over there to see for myself. But I fear that while we might be winning on the battlefield, the war is being lost at home because the American people are turning against it. People are losing faith in this war because their leaders haven't been telling them the truth. The pictures coming out of Vietnam are exposing the lies.

"However, Specialist Hayes observation about the pictures is very instructive. He made a good point. We have to be very careful, but I still believe people know the truth when they see it. Specialist Hayes here told the truth, and everyone in this room—even, I suspect, Miss Madrid—knows it. And I'm so grateful that he did tell the truth, because before he did, I was very afraid that Miss Madrid had it right. We came very close to making a terrible mistake. I am going to give more serious thought to what Hayes said concerning what we show on TV and what we say about it. But that's the point. Our leaders say one thing, but we keep seeing pictures that seem to show something else."

As Cronkite walked out the room, Hayes concluded that he had lied by omission. He hadn't told them he'd been stoned on LSD. But he had no regrets.

February 6, 8:50 p.m., New York

Hayes wrapped his arms around Gloria's naked body, thankful that at last they were alone and safe. They were in a luxurious suite in the Drake Hotel. Suggs and Frances Lincoln were in two other rooms in the hotel. He and Suggs were scheduled to fly out the next morning on the first leg of their journey back to Vietnam.

Gloria's financial prospects were continuing to rise. Logan Carlton had called to say that Matthew Doran had died intestate. He had no will, so Gloria was likely to inherit his fortune as well.

Hayes felt her bulging abdomen, and he was so ready and so anxious that he felt like he was going to explode. He could sense that she was anxious too.

"Can you can feel our baby moving?" she asked. She kissed his cheek and then his lips. It was a long kiss, and during it she took his hand and placed it on her belly. He felt movement against his hand—not much, but there was no doubt.

"Wow!" He laughed. "There's really something in there! You're not just fatter than I remember!" She punched his arm, but he kept caressing her swollen belly. When he felt no more movement, he allowed his fingers to wander over her body.

"My stepfather wanted to kill the baby." She didn't move away and she seemed to be enveloping him with her body. It had been so long. "There was this nurse at the clinic when I first found out I was pregnant. She said she could help me get rid of it."

The conversation stopped when he kissed her again.

"But I could never do that," she said when they broke.

"Me neither," Hayes mumbled, nibbling at her lip, then pulling back a little. "I mean it, Gloria. You're right."

He was concentrating on the things that elicited little moans and gasps when he touched her. He was remembering what she liked and he was trying to be gentle, even though he was so desperate. He kissed her hard and it lasted a long time.

Too long. He started thinking about the men he'd killed at the cabin, about perhaps killing his own father and about killing her stepfather. That led to thinking about Vietnam and the Headhunters, about Camp Johnson, the firefight at the bunker, combat assaults, Hollister and Major Lehman and the ARVN.

He remembered the look of horror on her face when he'd cut off the arrowheads sticking out of her stepfather and pulled the arrows out. He was doing everything he could to keep the police from finding out what he had done. She hadn't told him any details about seeing her stepfather kill her real father, just that she'd seen it. She didn't want to talk about it yet, and he didn't want to talk about what had happened at the cabin. But he was thinking that she must feel as surrounded by death as he did. He became aware that he was breathing faster and harder. "I've killed a lot of people," he said finally. "I killed all four of them at the cabin."

She shivered against him and emitted a little moan.

"I had to do it. It was just like I was still over there, you know? You have to kill and it's bad. Uncle Sepp warned me about it. I'm getting used to it, and that's bad too. You can't hesitate, even a little, when you kill. It's like playing in a band; you have to get your licks in just right or the whole song goes bad. Except, it's war and if it goes bad, you'll be dead. And you could be dead even if you don't mess up."

Soon as he said it, he realized he was sounding like Rivera. He had changed more than he wanted to admit, and he shouldn't be talking to her like that. He rolled away from her and found his cigarettes on the bedside table. Then he remembered again that she didn't like smoking. She had asked him to go outside when he had taken out a cigarette when they were at Mrs. Lincoln's house. He wished he had a joint so he could just get his head away from everything that was so hard to think about. But he had also promised to stop doing that. He dropped the cigarettes and lay still for a long time, trying to think about being a father. He thought about Rufus, who had never known his parents. Hayes hadn't known who his father was until Gloria told him, and the mother he could barely remember hadn't been his mother. But his mother and father hadn't gotten rid of him. He wondered whether they had ever wanted him. Then he knew he wanted the baby. "I could never hurt our baby, Gloria," he said. "I love him or her. It's us. And I love you too, more than anything in the world."

She rolled against him again. "Love," she said, in her singsong voice. "I sang 'All You Need Is Love' at that teach-in after that awful guy was screaming about soldiers being pigs. It seemed to mellow people out, though not him. They were singing along with me. So maybe the song is right."

"Yeah... at least talking about love is better than talking about killing," he said, starting to relax again. He marveled at her insight because it was so simple. "Love is the light that erases those deathly shadows when they're closing in on you."

Love me," she said with a new melody that came out in a whispered hum. Then the music and the love flowed through them.

EPILOGUE

26 August, 1968 0830 Hours

Staff Sergeant Jimmy Ray Suggs was inspecting the corpse of Jubal Sypher outside a latrine used mostly by senior NCOs in Long Binh. The body had been shredded by a Claymore mine. The Claymore contained 700 steel balls propelled by 682 grams—about 1.5 pounds—of C4, a plastic explosive. The Claymore would have been effective up to 50 meters—about 160 feet—but it looked to Suggs that Sypher had been facing the mine and probably less than 15 feet away. The killer had been hiding behind the wall of sandbags that went around the latrine and the mine had been placed on the same wall but on the other side of the latrine. *Up close and personal,* Suggs thought. *Too bad it was so quick.* The clacker used to detonate the mine was still there.

The mine had exploded a little after 0600 and two soldiers from Graves Registration were anxious for Suggs to finish so they could remove the body before it got any warmer. A news photographer who had somehow found out about the murder had arrived about the same time as Suggs. He was hovering in the background, camera ready, and Suggs had heard him throwing up. *Well, the bastard looks like hamburger. And the photographer's an idiot because no one's gonna publish such a gruesome image.* Suggs bent over and twisted one of the dog tags so he could read it. There was a hole in the tag but he could still see the name. "Jubal Sypher," he said and sighed. This was one murder he wasn't going to try too hard to solve. Whoever had done it deserved a medal as far Suggs was concerned.

Suggs had been trying to nail Sypher for months. When he had unearthed the Brendan McAlister ring of NCOs, Sypher had been one big fish he hadn't scooped up in the net. The Repo Depot Sergeant Collins had told them everything he knew, which in the larger scheme of things wasn't much. But it was enough to bounce half a dozen NCOs out the Army with less than honorable discharges that cost them their pensions. Collins got to keep his.

For months, pharmaceuticals had been disappearing from the 24th Evacuation Hospital. CID had sent in two men to work undercover. Both had been reporting to Suggs who was in charge of the case. When he found out that First Sergeant Jubal Sypher was the NCO in charge of supply, the investigation focused on him. Suggs had remembered hearing Sypher's name from Hayes, and the pharmaceuticals had started disappearing from 24th Evac not long after Sypher's arrival.

Sitting next to him for almost 20 hours flying back to Vietnam, Suggs had gotten to know Hayes better. He'd been worried Hayes would have trouble going back to Vietnam—clearly, he didn't like it—but Hayes had told Suggs, "I stayed in my Headhunters mindset until the last day or two. It'll be okay."

"What do you mean by the "Headhunters mindset?"

Hayes had a difficult time explaining. "Well, one day you take a long plane ride and you're suddenly in an uncivilized environment where you're expected to kill human beings, an act that's about the most evil and immoral thing you could do in the civilized world that you just left. They train you to do it but they don't talk about the right or the wrong of it. You gotta figure that one out for yourself. And you gotta get used to it, or you don't go home.

"Then, after a year of that, you take another long plane ride and suddenly you're in a place where everything that was right only yesterday is now wrong. Well, when I found myself back in the World, I knew I'd be going back to the bad place pretty quick so I just kept on pretending nothing had changed."

"What do you mean? Can you give me an example?"

"I really can't," Hayes had said, and then he'd stopped talking about it.

Later, Suggs understood it better.

Antoine Lincicombe had stayed in touch. In his first letter he described how the East Lansing police were struggling not only with who had killed Matthew Doran but exactly how he had died. At first they'd thought it was a couple of through-and-through shots from a high-powered rifle. Then the coroner told them it might have been a long knife or perhaps a sword. After thinking about it, he added arrows to the list. Gloria Doran was questioned but she was too upset to tell them much. And she suddenly had one of Detroit's top law firms, Parker, Cunniliffe and Papineau, representing her. Then a couple of months later, Lincicombe wrote that four bodies had been found in Lake George, which was just a wide part of the St. Mary's River on the east side of Sugar Island. One of the bodies was Vinnie Ayala and two of the others were a couple of Percy Dupree's little gang. The fourth was a sheriff's deputy from a neighboring county. Suggs found it interesting that Lincicombe made a point of telling him that the deputy and one Percy's pals had both been shot with the same gun and that the slugs were unusual because they were believed to be of Russian origin. Lincicombe said police in several jurisdictions had concluded that the four bodies pulled from the river, the dead Garganos and Doran were all victims of a Mafia war.

In the files in Doran's Detroit office, Lincicombe had found copies of letters to Brendan McAlister indicating the two were working together. One letter specifically asked McAlister to help Percy Dupree when he came to Vietnam. That was enough for Suggs to charge McAlister with being an accessory to murder, and along with the corruption that Collins' testimony exposed, McAlister was going to be locked up for a long time. Two of the NCOs exposed by Collins worked in Army aviation on aircraft that regularly went back and forth to the States. When Suggs went back to them, they both cut deals and gave evidence that cemented the case against McAlister and implicated some others. The NCOs smuggling heroin to the States had been bringing back pharmaceuticals diverted from Michigan plants and someone had been selling them on the black market. Suggs was sure that someone was Sypher, but he couldn't prove it.

At first, Suggs had thought drugs disappearing from 12th Evac was a completely separate case, but he soon realized it wasn't. He had talked to several soldiers in the 99th Assault Helicopter Company, including Hayes, about Sypher. Hayes had been about as angry as Suggs had ever seen him when he told him what he thought Sypher was doing. Some of the wounded soldiers who had been in pain or gotten infections because drugs had disappeared had been from the 99th. If Hayes hadn't already rotated home, Suggs would have thought he had killed Sypher. But Suggs had seen Hayes go home, an E-5 sergeant who had been the acting platoon sergeant his last month in-country. And Hayes had mailed him a picture of Gloria and him at their wedding holding their three-month old daughter.

Putting McAlister away had been immensely satisfying for Suggs, and he had learned what he wanted to do with his life.

He wanted to find the bad guys and lock them up. Al Checchi, whom he had never met, was his role model.

The meeting in New York had soured Suggs on the Army. The CIA had been there and done everything in its power to block Suggs' investigation of the Doran and Bonaventure drug ring. Once the Army's bad eggs had been found and thrown out, the Army was no longer interested in pursuing the investigation. Even the FBI seemed to have caved, though Suggs was sure they knew more than he did. Ovenden had been pulled off the case by Mosley-Williams, who was unhappy about it but unwilling to talk. At least that's what Lincicombe had told him. And Suggs' promotion to warrant officer had never come through. His embarrassed major counseled him to be patient, indicating he would be promoted in due time, but Suggs had decided against re-enlisting. Ads for jobs with stateside police departments plastered the bulletin boards in the MP compound. He would probably have to work the streets for a while, but he was confident he could join a police department and become an investigator before long. He was thinking of trying Detroit because he knew and liked Lincicombe.

He turned his attention to the Graves Registration guys. "You can take him. I've seen enough." Maybe he'd bag the clacker and take it back to Long Binh so he could dust it for prints. He didn't expect to find any, but if he did he might have to run them. So he decided he would take it, but he'd wipe it clean on the way back.

The news photographer squeezed past him and started shooting pictures of the bloody corpse with his Nikon. Suggs didn't like the press and this guy was particularly irritating. "Hey, let me see some identification," Suggs said. The man stopped taking pictures. He was dressed in faded jeans and what looked like an Army T-shirt. His camera looked brand new but unlike most of the news photographers, this guy had no extra lenses or rolls of film, and he was younger than most of them. Looking closely, Suggs saw numerous tiny scars on the man's face, and larger splotches that looked like healed burns. He took out his wallet and handed Suggs an I.D. card from a Spanish language publication in Miami.

"Francisco Rivera," Suggs said reading the I.D. "Francisco, do you really think anyone's gonna print a picture of this?"

"No habla ingles," Rivera replied.

Suggs didn't speak Spanish but he knew that phrase, and he didn't believe Rivera couldn't speak English. He was also sure he'd heard the name Francisco Rivera before, but was equally sure he'd never met him. But it was getting late and Suggs had rushed out before he'd had any coffee. "Fuck it," he said, and he walked away.

"Besides," Rivera said quietly, "these are for me. And a friend."

The End

ACKNOWLEDGEMENTS

This is a work of fiction. Although I served with the 187th Assault Helicopter Company for a year in Vietnam, the characters in this story are not modeled after the real people with whom I served. Specifically, the non-commissioned officers in the 187th were some of the finest individuals I have ever known and the two first sergeants with whom I served in the 187th were both outstanding soldiers. I feel the same way about the officers and enlisted men that I knew in Vietnam. Many have become lifelong friends. However, every story needs villains and not everyone in the U.S. Army in Vietnam was a saint.

It is no secret that American soldiers used drugs during the Vietnam War though it was more common among rear echelon troops than in combat units. During my tour in Vietnam marijuana was the only drug I personally saw but before the end of the war heroin would become a major problem for the military in Vietnam.

A few of the incidents described in this story resemble events that really happened. The 187th did lose a flare ship and all five on board died. One of our crew chiefs learned to fly a helicopter well enough to fly the ship to safety when both pilots were wounded. We had a couple of unauthorized dogs in our company and one of them did come to an unfortunate end in a cooking pot. However, virtually all of the actions in this story are completely made up. I've tried to make these events and all of the settings in my story as realistic as possible. The 99th Assault Helicopter Company is a fictional unit and Nui Binh is a fictional place. I'm not sure exactly where in Vietnam Nui Binh is supposed to be except that it's almost within sight of the Cambodian border and you can easily fly to Cu Chi or Long Binh from there. So it's probably not far from Tay Ninh Base Camp where the 187th was stationed.

The same is true for the events that take place in Michigan. I graduated from Michigan State University in 1967 and one of my dormitory acquaintances was an avid explorer of the campus steam tunnels. I began my first job after graduation in Detroit the week the Detroit Riot broke out. Later, I was a reporter for the *Detroit Free Press*, but that was about 10 years after this fictional story takes place. I have great respect for General William Westmoreland and Walter Cronkite, the real people who appear in this story. I never met either Cronkite or Westmoreland.

I followed the historical timeline for the Tet Offensive as closely as I could. In the second half of this story, action unfolds in several different time zones on either side of the international dateline. The time and date at the beginning of a chapter is the time and date for that location. Likewise, the times in Vietnam are based on the 24-hour military clock and those in the U.S. are based on the civilian 12-hour clock.

Getting a novel published in today's rapidly changing book world is no easy task. I will be forever indebted to my editor Harvey Stanbrough. He fixed many of my mistakes and counseled me to make other changes. In short, he made this story immeasurably better. Although this is my first attempt at fiction, I've been a writer and editor most of my life and have never met anyone who can deliver as much valuable editorial insight as quickly and succinctly as Harvey did. Working with him has truly been a delight.

I also want to thank my family for their patience and help. My oldest daughter Laura and her husband Stephen offered early feedback. Although she may not know it, my youngest daughter Vicky helped me avoid many pitfalls with her cynical comments on the state of today's fictional young adult dramas in books, television and movies. Then there's my wife Cyndy, who has put up with my long absences while I was locked in the embrace of my laptop mistress. I will try to make it up to her.

Finally, I have another family that requires acknowledgement, and that is the 187th Assault Helicopter Company Association. Every year we stage a reunion and every year, the war stories we tell each other get better and better. The 187th was one of the most distinguished aviation units in the Vietnam War. Readers interested in real war stories told by real people who were there should check our unit's website at:
www.187thahc.net/.

I take war stories with a grain of salt though. I know that people who were present at the same intense event often don't remember it the same way, especially after four-plus decades. That's why the stories keep improving. We incorporate the best elements from everyone's fading memories. So any inaccuracies in all of this are my fault. And if you feel strongly about it, I might even buy you a drink.

Thanks for reading my book.

About the Author

Bob Calverley has worked as a writer, editor, marketer and public relations consultant. He was born in rural northern Ontario and moved to the Upper Peninsula of Michigan when he was 16. He graduated from Soo High School in Sault Ste. Marie Michigan, attended Michigan Technological University, Soo Branch (now Lake Superior State University) and graduated with a BA in Journalism from Michigan State University in 1967.

Calverley was drafted into the U.S. Army in 1967 and served a year with the 187th Assault Helicopter Company in Tay Ninh, Vietnam. During that period, the 187th suffered heavy casualties and earned a Presidential Unit Citation. By the end of the war, it was one of that war's most decorated helicopter units. Calverley, however, spent most his tour in Vietnam as company clerk, and occasionally flew as a door gunner.

For most of the 1970s, Calverley worked as a newspaper reporter, first at the *Sun-Sentinel* in Fort Lauderdale, Florida, and then at the *Detroit Free Press* where he was the recipient of several awards for stories on a large environmental accident. His journalism career included stints as a medical writer, a general assignment reporter, and a reporter who covered local governments and police activity. He also reviewed books and records.

Since leaving newspapers, he has worked in public relations and communications, mostly for nonprofit organizations including the RAND Corporation in Santa Monica, the Los Angeles County Medical Association and the University of Southern California. He retired as Executive Director of Marketing and Public Relations at the USC Viterbi School of Engineering. After retiring, he has continued to work as a consultant and served for six years on the Board of Directors of the nonprofit 187th Assault Helicopter Company Association. The main activity of the association is to stage reunions and improve war stories.

Calverley lives in Southern California with his wife, his youngest daughter and feral lab mix dedicated to protecting them from rabbits, squirrels, lizards and birds.

Made in the USA
San Bernardino, CA
18 January 2016